BOLD MEN AND PASSIONATE WOMEN

Mattie Jo Hunter—She had defied her father and her husband. Now she would stand fast against scandal, the raging elements, and her aching need for Jesse.

Jesse McDade—He would die for Mattie, but could not live for her. He would try to go his own way.

Tom Miller—His love was deep, strong, and patient. He knew Mattie would never stop loving Jesse. But he was determined to share her heart.

Praise for D.R. Meredith's *A Time Too Late*:

"An enthralling and satisfying novel."
—Linda Lay Shuler, author of
She Who Remembers

"Meredith knows the wind-swept high plains' every mood, beauty, and danger, and has created characters who cast long shadows."
—Jeanne Williams, author of
No Roof But Heaven

Also by D.R. Meredith

A Time Too Late

Available from
HarperPaperbacks

ATTENTION: ORGANIZATIONS AND CORPORATIONS

Most HarperPaperbacks are available at special quantity discounts for bulk purchases for sales promotions, premiums, or fund-raising. For information, please call or write:
Special Markets Department, HarperCollins Publishers,
10 East 53rd Street, New York, N.Y. 10022.
Telephone: (212) 207-7528. Fax: (212) 207-7222.

The
RECKONING

D.R. MEREDITH

HarperPaperbacks
A Division of HarperCollinsPublishers

If you purchased this book without a cover, you should be aware that this book is stolen property. It was reported as "unsold and destroyed" to the publisher and neither the author nor the publisher has received any payment for this "stripped book."

This is a work of fiction. The characters, incidents, and dialogues are products of the author's imagination and are not to be construed as real. Any resemblance to actual events or persons, living or dead, is entirely coincidental.

HarperPaperbacks   *A Division of* HarperCollins*Publishers*
10 East 53rd Street, New York, N.Y. 10022

Copyright © 1993 by D. R. Meredith
All rights reserved. No part of this book may be used or reproduced in any manner whatsoever without written permission of the publisher, except in the case of brief quotations embodied in critical articles and reviews. For information address HarperCollins*Publishers,*
10 East 53rd Street, New York, N.Y. 10022.

Cover illustration by Peter Fiore

First printing: September 1993

Printed in the United States of America

HarperPaperbacks and colophon are trademarks of HarperCollins*Publishers*

❖ 10 9 8 7 6 5 4 3 2 1

To the pioneer woman in her ranch house or dugout, log cabin or frame shack, soddy or adobe hut, of whom so little is written and to whom so much is owed;
and
to Charles Goodnight and Temple Houston, two very different heroes alike in their respect for women.

Acknowledgments

Claire Kuehn and Betty Bustos—Panhandle Plains Museum Archives—whose assistance in searching for obscure facts and advice in selecting the most likely of divergent accounts of events went beyond what any author might reasonably expect, and I shall be forever grateful.

Sherman Harriman, who shared his knowledge of old Tascosa and its courthouse and served as a guide as I walked down its long-vanished streets.

Jay O'Brien, who took time to talk to me of cattle brands.

Megan Meredith, my daughter and only research assistant, whose skill in locating documents containing needed historical details leaves me in awe.

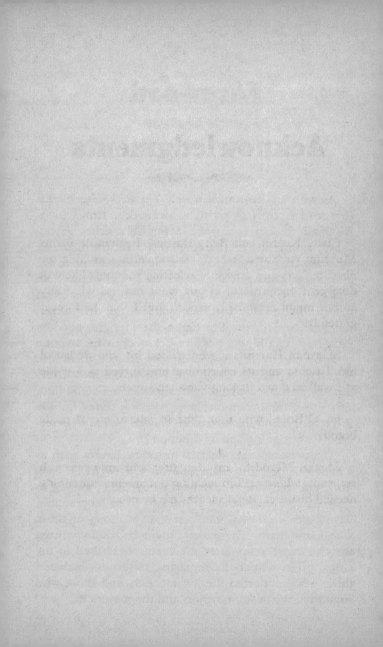

Foreword

As with any historical novel, *The Reckoning* blends fact and fiction to paint a picture of times past. Although the Bar H and the Flying MJ ranches are fictitious as are all the characters who live on them, all other ranches mentioned did in fact exist. Most of the events described actually occurred. The cowboy strike and the resulting blacklist is based on the historical record. The prairie fire, the blizzard, the drift fence, the Big Die Up, the Big Fight, the drought, and the grasshopper plague were re-created using written records left by those who survived these disasters. When these records disagreed, I chose the most likely account based on what empirical evidence I could find. When personal memoirs gave varying dates for the drought, I used moisture tables for the period to determine its beginning and its duration.

The personalities of actual historical figures such as Charles Goodnight, Temple Houston, W.M.D. Lee, Jim East, the various managers of the XIT, as well as lesser-known individuals are drawn from biographies, newspaper accounts, and personal memoirs of those who knew them. These same memoirs, many written forty or more years after the events described in my story, often reflect the lingering bitterness between those who supported the big ranchers and those who supported the nester ranchers and the mavericks.

Temple Houston's defense of Jesse is shamelessly based on his closing argument in defense of a "soiled dove" delivered in Woodward, Oklahoma Territory, May 26, 1899. I like to believe that if Mattie Hunter had actually existed, Temple Houston would have defended her in reality as passionately as he defended her in my fiction.

My fictional characters are creations of my imagination and are not intended to resemble any persons, living or dead. Their interpretations of and reactions to actual events and persons are their own and not necessarily mine. Although many of Mattie's ideas and reactions might be considered too "modern" for the times, her desire for equality was by no means unique to her. Texas history reveals many strong women who fought for an equal place in the male-dominated ranching industry. While most of these women did not stray so far from convention in their private lives as my character, there are infrequent glimpses of those who, like Mattie, loved unwisely but all too well.

—D.R.M.

CHAPTER

1

Texas Panhandle, 1882

The Colonel left for Pueblo the last day of September when the leaves on Mattie's cottonwood tree had turned as golden as her hair, and his daughter had proved as inhospitable as the land.

Not that Mattie had asked him to leave—she had not completely lost her manners—but her tarnished gold eyes reflected the same indifference to his presence as the flat Texas plains unbroken by the natural features expected by a man used to the mountains of Colorado. The Colonel felt naked in such emptiness, exposed to wind and sun and other men's curiosity, and wondered how Mattie tolerated it. What human habitation a man saw—provided he saw any—was generally a mean, sorry example of shelter often built of native stone and adobe as though everyone was afraid of imposing foreign, man-made materials upon the land. Even Mattie's new three-story house built of lumber freighted in from Dodge City rested upon a foundation of native stone. Inside murals of ranching scenes were painted on its interior plaster walls as if his daughter sought to placate an angry land by turning her home into a shrine.

The Colonel paused on the porch that circled Mattie's house and shivered from the very bleakness that surrounded the ranch house. "It's unnatural to my mind, Jubilee," he said to his ex-slave. "All this space empty of any sign of human commerce."

Jubilee leaned against one of the wooden posts that held up the porch roof. "We gots commerce. Must be more than two hundred thousand cows and Lord knows how many ranches in the Panhandle."

Col. Andrew J. Corley, late of the Confederate army, grimaced at the Negro's direct look. Darkies weren't supposed to look in a white man's eyes— nor contradict him either. "Cows, ranches, cowboys. A man can't step outside without smelling cow shit and swatting flies. The Panhandle is the hind end of Texas, Jubilee. No factories, no ironworks, no railroads, no brick streets anywhere in its twenty-five thousand square miles, and only three towns. None of them is any use to a man except to drink or gamble or whore in the case of Mobeetie and Tascosa. Clarendon isn't even good for that. Saints' Roost, the cowboys call it, and for damn good reason. It doesn't have a saloon, a gambling hall, or a single lady of ill repute."

"Reverend Carhart and his Methodists settled it, Colonel, and them Methodists is death on liquor."

"I find such rectitude uncharitable. A man ought to at least be allowed a glass of brandy to help him digest his supper."

"They is a God-fearing lot in Clarendon."

"Mattie's never been to Clarendon, has she,

Jubilee?" asked the Colonel, staring across the yard at his daughter leaning against the trunk of the huge cottonwood tree.

He heard the ex-slave shuffle his feet. Just like a darkie, he thought. Ask one a question he doesn't want to answer, and he shuffles around as though looking for a good lie.

"Clarendon's a good piece away, Colonel," Jubilee finally said. "Must be more than a hundred miles from this-here ranch. Ain't no sense in riding that far when Tascosa's just down the Canadian River from here. Besides, Miss Mattie don't have no close ties to them folks."

"I can't blame her, Jubilee. No point in Mattie getting a stiff neck trying to hold up her head, or asking folks there to stretch their Christian charity to the breaking point by ignoring that Hunter woman." He clenched his fist as he glared at Jubilee. "That Hunter woman! Name of God, but her mother would be turning in her grave if she knew her daughter was called by such a name, like some white-trash share-cropper, or possessed such a reputation for unseemly behavior. No one has ventured so far as to call her behavior unsavory—at least, not in my hearing—but they're thinking it! I know that as surely as I know Mattie Jo Corley Hunter—my only child—deserves her reputation!"

Jubilee glared at the colonel with disapproval. "You ought not listen to such talk about Miss Mattie. Folks in Clarendon don't know her."

"They talk about her in Mobeetie and Tascosa, too, Jubilee, but in my estimation, the number of citizens of either town who are without sin don't amount to enough people to organize a good stoning."

"You ain't hardly without sin yourself, Colonel."

"I'm a man! I'm supposed to have sown some wild oats in my time."

"You done planted enough for a bumper harvest!"

"I never committed adultery, Jubilee, and I've kept my fornication within gentlemanly limits."

Jubilee shook his head, his lower lip pushed out. "That ain't no excuse to be sitting in judgment on Miss Mattie."

The colonel pulled on his gloves and stepped off the porch. "She's my daughter. I must see to her moral character—and I have! I've seen to it that Jesse McDade will not share her bed or her table again! If he does, I'll see this damnable ranch she loves so much sown with salt and sold to the first British syndicate that wants it."

Jubilee straightened, the expression in his eyes foreboding. "Miss Mattie hates them British syndicates, Colonel. She don't think they treat their cowboys or the nester ranchers fair."

"I know that, and you know that, but what's more important is that Jesse McDade knows that." The colonel hesitated. "I give the man credit for being too fond of my daughter to go back on his word not to see her."

Jubilee followed him to the hitching post where his horse waited. "I backed you up, Colonel, when you twisted Jesse's arm into making that promise, 'cause he needed to leave her be. Wasn't nothing else for him to do, but I hopes we ain't gonna be sorry for what we done."

"We did what we had to do," said the colonel.

"So did Miss Mattie, Colonel."

Ignoring him, the colonel gathered his reins, but stood by his horse's side without mounting, studying the daughter who, until the past June, he had not seen for five years. Her hair was the same gold, her eyes the same pale, pale color that looked more yellow than brown. But she was different. The soft, childish contours of her face had vanished, leaving the chiseled features of a woman. Her cheekbones were more prominent, her jaw more firm, her eyes more dominant and filled with shadowy secrets she did not share. No woman should look a man in the face with such directness, such assurance, such lack of modesty, such *indifference*. Particularly if that man was her father.

It was unseemly and improper.

She was twenty-two years old, and the strength to be so indifferent was unnatural in one so young— particularly in a woman.

Unless.

He closed his eyes and caught his saddle horn, hanging on until he controlled his grief and fear. He knew now why Mattie refused to go to Clarendon. It was not because she was ashamed of her behavior, but because she was unrepentant.

"Mattie?"

Her father's voice was an intrusion on her thoughts. She resented his choosing to leave at barely past dawn. This was her private time when she looked to the west, toward Jesse's place, and thought of him. She imagined him standing in the bedroom meticulously shaving, dipping his straight razor in the steaming water, then raising his chin to shave his throat. He would be bare chested, the weather not being cool enough yet for a union suit, and drops of soapy water would catch on the curly body hair that had always intrigued her.

Her thoughts followed him into the kitchen where a grizzled, bowlegged old man named Charlie fed him breakfast before Jesse walked out into the cool dawn, drawing on his riding gloves and running through a checklist of jobs to be done by himself and his twenty men. He looked the same as he always had—except harder, the grin that revealed a dimple on one cheek seen less often, his eyes the silver color of lightning before a storm and just as dangerous.

Or so Jubilee said.

Mattie hadn't seen Jesse since her housewarming when her father had terminated his contract as manager of the Bar H Ranch and paid him his bonus.

"Mattie?"

Jubilee touched her shoulder. "Yore daddy is talking to you."

She turned her head reluctantly to look at her father. "I hope you enjoyed your visit, Papa, and will come again soon. Leon will miss you." Her voice was as flat and colorless as the plains and she wondered if it would always be so, or if time would give back something of her life.

The Colonel's eyes were pleading. "Come home with me, Mattie. Leon is six years old and needs to be in school, not taught by you at the dining-room table. He needs playmates his own age who are children of good families. Not these ignorant cowboys."

"I will send Leon to Tascosa as soon as they open a school," replied Mattie. "I'll board him with a respectable family."

"Tascosa! And what will he learn there, young lady? How to gamble and indulge in less respectable pastimes? There are even games of chance held in the livery stable, and the stakes are as high as any mining town could boast. And that's in the so-called best part of town. The Hogtown section is even worse. The women in those two- and three-room shacks behind the saloons in Hogtown don't make their living by taking in sewing."

Mattie flushed. "I know Tascosa's reputation better than you, Papa, but it is the only close town. Mobeetie is no better. Besides, Leon is not the first child to learn to read and write at home."

"Mama and I can't go to Pueblo, Grandpa," said Leon, his blue eyes as serious as ever, too old for Mattie's liking. "Fall roundup is next month, then we're trailing a herd to Dodge. Mostly the last of the culls Mama wants to sell. Then our herd will be almost all the crossbreed that Mama and Jesse bred. Have you looked at them, Grandpa? The yearlings are mostly red with white faces and very short horns. Jesse says that shorthorn cattle are better than the Texas longhorn. He says it is a noble breed, but not practical because their horns take up too much space in a cattle car. Their meat is stringy, too."

The Colonel's face took on a desperate expression as he looked at Mattie. "Do you suppose Leon knows more than three sentences that don't include that man's name?"

"Jesse's?" she asked, drawing out the name, relishing the opportunity to say it aloud. "No, I don't. He taught us both all he knew."

The Colonel glanced over his shoulder as if expecting to see the former trail boss behind him, then turned back to catch her eyes. "Mattie, I understand more now than I did. The land's hard and the work's hard, and a woman needs a hard man to look out for her, and you didn't have one in your husband, Samuel. I don't blame you as much as I did. You were lonely, and there weren't many other women, and a man like Jesse has needs. I see now how it could have happened. A woman has to survive."

"If it makes you happy to think so, Papa," said Mattie.

"It doesn't make me happy, but it makes me less sorrowful than thinking you were grabbing what might have been—maybe what should have been.

We might regret the things we do to survive, but not as much as we regret the things we want and can't have. A man never gets over that kind of regret."

"Or a woman," whispered Mattie, turning her eyes blindly toward the west.

"I'm sorry, Mattie."

She swallowed. "You best go, or you'll miss the freight wagons leaving Tascosa. Then you'll never find your way across the prairie to Mobeetie. As you're so fond of pointing out, we have no roads in the Panhandle."

He nodded, his gaze falling involuntarily to Mattie's swelling belly. "I'll send Aunt Patty for your confinement."

Mattie laid a hand on her stomach in time to feel the baby kick. "Travel is dangerous in this country in the late winter. Besides," she continued to distract his counting months, "if you send Aunt Patty to me, you'll have no one left."

His eyes strayed to Jubilee, then back to her. "I have no one now." He cleared his throat. "I'll be fine, Mattie, and so will you and Samuel. A new baby always puts starch in a man. You'll see."

She heard the unspoken question in his voice and ignored it. Whether she was carrying Jesse's baby or her husband Samuel's was her business and none of his. As Jubilee said, what folks suspect is not the same as knowing. The less she said about her baby's parentage, the less chance it would be branded a bastard.

That was the only reason she hadn't revealed that Samuel had raped her the night Jesse left.

That was the only reason she hadn't killed him afterwards.

"Good-bye, Papa."

She saw his lips tremble for a second before he lifted his head to look at the silent figure standing beside her. "You're too old to be working like a field hand, Jubilee. Best come back to Pueblo with me."

"There's life in these bones yet, Colonel. Reckon I'll stay."

The Colonel mounted his horse with a creaking of leather and aging joints. "Jubilee, take care of Mattie and Leon."

"Don't you worry none, Colonel. I be watching out for her like I always done."

Finally the Colonel sighed and tipped his hat to his ex-slave. "Watch out for yourself, too, you old reprobate. We spent too many years together for me to take kindly to your leaving this world without a last farewell. It's tradition, Jubilee."

Mattie was close enough to see the tear that escaped Jubilee's eye. "I reckon I'll outlast you, Colonel."

Mattie's father nodded. "You would, too, just to get in the last word. You always were an uppity nigger, and Texas hasn't improved you any."

Mattie watched him ride off, the father she loved and hated.

Clint rode in on the first of October.

Maggie knew who walked into the kitchen even though she had her back to the door. Clint Murray had his own personal smell of corruption. How many years since the ex-gambler had first crossed her threshold, leeching onto Samuel and draining away his strength and decency—what little her husband had? Three years? No, four years, nearly five, and for most of that time, she had forbidden him to live in the old Mexican sheepherder's plaza that served as headquarters before she built this house. Nothing had changed. She had no intention of allowing Murray to live in her new headquarters any more than she had allowed him to live in the old one. She didn't intend to make it any easier for him to influence Samuel.

She brushed back a lock of hair and considered that influence. She must make an effort to decipher its source. As long as Jesse was manager, it was enough to know that Clint Murray made her skin turn cold without delving into why. But Jesse was gone, moved to his own ranch, and she sensed it was important that she dissect Samuel's and Clint's relationship. Ignorance was a hindrance to survival. That was one of the first lessons Jesse taught her. Know the land and the men on it because both can kill you—one with the brutal indifference of nature and the other with deliberate malice.

Jesse taught her one other technique for survival. Respect yourself.

She added another stick of wood to the stove before turning around. No need to ruin five loaves of bread by letting the fire burn too low just because a piece of filth was standing behind her.

"You hardly let the dust settle from my father's horse before coming back, did you?"

Clint Murray wore an ugly smile as he pulled out a chair and sat down at the kitchen table. "Not a very warm welcome for an old friend, Mattie."

"You're not a friend, and you're not welcome. Get out of my house."

"You're being inhospitable, Mattie." Samuel's smile was equally ugly, but with a touch of cockiness that set Mattie's teeth to clenching. He dropped into the chair next to Clint's and laid his hand on the other man's shoulder. The gesture only added to Mattie's usual morning nausea. "Now be a good little wife and fix Clint and me some breakfast."

Mattie heard Jubilee move up behind her. "Didn't

you hear me, Samuel? Clint Murray is not welcome in my house."

Samuel leaned back in his chair with the air of a potentate. "It's not *your* house, Mattie. It's mine. You do not seem to understand yet that things are different now. You no longer have that poor white trash McDade to interfere with my rights. And your father has gone back to Pueblo, leaving affairs in my hands. Your name on the ranching accounts and on the deed is a mere gesture on his part. Practically, it means nothing. I am in charge, and Clint is the new manager of the Rocking H."

"Red's the manager, Pa," said Leon, who had been sitting quietly at the other end of the table, but Mattie had noticed his serious expression as he had listened to the exchange. "Clint Murray doesn't know enough about ranching."

Samuel's face turned ruddy with anger. "Shut up, Leon. I'll not have you arguing with me. Your behavior is your mother's fault. She turned you against me. You break my heart, son."

Leon's face turned white, and Mattie saw his lower lip tremble as the child broke through his mask of maturity. No one had ever spoken so harshly to him. Certainly not his father who generally ignored his presence. She put her hands on his thin shoulders and felt their rigidity. "Ask Danny to saddle your horse, Leon. You're late this morning, and Red will be wondering where his youngest hand is."

Leon scrambled away from the table, grabbed his hat off the hat rack, and ran out the back door. Red, the young cowboy she had appointed manager after Jesse left, would protect Leon. She was certain of that. Red had worked for her—for her and Jesse, she silently amended—since the day when they trailed the first cattle herd down from Pueblo, Colorado, to the empty Texas Panhandle. Red knew and despised Samuel and Clint. He would protect Leon from them until Mattie solved this latest crisis.

She braced her hands on the table and leaned over to look directly at Samuel. "Don't ever talk to him like that again. Leave him be. This fight is between us and Leon has nothing to do with it. I haven't turned him against you, much as I've wanted to, because I don't want him caught between us, never knowing whom to believe, whom to trust. I'm begging you, Samuel, if you have any decency at all, if you have any real feelings left for your son, *leave him be!*"

She thought she saw indecision in his eyes, and closed her own, praying that she might win this one argument.

She heard a chair creak and opened her eyes to see Clint Murray lean over to whisper something to Samuel. Her husband clenched his hands together and stared down at them as if they mirrored an internal struggle. Mattie watched also, hypnotized by those hands that twisted and pulled at one another. There was no sound in the room but Samuel's rasping breaths and the billowing of the curtains from a cool fall wind that blew in the window, bringing the scent of cattle and horses to blend with that of baking bread.

Finally Samuel raised his head. "He is my son, and I will deal with him as I see fit."

Mattie straightened. "Jubilee, if you will bring coffee to my sitting room, please. I have need of clean air to breathe."

Samuel grabbed her arm. "Fix our breakfast."

"Fix your own breakfast, damn you!" she yelled, clawing furrows with her nails in the top of his hand and stumbling awkwardly backward when he let go of her to cradle his bleeding hand.

"Bitch! You marked me!" He knocked his chair over getting up, his teeth showing in that feral grimace that always frightened her so.

Years later Mattie wondered what might have happened if Hank Wilson had not come bursting through the back door, if time had stood still a moment longer and Jubilee had killed Samuel and Clint with the shotgun he always kept close at hand.

But time had ever been her enemy.

"Miss Mattie, men—freighters—are down on the creek chopping down every damn tree more than waist high. They said your husband sold them all the wood they could cut to fill their empty wagons."

"What?" screamed Mattie.

Samuel's expression had turned from feral to triumphant. "Driving empty wagons back to Dodge from Tascosa costs the freighting companies money. If those wagons are full of goods for resale, then the freighters turn a handsome profit—and so do I. Wood for fence posts, Mattie. Charlie Goodnight made the same kind of deal over on the JA ranch."

"And Goodnight regretted it!" Mattie's belly churned with a sickness that had nothing to do with her pregnancy. "The freighters nearly stripped the Palo Duro, leaving nothing but stumps and ugliness. I won't have it here!" She ran for the back door and Hank's horse.

Samuel laughed. "You can't stop it, Mattie. You're just a woman with no say."

His words followed her out the door and lingered on her mind long after she mounted, her skirt ruffled up showing her ankles and calves, Hank's Winchester balanced across the saddle in front of her. She kicked her horse into a gallop toward the creek. Samuel was right. She had no say—not directly at least—but her husband had underestimated her influence. Her reputation as a lady might be tarnished, but her reputation as that Hunter woman was intact.

And so was her army, she noticed as she reined in her horse. Freighters and cowboys faced one another against a backdrop of fallen trees. The red and gold leaves scattered on the creek banks crackled under her horse's hooves like colored glass.

She quickly picked out the leader of the freighters—a tall, barrel-chested man with a face as hard as the land before a rain. "Get your men and wagons off my land. I'm not selling timber to outsiders now or ever. There are few enough trees in this country, and what I own, I'll keep for my own use."

The freighter shifted a wad of tobacco from one cheek to the other and spat. He wiped his mouth with the back of his hand and looked up at her. "You must be Mrs. Hunter."

Mattie nodded. "Obviously—or I wouldn't be chasing you off my land."

"Begging your pardon, ma'am, but your husband sold us these trees. Closed the deal in Tascosa yesterday."

While she had been saying good-bye to her father, thought Mattie, keeping her face as impassive as she was able. Samuel had not waited overlong to snipe at her. "My husband did so without consulting with me. I don't intend to abide by his decision."

The freighter looked over her shoulder. "Reckon you best take that up with your husband, Mrs. Hunter. That's him riding up now."

"Mattie! Go back to the house! You have no business talking to men in your condition." Samuel jerked on his reins and slid off his horse to swagger up to the freighter. "I'm sorry about this, Mr.

Blanchard. My wife is a little upset about her trees. We have to coddle women who are in the family way."

Mattie gasped with outrage. To speak of her pregnancy in front of strange men was worse than her appearing in front of them. Damn Samuel. "I won't go back to the house until these men are either off my land or arrested by the sheriff for trespassing."

Blanchard frowned. "I didn't count on no conversation with the sheriff, Hunter."

"Mrs. Hunter's threat is just so much hot air," added Clint Murray, casting a malicious glance at Mattie. "She is powerless to do anything."

Mattie lifted her Winchester. Behind her she heard her cowboys cock their pistols. "By all means, Mr. Blanchard, let us discuss power. At present I have Winchester power. In a few hours there will be warrants here and I will have legal power. I sent one of my men to Tascosa to bring charges against you for trespassing."

Samuel laughed and clapped the freighter's shoulder. "Don't worry, Blanchard. The sheriff can't arrest you for trespassing if I've given you permission to be here."

"The sheriff will have to serve those warrants, Mr. Blanchard," said Mattie. "And he will do so in spite of Mr. Hunter's protests, and let the matter be settled in court. The judge may refuse the case—but not before you have been inconvenienced."

Leather creaked as Mattie leaned back in the saddle seeking a more comfortable position. "There is also the nature of democracy to consider. I do not have a vote, but I control votes. My cowboys and those of Jesse McDade are registered voters of Oldham County. They far outnumber my husband and Clint Murray. If elected officials, such as the sheriff and the county judge, fail to support my charges, my men and Jesse's men will fail to support them in the next election. I may be a woman, but I am not ignorant of how government works." She heard one of her cowboys whistle and another snicker.

Accolades came in all forms.

Blanchard spat a brown stream of tobacco juice on the ground. "I don't believe I'll wait around for them warrants, ma'am. The Winchesters will do."

Mattie smiled and lowered her rifle. "Have a pleasant trip back to Dodge, Mr. Blanchard."

Samuel grabbed for the freighter's arm. "You're not going to listen to her?"

Blanchard shoved him away. "Don't be reaching for me. I'll take my bullwhip to you. I ain't getting mixed up with the law, Hunter. I don't much like you anyway, and your wife's got you over a barrel best I can tell. Next time you pull a stunt like this, you best talk to her first." He lifted his hat to Mattie. "Good day, ma'am."

Samuel rounded on her, his eyes so vicious that Mattie barely kept from flinching. "So this is the way it'll be."

Mattie nodded. "Leave my ranch alone, Samuel." She turned her horse and rode back home to prepare for what she knew would be an unrelenting war.

CHAPTER

2

In Jesse's opinion Tascosa was easy on the eyes and the nose only in early October when the cotton-woods turned golden and the cool fall weather lessened the stench. In the winter the town huddled under the cottonwood's bare limbs like so many mud huts in a grove of sticks, while in the spring and summer flies and heat and the smell of cattle and sweaty men crept along its streets and circled its buildings like an invisible noxious fog. But in all seasons Tascosa echoed with the noise of wagon wheels, horses' hooves, the slap of cards on a bare tabletop, the clinking of poker chips, men's husky laughter or harsh tones of an argument, the cheerful conversation of respectable women as they went about their daily chores, and the shrill voices of children playing in sandy streets. And rumors. Surrounded by ranches, with no newspaper, isolated by empty miles from the larger world, Tascosa wrung every last drop of entertainment and information from rumor and gossip and half-understood stories. It was in Tascosa where Mattie's reputation as that Hunter woman first took root, and it was in Tascosa where Jesse heard of the first skirmish in Mattie's war when he ran into Jubilee in Mickey McCormick's livery stable. The ex-slave looked as if he had aged years in the four months since the night of Mattie's housewarming party. There was more white in his kinky black hair and the furrows on his forehead were deeper. His eyes darted restlessly as if he were searching out an ambush.

Jesse slid off his horse and tossed the reins to a waiting stable boy, then strolled over to slap Jubilee on the back. "You worthless no 'count, what are you doing in Tascosa? Did Mattie give you a day off for a spree? Or is Mattie here?"

A foolish question, he thought as he glanced quickly around the stable's dark interior, searching for a glint of golden hair, the flash of topaz eyes. If Mattie had been anywhere in Tascosa, he would have sensed her presence in the same way he did a coming storm before the clouds had even gathered, in some ancient part of his soul reserved for sensing life-giving things.

Jubilee leapt as though Jesse's hand had burned him, and whirled around, clawing at his holster. He closed his eyes and sagged against one of the stable's walls when he recognized Jesse. "Lordy, don't sneak up on me like that. I coulda kilt you 'fore I knowed what I was doing."

Jesse smiled, an uneasy feeling tightening the skin across his shoulder blades. "I doubt it, Jubilee. You couldn't outdraw Leon, much less me. What are you so fidgety about?"

Jubilee wiped his sleeve across his forehead. "I thought you might be Hunter."

"What about Hunter?" He suddenly noticed the

expression in the black man's eyes and caught his arm, drawing him to a corner away from the curious eyes of the stable boy. "What's going on, Jubilee? Why do you look scared to death?"

"I just finished catching up with the Colonel, taking Leon to him so he can go to Pueblo with his grandpa. Miss Mattie had me sneak him out of the house and ride like thunder. I hopes I never lives through nothing like that again. I ain't never been much on a horse—house servants never had much call to ride—and between the horse and Leon crying like I was beating him, I'm wrung out like a dishrag. I had to stop here in Tascosa and let my hindquarters rest even iffen I was plumb scairt out of my hide. I figured you was Hunter fixing to shoot me for taking the boy without his knowing about it."

Jesse drew a breath and slowly let it out. "I think you better tell me what's happening." Jubilee did, and Jesse felt his muscles go rigid. "So Mattie sent Leon to Pueblo with the Colonel so he'd be safe from Hunter?"

Jubilee nodded. "Poor little feller didn't want to go. Kept looking at me with them eyes of his that looks too old for a chile his age, and asking why he'd done wrong. I told him his mama wanted him to go to school. I lied to that boy, Jesse, 'cause I couldn't tell him his mama was afraid his pa would hurt him."

"What about Mattie?" demanded Jesse. "Why the hell didn't you throw her across a horse and take her along?"

"I tole her and tole her she better come, too. Hunter was madder than a wet hen over that tree business, and I don't know what he's planning next. But Miss Mattie, she say she's not gonna hide. That she ain't about to walk off and let Hunter have that ranch, not after you and her worked so hard building it up while Hunter done nothing but sit on his behind, and that she for certain ain't about to go back to being the Colonel's little girl. And she threatened to skin me if I told her daddy. She said there was nothing he could do seeing as how she'd paid off the mortgage he'd done held on to the ranch, and besides, she didn't want two men telling her what to do. She ain't no coward, Jesse, but she is for certain a fool. Woman can't live like that— allus fighting and looking behind her so nobody sneaks up."

Jesse spat out the bile that choked him. "I should have told the Colonel that Samuel was a damn pederast."

Jubilee shook his head. "Iffen that means what I reckons it does, the Colonel wouldn't have believed it. Not coming from you, anyhow. He'd figured you was just trying to get Miss Mattie. He probably wouldn't have believed me none either. The Colonel ain't much on taking a nigger's word over a white man's. Comes from his raising, and I guess he ain't ever gonna change. Besides, he ain't forgive me for leaving him to come to Texas with Miss Mattie. I been with him since we was both five years old, and I hurt him bad when I left. I knowed it when I done it, but I figured after fifty years, it was time he learned to shave hisself. And Miss Mattie needed family— somebody besides that worthless husband—and she needed somebody to stand between her and you. I saw that heat in your eyes the first time you looked at her in the Colonel's office back in Pueblo before he even hired you to trail that first herd to Texas and set up a ranch. I knowed then you was trouble." He looked away, embarrassed. "I just didn't figure my Miss Mattie would grow up to want that kind of trouble."

Jesse searched for feelings of regret or shame for lying with Mattie, but found his grief instead. He wondered how long he would grieve for Mattie, and if she grieved for him.

Or if she believed he had betrayed her.

"Where's Hunter now?" asked Jesse, pulling off his right glove and flexing his hand.

Jubilee grabbed his arms. "Don't go shooting him, Jesse. It would plumb ruin Miss Mattie, and the law would be after you."

Jesse pushed him away. "I'll risk it."

The black man shook his head. "I ain't gonna let you. Hunter ain't hurt her yet, and he ain't going to. She's got the cowboys and she's got me. Miss Mattie thinks if she can hang on, Hunter will get tired of warting her, and she can buy him out. She ain't far wrong, Jesse. He hates that ranch and he hates Texas. He'll go off one of these days—him and that low-down Clint Murray."

Jesse patted the other man's arm. "I won't kill him then, Jubilee. I'll just encourage him to find a place he likes better a little faster. Now, where is the son of a bitch?"

"I heared he was down to the Equity Bar. That's why I was hightailing it out of town just as soon as I could feel my hindquarters again 'fore he knowed I was here. I weren't too anxious to take him on in front of a bunch of drunk white men who might not take kindly to a nigger beating up on another white man. Cowboys at the ranch don't care. They'd just as soon spit on Hunter as look at him."

"I'm going down to the Equity and have a drink—among other things. No one will take notice of one white man beating up another."

"They will if it's Jesse McDade and Samuel Hunter," warned Jubilee.

"I left her, Jubilee. And I promised her father I'd leave her be—and I'll keep my word—but I don't want Samuel getting the idea that means she's alone.

Because she's not. I'm always there—whether anybody else can see me or not. Until all the grass dies and the Canadian runs dry, I'm always with her." He squeezed Jubilee's arm and walked down the sandy street to the Equity Bar.

"Hunter!"

Jesse stopped in the archway leading to the back room of the Equity Bar where chairs and gaming tables were set up. Even though it was only late afternoon, the tables were full, the air heavy with the odors of tobacco, sweat, and cheap whiskey, and women of various ages and looks but of equal availability stood ready to hand a man a drink or themselves, depending on which thirst was the greater at any given moment. The drinks were cheaper, but the price of a woman was not above what a cowboy could afford on his wages—provided he practiced economy and didn't try to sample all the available wares and gamble too much besides. A man had to pace himself in Tascosa.

"Hunter!"

At a table in the far corner of the room, Samuel threw down his cards and kicked back his chair. He swatted away a woman too newly arrived in town to know she was scattering the seeds of her allure on sterile ground, and faced Jesse.

"What do you want, McDade?" he asked, a higher pitch to his voice than Jesse remembered.

Jesse stalked across the room, barely noticing the men abandoning their money and cards on the tables to scatter out of the way of possible gunfire. He stopped in front of Samuel, grabbed the edge of the table, and tipped it out of the way. "To talk to you. Outside—unless you want the whole town to know our business."

Samuel's glanced skittered toward Clint Murray, and Jesse's eyes flickered over the other man, noticing no gun belt, but recognizing the awkward bend of Murray's arm. In violation of the Equity's rules—and all other saloons' rules so far as Jesse knew—Murray no doubt carried a hideout pistol under his sleeve.

Without further reflection, Jesse hooked his boot in the chair rung and yanked it over, spilling Murray backward on the floor. Murray's arms splayed out in a futile motion to catch himself, and with a reflex so quick spectators later said they could hardly see it, Jesse vaulted over the prone figure and stomped on Murray's gun hand. The crack of breaking bone was followed by Samuel's scream.

"You bastard!"

Jesse leaned over and removed Murray's hideout gun from its spring-loaded holster and tossed it to a watching cowboy. "I want a fair fight, boys."

The cowboy caught the gun and nodded. "Sure enough, Jesse."

Samuel launched himself at Jesse, landing the first blow high on Jesse's chest. "I'll kill you."

Jesse retaliated, catching Samuel with an upper cut that knocked him back against the wall. He followed it up with a belly punch that doubled Samuel over. Another upper cut straightened him up again so Jesse could switch to openhanded blows that whipped Samuel's face from right to left to right again, reducing the man's countenance to stinging flesh. Grabbing Samuel's collar, he pulled him out of the game room, through the main saloon with its fancy display bar, and out into the street. Turning right, he dragged the blubbering man past Joe Krause's livery stable and an adobe residence, to the banks of Tascosa Creek, once a pretty, tree-lined stream, but now mostly denuded of its vegetation.

With a grunt, Jesse rolled Samuel's inert body into the creek, watched him gasp and cough up the dirty, cold water, then reached down and dragged him onto the muddy bank. Squatting down, Jesse grasped his hair and jerked Samuel's face out of the mud.

"Don't ever do anything to threaten Mattie again, you piece of cow shit. Don't interfere with her managing the ranch, and don't use her son against her. If you do, there's no place far enough that I won't find you. And next time, Samuel, I'll kill you."

Samuel's pale blond hair lay plastered to his head with mud, and spare, wet lashes emphasized the protuberant blue eyes. "You're crazy, McDade, crazy because she threw you out of her bed. I saw her at that housewarming party, dancing with every man, cutting you dead. I guess she thinks you should have turned down the Colonel's fat bonus and begged the old bastard to give you another five year contract so you could sniff around her like a dog in heat. I told her no woman's tail was worth that kind of money—not even that Hunter woman's."

Jesse backhanded him again. "Don't be talking about Mattie that way."

Samuel's eyes were maniacal with hatred. "Can't stand it that her belly's swelling up again, can you, McDade? Can't stand to think that she welcomed me—*me*—into her bed the very night she cut you out. All those months you sweated over her, and I planted her in one try. You can beat me senseless, but I'm more of a man than you."

All of Jesse's strength was behind his last blow, the sound of Samuel's ribs cracking under his fist louder than a pistol shot. Staggering up, he walked away, shoving the curious out of the way as he stumbled down Main Street toward Mickey McCormick's livery stable.

Mattie was pregnant again! Pregnant by Samuel. She would always be pregnant by Samuel—always be his wife. And Jesse McDade would build a dream for children he would never have, and his land would pass to strangers, and his body molder in the grave with no one to mourn but another man's wife.

He stopped abruptly, his legs spread wide and his feet braced against the shifting sand and raised a clenched fist toward the empty sky. "No!"

CHAPTER

Aunt Patty arrived the first of February 1883, the year of the rainless, snowless winter. The Canadian had dried to cracked red chips where it ran through Tascosa, and the townspeople and ranchers watched the north for snow clouds and the southwest for thunderstorms. Tempers frayed in the unseasonable weather, and the cold, dry air sucked moisture from lips and skin, leaving hands and mouths cracked and bleeding. Cattle lost flesh and turned gaunt as water holes disappeared in the arid pastures north of the Canadian. Instead of drifting before a blizzard, the cattle drifted before the drought and scattered in search of grazing and water. With water scarce, ranchers clamped down harder on nesters and on their own men. Rules against mavericking became harsher, and the cowboy, once an independent knight on horseback and loyal unto death to the brand for which he rode, found himself truly just a hired hand. A laborer on horseback, ill paid and unappreciated.

To Mattie, the discontent of land and men had seemed distant as her pregnancy constricted her world to the ranch headquarters and the house she had built. Not that she ignored her sense of trouble gathering, but she lacked the strength to face it. It seemed unimportant compared to Jesse's child, the child she had labored to deliver since yesterday at noon. As she watched the long night hours pass in the flickering shadows cast by the lamplight, the pain of Jesse's absence nearly equaled the pain of labor, and her cries became more of loss than of childbirth.

But never once did she call his name.

"Lord above, Miss Mattie, I wish you would just once say something instead of that awful screaming," said Aunty Patty, wiping Mattie's sweating face. "It's enough to make a body's hair stand on end. Most women at your stage would be begging the Lord and the devil both to send their husbands to perdition without their male parts. There ain't no shame in feeling that way about this time in birthing a baby. A woman feels like her vitals is being tore out while her husband is waiting out her pain guzzling liquor."

Mattie flexed her hands, stiff from clutching the rawhide rope tied to the bedposts, then gripped it again as her belly contracted. "He had no part of this," she gasped, drawing up her knees and pushing down.

Not until her muscles eased did she realize what she had said, and looked up at the old mountain woman she'd known most of her life. "Aunt Patty," she said, her voice hoarse from her screams. "Give me your word you'll hold your tongue."

Aunt Patty's pale blue eyes held no condemnation that Mattie could see. Nor did they hold any surprise. "When your pa found me burying my last child beside the trail, he could have given me food and told me where the nearest town was. But he didn't. He offered to bury my boy for me, then he hired me—an old mountain woman in a patched gingham dress who he didn't know from Adam. I promised him I'd look after his women-folk—you and your mama—and I did until your mama died and you moved to Texas. I don't figure nothing has changed. You need looking after and your pa trusts me to do it, but birthing is woman's business, and I don't reckon there's any man has a right to know what's on your mind while you're at it. Nor any woman either, for that matter."

Aunt Patty lifted the sheet covering Mattie's legs. "I see the head, Miss Mattie. Just a little more work, and we'll have this young'un born."

Mattie propped herself up on her elbows and pushed down again. Her hair, braided in a waist-length cord, was dark with sweat, and her lips reddish brown with dried blood where she had bitten them before finally giving in to the urge to scream as her labor and loneliness dragged on through the night. She braced herself again as the ungovernable urge to push caught her up and her muscles tightened, then relaxed as she felt the indefinable sensation of her baby sliding from her body. She fell back with a gasp of relief and blinked as the sun threw a sunbeam across her pillow, and a newborn's first cry broke the silence of dawn.

"It's a boy, Miss Mattie, a mighty big one, too," said Aunt Patty with no discernable question in her voice.

"Let me see him!" demanded Mattie, reaching up her arms.

Aunt Patty laid the baby on Mattie's stomach and

cut the umbilical cord. "You just lie still until you finishes what you have to do. This child's not going anywhere."

Mattie twisted her head for a better look at the infant lying on her stomach, tiny fists clenched in anger at his unceremonious arrival. "Hold him up, Aunt Patty!"

The old woman threw her a sharp glance. "Don't go using that tone of voice with me. I ain't one of your cowboys, and I ain't gonna jump every time you open your mouth." She relented as she seemed to feel the anxiety that Mattie had strove to hide. "He looks like you, Miss Mattie, if that's what's worrying you. Gonna have gold eyes like yours. Hair's liable to be a powerful lot darker—maybe like tobacco—but sometimes that happens. Your pa's was brown when he was younger, so you can rest easy. This young'un ain't gonna have black hair."

Mattie lay back. "Thank you, Aunt Patty."

"Is that all you got to say?" asked Aunt Patty, bathing Mattie's womanly parts and binding her up with soft, clean cloths.

Mattie touched the fine down on her baby's head. "His name is Robert Corley—Hunter. Born on February twenty-third, 1883, to Mattie Jo Hunter. My Bible is on the dresser. Record the birth, please, Aunt Patty."

The old woman picked up the infant and began to bathe him. "Time enough for that when you're sure about the name you've picked. Don't want to be crossing out things in the family record, nor lying neither."

"I'm very sure, and I'm not lying. He is my son."

"Secrets got a way of coming out when you don't want them to, Miss Mattie, and they generally come out a little worse for being hidden. Best have one place where the truth is written—for them who come after you if for no better reason. Otherwise, you're storing up trouble."

Mattie was certain her eyes were as hard and bright as newly minted coins. "Write it down, Aunt Patty, exactly as I said it. Born on February twenty-third, 1883, to Mattie Jo Hunter. Nothing more."

Aunt Patty sighed as she blotted the squirming baby dry, then bound his belly where the umbilical cord was cut before diapering him and wrapping him in a blanket. "You was five years old or there-about when I first seen you, and I didn't know whether you'd grow up strong like a woman needs to, or weak and needing to cling to a man like your mama. I believe you growed up stronger than me, Miss Mattie. I sure hope so. I got a suspicion you're gonna need that strength 'cause when a woman sins and gets caught, she ain't got nobody to depend on but herself."

"I earned the right to sin, Aunt Patty."

"Knowing what a sorry specimen you married, I don't doubt but what you did. You best remember, though, it was a man who said the wages of sin is death. A woman knows better. The wages of sin is livin'."

"I'll survive." Mattie struggled out of bed and sank into a rocking chair, holding out her arms for her baby. She cuddled the newborn while she studied his face in the sunbeams shining through the bare limbs of the cottonwood tree outside her window.

Tom Miller huddled next to the campfire at the LS supply depot, a native stone and frame building near the mouth of Frio Creek south of the Canadian River. Besides the LS, cowboys of two other floating outfits, from the LIT and the LX, stood or sat eating beef, corn, tomatoes, molasses, and sourdough biscuits. Spoons clinked against the tin plates, and low, husky laughter occasionally punctuated the conversation. After weeks of chasing after drifting cattle and herding them back to their home ranges, Tom reckoned everyone was as tired as he was. Being assigned to the floating outfit that followed on the heels of drifting cattle rather than working out of the LS headquarters meant sleeping rolled up in a blanket on the prairie rather than in the bunkhouse or a line shack, eating off a chuckwagon, and bathing in a creek or water hole—if a man bathed at all. Mostly he didn't, especially in the wintertime or early spring. Too damn cold for a man to do more than wash his face and hands. Tom was weary of his own smell.

He was weary of more than that. He was thirty-seven years old and looked every day of it, and he'd been following the rear ends of cows since he was sixteen and left the dirt farm in east Texas after his father had laid a razor strap across his back one too many times for dreaming harder than he worked. Tom dropped his plate in the tub of soapy water and poured another cup of coffee as he thought about his father. His pa hadn't been a wicked man, just couldn't dream any farther than the end of a plowed furrow and a dogtrot cabin nestled under the pine trees. He hadn't hankered after a sky a man didn't have to peer at through the tree branches, or a land that stretched out to meet the edge of the world.

Tom figured that dreamers were mostly people born in the wrong place who drifted like cattle until they found the range where the grass was green and the water sweet. Some folks never found that place. He had. It took a few years of trying out different parts of the country, but he was finally home.

And now barbed wire, foreign syndicates, and big ranchers who never spent a day working alongside their own cowboys were trying to deny him his home. He'd left the LX when the syndicate forbade his running his small herd with their brand, then fenced off a pasture where his two sections were located and gave him the choice of selling up or being arrested for trespassing every time he rode across LX land to his place. He'd sold up for a good price because he couldn't see that he had much choice, but it galled him to do it. Now he was riding for the LS brand, and Mr. Lee and Mr. Scott who owned it weren't much better than the syndicate. Mr. Lee was a powerful believer that if his cows were eating the grass, then the land it grew on was his regardless of whether that particular section was public land or not. Tom could understand a man who held what he owned, but neither Lee nor any of the other big ranchers owned the public school land. A lot of them didn't even legally lease it from the state.

Except Mattie Hunter and Jesse McDade.

They were two ranchers who played fair. They owned or leased every acre they claimed, and the few they didn't belonged to their cowboys, and not a word about running them off their land. They were a hell of a pair, those two, and Tom didn't give a hang what any of the other ranchers said. They were holding true to all the best customs for as long as they could.

Tom sipped his coffee, strong and black as a villain's heart, and let loose his dreams about Mattie Jo Hunter. The day he rode up and saw her holding a gun on that trail boss to keep him from driving cattle carrying Texas fever across her land, Tom knew that he had found one of his dreams all fleshed out with gold hair and skin. When her standoff ended in gunfire and she cried out a name when a bullet left a bloody furrow across her arm, he had no way of knowing who she was calling. He hadn't known at that moment that she was married to one man and her soul claimed by another.

He did now.

In fact, he knew almost everything about Mattie that listening and watching could teach him, and some things that he sensed without knowing for sure. Like for instance, he knew without being told that she and Jesse had spent most of a year enjoying what most folks called the sins of the flesh. He didn't condemn her for that—or Jesse either—but it burned his gut all the same. She'd earned better than the choice between a man she couldn't have and a husband not worth the rope it would take to hang him. But things changed. If there was one lesson he'd learned in his years, it was that nothing ever stayed the same, and life was as risky as a poker game. But Tom Miller was a hell of a poker player, a hell of a patient man, and he'd wait until the end of the game before throwing in his hand, because one of these days life would deal Mattie Jo Hunter new cards, and he planned to place a bet when it did. If he was wrong, if he was dreaming of cards that would never be dealt, so be it.

Tom Miller had lost poker games before.

"Hey, Tom, what do you think of the Panhandle Stock Association inspectors at the railhead cutting out our brands and claiming they're stolen? Hell, those big ranchers and syndicates lose more cattle in the Canadian River quicksand in a month than what few mavericks we claim. What's a couple hundred head when just one of them runs forty or fifty thousand head?"

The speaker was an LIT cowboy named Higgins, a quick-tempered fellow so short he was hardly frying size, but Tom respected his opinions. "I reckon there is some rustling going on, Higgins. Some men think it ain't a crime to rope a syndicate cow."

Higgins opened his eyes as wide as possible and let his mouth drop open. "You mean it is?" There was a roar of laughter from the other men around the campfire. "Listen, Tom, me and the other boys was talking, and we figure that if the ranchers ain't gonna let the cowboys run a few steers and horses alongside theirs, and if they're gonna call us all rustlers, then by God, they ought to pay for the privilege of insulting us. If I'm gonna be a hired hand on horseback, then I'm gonna be a well-paid one. Harris, wagon boss of the LS, has drawed up an agreement for us to sign."

Tom frowned at Higgins. "I know who Harris is. He's my wagon boss and he's squatting across the fire from me." He looked at the man who, next to Jesse McDade and Charlie Goodnight, was probably one of the most forceful men in the Panhandle, a natural leader frustrated by his powerless position. It suddenly struck Tom what a dangerous combination that was. "What kind of an agreement are you talking about, Harris?"

Tom Harris stood up, a piece of paper in his hand. "While you've been staring at your coffee cup, the rest of us have been talking about something besides horses, cows, and women. We're talking strike, Miller. A cowboy strike. Let these big ranchers with their slave wages and their account books find out that a cattle ranch boils down to hooves and horns. Men have to herd those cattle, brand them, treat them for screw worm, pull them out of the river when they bog down, drive them to market. Cows are real, not just marks on some manager's tally book, and real men have to work them. We earn a decent wage, and they can't do without us. They're making money hand over fist and denying us the right to make a little of our own, so I say we strike."

He held out the sheet and began to read. "We, the undersigned cowboys of Canadian River, do by these presents agree to bind ourselves into the following obligations, viz—First, that we will not work for less than $50 per month, and we furthermore agree no one shall work for less than $50 per month, after 31st of March.

"Second, good cooks shall also receive $50 per month.

"Third, anyone running an outfit shall not work for less than $75 per month. Anyone violating the above obligations shall suffer the consequences. Those not having funds to pay board after March 31st will be provided for 30 days at Tascosa."

Harris looked across at Tom. "All these boys have signed, and we're gonna put out a general call for cowboys on the rest of the ranches to join us. What do you say? Are you throwing in with us?"

Tom cleared his throat. "The demands seem fair enough, but some hands already make that much and more. McDade and Mattie Hunter pay their cowboys seventy-five and I hear Red gets a hundred, plus they can still run their own brands and throw a noose around a maverick. It'll be a cold day in hell before any cowboy strikes against the Flying MJ or the Bar H."

Harris raised his eyebrows. "McDade's always been a fair man, I'll give him that. But Mattie Hunter's been sticking close to home with that new young'un of hers, and that bastard she's married to has hired a fencing crew. I hear he's going to throw up his share of the drift fence in the north, and fence off his southern pastures. Any nester caught between the two fences is liable to find his hindquarters hanging out to dry. Mattie Hunter might not find her hands as loyal as she thinks."

"Samuel Hunter's come out on the short end of

the stick every time he's crossed his wife, usually with Jesse McDade holding the other end," said Tom.

Harris rubbed his jaw. "That's true, but I hear they aren't keeping company anymore."

Tom had heard that, too, heard in fact that Jesse and Mattie had not met face to face in nearly a year. Not that he figured that made any difference. It just meant that when they met again, the stakes for both would be higher for all the time and feelings they'd stored up.

Mattie was nursing Robert when her cowboys quit.

"Strike?" asked Mattie, pulling her shawl more tightly about her shoulders against the early morning chill. She could hear Robert upstairs crying in protest that his feeding had been interrupted, and she felt her milk-laden breasts ache in response. She had sent Aunt Patty up with a bottle of canned milk mixed with water, but obviously Robert found such a concoction not to his taste. He was a demanding baby and a poor sleeper, and she felt as if she had been only half awake at best the past month. Now, when she needed all of her faculties, she found herself wanting to lean her head against the side of the house and sleep standing up.

"Strike?" she asked again, shaking her head to clear it. Surely in her state of semiconsciousness, she had misunderstood.

"Yes, ma'am," replied a sullen-faced Red, handing her a piece of paper. "The boys voted to join Harris's strike. We drawed up a list of demands for you, and nobody works until they're met. I reckon Mr. Hunter and that Murray are gonna have to herd their own cattle for a change. They better get after it, too. The heel flies are nipping already, and might' near driving some of the cows loco. I figure there'll be some need to be pulled out of the Canadian."

"Everybody voted to strike, even you, Red?" she asked, putting out a hand to brace herself against the side of the house.

He shook his head, his eyes bitter. "Not me, but then I don't have much of a choice, do I? Me and Hank and Danny. We all run a few cattle under our own brand on your range, and we each got a section or two inside your property that we own. We strike and your husband's gonna squeeze us out."

She might have known Samuel was behind this. He'd taken advantage of her confinement to promote some nefarious scheme. Well, he had underestimated her. Childbirth made her tired. It did not make her helpless.

"He'll do nothing of the kind. You're my manager, Red, the man I trust more than any other on the place except Jubilee. I won't allow anyone to push you off your land."

Red leaned over the edge of the porch and spat on the ground, then looked at her. "I ain't your manager anymore, ma'am. Your husband fired me, and put Clint Murray in."

Mattie felt scalded with anger. "I did not authorize your firing. As far as I'm concerned you're still my manager. Now, get these men back to work, and I'll handle Samuel."

Red slapped his hat against his thigh. "Begging your pardon, ma'am, but I think you best read our demands."

"All right," she said, unfolding the paper and rapidly scanning the penciled lines, then closing her eyes to shut out the injustice of it. "He cut your wages."

He nodded. "Yes, ma'am—down to twenty-five dollars a month for everybody. Some of the boys quit—the ones who ain't worked for you long—but the rest just went on strike."

She pushed herself upright and fumbled to open the front door. "Come in the house and I'll write bank drafts to bring your wages up to what they were. But I don't want to hire back the men who quit. They should have trusted me, Red. You all should have trusted me."

Red flushed and avoided her eyes. "It ain't that we don't trust you, Miss Mattie. We just ain't sure you can beat your husband this time."

"Of course I can. I'm a hard woman."

When she discovered that Samuel had removed the ranch's books from the office, she hid her rage behind a smile and paid Red and the rest of the cowboys from her private account. *Those* bank drafts she kept locked in her room. Not until she watched the front door close behind Red did she let the killing anger she felt sweep her up the stairs to Samuel's room.

She slammed open his bedroom door and not even the sight of Clint sleeping next to her husband prevented her from ripping off the covers and pouring the pitcher of cold water from the washstand over his body.

Samuel leapt upright, shivering in the cold room and shaking water from his face. "What the hell?"

"I'll speak to you downstairs," she replied, and slammed the door behind her. While she waited behind the desk in the office, she wondered why Clint Murray had slept in Samuel's room. There were three empty bedrooms upstairs, and as long as Samuel was disregarding her wishes and allowing Clint to stay in the house, she wondered why her husband hadn't given him a room of his own.

"What was the meaning of your disgraceful behavior?" demanded Samuel, flinging open the door and marching in the office to lean over her desk.

Mattie studied the face of the man she'd married when she was fifteen. Samuel's pale blond hair was thinner, his eyes and nose laced with red veins from indulgence in whiskey, his body no longer slender, but bloated and soft looking like a hairless, white slug. She wondered why she had ever thought him handsome. She wondered why she had been so ignorant as to marry him. Youth and stupidity, she decided.

Eight years of marriage had cured her of both.

"Sit down, please," said Mattie. "I have no intention of being intimidated by your standing over me."

"And what are your intentions, Mrs. Hunter?" asked Clint Murray, following Samuel in and seating himself comfortably in a chair. "Now that you know that your husband is firmly in control of the ranch, as I assume you do since your little demonstration upstairs was that of a woman thwarted."

He made no effort to disguise the gloating expression in his eyes, and Mattie knew that defeating her gave him pleasure—much as she imagined his torturing animals might. But she wasn't an animal nor was she as defeated as he believed.

She focused her attention on Samuel. "The cowboys joined the strike because you cut their wages."

Samuel laughed. "Then I'll fire them like Reynolds of the LE did to his strikers. Or I'll cut off their food like Lee of the LS did."

"You can't treat our men like that! Don't you feel any loyalty to men who rode with us on the drive from Pueblo? Don't you think men who ride out in blizzards and drought, who spend weeks in miserable line shacks, who work until they fall exhausted into their blankets deserve more than the shabby treatment you've given them? For heavens' sake, you've never even thanked them!"

He waved a languid hand in total indifference. "I can hire all the cowboys I want for my own price."

Mattie sat back, sickened by his ingratitude, amazed at his foolishness. "For twenty-five dollars a month? All you can hire at that price are inexperienced children and the scrapings out of the gutters of Mobeetie and Tascosa. We need good men, Samuel, experienced men. We cannot risk our cattle to careless handling. Surely you can see that."

Samuel sat down and crossed his legs, a relaxed pose that Mattie distrusted. "I can see you indulging in womanly exaggeration—as you did over the woodcutting on that miserable little creek."

"That's what this is all about, isn't it, Samuel? You're getting back at me."

He studied his nails, then slapped his hands on the chair arms. "I have warned you in the past not to humiliate me, my dear. Now is the time to pay the piper. The striking men may either quit or be fired. That is their choice."

She shook her head. "I have made up their wages out of my personal account. They are staying."

"Then they will go to jail for rustling."

She stared at him, feeling a chill that had nothing to do with the cold room. "What are you talking about?"

"Those cattle they run under their own brands, my dear. The Stock Association looks with disfavor on that practice. Too many of the cowboys simply brand their employers' calves under the pretense that they are mavericks. I shall testify that is the case on the Bar H—with the appropriate histrionics, of course."

"And I shall testify that you are lying, and who do you think a jury of cowboys will believe?"

"Mattie, my dear, you don't understand. The other ranchers have fired their striking cowboys, and your men as the defendants cannot sit on a jury. Any new cowboys hired by the LS or the LX or the other large ranches will know which side of their bread is buttered. They will not acquit your men. You have lost your power."

Mattie swallowed bile. "Not quite. I'll buy their herds."

Samuel looked pleased. "That would solve the problem of their cattle eating our grass. However, I shall still fire them and hire new men."

She rose and leaned over the desk. "And I will pay my cowboys. We'll have our own private range war, Samuel. My men against yours. Experienced, hard men against whatever dregs you can hire for your pittance. I'll win that war, but in the meantime, there'll be no one to work the cattle. We'll lose money—a lot of money. I have my own resources, remember? You don't."

"You are a passionate woman, Mattie, but your passion works against you. Are you willing to see your precious ranch ruined? Are you willing to see those smelly beasts drift into the hands of rustlers during our so-called range war? Are you willing to see them suffer from screw worms and mange and God only knows what other filthy ailments while our men fight?"

Mattie sat down and hid her shaking hands under the desk. "I will not turn against men who have served me well. Men who are my friends!"

Samuel smiled, and Mattie shuddered at the cruelty of it. "Then perhaps we may compromise?"

She felt as if she were stepping into the Canadian without knowing where the quicksand was. "What kind of compromise?"

"I have hired Perry LeFors to build our share of

the drift fence plus another fence across our pastures to the south."

"Never! I've already told Lee and the other Canadian River valley ranchers that I'll have no part of a drift fence. Cattle will stack up against it and freeze to death in a hard winter." She swallowed as a memory of stiff, ice-encrusted cattle threatened to make her lose control. "Don't you remember our first winter, Samuel? Don't you remember the herd that drifted against the mesa and lacked the sense to walk around it? Don't you remember their frozen bodies and the stench and flies when the sun thawed them out? The same thing would happen with a drift fence."

Samuel brushed lint from his black wool waistcoat. "I remember losing a few cows."

"A few! We lost over three hundred head, Samuel!" She folded her hands. "No! I'll never consent to a drift fence across my land."

He nodded. "I rather thought that would be your reaction. That's why I have a written contract and have already paid Mr. LeFors for his labor and materials. You can hardly claim trespassing this time— not that it would do you any good with your power base so eroded by the strike."

"That's over eighty miles at an average of two hundred and fifty to four hundred dollars a mile. That's over thirty thousand dollars, Samuel! Are you insane? What if the spring rains don't come and grazing is poor? Gaunt cattle don't bring a good price. Your foolishness might well bankrupt us. How else have you recklessly spent money? Where are the account books? I want to see them *now!*"

"I shall keep the books, my dear. I'm rather tired of your penny-pinching ways."

"My penny-pinching ways and Jesse's management earned us nearly a half million dollars above overhead and capital investment in the last six years, Samuel. How much of it is left?"

"You and that brat of yours won't starve. However, I will admit that you are much better at the mundane task of figuring. Such a tedious chore. Perhaps I should be persuaded to allow you to play bookkeeper—under adequate supervision, of course." He turned to Murray. "What is your opinion, Clint?"

Clint Murray lit a cigar and inhaled while studying Mattie's face. "I think you should first exact her promise about the fence, Samuel."

Mattie felt chills course up and down her arms as she realized that Samuel's strategy wasn't his at all; it was Murray's. "I won't have that fence built. I'll cut it as fast as LeFors builds it."

Samuel looked at Clint. "You were right, as always." His eyes were cold and indifferent when he turned back to Mattie. "In exchange for your precious cowboys' jobs, you will allow the fence to go up without hinderance. In exchange for my not fencing off their access to their pitiful little sections of land, you will be given the ranch's accounts to manage—minus one-fourth of all receipts for my personal use. I'll not hang my head in front of the other ranchers again!"

Murray nudged his arm. "Remember McDade."

Samuel smiled. "Of course. McDade. If you should divulge our compromise to McDade, then I am prepared to carry out every threat I've made. Which is it to be, Mattie? Your cowboys and a prosperous ranch under your control? Or range war and the slow bleeding death of the Bar H?"

Mattie turned to Murray. "This is your idea, isn't it? You knew I wouldn't sacrifice my men and this ranch. You used my decency and loyalty against me. Why? Why are you doing this?"

His hatred turned his eyes hot, like a boiling swamp. "I never forget a wrong. Your father humiliated me years ago in Pueblo. He had one of his tame constables throw me in a cattle car on a train out of town with only the clothes on my back. And for what? For playing a friendly game of chance with your husband."

"A friendly game of chance! You were stealing every dime Samuel and I had with your crooked playing. Papa was trying to save Samuel," retorted Mattie. "You're a gambler. Pueblo can't have been the first town where you wore out your welcome, and Papa can't be the first man who interfered with your games, yet you've spent five years on the Bar H turning my husband against me. Whatever chance Samuel and I had to live out our lives in some kind of decency and respect, you deliberately destroyed with your filthy talk. You've even encouraged him to use his own son against me, damn you! Now you want to destroy the Bar H. Why? What do you want?"

Clint Murray licked his lips. "Perhaps the score is even with your father, but not with you. You threw me out of that miserable mud plaza you used to call headquarters. You humiliated me in front of filthy, ignorant cowboys. You forced me to sleep in the storeroom. I'm only getting my own back."

"How long will you exact revenge, Murray? How long will you torture me and mine?"

"For as long as it amuses me."

CHAPTER

4

Tom Miller figured the strike would fail for at least a couple of reasons, one being that all the ranchers could simply fire the strikers. There were always men drifting into the Panhandle looking for work. He figured the ranchers wouldn't have any trouble replacing the strikers even if the new men didn't know one end of a cow from the other. They'd learn, and ranchers like Lee of the LS and Reynolds of the LE, not to mention the syndicates, were willing to put up with green hands until they did. The fact that the big cooperative roundup was a month away wasn't going to change those ranchers' minds. They'd make do with what they had until they could hire something better. It was the way of things no matter how it galled a man.

The other reason Tom knew the strike would fail was that the strikers' camp was just too damn close to Tascosa and Harris's brother-in-law's saloon. Whatever money the cowboys had in their pockets would soon find its way into other pockets in exchange for liquor and entertainment, and Tascosa had plenty of both. When all their money was gone, the cowboys would either have to find some other kind of job or leave the Panhandle.

He was right in all regards.

The ranchers fired the strikers, the cowboys spent their last wages on cards, whiskey, and women, and the strike was over in a month. The cowboys found themselves out of jobs and blacklisted besides.

By the middle of May, Tom faced some hard choices. He could drift to another big ranching country—south Texas, New Mexico, Montana, or Wyoming—or he could settle down as a nester next to his former employer like some of the boys were doing, and brand any cow that happened to drift his way. He figured brand changing was soon going to be a way of life and a thorn in the side of any big rancher. While he still didn't quite believe that it was much of a crime to brand a syndicate calf, he knew he couldn't do it. Too many years of being too honest for his own good, he reckoned.

But he wasn't going to leave the Panhandle either— or go to work driving freight wagons or clerking in a store. He was a cowboy. It was all he knew—and all he wanted to do. Someday he'd own his own spread—he hadn't given up that dream—but until then he'd have to be content with what he could have. Which was why he was sitting on his horse in a soaking rain waiting for the gray-eyed man to finish his tally.

"McDade."

Jesse McDade crossed his hands over his saddle horn and gazed back at Tom from under his dripping hat brim. "Miller."

"I heard you were hiring a few hands for the roundup and weren't asking questions about what a man did during the strike—provided he was a top hand and worth the wages you paid. I figure I'm both."

Tom felt as if those gray eyes were looking straight through his skull to his brain. Finally Jesse spoke. "I heard you got squeezed off your place and that you were one of the cowboys who signed Harris's original ultimatum."

"That's right. One wasn't a fair shake and the other was," Tom replied, studying the other man. Jesse McDade looked older, harder, than when he'd seen him last, like a man who'd forgotten how to smile.

Jesse shifted restlessly in his saddle. "I won't insult you by warning against throwing a wide loop anywhere near my brand."

"Best you don't."

Jesse smiled reluctantly. "For a man in need of a job, you're not very humble."

"I'm broke, McDade. I'm not beaten."

Jesse nodded, then glanced toward the east— toward the Hunter place. Tom suspected he'd done it so often, he didn't even know anymore that he did it. "I don't need another permanent man. I've got enough if I spread them thin. Mattie Hunter needs another good hand or two."

Tom felt his hand quiver once, but managed to keep his face impassive. "I figure Mrs. Hunter has enough on her plate with that husband of hers without having to contend with Mr. Lee of the LS yapping at her for not going along with the blacklist."

"Mattie's hired other striking cowboys."

"But not one who signed the ultimatum. I figure I'm about as welcome in the Panhandle as Texas fever and would cause her about as much trouble."

"I thought there might be another reason."

"You ain't ever scared me, McDade, if that's what you mean." The gray eyes acknowledged his claim, and Tom continued. "But you've always been a little watchful of me."

Jesse turned his head toward the east, his profile sharply etched against the canopy of gray clouds. "You're the only man besides me who ever respected her for what she is."

"And what might that be?" asked Tom, curious to see inside Jesse's mind, and certain that few people ever had—except Mattie.

"A woman, a whole woman, not a china doll full of emptiness, and not a mirage that disappears when you approach her. A man can hold her, and she holds him back." He turned suddenly to look at Tom. "You don't think much of me in some respects, do you, Miller?"

"Just one respect, McDade. You should have let her be."

"Don't you think I know that?"

Tom heard the hunger in his voice, and decided that if ever there was a man in torment, it was Jesse McDade.

"I reckon it takes a decent man to admit it, McDade."

His eyes glittered silver in the light. "I walked away because I had no right choices, not because I was decent. That doesn't mean I've changed, and neither has she. I'd know it if she had."

"You heard her call your name that day she was shot, didn't you, McDade?"

"Sometimes a man thinks he hears things he can't possibly hear and comes running. But I would've been too late if you hadn't stepped in. I'll always come running, Miller. I don't want you thinking otherwise. No matter how my life or hers might change, that never will. But I might be too late. I haven't seen Mattie in nearly a year, and she weights on my mind. I think Samuel forced her into changing her mind on the drift fence even though I hear from Jubilee that she says otherwise. She's not as hard as she thinks she is, and without me to stop him, there's no telling what else he may force her to do. She's a strong woman, but she's still a woman, and he's her husband. I can't change that, but I have to know she's safe. Go hire on with her, Miller. She'll have need of a good man."

A gust of rain obscured Jesse's face, but not before Tom caught a glimpse of his eyes. He had seen eyes like those once before—in a young cowboy who had just been told that his leg mangled in a stampede would have to be amputated. The cowboy knew he'd live, but he wasn't sure he wanted to.

The grass greened up after the late spring rains, and the cattle lost their gauntness and took on weight. Perry LeFors and his fencing crew dug post holes and strung wire, and Mattie avoided the north and south boundaries of her land, being satisfied with the cowboys' reports of full watering holes and good grazing. She pondered the strands of barbed wire cutting across her property, both as a symbol of her defeat by Samuel and of the final and inevitable end of open range. Even though she and Jesse had fenced off pastures before anyone else in the Panhandle, their endeavors had been limited compared to the latest orgy of fence building. Two hundred miles of barbed wire stretching across the width of the Panhandle north of the Canadian River to stop the cattle drifting south before the winter storms, with each rancher building the section along his boundary. As a means of saving the grass along the Canadian River for the cattle of those who owned the land, it was a brilliant idea.

As long as winters were mild and storms of short duration.

Otherwise, the cattle would drift before the

storms into the fence and freeze where they stood. To Mattie's mind, barbed wire meant the stench of rotting carcasses and the end of a way of life. To the ranchers and farmers of the West, barbed wire meant at last that grazing land and crops would be protected against trespass by man or animal.

Mattie braced herself against the winds of change blowing across the land.

But the summer passed, the cowboys trailed herds to Dodge City, the ranch prospered, September brought the first of the winter's blue northers, and nothing changed. She often rode out to check her herds, Robert lying on a pillow across her thighs, talked to her men of cattle and horses and cutting hay for the coming winter, and nothing changed. The Stock Association finally declared mavericking to be cattle rustling, and in Mobeetie and Tascosa and at ranch headquarters up and down the Canadian there was talk again of that Hunter woman as the old year passed into the late winter of 1884.

Clad in a soft blue wool shirtwaist against the cold wind of a March as bleak as her life, her hair pinned on top her head in a loose coronet of braids, and Robert lying on a blanket chewing on a stuffed cow Aunt Patty made for him, Mattie sat in her office behind the lovely rosewood desk that had been her father's and smiled at the leader of the delegation from the Stock Association.

"Mr. Lee, I'm beginning to think you have moved to the LS permanently. We see you so often in the Panhandle these days. I'm flattered that you would neglect your other business affairs in Kansas or wherever to discuss my differences with the Association."

Lee didn't lose his composure as Mattie had rather hoped he would. "I think you're spoiling for a fight, Mrs. Hunter."

Mattie arched her eyebrows. "I would not shrink

from one by having an attack of the vapors, Mr. Lee, and you should not expect any such feminine distractions. When I shoot, I shoot straight. I expect the same from you. Being condescended to makes me angry—more angry than I already am."

Lee smiled. "I can't imagine you with the vapors, Mrs. Hunter."

"I can't either, Mr. Lee. The vapors make a woman helpless, and a helpless woman is at a disadvantage in a man's world." She glanced at the watch pinned on her bodice. "I'm short of time, gentlemen. My son will need his nap in a few minutes, so why don't I enumerate my offenses against the Association. One, I will not forbid the nester ranchers living within my property boundaries to participate in the cooperative roundups, and if any cattle wearing one of my lesser brands are rounded up as maverick brands and thus sold by the county, I shall file suit against the county."

"You registered those lesser brands under your name to defy the Stock Association resolutions, but the damn cows wearing them belong to your men, and you know it, Mrs. Hunter!" exclaimed a representative from the LIT.

Mattie tapped her fingers on the desk. "You would have to prove that in court, sir, and you can't. If you try, it would appear you were calling me a liar, and even if my behavior is occasionally unseemly—in your opinion—no jury would find for a man who called a woman a liar. After years of being at the mercy of social custom, I would relish using that same social custom to my advantage."

"You are ignoring the amount of brand changing going on, Mrs. Hunter," said Lee. "Most of those maverick brands are on rustled cattle."

"I'm not ignoring that, but I don't see how punishing my men for branding a few mavericks will stop rustling on your ranches." She smiled at him. "It is not my fault if Pat Garrett and the Home Rangers have failed to measure up as a private army."

Lee's face turned red, then white. "Garrett is a captain in the Texas Rangers and his men are duly commissioned."

"Since when are the wages and expenses of a duly commissioned Texas Ranger paid by a private citizen as Garrett's are? How much is it costing you and the other large Canadian River ranchers to keep Garrett and his men on a leash and unloose them on defenseless men soon to be disarmed by Governor Hogg's proclamation forbidding Texans from carrying guns? A proclamation you have persuaded him to issue, Mr. Lee."

She smiled at the look of surprise he couldn't quite hide. W.M.D. Lee should know better than to think his actions could be kept secret. "And please include in your estimate the twenty-five thousand you *loaned* to Oldham County to build a fine stone courthouse, and the money it cost you to buy each of your cowboys a lot in Tascosa."

Lee's blue eyes glittered. "One has nothing to do with the other, Mrs. Hunter."

Mattie wagged her finger. "Please don't insult me, Mr. Lee, by insinuating that I am a fool. A new courthouse means a grand jury, and with all your cowboys now property owners in Tascosa, they will be eligible to serve on that grand jury. You will excuse my mostly distrusting any indictments handed down by such a grand jury if those indictments rest on less evidence than it would take to arrest a child stealing cookies, and result in search warrants and arrest warrants to be used against my neighbors by Mr. Garrett. I plan to pay the defense costs of those who find themselves jailed on spurious charges."

"I don't like your insinuations, Mrs. Hunter," said

Lee. Mattie noticed that he failed to deny her charges.

"And I don't like your methods, Mr. Lee." She counted on her fingers. "Oh, yes, my second offense is my refusal to fire Tom Miller."

She leaned back in her chair, careful to keep her back straight, and waited.

Finally, the LX delegate broke the silence. "Go on, Mrs. Hunter. What about your refusal?"

"There's nothing *about* my refusal. I simply refuse. Tom Miller is loyal, trustworthy, and an excellent cowboy, all good reasons for retaining him in my employ."

"He signed that damn ultimatum to strike, Mrs. Hunter. He's not so damn loyal." The LX delegate folded his arms as if there were no reasonable rejoinder a rancher could make.

Mattie smiled. She had learned that smiling while pricking swelled-up male stupidity rendered men unable to retaliate. Another social custom. A gentleman was not rude to a polite lady. "Perhaps the best way to gain loyalty is to give loyalty—along with a decent wage and fair treatment."

The delegate's face turned red. "Your husband said that your womanly sentiment set you against his wishes, but he had hoped you would listen to common sense from the Association."

The rage nearly broke through her control at the mention of Samuel—Samuel who threatened to use Leon against her; Samuel who was building that damn drift fence; Samuel who consumed one-fourth of the ranch's profits and contributed nothing. Now he was using the Association in an attempt to bring her to heel. Damn him!

"It is *my* wishes which are law on the Bar H, sir, and don't—ever—doubt—it!" She rose and picked up the squirming Robert. "I believe that's all, gentlemen."

"All?" asked the LIT man. "Not by a long shot, Mrs. Hunter. We warned your husband that the Stock Association would take action against the Bar H. We will strip you of membership."

Mattie shifted Robert to one hip. "Go ahead. I don't have a vote anyway. I do, however, have seven hundred thousand acres. Jesse McDade has another quarter of a million or so. We stand together, and between us, we have over one hundred well-armed and absolutely loyal men. So don't threaten me! And keep Mr. Garrett and his search warrants off my land!"

She snuggled her son against her body, her heart beating so violently that she feared the men might see it pounding otherwise, might guess that Hunter woman was betting her hand without ever looking at her cards. She hadn't seen Jesse in well over a year. She had no idea whether he would stand by her or not. She had nothing with which to bet but her memories.

"I trust you gentlemen can find the front door on your own? I must take Robert upstairs."

"Mrs. Hunter," said Lee. "You are deliberately defying the Association. It's not in your best interest to do that. You might appreciate our support one day."

"So I have been told—several times. I should think you gentlemen would tire of hearing your voices rattling around in your heads. I certainly have. Good afternoon," she added, sweeping from the office.

She regained her self-control and indeed felt an unnatural calm while she waited for Samuel and Clint to come downstairs for supper that night. She had long since given up putting a good face on her disagreements with Samuel, and her allies waited in the living room with her: Aunt Patty, Red, Hank,

Jubilee, and the man whose quiet ways most comforted her—Tom Miller.

Samuel descended the stairs followed by Murray, and Mattie frowned at the pleased expression on her husband's face. He paused on the landing, his protuberant blue eyes meeting hers. "My dear, is this reception for me? Is there a special occasion I am unaware of?"

Mattie carefully set her coffee cup on the mantel. "I had a most interesting conversation with a delegation from the Stock Association this afternoon, Samuel."

He gracefully descended the rest of the stairs. "Please don't keep me in suspense, Mattie. Did you listen to their advice?"

"I do not intend to allow the Association or anyone else to tell me how to run my ranch or whom to hire or fire."

Samuel removed a cigar from his waistcoat pocket. "The matter of your nester ranchers and of Mr. Miller." He glanced at the three cowboys. "Your mistress has once again upheld your piffling rights—or what she sees as your rights."

"We appreciate it, too, Hunter," said Hank, not bothering to hide the dislike in his voice.

"No doubt," said Samuel, his gaze passing over the old cowboy to settle on the tall figure leaning casually against the fireplace. "Are you appreciative, Miller, seeing as how my wife suffered some loss of face in defending her action in hiring a striker?"

Tom's face was impassive. "I reckon Mattie knows she can count on me."

"I'm certain that must be comforting to her," replied Samuel, dismissing Tom's laconic remark and Tom with a wave of his hand.

Mattie didn't dismiss it. Tom had worn that same

impassive face the day he shot a man out of his saddle defending her.

Clint Murray spoke for the first time, his voice as sugary with false kindness as ever. "Pour Mattie a glass of wine, Samuel. After being expelled from the Association, she must be feeling undone. Being isolated from her fellow ranchers puts her in an uncomfortable position. She'll have no one to call on for help."

"I still have Jesse McDade," retorted Mattie. "Have you forgotten Jesse?"

Samuel's eyes were bland. "No, but he apparently has forgotten about you. What has it been, Mattie, nearly a year and a half since your last meeting with Mr. McDade? Perhaps you have overestimated the depth of his regard."

A cold spot formed in Mattie's chest, and she felt numbness spreading through her body as she caught her husband's sly look at Clint Murray. "What have you done, Samuel? What are you planning now, you and your bastard friend, Murray?"

Samuel lit his cigar and tossed the match in the fireplace. "You were the one who described our relationship as a war, Mattie. Don't expect me to reveal my battle strategy."

"Damn you, Samuel!"

For a split second his eyes held an expression of pity and confusion. "I suspect we both are, Mattie, and sometimes I even regret it."

"Then leave me alone, Samuel."

Clint squeezed Samuel's arm, and Mattie watched her husband's pity melt away. "I plan to, Mattie. I plan to leave you all alone."

Winter faded into early summer before the meaning behind Samuel's ominous words ripped open Mattie's numbed heart and the Panhandle gathered at Jesse McDade's wedding to watch it bleed.

CHAPTER

5

June 1884

Samuel's announcement at supper, after the June roundup was done and Mattie had sent a herd of three thousand head up the trail to Dodge City, was not her first inkling that something was wrong. Throughout late winter and early spring she had noticed Jubilee and her cowboys falling silent when she was near. On her infrequent trips to Tascosa, she only had to step into a store for conversation to die away, and speculative looks to replace the respectful expressions that usually greeted the woman who owned the Bar H. Folks in Tascosa might not approve of her, but Mattie knew they respected the power she wielded.

Lately, no one even seemed to grant her that much.

She existed in the center of ever widening circles of silence and curiosity.

Not once in over a half year had anyone mentioned Jesse's name, nor answered any question about him in her presence. Certainly she knew he still owned the Flying MJ. Certainly she knew he was well. She even knew how many cows wore his brand and how much profit he was expected to make on this year's herd. She knew the same information about all the ranchers along the Canadian River valley and as far northeast as Lipscomb County and the ranches along Wolf Creek. But no one refused to share gossip and rumor about the other ranchers. She knew who was drinking and who was courting. She knew who was planning to expand their holdings, who owed money, who was losing cows to the brand changers.

About Jesse she heard nothing, and foreboding had deadened her appetite and taken away her laughter—what little she had of either—long before Samuel tapped his whiskey glass and gazed down the length of the dining table at her.

"I'm certain by now you have heard of Jesse McDade's plans to marry," he said, drawing out the announcement as though he savored it. "I have volunteered to host the wedding."

If Samuel had pinned her to her chair with an icy steel blade, Mattie could not have sat so still nor could her body have felt so cold. Too cold to bleed. That would come later. Now she could only stare at Samuel, barely hearing Jubilee's outraged voice.

"I hopes I didn't hear what I thinks I did."

Hank pushed his plate away. "And I think I want to hear it again, Hunter. Just what the hell did you do?"

Samuel drank a swallow of whiskey before answering, his amused gaze dancing from one outraged face to the other. "I offered the poor girl our house for her wedding. There isn't a more appropriate or larger home this side of the Goodnight place in the Palo Duro, and that is such a distance from McDade's ranch." He looked down the table at Mattie, sly amusement curling his lips. "Besides, since the groom is a former employee who meant so much to my wife, I felt it the decent thing to do."

Red threw down his napkin and kicked his chair back. "You ain't even got a nodding acquaintance with decency, Hunter, and I always knowed it. Jesse won't allow this, Miss Mattie," he said, looking at her. "See if he does."

Mattie had always known without admitting it that the cowboys had guessed the truth about her and Jesse, but to hear them forced to defend her, to hear the outrage and sympathy in their voices, stripped away her mask to expose the hurt beneath it. The silent voices that had guarded her private time with Jesse were silent no longer.

Samuel's smile widened into the most malicious expression Mattie had ever seen. "McDade is driving a herd to Dodge at present. I believe he isn't scheduled to return until the day before the nuptials. A bit late to change the arrangements, I am afraid, since I graciously offered to deliver the invitations yesterday."

"How dare you!"

Samuel cocked an eyebrow. "It was the least I could do, my dear. Poor sweet Caroline is a newcomer to the Panhandle from the east—St. Louis, I believe—and is orphaned. She was journeying to live with a distant cousin on some nester ranch that Mr. Lee recently bought, and found herself stranded in Tascosa. McDade rescued her from an unpleasant drunk—who I understand will recover soon from his attentions—and escorted her to Mrs. Russell's. Miss Knight—Caroline—was quite enamored by McDade's chivalry, and he was quite taken by her ladylike demeanor." He rolled his eyes toward the ceiling and clasped his hands over his heart. "Ah, true love."

Aunt Patty glared at him, her gray-red hair nearly bristling with disgust. "You're so damn mean, the pigs wouldn't eat you."

"You dinner conversation is eloquent as usual, Aunt Patty," replied Samuel. He patted his mouth and looked down the length of the table at Mattie. "Of course, my dear, if you find my arrangements too presumptuous, you are at liberty to cancel them. Unfortunately, it would humiliate the bride and provide fodder for gossip. I realize you *are* used to gossip, but you've never been pitied before. I doubt you would enjoy it. Poor Mattie Hunter. Thrown over by Jesse McDade, and so upset that she cancelled her offer to host the wedding because she couldn't stand to watch the ceremony. I imagine that's the sort of thing that would be said as well as other remarks less kind. How do you ladies put it? You would never be able to hold up your head again."

Samuel pulled a cigar from his vest pocket and rolled it around in his mouth to wet the end. Finally, he lit it and blew a cloud of smoke toward the ceiling. "What is it to be, Mattie? Will you cancel the bride's arrangements?"

Mattie felt as though she were standing outside herself observing the scene. She could see and hear everything, including herself staring at Samuel from glazed golden eyes sunken in a white, white face. Like a gunshot victim, she could feel nothing the first seconds after being wounded, but soon the shock would wear off and the pain would be beyond anything she had ever imagined.

She hoped she might die of it.

Folding her napkin, she rose and slowly walked

out of the room, step by deliberate, unhurried step, her back as straight as if she were balancing a book on top of her head as she had done when she was a child and her mother was teaching her how a proud lady walks.

Mattie's headquarters had changed very little in the two years since Jesse had ridden away for the last time. The gigantic cottonwood tree still shaded the front of the three-story house. The covered veranda still circled it, and the hitching post was still fifty yards from the front door. Mattie abhorred flies and didn't intend having horse manure close enough to the house to attract any.

The only notable difference were the garlands of red cedar and wildflowers decorating the veranda and the benches made of scrap lumber nailed to apple crates, rows and rows of them in the yard, all facing the improvised altar on the veranda. There were no benches under the cottonwood tree, he noticed, and a fierce gladness swept over him like a rain-moist wind. Before there was a house, before there were corrals, barns, stables, a bunkhouse or storerooms on this wide, grassy plain that swept down from a mesa to a narrow creek that emptied into the Canadian a few miles away, Jesse had lain for the first time with Mattie beneath that cottonwood tree. He had joined his body to hers in the leaf-shadowed moonlight, completing the bond between them the only way a man knew how. They had shared their bodies as they shared their lives, until time ran out and they used up the sin they had earned.

The cottonwood tree was hallowed ground.

He didn't want anybody sitting under its shade watching Mattie Jo Hunter's reaction to the wedding and to ogle the bride.

His bride.

Jesse McDade's.

Jesse viciously kicked one of the benches on his way to the house. He wished it were Samuel Hunter's head.

He jerked open the screen door and walked into Mattie's living room. The house smelled of freshly baked cakes and pies, roasting turkey and beef, roses and wildflowers, lemon oil—and sorrow.

"Lordy, Jesse! What's you doing here so early and looking like you just rode in off the trail? Your wedding ain't till eight o'clock, and it be just barely noon," said Jubilee, walking through the open French doors from the dining room, followed by Aunt Patty and Tom Miller.

Jubilee's words were polite enough, but his tone of voice sent a chill through Jesse. To Mattie's surrogate father, Jesse had done her wrong.

"Where's Hunter?" demanded Jesse.

Jubilee looked over Jesse's shoulder. "I sees him slithering down the stairs. That man be the only snake I knows who walks on two legs."

"A person can see a snakebite and can suck out the poison before it kills him," said Aunt Patty. "Samuel Hunter don't leave no fang marks. His poison just festers inside Miss Mattie with nobody able to help her 'cause nobody knows where he bit her."

Jesse turned around. "Hunter!"

"McDade! Did you come to see if the wedding arrangements met your high expectations?" asked Samuel, walking gracefully down the stairs, Clint Murray by his side. "You should have known that I wouldn't skimp on the nuptial arrangements. I do feel a need to repay you for the service you rendered my wife—and me, of course."

Jesse reached him in two strides, grabbed his lapels, and jerked Samuel up until the shorter man's toes barely brushed the floor. "You son of a bitch! This was your idea, wasn't it? Mattie had nothing to do with it."

Samuel pulled at Jesse's wrists in an effort to free himself. "Put me down, you ill-bred bastard."

"Thanks for the invitation. I believe I will," said Jesse, releasing Samuel, then dropping him to the floor with a powerful blow to his face.

Jesse stood over the sprawled body wondering why, when he'd been so dishonorable about so much, he'd been too decent to kill Samuel years ago.

"Take him upstairs, Murray, or out to the horse tank—anywhere out of my sight."

Murray knelt down and hoisted the unconscious Samuel over his shoulder. "You didn't change a thing, McDade."

Jesse rubbed one knuckle he'd cut on Samuel's tooth. He hoped the man's bite wasn't as poisonous as his mind, or if it was, at least this time the fang marks were visible. "See how many of his teeth are loose before you say that, Murray. I may have changed his charming smile permanently."

He waited until Murray disappeared upstairs with his burden, then turned to Jubilee. "Where's Mattie?"

The ex-slave's eyes met his. "Like Murray said, you ain't changed a thing. Ain't you done enough without tormenting her any more?"

Jesse rubbed his hands over his red eyes. "I've gone without sleep for two days and nearly killed three good horses riding the two hundred fifty miles between this ranch and Dodge City to stop the torment, Jubilee. I left as soon as I got Caroline's letter telling me of the Hunters'"—his teeth clenched— "generous offer. I didn't know a damn thing about the final arrangements until then. Do you believe I'd shame Mattie like this if I had known?"

"I purely don't know what to think, Jesse, and that's the truth," said Jubilee.

"Think a lot of yourself, don't you, young man?" asked Aunt Patty. "You think the sight of you wouldn't make Miss Mattie sick to her stomach? You think you got anything to say she might want to hear?"

Jesse felt his face turn hot and his belly cold at the truth of Aunt Patty's words. He had nothing to say that Mattie would want to hear, but it had to be said. Samuel had left them no choice. There was no gentle way out for her—no way to be kind for him.

"This is between Mattie and me."

Tom pressed Jubilee's shoulder. "Best they talk." He met Jesse's eyes with that same direct look that Jubilee had. "I can't protect her against you, McDade, and you're the one she needs protection against the most."

Mattie obliged the wedding guests by sitting on the front row so everyone could get a good look. It would be a shame to disappoint all those people who had ridden hours, and in some instances, days, to watch Mattie Jo Hunter. She gave only the Goodnights, the Bugbees, and Hank Cresswell the benefit of a doubt. Everyone else came mostly to gauge her reaction to the bride Jesse McDade preferred over that Hunter woman.

The bride.

Mattie hated her on sight.

Hated her dark chestnut hair all pulled up high on top of her head and hidden by her veil. Hated her wide-set hazel eyes and thick lashes. Hated her small, heart-shaped face with its oh-so-pointed chin. Hated the fashionably pursed lips. Hated her soft voice. Hated her lace-and-gauze wedding dress with its short train and bustle. Hated her.

"My mama always said if you look a snake right in the eye, it'll crawl off without biting you," whispered Tom Miller, inclining his head toward hers. "That's what you have to do tonight. Look all your guests straight in the eye, and maybe they'll crawl off without biting you."

Mattie snapped open her silk fan. "Samuel never has."

She heard Tom chuckle. "You'll do all right, Mattie Jo Hunter."

She doubted that, but she kept her doubts to herself—as she had kept her conversation with Jesse earlier this afternoon to herself.

She had been standing at the window of her office, staring out at nothing, and waiting for him. She had known he would come to her eventually—known it with a certainty she had never doubted—and barricaded herself behind pride. She lifted her head when she heard the door behind her open, heard his boots thud on the floor in that old remembered rhythm, smelled the scent of man and sweat and leather and sun.

"Mattie."

The husky voice breached the fragile wall she had erected and touched her raw soul.

"My father was right. He said a man never buys a milk cow if he can get the milk for free. He said you'd marry some proper young lady who hadn't shamed herself."

"Your father was wrong."

She didn't turn around. "About what, Jesse? The milk cow or the proper young lady?"

"About you—and about me."

His words dragged her around even though she knew she shouldn't look at him—shouldn't remember what had been. A lady would ignore their shared past as if it hadn't existed. A lady would never acknowledge that she had lain naked in his arms smelling of his sweat and seed. A lady would never sound like a cast-off doxy.

But then she hadn't been a lady for such a long time.

She faced him—holding herself less than an arm's length from the lean, broad-shouldered body she had known so well—stared into the gray eyes that could change from pewter to silver depending on his mood. "Two years, Jesse, and not a word from you. But then you'd already said all the words you needed to, didn't you? Lying words about how I made you whole. Sweet words about building your headquarters with me in your mind. You even lied to me about your brand. The Flying MJ stood for Mattie and Jesse, not your initials in reverse. And I *believed* it! I believed it all. Even after you took my father's money and you walked away after lying again about how you didn't want people thinking I was sleeping with the hired hand, I believed you."

His body stiffened, and she wondered at the anger in his face. He had no *right* to be angry when she was the one wronged. "I didn't lie, Mattie. I didn't have to."

"How dare you!"

He caught her arms in his strong hands and held her immobile. "You can curse me or shoot me, but I won't let you call me a liar, and I won't let you hold yourself up as a trusting fool. I didn't lie my way into your bed and I didn't seduce you. We came together because for a time it was right. What we shared was right. I claimed you, and you claimed me, and there were no lies between us."

She pulled away. "Then why did you walk away? Why did you leave me alone?"

"Because I was hurting you, and if your father hadn't stopped me, I'd still be hurting you. You'd have nothing left of your self-respect."

"It's my choice, not my father's."

"What's my choice, Mattie? To climb up the cottonwood tree and sneak into your bedroom window? To bed you on the prairie in the dirt? To meet you in some filthy line shack? Rent a room at the Exchange Hotel in Tascosa and lie with you like you were a woman from one of the cribs in back of the saloons? Would we send notes by one of the cowboys to arrange our meetings?" He drew a quick breath, his features rigid like those of a hunter stumbling across a mortally wounded doe he knows he must kill, but who hates the necessity of doing so. "I can't do it, Mattie. I can't turn you into Jesse McDade's whore, and I can't be Mattie Hunter's kept man. The only way to keep what's right between us is to let it go."

She pressed her hands over her mouth to keep from screaming as he shook his head and continued, those terrible silver eyes never leaving hers. "You're another man's wife, Mattie, and no amount of dreaming is going to change it. I've finally accepted that. We have a past together, but we don't have a future together, and I've finally accepted that, too."

"No! I don't accept it!"

"Do you think I wanted to?" he asked. "It took two years to accept that I can't live off the crumbs left over from your marriage. I would die for you, Mattie, but I can't live for you. I want a future. I want a family, a home, something to fill the empty place in my life. I'll be another woman's husband, and you'll have to accept that."

He looked like anything but a bridegroom. He was too weary, too wounded, and his eyes too tormented. If she was hurting, so was he. If she felt betrayed, he suffered the guilt of the betrayer. If she felt bereaved, he knelt by the same grave. The hunter had shot the doe and wounded himself beyond healing while doing it. She wanted to tell him he already had a family—that they had a son together—but she couldn't. The son of Jesse McDade's whore would have no future.

"Dear God, Jesse, why didn't you tell me? Why did it have to be Samuel?" Her voice broke on his name and she wrapped her arms around herself, bending over with the agony of loss. "I'm hurting," she whispered.

She felt his hands first on her shoulders, then felt them slide down her back and pull her full against him. He bent his head and pressed his cheek hard against hers. His hot breath stirred the loose wisps of hair above her ear. "I've fought the Comanche and I've faced down men so vicious that they would shoot a man in the back, then steal his boots and leave his body unburied, but I was afraid to face you. And I was afraid to face myself. This damnable bond between us is still stronger than decency, and I didn't trust myself not to grab at you just like I'm doing and try to bring back a time we can't have. I put off telling you until I knew the time and place of the wedding so it would be too late to turn away from the future. I was a coward and I was selfish. I wanted to hold on to the past as long as I could. But I didn't count on Samuel's interference. I didn't count on his humiliating you like this. Good God, Mattie, cancel the ceremony. Caroline and I can get married in Tascosa."

She slipped her arms around his waist, dug her fingers into the hard muscles of his back, and held on to her life for a few more minutes before she closed it away behind a locked door in her mind.

"The wages of sin is livin'."

Aunt Patty's words echoed through her memory,

and she felt shamed—not because she had sinned, but because for a few short minutes she had lacked the courage to do what had to be done: to live.

She raised her head to meet those silver eyes. "The wedding plans are already made, and I won't have it said that Mattie Jo Hunter is a coward. Kiss me good-bye, Jesse. One last time."

She met his descending mouth and time stopped to let them store up memories for the lonely future.

And now she sat on a hard bench, wrapped in pride, and waited to hear Jesse McDade exchange vows with Caroline Knight while she touched the heart-shaped locket she wore around her neck. It and her memories were all she had left of her time with Jesse that were hers alone.

His son and seven hundred thousand acres she shared with Samuel.

CHAPTER

The summer of 1884 brought copious rains to the Panhandle and drought to the rest of the plains. The grass grew thick and green on the arid range north of the Canadian, and water silvered the shallow playa lakes. The ranchers trailed fat, sleek cattle to Dodge throughout the warm months and brought back high profits. The smell of money brought more foreign syndicates scurrying to buy a share of the beef bonanza. W. H. Bates and D. T. Beals sold the LX to the British while the Box T went to the Canadians. Even Reverend Carhart, founder of Clarendon, sold his Quarter Circle Heart brand to the British. One by one the pioneer ranches were sold, and absentee owners became the rule rather than the exception. For the most part Mattie was surrounded by syndicate ranches. The winds of change she had expected in 1883 blew away what remained of the old customs in 1884. In the fall the grand jury handed down 159 indictments mostly for theft, and Pat Garrett and his rangers rode out with legal authority to search a man's property and to arrest him for suspected rustling. The battle lines were drawn and the Panhandle split into factions with Mattie and Jessie on the side of the nester rancher and the small stockman. But it was a romantic gesture that did nothing to turn back time. On the big ranches the bookkeeper became a more important employee than an experienced wagon boss, a double entry ledger more valuable than a cowboy's tally book, and dollars and cents watched after more carefully than men and horses.

Cattle ranching had finally become a business.

As summer turned to fall the Bar H prospered, the Panhandle changed around her, and Mattie retreated within herself where she searched her mind for any feelings, but found only locked doors. One day she must open those doors, sort through the memories stored in the rooms behind them, discard what was of no use, and air out those that were.

One day—but not tonight.

Wrapped in a heavy shawl, Mattie huddled on the front steps protected from the cold wind that blew out of the north and shrieked around the corners of the house. Gray clouds bunched together in the sky to the northwest like a herd of ghostly gray cattle drifting before a storm, and she supposed it would snow before morning. The weather suited her because it matched her life. A frozen lady living a frozen life against the backdrop of a frozen landscape.

"Getting a tad cold to be sitting outside to watch the sunset, isn't it, Mattie?"

She could no more explain how her habit of sitting on the steps every evening with Tom Miller had begun than she could remember at what point he had starting calling her Mattie instead of Miss Mattie. It was one more change that had slipped by her since Jesse's wedding, and one she didn't care to ponder. It was enough that he had become a refuge from her own emptiness.

"I had about decided you weren't planning to join me, Tom."

He settled his lanky body on the step below her and leaned back on his elbows, turning his head to grin at her. "A man would be a fool to pass up a chance to sit for a spell by the prettiest woman in Texas, and I've been called lots of names, but never a fool."

She felt a little less frozen and smiled back at him. "Your compliments would turn a woman's head if she let them."

"That wasn't my intention. Just thought you might need to hear an admiring remark for a change. Been an unsettling time for you lately."

Mattie smoothed her skirt over her knees and wrapped her shawl more tightly about her shoulders. "Is that what you call it, Tom? I call it being besieged. I'm cut off from everyone. The other ranchers except Charlie Goodnight and Mr. Cresswell and Mr. Bugbee find my company as desirable as lice in a bedroll. My son is in Pueblo with his grandfather and hardly spoke to me when he and Papa came to visit this summer. And Jesse . . ." She looked to the west. And her glance lingered.

Tom's broad shoulders blocked her view, his gloved hand settling over hers, and she looked up to see him leaning over her. His hazel eyes mirrored all the colors of the Panhandle—the brown land, the green of spring grass, a hint of blue like the color left in the sky at midday after the summer heat bleaches it almost white—and they were no softer than the land.

"Best you give him up now, Mattie."

"You presume too much, Tom. I never gave you leave to mention his name."

"I reckon I'll do it anyway, Mattie. I'm not a man to put off what needs to be said. I'll not have you learn of this from Samuel or from some store clerk in Tascosa gossiping about it with a customer just loud enough so you can hear. I'll not have folks staring sideways at you to see how you take the news. I'll tell you myself. Jesse's wife is in the family way."

She felt her body tighten as locked doors threatened to burst open from the pressure of the memories behind them. "Let me go."

He tightened his grip on her hands. "Did you hope Jesse would live apart from his wife, Mattie?"

"Of course not," she said, and knew she lied. Tom knew it, too—she saw it in his eyes.

"It's a foolish notion, Mattie. Jesse has made his bed and he's lying in it with Caroline Knight."

She licked her lips and tasted salt. Odd that she hadn't known she was crying. "You're not a gentle man, Tom Miller, or you wouldn't speak to me so."

His eyes didn't soften nor did his face. "I can be gentle, Mattie, but no, I don't reckon you can call me a gentle man. Kind, maybe. A man can be hard and still be kind, but a man who starts out gentle in this country doesn't often live long enough to grow hard."

She could feel the tears now as icy droplets running down her cheeks. "I've had enough of hard men."

Tom lifted his hand and smoothed it over one wet cheek, then closed it gently around the nape of her neck and pressed her face against his heavy woolen coat. "You ever see one of those carousels, Mattie, with the wooden horses that go around and around? That's what you and Jesse were riding—a carousel—and you can't ride one forever because they don't go anywhere. A man like Jesse can't be happy not going anywhere. And neither can you. It's not in your natures."

She raised her head to look at him. Cold night had fallen, and she could hardly see the hazel eyes anymore—just a faint glitter in the darkness of his face. "And just what is my nature, Tom Miller?"

"You're too strong a woman to be running away to hide inside yourself like you've been doing since Jesse's wedding." He rose and tugged on her hand. "Walk with me."

Hanging on to his hand she stumbled after him, the wind whipping her skirts against her legs, her wet cheeks turning numb in the cold air. Frozen tufts of grass crunched beneath their feet as Tom pulled her along toward the open pasture that stretched toward the creek. He stopped abruptly and released her hand.

"Look around you, Mattie. There's nothing but short grass and sky and a sand-choked river not much more than waist deep. Nothing gentle about this land that a lady might like. Nothing soft about it but the coat on a newborn calf. It's a hard man's country and it won't answer to a woman who hides inside herself."

She clutched her shawl and shivered from more than exposure to the cold wind blowing across the bleak plains. Weakness brought on trembling as fast as freezing temperatures did. She wished Tom had waited until daylight to tell her about Jesse. She had never liked the night, never found anything particularly romantic about the moonlight; it never softened the world, but hid its dangers in shadows. She preferred the sun. She drew strength as well as heat from its light.

But there would be no sun tomorrow, not with a storm coming.

There was only the land to give her strength as the hard man standing beside her knew. If Jesse was her heart, the land was her soul, and Tom Miller knew that, too. If she must give up one, she still possessed the other—and it she would not lose.

Mattie straightened her shoulders and lifted her face to the wind.

"Thank you."

Tom heard Mattie's whispered words and sighed as he reached out to stroke her cheek. He wished he'd left his gloves off so he could touch her skin with his bare hands, but he wasn't a man to leave himself open to temptation. He didn't intend for Mattie Hunter to be sorry she ever said thank you to Tom Miller—even if it meant he never claimed more of her than her company on the porch every evening.

It was more than Jesse McDade had.

"Mattie."

She turned her head up to look at him, and he could just see her face in the cold moonlight. "Yes, Tom?"

"We best go back to the house. It's too cold for you to be standing out here with nothing on but that shawl."

She smiled. "You go on, Tom. Tell Jubilee to heat up the coffee, and I'll be there in a minute. I need to stay here a little longer. I need to see if I remember how to stand alone."

"You aren't alone, Mattie. Any time you reach out, I'll take your hand."

She tilted her head to one side while she studied him, and he wished he didn't show so many signs of wear. He wished he was a handsome man instead of looking so harsh featured with his strong nose and wide mouth and so much of his hair streaked with that yellow-gray like the wind had blown away part of its color. But he was what he was, and there was no changing it.

She nodded, then looked away. "Pray I never accept your offer, Tom Miller. I doubt that I would bring you much content."

He hesitated. "I reckon I'll cross that bridge when I come to it, Mattie." He stroked her cheek again. "Don't stay out too long, or I'll come looking for you."

He walked back to the house and hung his coat on the rack in the kitchen. He accepted a cup of coffee from Jubilee and collapsed into a chair. "I told her."

The former slave sat down on the opposite side of the table. "I thanks you, Tom. I knowed I should say something to her, but I was just plain too scared. Seems like every time she gets her feet under her real good, something else happens to knock her down again. I didn't want to be the one to do it this time, and that's the truth." He rubbed at a stain on the cottonwood plank table for a moment, then looked up. "You ain't said nothing about how she took it."

Tom wrapped his hands around the coffee cup and debated how to answer. He decided there was no sense in lying. "I felt her go rigid like every muscle in her body was fighting to throw off some poison. I've seen men bitten by rattlers stiffen up the same way the instant they felt the snake's fangs. Sometimes they lived if the snake bit a leg or an arm, and somebody who was thinking fast sucked out the poison. Sometimes they took days to die while they bled beneath the skin and their bodies swelled up and gangrene set in."

He met Jubilee's eyes. "Mattie took the bite right in the heart, and I don't know if anyone could suck out the poison, but I figured I had to try. She had a foolish notion that Jesse's marriage is like some kind of false-front building with nothing but daylight behind it."

Jubilee wiped his eyes on his shirt sleeve. "And you told her different?"

Tom nodded. "And I told her different."

Jubilee nodded and rubbed his hands over his hair that Tom suddenly noticed had turned completely gray in the past few months. "I remembers when I first heared about Lincoln freeing the slaves. A young Yankee captain rode up to the Colonel's house with a bunch of soldiers and herded us up on the veranda. When he read us the Emancipation Proclamation from off a dirty and wrinkled piece of paper what looked like he'd been carrying around stuffed in his pocket, I pondered how a few words by some white man I didn't know was supposed to change the world I did know. I grew up with the Colonel, and he grew up with me, and our lives got tangled together through no fault of our own. Mr. Lincoln's words freed my body, but they didn't free up my heart along with it. Jesse and Miss Mattie got their lives tangled together, too, and them words that Judge Willis said over him and Caroline Knight didn't free up his heart any more than them words that young captain read freed mine."

Tom sipped his coffee and found its lukewarm flavor no more to his liking than Jubilee's words. He set his cup on the table and rolled a cigarette while he considered what the old man had said. "There's one difference between you and Jesse. You never turned your back on the Colonel and went looking for the future. You stayed with Mattie, which is nearly the same thing. Jesse broke away from Mattie."

Jubilee shook his head. "But he ain't turned his back on her."

"I don't expect him to—just as long as he keeps his interest neighborly."

"It don't matter how many women he marries or how many young'uns call him Pa, Miss Mattie always gonna own a part of him."

"I figure Jesse's strong enough to live with that. It's a lucky man who doesn't leave parts of himself behind whenever he moves on. So long as he don't come back to pick up the pieces and try to build them into something."

"He always gonna own a part of her, too," said Jubilee slowly in the tones of a man admitting facts Tom figured he'd rather not admit.

Tom lit his cigarette and peered at Jubilee through the smoke. "And I reckon I'll have to live with that."

Jubilee grabbed his wrist. "I hopes you ain't thinking to take up where Jesse left off 'cause I'll have to kill you if you does. I ain't stepping aside again for no man to lead my chile into sin."

"I suspect it was six of one and half a dozen of the other, Jubilee, but you don't need to fret about my intentions. Mattie's safe with me. I won't shame her in front of folks."

Jubilee sighed and released Tom's wrist. "I believes you and I feels some better."

"Jubilee." Tom waited until the ex-slave met his eyes. "That don't mean I'm more decent that Jesse. It means I'm older than him, and my blood don't run as hot. And I'm patient. I'm content to wait."

CHAPTER
7

March 1885

Mattie frowned as she entered the figures in her ledger. The winter had been a hard one with temperatures plummeting below zero on several occasions. Had her cattle not been so fat from good grazing over the summer and early fall, and had Tom not ordered hay cut and stored during that period when she was without interest in the ranch, the Bar H would be much worse off. As it was, losses of cattle due to weather were running above average.

Losses due to brand changing or rustling were nil.

Mattie might be anathema to the big ranchers, but to blacklisted cowboys and nester ranchers fighting to survive by branding mavericks and running their herds on public school land, she was a heroine. Her refusal to support the hiring of Pat

Garrett and his Home Rangers and her threat to press trespassing charges against Garrett if he rode across her land in search of rustlers left W.M.D. Lee frothing with rage and the smaller ranchers laughing. Her audacity in paying for the defense of many cowboys charged in the indictments handed down by Tascosa's grand jury kept her own herds safe. If many of those charged were guilty of swinging too wide a loop, and Mattie admitted to herself that many were, then there was honor among thieves and they honored her by not rustling her cattle.

Between one thing and another, she had survived the winter with fewer losses than expected. Better surely than the syndicate ranches where managers made decisions, always subject to the wishes of absent owners. Usually high-toned Scots or English.

Mattie hated the sound of a Scots burr, but she supposed now that spring had arrived, she would be hearing it again as the younger sons, cousins, brothers, nephews, and friends of Lord Somebody or the other, investor in this syndicate or that, would also be arriving for a few weeks of hunting, picnicking, riding, and generally making a nuisance of themselves. They would make remarks about the "uncivilized accommodations," wave perfumed linen handkerchiefs beneath their well-bred but skinny noses, order the cowboys about like common laborers, and generally make themselves unpopular and unwelcome to all who had the misfortune to be forced into their company. By late summer they would be gone, leaving the land to those who knew it best.

She rested her chin in her hand. There were so few of the old-timers left: herself, the Rowe brothers—British by birth, Texan by inclination, Charlie Goodnight, Hank Cresswell, a few others. W.M.D. Lee owned the LS, of course, but Mattie didn't count him in her camp. The balance of power was shifting from the pioneer rancher to the syndicate, and the most powerful syndicate was the Capitol Freehold Land Investment Company, Ltd.

Fathered in 1882 by the Texas legislature in return for the building of a new state capitol, nurtured in the womb of a Chicago syndicate, and delivered with the aid of bonds sold to English and Scottish investors, an immense ranch of three million acres was born in 1884 to the Capitol Freehold Land Investment Company. The giant, as Mattie thought of it, stretched some two hundred miles from the border of No Man's Land on the north to past the Yellow House region in the south, and covered most of ten Panhandle counties along the New Mexico border. Rumor said that all three million acres were to be fenced in—six thousand miles' worth of barbed wire by the time the fencing crews finished.

At present the giant slept undisturbed, but soon it would wake to receive its subjects: cattle—thousands upon thousands of cattle. As cattle poured onto its fenced pastures in an endless river and more and more men hired on to ride for its brand, the giant would grow, flex its muscles, and cast its shadow across the Panhandle. Mattie would need all the consolidated power of her seven hundred thousand acres, its men and cattle, to face the giant's challenge.

With an uneasy glance toward the west where the sleeping giant lay, Mattie closed her ledger. So many changes during the time she was hiding inside herself, as Tom put it, but none she could have stopped any more than she had been able to stop Jesse's wedding. She felt her eyes sting at the thought of Jesse and turned her thoughts to more pleasant changes. At least, she finally had clear title to all the railroad lands within her boundaries, and by hook and crook—mostly crook—she had title to much of the school land. The world outside might not turn according to Mattie Jo Hunter's wishes, but on the Bar H it revolved by her will.

If she was not happy, she at least survived. If she sometimes couldn't sleep and spent much of the night sitting in her rocking chair looking out her bedroom window at the giant cottonwood tree and visiting her memories, that was her business. If her body sometimes felt empty and her breasts in need of Jesse's caress, that was her business, too. If she still licked her wounds, she did so in the privacy of her bedroom.

At least Samuel was not present to pour salt in those wounds.

But he would be soon.

Mattie picked up his letter and smoothed out the creases from where she had crushed it in her fist. Like vultures waiting for her to die, he and Clint Murray had circled her all summer and much of the fall until even they noticed their taunts no longer touched her—but then nothing much had. They had ridden off in search of more agreeable climates in which to winter—Chicago, New York, Kansas City, Denver—strange choices for a Southerner who claimed to hate Yankees as much as Samuel did. Not that she cared where he went—as long he stayed away from the Bar H.

But like a snake who crawled out of his hole to sun himself on a rock when warm weather came, Samuel was returning to the Panhandle.

Today.

The Ides of March.

Caesar hadn't expected treachery. Mattie expected nothing less.

She made her plans accordingly.

* * *

Samuel rode in at noon, but he did not ride in alone.

Clutching a long shawl around her shoulders so that its trailing ends covered the bulge of a Colt .45 hidden in her skirt pocket, Mattie watched silently as Samuel rode his gray gelding in a circuit around the ranch outbuildings. She watched, shivering in the cool air, while he gestured toward the corrals, the barn, the storage sheds, and the long, rectangular adobe bunkhouse. She watched his easy smile flashing like the sun on fool's gold as he spoke to the taller of the two strangers who had accompanied him and Clint Murray. She could not hear what her husband was saying, but he was obviously bragging about the well-kept and prosperous headquarters he had nothing to do with building.

Mattie felt a coldness inside her belly as though she had swallowed a handful of snow. Samuel's sudden interest in the ranch, his close scrutiny of the outbuildings, violated her as surely as rape. Insofar as adobe mud and cottonwood logs and lumber and hooves and horns could symbolize a person, she *was* this ranch. Defile it with unworthy intentions, and you defiled her. Whatever Samuel's intentions were, they were most certainly unworthy.

Clint Murray rode by Samuel's side, turning his head every so often to watch Mattie, and she fancied she could see his muddy green eyes despite the distance that separated them. Being the object of his attention made her feel unclean as though whatever taint of some moral decay infected Murray had rubbed off on her.

She turned her eyes toward the strangers and smoothed her skirt, feeling the hard shape of the Colt in her pocket. She did not know who they were or why they were riding with Samuel and she did not care. She did not intend to offer them hospitality. No one worthy kept company with her husband

and Clint Murray, and she would be damned if she would allow any other worthless men Samuel picked up during his travels to set foot inside her house. She had shot a man once before for trespassing on what was hers. She could do so again.

She waited for the confrontation.

Finally, Samuel spurred his gelding toward the house and dismounted, leaving Clint Murray and the strangers in front of the bunkhouse.

"Mattie?"

Mattie did not return his smile as Samuel paused at the edge of the porch, then walked toward her with a step neither so light nor so graceful as in the past. She did not owe him that welcoming courtesy, had not owed it to him in years.

"Samuel."

Samuel removed his butter-soft leather gloves and slapped them against his thigh as he studied her. "You're looking gaunt and brown, Mattie. It is as I feared. This climate is making a bony old woman of you before your time."

"You, however, have filled out some, Samuel," she said, studying her husband's thickened body and his features blurred by too much good living—paid for with the sweat of everyone on the Bar H. "If you were a steer, you'd fetch a high price for such goodly beef on the hoof."

Samuel's pasty complexion turned red, Mattie noticed, even where thinning blond hair revealed his scalp. "I see you're still lacking in respect, Mattie." He took a step closer, raising his hand to strike her.

"Samuel!" snapped Clint Murray as he stepped on the porch.

Samuel turned his blow into a caress and patted Mattie's cheek. "My long absence from you has made me forget my manners."

Mattie choked back a cry of revulsion as she jerked away from his touch. She caught the amused expression in his eyes and knew he had mistaken her revulsion for fear. Samuel fed on signs of fear as other men fed on beef and beans.

Samuel was wrong. She did not fear him; she despised him.

She straightened her back and lifted her chin. "Don't touch me again, Samuel. You make my skin crawl and my belly sick."

Samuel shook his head, his eyes still holding that amused look. "Your speech is as coarse as your behavior, Mattie. I'll ask you to remember you are supposed to be a lady of refinement and to act like one—if you remember how. Once a woman has taken to whoring and living among rough men, she's ruined for polite society. The vileness shows through the fancy clothes."

Mattie thought briefly of jerking her Colt out of her pocket and ending Samuel's filthy tirade by ending Samuel's life, but dismissed the temptation. She would not kill over words. She was not a man with a man's pride. A too-proud woman was soon broken in a man's world. Self-respect, not pride, held a woman together.

She would shoot Samuel only if he physically mistreated her. Or if he threatened her self-respect.

"The only rough men I've lived among have been you and Murray. If you find my behavior toward the two of you unseemly, you only have yourselves to blame. Beat a horse often enough and it will turn on you and kick you to death."

Samuel clenched his fists. "Shut your mouth or I'll . . ."

"You'll what, Samuel?" she asked softly when he hesitated. "Rape me again?"

"Punish you," he finished.

"I think not, Samuel. I'll not allow you to exercise your idea of husbandly authority."

"We failed to consider that she might recover from McDade's disaffection, Samuel," said Clint as he studied her, his muddy green eyes holding the same expression Mattie had seen a score of times in her father's eyes: that of a man reassessing an adversary after underestimating him. "You were beaten last summer, Mattie. As a gambler I've sat across the poker table from a hundred men as arrogant and certain of themselves as you and watched them stagger away with their pride broken. Such men are no longer a threat. Break a man's pride and you break him."

"I'm not a man, Clint Murray. It was a mistake to judge me by a man's standards." She did not speak of self-respect because she sensed that to do so was to give Murray a weapon to use against her.

Murray nodded. "Perhaps so. Or perhaps you recovered because we did not strip you of all that pride after all. At any rate, I'm pleased you've regained your sharp tongue. I dislike kicking a cowering dog. There's no sport in it. A spirited opponent makes this final victory more pleasurable."

Mattie shivered again—whether from the cold wind that blew across the porch or the sense of uneasiness brought on by Clint Murray's words, she didn't know. "What do you want, Samuel? More money? Did you come back to raid the accounts again? And who are those two strangers?"

As Samuel and Clint exchanged amused glances, she wished Jubilee or Tom would cut short their chores to return to the house. Tom in particular had not wanted her to greet Samuel alone, but she had refused his offer of company. Now that winter was over there was too much work to spare a single man to watch over her. Cattle that had drifted south in front of winter storms had to be rounded up, fences had to be mended, water holes and grazing had to be checked, and fresh supplies bought.

Besides, to Samuel, Tom's presence would be a sign of her feminine weakness, and she could no longer afford an appearance of weakness.

"You are partly right, my dear," said Samuel, turning to watch a tall man striding toward the porch, followed by a shorter, older man walking a respectful distance behind him. A servant, Mattie immediately thought, and one who knows his place.

"It is the Bar H accounts which concern us, and I have found a way to swell them beyond even your avarice." Samuel stopped and smiled, gesturing with his right hand. "Mattie, may I introduce George Henry Edward Faulkner, Esquire. Mr. Faulkner, my wife."

He did not introduce the servant, Mattie noticed without surprise. Samuel didn't consider hired help worthy of an introduction.

George Faulkner, a tall, broad-shouldered man with a lean face, square jaw, and thick auburn hair, gazed at Mattie from eyes the exact gray-green color as the leaves of a sagebrush plant. Surprise followed by male appreciation flickered momentarily across his face before his features assumed an expression of bored politeness. Tucking a riding quirt under his arm he strolled across the porch with a languid grace Mattie thought at odds with the hard muscles so clearly revealed by his tight-fitting English riding pants.

"Never thought you were short of words, Hunter, but you were certainly close-mouthed about your wife's beauty. Can't blame you. Any words that would do her justice would have only convinced me you were lying." He paused and bowed just slightly. "Madam, your beauty leaves me speechless—as it does your husband."

Mattie felt her belly clench as much from the sound of the man's slow Scots burr as from his false compliments and bland expression. Another useless, misbegotten offspring of a foreign investor on his way to make some ranch manager's life miserable. "I have never known Samuel to withhold his opinions of either my virtues or my faults, Mr. Faulkner, so please don't exaggerate on my account."

George Faulkner didn't change expression but Mattie caught a narrowing of his gray-green eyes that told her he had heard the cold dislike in her voice and was both displeased and puzzled. Clearly Mr. Faulkner was a man used to female approval and adoration. Mattie wasted neither on British fops.

"What faults could so lovely and charming a woman possibly have, Mrs. Hunter?" asked Faulkner with a smile that revealed a dimple in one lean cheek.

"I don't like to be patronized and I'm not an empty-headed female who needs a man to convince her of what her own mirror tells her. I've learned that most gentlemen find either attribute unattractive."

Samuel grabbed her wrist. "Your behavior toward our guest is unseemly, Mattie."

Faulkner poked the end of his quirt in Samuel's chest hard enough to draw a gasp. "No offense taken, Hunter. I like a spirited woman. Keeps a man up to snuff."

Mattie rubbed her wrist and choked back hysterical laughter. Two men had complimented her on her spirit: Clint Murray and this Scotsman. She trusted the motives of neither.

Samuel's flushed cheeks gave away his rage, and Mattie expected him to lash out at the Scotsman for protecting her. She was surprised when he spoke to her instead. "Mattie, our guest is in need of refreshment and to warm himself. Surely your lack of my civilized company the past few months hasn't made you forget how to be hospitable. Let's go inside and you fetch us a decanter of bourbon and three glasses."

Mattie smiled as she stepped in front of the door, blocking Samuel's attempt to open it. "Mr. Faulkner will have to do without. The only liquor on the Bar H is a bottle of Taos Lightning Jubilee keeps in the kitchen for snakebite, and I don't recommend drinking it. The resulting headache is without parallel. Or so I understand. I have not ever drunk any myself."

Faulkner arched one eyebrow and Mattie suddenly clenched her hands. Jesse always arched one brow in that same manner. "Are you one of these temperance ladies I've been hearing about, Mrs. Hunter?" he asked, a faint hint of amusement in his voice—like Jesse when he teased her.

"Mattie is a woman of strong convictions but peculiar notions," said Clint Murray with a smile that did nothing to warm the cold viciousness in his eyes.

Mattie expelled a slow breath. Faulkner was not like Jesse. Jesse would never associate with men like Clint Murray and Samuel. "Cattle and alcohol don't mix, Mr. Faulkner. I allow no drunkenness on my ranch. If you want whiskey, I suggest the nearest saloon—which happens to be in Tascosa. It's where my cowboys go when they work up a thirst. There is also a hotel in Tascosa—one with clean sheets and no lice."

"Mattie!"

Samuel's face was red, his lips thinned with anger. "You see why I sought you out when I heard of your interest in Texas, Faulkner. Life on a ranch is simply too hard on my wife. I hardly recognize the gentle, biddable young girl I married in this hard-talking creature." He took Mattie's arm. "Move out of the way so our guest can get out of this damnable wind."

"He is not *our* guest, Samuel. He is yours, and I have not the time or the patience to put up with another bourbon-swilling, card-playing friend of yours sleeping on my sheets and eating at my table."

Samuel squeezed Mattie's arm until she grimaced with pain. "Shut up before you ruin everything."

Faulkner held up his hand, a grimace of distaste twisting his mouth. "Please, sir, I don't wish to be the cause of any further marital discord. If Mrs. Hunter will excuse us, perhaps you could send for your man of business and I could examine your books. Tomorrow I should like to take a closer look at the property, although I am favorably impressed by the condition of the outbuildings I briefly examined, while allowing you to greet your lovely wife privately and acquaint her with my purpose."

Mattie leaned back against the door, her knees suddenly weak. "What purpose, Mr. Faulkner? What interest do you have in the Bar H?"

Faulkner glanced at Samuel with an expression of surprise before looking back at Mattie. "Your husband has offered to sell me the Bar H, Mrs. Hunter. Or rather, sell it to the syndicate headed by my father. I'm here to appraise the property."

He tapped his quirt against the palm of one hand. "Speaking of property, Hunter, I shall want an actual count of your herds. My father and I are aware of too many instances in which the book count and the number of animals actually present differ by several thousand head. I will not pay for nonexistent cattle."

"No!"

Mattie felt the doors in her mind burst open even as her denial burst from her lips. Memories swirled out like dried leaves blown by the wind, memories of the trail drive to Texas, memories of that first horrible year of flies and heat and bone-deep cold and a stillborn daughter's grave on a windswept cliff above the Canadian. And memories of Jesse—Jesse who respected her and taught her to respect herself.

But more powerful than memories were the ghosts who walked among them, and none was more powerful than the ghost of herself as she used to be before Jesse called her out of hiding in the opinions of others—called her out to root herself and grow whole and proud in this land.

Her land.

She saw Clint Murray licking his lips like a wolf ready to feed on a dying cow. If Samuel had returned to sell the ranch, then Murray had returned to watch her uprooted soul die.

"No," Mattie repeated quietly as she straightened and stepped forward into the sunshine that slanted across the porch. "You'll not pay for existing cattle either, Mr. Faulkner, nor for outbuildings nor wagons nor horses, because my land is not for sale!"

Samuel interrupted. "You needn't worry about my wife, Faulkner. My absence has unsettled her mind until she believes she has a say in a man's business. If necessary, I'll sign her name as well as my own to the deed."

Mattie shook her head without looking at him. "Then the deed won't be legal, Samuel, and Mr. Faulkner and his syndicate will find themselves inconvenienced by a lawsuit if they attempt to exercise authority over my ranch."

Samuel's eyes narrowed. "Don't listen to her, Faulkner. She's deranged."

Faulkner ignored Samuel, folding his arms and staring at Mattie instead, his eyes revealing a sharp intelligence. "Doesn't sound as though you're ready for Bedlam yet, Mrs. Hunter, so why don't you explain yourself? Why can't your husband sell his property to me?"

Mattie met his eyes. "Because this is Texas, Mr. Faulkner, and this ranch is not my husband's property. Legally it is *our* property, and unlike the property laws in England or in most states, Samuel cannot sell this ranch unless I agree. A woman may not be able to vote, and she may not borrow money without her husband's permission, but she is not totally without rights. In order for Samuel to sell this ranch legally, I must sign the deed outside of his presence and swear in front of witnesses that he has not coerced me."

She whirled around to face Samuel. "I am not your chattel, and I will not sign that deed!" She saw his mouth gape open and the blood drain from his face, and knew that one way or another her war with Samuel would end today. There was no going back; he had threatened her once too many times, and she had defied him once too often.

She reached behind her and opened the screen door, slipped inside, and latched it. "I'm sorry you wasted your time, Mr. Faulkner. Have a pleasant journey back to Scotland. Good day."

She closed her oak-plank front door and slid the bolt home, locking herself inside her house. She wasn't hiding; she was making a strategic retreat.

She heard Faulkner slap his riding quirt against his English riding boot, its crack audible over the sound of Samuel's cursing. "Texas has some damnably strange laws that an Englishman wouldn't permit."

"I'll see to my wife, Faulkner. I'll make her change her mind!" Mattie heard Samuel exclaim.

"I dislike being misled, Hunter, and I dislike fools. You have done one, and you are the other. Don't bother calling upon me when I find lodgings. I shall not be receiving you."

She heard him step off the porch, then listened as the sound of hoofbeats faded away. Except for Robert asleep in her bedroom, she was alone with two men poised outside her door like two rattlers ready to strike. She glanced at the murals on the walls of the empty front room—a history in pictures of the Bar H and the men who rode for the brand. Including Jesse.

"The only way to keep what's right between us is to let it go."

"Thank you, Jesse, for those words," she whispered as she turned back toward the door. She straightened her shoulders. The only way to save her land was to let it go.

She heard the sound of a knife cutting through the screen, then the heavy thud of boots against the wooden door, and drew her Colt. "Samuel!" she shouted over the pounding. "I'll sign that deed, but only if you sell the Bar H to Tom Miller."

The pounding stopped, but Mattie could hear nothing from the two men. The coldness she'd felt while she watched Samuel showing Faulkner the outbuildings was back. She refused to call it fear, preferring to call it anticipation instead. Anticipation also speeded up the heart and shortened the breath. Her legs trembled and she locked her knees to keep from falling. Dear God, where were they?

The front window shattered, a small round table tipped over, sending a lamp crashing onto the floor in a tiny, ill-smelling puddle of kerosene and glass shards, and Samuel crawled inside. He staggered toward her, his eyes maniacal, his hands reaching. "I'll kill you."

Mattie backed up and pointed the Colt at him. "Three hundred thousand dollars, Samuel, for your signature on that deed."

Samuel stared at her, his chest heaving, his eyes less sane than before. "Faulkner offered three times that much, you stupid bitch."

Clint Murray ducked in the window. "Pardon me

for eavesdropping, Mattie, but where would your battered Galahad find three hundred thousand dollars?"

She ignored him, concentrating on Samuel instead. "You'll be free, Samuel."

Clint smiled. "It's your money, isn't it, Mattie? You'll give Miller the money. You have to do it that way, don't you? As you pointed out to Faulkner, this is Texas. You own the property jointly with Samuel. You can't buy him out. You must both sell to a third party—a straw man I believe he's called—who in turn may sell it back to you." He stroked his chin. "With all the proper papers designating such property as being separate from that owned by your husband, of course."

Mattie turned her head slowly toward him. It was strange how she'd never noticed how seldom he blinked. A snake never blinked either. "If you know so much about Texas community property law, why didn't you tell Samuel that he couldn't sign my name on the deed?"

If anything, Clint Murray looked even more amused. "I only warn Samuel if a game is crooked in the house's favor. This one wasn't. There was no way I could lose, Mattie. If you quietly signed, you lost this ranch and ended up living with your daddy again—far away from Jesse McDade—and miserable. Or it might have been amusing to keep you and your brat with us for a while—until we tired of you."

He pulled a cigar from his waistcoat pocket and inhaled the aroma. "On the other hand, if you had refused to sign, then Samuel's revenge promised to be exceptional. Either way, you suffered and I won." He fished a tin of matches from his coat pocket and struck one, lighting his cigar. "I hadn't anticipated your holding a gun on us, though. Our game truly becomes a game of chance. Tell me, Mattie, if we refuse your offer, what will you do then? Shoot us?"

Mattie felt a trickle of sweat roll down her spine. "Yes."

His teeth bared, Samuel took a step closer to her before Clint grabbed his arm. "Don't push her, Samuel! Most women holding a gun are unpredictable."

He stroked Samuel's arm and back with a familiarity that made Mattie's muscles tighten with revulsion. "You've always allowed Clint to advise you, Samuel. I suggest you do so this time also."

Clint looked at her as he continued to stroke Samuel. "You, however, are very predictable, Mattie."

"She's mad!" Samuel exclaimed, his eyes so filled with hatred that Mattie almost flinched.

Clint ignored him, his gaze never leaving her. "You intend to murder Samuel if he doesn't sign?"

Mattie swallowed. "There's no need for me to kill anyone. I have made Samuel a fair offer. However, if he refuses, I intend to kill you. You are the venom in his blood. Without you poisoning him, he'll sign. He hates me and he hates the Panhandle and this ranch. He'll be glad to be rid of all three."

Clint shook his head. "Your womanly sentiment is misleading you. As much as you've tried, you still aren't the cold, hard woman you want to be—that you *need* to be if you plan to win this hand. And this will be the last hand you ever play, Mattie, and you know it, too. That's why you chose to play it alone. And you are alone, aren't you?"

Mattie swallowed and nodded. "Yes."

"Foolish sentiment again. And the pride you deny. You don't want anyone else hurt, and you don't want any witnesses to your defeat."

"I can stand on my own without a man's crutch. If you see that as pride, then nothing I say will change your mind."

Murray smiled—the slow smile of man enjoying

his self-professed superiority over woman. "Foolish, foolish Mattie."

"Why won't you let Samuel accept my offer?" she asked, careful to keep her voice from revealing her desperation.

He looked at her impatiently. "It is not in my nature to be kind, Mattie. Some men live to defeat and destroy. Others live to nurture and build. I am one and you are the other. There is no compromise between us. This hand can't end in a draw. So what's it to be, Mattie? You can't leave a witness to murder. You'll have to kill Samuel, too, or you'll never be sure he won't go to the sheriff. Being a woman might save you from the hangman, but it won't save you from prison. Will you murder your husband, Mattie?"

Mattie felt her hands tremble and bile fill her throat. She swallowed. "I won't be tortured again. I won't be humiliated or hit or raped again. I won't see my children threatened. Neither God nor the law has any right to ask me to live the way I have since Jesse left."

Clint smiled. "Perhaps it's your reckoning for breaking your wedding vows."

"I've paid enough!"

Clint released Samuel's arm and walked toward her. "Give me the gun, Mattie."

Mattie's hands were greasy with sweat and she was afraid her finger would slip off the trigger. "Never gamble on a woman's sentiment, Clint. It's the first thing we sacrifice to survival."

She shot him.

CHAPTER

But she didn't kill him.

Just as she pulled the trigger Samuel grabbed her arm, and the bullet missed.

But not entirely.

Mattie saw the ragged hole appear in Clint Murray's coat near the waist and to the left side. Had she hit any vital organ? She didn't know and didn't have time to worry about it as she curled her left hand into a claw and raked it down Samuel's face, missing his eye and leaving deep, bloody furrows on his cheek.

"I'll kill you!" he screamed, and twisted Mattie's wrist until incredible pain streaked up her right arm and she heard the bone snap.

Samuel snatched the gun from her suddenly numb fingers and shoved her away. Mattie's feet skidded on the waxed floor and she fell backward, narrowing missing slamming her head into the corner of the stone hearth as she landed heavily on her back in front of the fireplace. She saw Samuel cock her own gun and aim it at her chest and tried to crawl away. But she couldn't. Her wrist was a limp piece of white-hot pain and she had no breath left in her lungs. Her body demanded that she breathe before she moved, and her mind demanded that she find words to stop her own murder. To survive she must do both.

"No!" shouted Clint as he grabbed Samuel's hand.

Mattie finally drew a breath, then several more as she watched Clint grapple with Samuel. The pain in her wrist had settled into a throbbing that made her grit her teeth, and shock confused her mind. Clint fighting Samuel to save her? It denied everything she knew about the man.

She rolled over and pushed herself to her knees using her left hand and arm, cradling her right wrist to her chest as she tried to concentrate on her next move. The kitchen! She must get to the kitchen. There were guns there.

In the next instant someone kicked her between the shoulders, and she sprawled face down on the floor, landing on her broken arm. She forgot not to scream.

"If you move, your arm will hurt worse, Mattie," said Clint.

She lifted her head and turned it until she could see him from the corner of her eye. He must have kicked her instead of Samuel since it was his booted foot pressing on her shoulders.

"Let me up," she ordered.

Clint laughed in spite of the white lines bracketing his mouth that spoke of a man in pain. "Still spirited, Mattie? Samuel broke your arm but not your spirit?"

She licked her lips and tasted dust. The floor hadn't been swept today, she thought, and nearly laughed herself. She was going to die and she was worrying about household matters. "Samuel will never break me and neither will you."

"Let me kill her," begged Samuel, his voice like that of a petulant child asking for a treat. "She deserves it. She shot you."

She saw Clint shake his head. "Only a flesh wound. And we can't kill her. A man can't kill his wife, Samuel. The law doesn't allow it, and I don't intend to see my face on wanted posters."

He pressed his boot harder against Mattie's back, until she could feel her breast bone grinding against her broken wrist. She couldn't stop her scream.

"You may discipline her, Samuel. No one will say anything against you for that. After word of her rudeness and lack of hospitality toward Faulkner gets around—and it will—no one will wonder that you finally lost your temper." He lifted his boot and leaned down to grab Mattie's hair, digging his fingers into the mass of golden curls pinned on the back of her head.

Mattie's eyes watered as Clint jerked on her hair until he pulled her up to her knees, her head tilted backward by his inexorable grip. She bit her lip to prevent another scream. So help her God, she would not give either one of them the satisfaction of hearing her scream again.

Samuel grabbed the front of her blouse and jerked her to her feet, ripping a shoulder seam in the process. Mattie didn't scream at the expression of anticipation in her husband's eyes, but she couldn't stop herself from shuddering. Caught between the two men, she smelled Samuel's sweat and her own mixed with the sweet coppery odor of Clint's blood and gagged.

Samuel's first blow split her lip and dazed her mind. His second glanced off her cheekbone, and his third scraped her eyebrow, leaving stinging flesh around her right eye. Instinctively, she jerked her head back and stretched up on her toes, easing the pressure on Clint's grip on her hair, then rammed her left elbow backward into his wounded side. She heard him grunt and loosen his grip, and she spun away, feeling a sharp sting as he pulled out several strands of her hair.

But she reckoned without Samuel. Again.

"Bitch!" he shouted as he grabbed the back of her blouse and kicked her feet out from under her.

She heard her blouse rip up the back as she fell heavily to the floor, this time twisting her body so she didn't land on her wrist. Samuel kicked her in the chest, narrowing missing her breast. She didn't waste her energy trying to crawl away, or even to push herself up to her knees. Doing so would leave her chest and belly vulnerable to repeated kicks. Broken bones would heal, but ruptured organs would not. Fighting to the death was the choice of a proud man. She wasn't a man. There was a time to resist and a time to endure. Instinctively, she knew this was the time to endure.

Resistance would come later, and so would revenge.

She rolled herself into a ball, her knees against her chest, her one good arm protecting her head. Not that her position stopped the hurting, because it didn't. Samuel just wasn't able to kick her belly or breasts. The rest of her was open and vulnerable, and he was generous in his attention. Samuel's panting breath, the soft thud of a leather boot on flesh, the groans she could no longer contain, the wind whistling like the sound of a crying child through the broken window, were the only sounds in an otherwise quiet room. Mattie felt herself begin to slip from endurance into submission.

First she lost her breath, then her consciousness. Her last thought was a cry for help no one could hear.

"Jesse!"

"Will you sign the deed now, Mattie?"

Mattie heard Samuel's voice and shivered. Her face and hair and blouse were wet and the cold wind with the wailing child was turning her to ice at the same time she felt the fireplace's heat searing her back. She sucked in a deep breath and nearly screamed as pain sharp as knives stabbed her chest. Not that her broken ribs hurt much worse than the horrible aches in her thighs and hips which Samuel had taken particular pleasure in kicking, but the pain constricted her movements more.

Samuel grabbed her hair and pulled her head off the floor. "Are you listening, Mattie? Will you sign the deed now?"

Mattie heard and she even understood him, but she was listening to the voice of the wind—the wind that sounded so much like a child—and felt afraid for the first time. Robert's thin cry blended so well with the shriek of the wind that neither man had distinguished one from the other. But if the wind fell, and they heard Robert, then there was no end to the evil of which they were capable. The least they would do was hold Robert captive to ensure her cooperation. The most they might do she dared not imagine lest her mind break.

Keeping her eyes shut as if she were still unconscious, she clenched her left hand and found it bruised but uninjured. Any injury whose pain did not threaten to make her mad was not worth considering.

Samuel released her hair and stood up. "She won't answer me, Clint."

Mattie opened one eye and peered through her lashes. Clint was sitting on the sofa holding his side. Blood had soaked through his coat and his face was pale. Perhaps he was more badly wounded than she had first thought. There was always a reckoning, and perhaps Clint's was to die slowly and painfully by her hands.

She hoped so.

But Samuel was not wounded. He was, however, visibly tired. He had removed his coat and sweat plastered his shirt to his back. His shoulders slumped and she could hear him panting. Too much soft living on ranch profits, she thought silently. She, on the other hand, was not soft. She rode with her men and often worked alongside them. Even terribly battered, she was stronger than most women. But not as strong as Samuel even in his poor condition. He was taller—if not by much—and weighed much more. But his weight made him awkward, the floor was slick, and he hated pain and was predictable.

So very predictable.

And so was Clint. He would oppose her wishes and thwart her acts no matter if it was foolish to do so or not.

She moaned and wiggled closer to the fireplace until her fingers touched the basket of cedar logs on the hearth—cedar logs from her land.

"She's awake, Samuel," said Clint. "You were too impatient before."

Samuel whirled around and started toward her. "Will you sign that deed, Mattie?"

She rolled to her right side and crossed her left arm over her chest. "Don't you dare kick me again, you fat, worthless bastard!"

Her lips were swollen from his blows and her words slurred, but she saw he understood. Blood suffused his face and he drew back his leg to kick her. This time she was ready. She caught the toe of his boot with her left hand and pushed. The waxed floor did the rest. Off-balance he fell backward, hitting the floor and stunning himself when his head bounced on the hard wood. Mattie didn't waste time gloating. She pushed herself to her knees, grabbed a cedar log from the basket and, fighting the pain from her broken ribs, slammed it down on Samuel's knee, then across his groin.

"I'm sure you enjoyed that, Mattie, but it gained you nothing except more pain when Samuel recovers," said Clint over the sound of Samuel's screams. Clutching his wounded side with his left hand, he cocked Mattie's Colt with his right. "Drop the log in the fire, please. It's cold in here and you might as well make yourself useful while we wait."

Mattie almost smiled. She hadn't counted on Clint's cooperation in his own defeat. She stuck the log into the fire and watched the sap on the end of it burst into flame like a torch.

"Catch it!" she screamed as she staggered up and threw the flaming log at the wounded man, then limped toward the stairs.

Clint Murray dropped the Colt and jerked his right arm up to protect his face as she had anticipated. It was a useless gesture—if predictable—since Mattie had aimed the log not at Clint, but at the puddle of spilled kerosene at the end of the sofa.

Her aim was true, and the kerosene burst into a sheet of flame that the wind blowing through the broken window fanned into a conflagration that spread in an instant across the floor, giving Mattie time to reach the stairs and force her bruised legs to climb its steps. "I'll burn down this house and the sparks will set fire to my grazing land all the way to the Canadian. You'll find no one to buy burned-out pastures and dead cattle, and I'll win this hand, Clint Murray."

She heard him cursing her as she hurried up the rest of the stairs and into her bedroom. More importantly, she heard the crash of another small table and knew he had jerked the rag rug out from under it. Clint was predictable. He would beat out the fire to thwart her.

She dropped the wooden bar across her door and gasped as the sobbing Robert clutched her bruised and throbbing legs. Not daring to kneel down to hug him because she could not risk his squeezing her broken ribs, she stroked his dark, curly hair and locked away her guilt for the time being. Later she would ask herself why she had not seen to her son's safety before confronting Samuel. Later she would ask herself if her love for this hard land had blinded her to the needs of those who lived upon it.

"Hush, baby, Mama's here. Everything's fine now."

But it wasn't, and she knew it. She was locked in the second-floor bedroom of a burning house and the only way out was to climb out the window, down her giant cottonwood tree, and ride to the nearest neighbor for help.

Ride to Jesse's.

Jesse's headquarters was unchanged since Mattie's first and last visit two years ago—a large main house of logs with outbuildings of adobe tucked within the loop of a tiny creek—but she lacked the time or the strength to admire it. She reined in her horse and slid off its back, clutching its mane to support herself until the swirling blackness that threatened to pull her under receded. She was light-headed from taking shallow breaths, and every movement was an agony beyond anything she'd ever known. She had tied Robert onto her back in a

sling made from a sheet, and his weight added to
her pain as his terrified silence added to her fear.
Her right wrist and hand had swollen nearly double
since she had fashioned a splint from the shovel
brim of a sunbonnet. Her fingers were cold from lack
of circulation and tingled painfully in each new gust
of wind.

Letting go of her horse's mane, she staggered
toward Jesse's door, bending over under the weight
of Robert and to ease the pain of her broken ribs.
With one eye swollen shut and the other blurring
from exhaustion, she saw the figure standing in the
doorway as only an indistinct shadow. Soon he
would take her hand and ease her burden and she
would no longer stand alone against Samuel.

"Jesse," she whispered, stretching out her hand
toward the figure. "Help me. Samuel wanted to sell
the ranch and—and beat me when I refused to sign
the papers."

"My husband is in Tascosa, Mrs. Hunter."

The voice was colder than the wind, and Mattie at
first denied its words. Jesse must be here. She
blinked several times before finally focusing on
Caroline McDade. What Samuel's beating had failed
to do, the sight of Caroline's pregnant belly accomplished. She swayed and finally sank to her knees in
front of Jesse's wife, her spirit broken.

"Jesse!" she keened, and leaning over, she vomit-
ed up the taste of betrayal.

"How dare you call for my husband," said
Caroline. "You are as shameless as everyone told
me. You have no right to bring your problems to
Jesse, and I'll not have you chasing after him. Go
back to your own husband."

Mattie wiped her mouth and raised her head to
look at Caroline. "I can't. He'll kill me this time.
Please help me."

Caroline's delicate face flushed and her eyes looked hard as agate. She pursed her lips with disapproval before speaking. "Only a disloyal wife speaks of marital disagreements in public, but then I've heard of your behavior with Jesse. You don't know the meaning of loyalty."

Caroline's words stung Mattie like rawhide lashes, and Mattie discovered she was not so broken as she thought. "And you don't know the meaning of charity, *Caroline*."

Caroline stiffened. "Mrs. McDade to you."

Mattie climbed to her feet on will alone. "I'll never call you that, *Caroline*."

"Get off my property, Mrs. Hunter. There's no place for you here."

Mattie never knew where the strength came from to swallow back her bitter words before she spoke them, words that served no purpose but to reveal her own black jealousy by sowing distrust between Jesse and his wife. No need to point out that the Flying MJ was not Caroline's property; it was Jesse's dream, and the only woman he had ever shared it with was Mattie Hunter.

CHAPTER

Burdened by a sense of uneasiness he couldn't explain or shrug away, Jesse cut short his business in Tascosa and rode for home at noon. As he spurred the black gelding into a gallop, he chided himself for his foolishness. There was no reason to hurry back to the ranch. Caroline was in good health, the baby not due for another two months or more, and she didn't indulge in any activity that might bring on premature birth. Jesse grimaced. One activity Caroline considered "not good for baby" was sleeping with him.

Or rather, lying with him.

Caroline liked to be cuddled but she never cuddled a man back. She never held a man while he held her.

Not like Mattie.

He clenched his teeth. Damn, but he needed to ride herd on his thoughts a little better, to keep his eye on the future and his mind out of the past. Caroline didn't deserve a man whose thoughts kept visiting another woman's bed. She had done nothing to earn such disloyalty, and done everything to earn his respect. She was soft-spoken, gentle, clever with a needle, a good cook, and always submissive to his needs—even though such submissiveness served to chill those needs as often as it stoked them. She listened to his plans for the ranch with attentive eyes and a smile on her lips and never made a suggestion or a comment.

He was never sure if she actually heard anything he said or only pretended she did.

She never laughed, but only smiled until his hunger for a woman's laughter drove him away from headquarters and onto the flat prairies to work cattle, mend fence, talk with his cowboys around the campfire—and to forget.

The only time Caroline had ever shown any emotion deeper than a shallow pond was when he had inadvertently mentioned Mattie's name at supper one night.

Caroline had slammed her cup back in its saucer so hard that both had cracked. "I don't want to hear that woman's name spoken in my house."

Jesse had flushed with guilt or embarrassment— he couldn't decide which—and tried to recall anything about his comment to bring on such a fit. "I only said that Mattie was buying more Hereford bulls to breed with her cows, and that I needed to do the same."

Caroline's face was red and her lips had thinned to the point of disappearing. "Breeding is not a fit subject for the supper table, and neither is that woman's name."

"Caroline, this is a ranch. Breeding cattle for a better herd is one of the things I do," he said, carefully avoiding an angry tone of voice. "And Mattie is a rancher and a good one."

She covered her ears. "Don't say her name."

Jesse threw down his napkin, shoved his chair back, and walked around the table to kneel by her side. Gently he pried her hands away from her ears and held them between his own. "Caroline, what have you heard about Mattie Hunter?"

She tipped her chin up and met his eyes. "She is a bad woman."

Jesse rose and paced around the kitchen. "I worked for Mattie Hunter for five years. We settled this country and we lived through some rough times together doing it. People didn't always understand Mattie, and still don't. She is what she needed to be to survive this land and to hold it, but she is *not* a bad woman. She's a woman who doesn't suffer fools and ignorant men and isn't afraid to go against what's custom." *And isn't afraid to sin*, he added silently.

"Folks say you kept company with her," said Caroline, her eyes so filled with jealousy that Jesse wondered they didn't turn completely green.

He lifted Caroline from her chair and held her in his arms, stroking her hair. "This is the West. It's not polite to ask about a man's past even if that man is your husband. What I did before I married you is over and done with and not something I'd talk about in any event. I started fresh when I married you, Caroline."

Tears ran down her cheeks. "Please, Jesse, if you care for me at all, don't ever mention her name again."

He had promised her he wouldn't, then he had taken her to bed and made love to her. Afterwards, he left her sleeping and walked out on the porch and faced east—toward the Bar H—and whispered, "Good-bye, Mattie."

The bond was finally broken.

He slowed his horse as he rode across the flat plain toward his ranch. The boundary line between his property and Mattie's ran right down the middle of this plain and he was on the Hunter side. It was the only part of Mattie's land that lay directly between Tascosa and his ranch and he always rode across it, knowing she wouldn't mind. Going around would add several miles to his trip, and Mattie trusted her neighbors to cross her land without abusing her good nature—such as leaving gates down or taking too close an interest in an unbranded calf.

He glanced toward the horizon and felt his heartbeat jerk, then settle into a faster rhythm. There was another rider on the plain, three miles north of him as nearly as he could figure, and it looked like Mattie with a pack of some kind on her back. He sucked in his breath when a gust of wind blew the rider's hair over her shoulders. It was Mattie. No other woman had hair the color of a golddigger's dream. But what in hell was she doing with her hair undone and without a hat? And why was she riding away from his place?

He clenched the reins in his fist as he watched her lonely figure riding toward the Bar H. His belly cramped and he told himself it was hunger. His eyes watered and he told himself it was dust blowing in the wind.

He spurred his gelding toward his own land and wondered when he'd taken up the habit of lying to himself.

By the time he slid off his horse, his thoughts were back on a short leash but his uneasiness was riding him hard. The hair on the back of his neck prickled as it used to when he was an Indian fighter and knew a band of Comanches waited in ambush over the next break.

Leaving his horse saddled and tied to the hitching post, he stepped up on the porch and immediately froze. Even the wind had not blown away the sour smell of vomit, nor had it dried the wet scrub marks on the cottonwood planks.

He slammed open the door. "Caroline!"

"Jesse?" Caroline walked into the parlor from the kitchen, tucking a strand of chestnut hair back into her smooth chignon. "You're home early. I didn't expect you so soon."

He grasped her shoulders. "Are you well?"

She smiled, her eyes downcast, and she folded her hands over her belly. "Is any woman every really 'well' in my condition? But I'm not unwell either. I was just having a cup of tea. Come into the kitchen and tell me about your trip to Tascosa?"

"You haven't been sick this morning?" he asked.

For just an instant he thought he felt her stiffen under his hands. She looked up, her hazel eyes meeting his. "Yes, earlier this morning. But I'm better now."

She was lying. Her breath was fresh and clean with no sour taint. Someone else had been sick outside his own front door and been denied comfort. He knew it as surely as he knew his own name.

He released Caroline and took off his hat. He wiped his forehead on his sleeve and was surprised to find he was sweating. "I saw a woman riding away from the house a little while ago."

Her head jerked up and she licked her lips. "Did you speak to her?"

He shook his head, his belly cramping and his mouth tasting of a sickness of his own.

"Then how do you know it was a woman?" Caroline asked, licking her lips again.

She can't lick away the lies, he thought. "A man can see another rider for more than five miles on these flat plains, Caroline, and I wasn't any five miles away. I was close enough to see the color of her hair. Did Mattie Hunter stop by here while I was gone?"

Her eyes didn't change, but her tongue flicked over her mouth again, and Jesse saw his future turn dark. Her lying didn't disgust him as much as the fact that she did it so well. Had he not seen Mattie, he would not have known.

"Don't lie to me again, Caroline. Mattie's the only woman closer than fifty miles from our door, and she's the only woman with golden hair."

Caroline clenched her fists. "Yes! She stopped by, and she's worse than even gossip says. She's peculiar—and brazen. How dare she stand on my porch in her ragged clothes and wild hair and demand to see you! No decent woman would visit in such an unkept state and then demand to talk to another woman's husband. I sent her off—her and that boy of hers! Imagine tying a baby on your back with an old torn sheet. No wonder folks gossip about her."

She took a deep breath and laid her hands on Jesse's arm. "Please, Jesse, I don't want to talk about her anymore. It upsets me and that's not good for Baby."

He pulled his arm away from her clutching hands. "I have never seen Mattie leave her ranch even to buy supplies without looking like she just stepped out of a bandbox. I know damn well she wouldn't make a social call without being groomed. And she's not peculiar unless you consider the courage to stand on her own two feet peculiar."

He turned and lifted his gunbelt off its peg by the door. Since W.M.D. Lee and the other big ranchers had railroaded Gov. Jim Hogg into issuing a proclamation banning a man from wearing his guns, Jesse had gone unarmed except for his Winchester whenever he left his property. The governor, Mr. Lee, and Lee's band of so-called Home Rangers could go to hell. He didn't intend to ride into trouble without his Colt.

Caroline clutched his arm again. "Where are you going, Jesse?"

He freed his arm again and strapped on his gunbelt. "Mattie would never ride over here to pass the time of day with you, Caroline. She's in trouble, worse trouble than she's known before, or she wouldn't have come asking for me." *She wouldn't have forgotten her pride and sense of betrayal unless she was desperate, he thought.*

Caroline slapped him, her eyes so filled with rage that he doubted she knew what she was doing. "You're carrying on with that Hunter woman, aren't you?"

He opened the door. "I give you my word that I haven't seen Mattie Hunter since our marriage."

She followed him outside and gripped the porch railing as she watched him mount his horse. "Then why are you riding over there?"

He gripped the reins. "She's a neighbor, Caroline, and I've got to see what's wrong. That's what neighbors do in this country."

"I won't stand for it, Jesse! It's not fitting!"

He turned his horse toward the east. "Go in the house, Caroline. It's too cold for you to be out. I'll be back as soon as I can."

He spurred his horse into a run, sick with fear and his own lies. He wasn't riding to Mattie's because she was a neighbor; he was riding to her because she was a part of himself whether it was fitting or not.

The bond was not broken.

* * *

Tom Miller rinsed out his mouth with a swig of water, then spat it out and hung his canteen over his saddle horn. He nudged the big sorrel gelding and rode over to the wiry ranch manager. "I'm going back to the house, Red. Mattie's been alone long enough what with Jubilee in Tascosa with a list of supplies and doodads longer than my arm."

The redheaded manager squinted at the sky. "Ain't three o'clock yet, Tom. Lot of hours till the sun goes down and a lot of work to get done." He rested his forearms across his saddle horn. "How come you're in such an all-fired hurry? Miss Mattie's been alone before. You got such a high opinion of your company that you think she can't do without it till you finish your chores?"

Tom heard the bite beneath Red's words and shrugged it off. He got along with the ramrod well enough most of the time, and he didn't intend to fight with Red over who was higher in Mattie's pecking order. Red just couldn't resist pushing sometimes because, right or wrong, he figured Mattie carried Jesse's brand still and he didn't cotton to another cowboy with a hot iron trying to alter it.

"Hunter's due in today, and Mattie figures to meet him and that no-good Clint Murray alone. She found chores away from the main house for everybody on the place. She's got something up her sleeve, but I don't like the odds. Hunter by himself she could handle, but Hunter and Murray together compound meanness faster than a banker compounds interest."

Red rolled a cigarette and lit it. "Jesse should have killed those two and left them for the buzzards years ago. Hell, *I* should have done it. I offered to, but Jesse turned me down."

"It wasn't your place," said Tom. "And Jesse couldn't shoot Mattie's husband."

Red looked at him. "I don't see it that way. Hunter

needed killing, and none of us would have thought any less of Jesse. And for damn sure, no cowboy on the place would have said anything against him. Still wouldn't for that matter."

"Killing's a mighty serious business, Red. Man oughtn't to do it unless his conscience is clear. God said an eye for an eye and a tooth for a tooth, but I don't recall His ever saying anything about shooting a husband so you can have the wife."

Red looked uneasy. "Hell, that wouldn't have been his only reason."

"Maybe, maybe not, but I reckon Jesse wasn't clear in his own mind which it was." He turned his horse toward the south and headquarters. "I'll be leaving now. Anything you want me to tell Mattie?"

"I can't figure you out, Miller. I tell you to go mend a fence or check a herd, and you do it without arguing just like you were any top hand, but if I was to tell you to get back to work and I'd check on Miss Mattie, I'd be looking down the barrel of your gun. Ain't that right?"

"Be best for everybody if it didn't come to that, Red."

"Then you mind telling me just why you think it's more your place to look after Miss Mattie than the men who followed her to the Panhandle?" asked Red.

"Time's wasting. Hunter ought to be there by now."

Red sighed. "Didn't figure I'd get an answer out of you, but I reckon if Miss Mattie takes to your company every evening after supper like a duck takes to water, then I better stay out of the pond."

Tom nodded and spurred his horse, glad that Red hadn't pushed harder for an answer he wasn't ready to give. His feelings for Mattie wasn't a subject he cared to have cowboys gossiping about around the campfire. There was too much gossip about Mattie as it was.

Tom rounded the mesa that lay northwest of headquarters before he smelled the smoke. He reined in the sorrel and sniffed the air. He was downwind from the house, so the odor was strong. And it wasn't smoke, he decided. It was the scorched smell fire left after it was extinguished. Neither the house or the outbuildings looked to be burned. Despite his sense of urgency, he slowed his horse to a walk so its hoofbeats didn't announce his coming. There was an air of wrongness hanging over the place, and he thought it best to check out the terrain before he went galloping in.

He rode south, then cut back east to keep the bunkhouse between him and the main house. He slid off his horse, slipped around the end of the bunkhouse, and saw a bareback horse tied to the hitching rail in front of the building's porch. It was a horse from the ranch remuda, but no cowboy he knew rode a horse bareback, and he saw no riders in any case. But Samuel and Murray were here because Hunter's gray gelding was tied up in front of the big house along with that chestnut Murray rode. He cocked his head to listen and silently cursed the wind that whistled around the bunkhouse and rustled through the bare limbs of the young cottonwoods Mattie had planted for shade. He heard what sounded like a groan coming from the far end of the bunkhouse, and unbuckled his spurs so their jangling wouldn't give him away. He drew his Colt and slipped along the porch toward the door at the far end that opened into the cowboys' sleeping quarters. He flattened himself against the adobe wall and eased down to the open door. He held his breath and heard furtive, rustling sounds. Tensing his muscles, he leapt through the door, slamming it back against the wall and cocking his gun at the same time.

"Don't move!"

The woman crouching by one of the tiers of bunks and pawing through a pair of saddlebags looked up and Tom recognized the golden hair. There was little else of Mattie Jo Hunter to recognize. Both lips were split and double their size. One eye was swollen shut and the other nearly so while a purple-black bruise surrounded both. One cut bisected her right eyebrow while another slashed a narrow red line across the point of her chin. Her cheeks were a deep red plum color and puffy—as though she had been slapped repeatedly.

But the battering of Mattie didn't stop with her face. Bruises—ugly bruises already turning black as sin—covered every inch of her exposed flesh and Tom had no doubt that the rest of her body was equally abused.

"God Almighty, Mattie," he whispered as he holstered his gun and dropped to his knees beside her.

Mattie lifted a pistol from the saddlebags. "Lost my Colt—the one Jesse gave me." Tom heard a sob catch in her throat. "No, that's wrong. Samuel took it away from me and gave it to Clint. He dropped it to put out the fire and I don't know where it is now." She peered at Tom through her half-open eye. "I'll borrow this one. I don't know which cowboy it belongs to, but when he asks, tell him I'll be careful with it. I won't lose this one."

Her hand shook violently and Tom held his breath, afraid that she would pull the trigger without meaning to. "Will you watch Robert for me, Tom? He's in that bunk over there. He's asleep. He's so tired. It wasn't such a long ride, but he rode in a sling on my back and I don't think he felt safe. You get so tired when you don't feel safe."

"Where did you ride, Mattie?" he asked softly.

She glanced away and he heard another sob. "To Jesse's—but he wasn't home. *She* said he was in Tascosa. I rode back here. There was no place else to go, and I didn't know where you were. I couldn't just ride without knowing where I was going. They might have followed me and caught me. I couldn't gallop—I rode bareback. Couldn't lift the saddle. Hurt too bad."

Tom glanced at her chest, saw the way she rounded her shoulders, and heard her quick, shallow breaths. A broken rib—more than one by the looks of her. "God, Mattie."

"No, I don't think He'll help me, Tom. I'll have to do it. If you'll watch Robert, I'll go back to the house. I won't talk this time. I'll just shoot. One and then the other."

"Why, Mattie?"

She glanced up at him again. "To kill them, of course."

"No, Mattie. I mean why did they beat you?"

Her one eye closed and she swayed and Tom grasped her shoulders to hold her up. He was almost afraid to touch her for fear of hurting her more.

She leaned against his hands and opened her eye again. "Samuel beat me. Clint watched."

She took a breath and gasped. He saw drops of sweat form on her forehead and knew she must be in agony. Then he listened to her weak, incoherent voice as the rest of the story poured out: her refusal to sell the ranch, her escape, her ride to Jesse's.

Gently he pulled the pistol out of her fingers. "You stay here, Mattie. I'll help you into one of the bunks and rest until I get back. I'll go see Samuel and Murray."

She shook her head and caught her breath at the

pain. "No. I have to do it. I have to stand alone to hold the land."

Tom hadn't cried since he was ten and his younger sister died of diphtheria, but he felt tears sting his eyes now. "No one can stand alone forever—not even that Hunter woman—and everyone knows how hard she is." He thought he saw her try to smile and blinked the tears out of his eyes. "Everyone needs help over the rough spots, and this is as rough a spot as you're likely to hit."

He released her shoulders and rocked back on his heels so he didn't crowd her. She'd been crowded enough and this choice had to be freely made. "I told you that if you needed help, to reach out and take my hand. I won't pull you along behind me because a strong woman walks by a man's side." He smiled and thought he felt his lips tremble. "Will you take my hand, Mattie?"

She didn't move, and he closed his eyes to hide his hurt from her when he felt her cold, trembling hand clasp his.

Tom went in through the kitchen window. He didn't figure Samuel and Murray would be keeping too close a watch on the back of the house. Nobody lived in that direction any closer than the border with No Man's Land. No, they would be watching out the front windows toward the south. Everybody, strangers or men who rode for the Bar H brand, came to the front door. Mattie respected her men too much to send them around to the back door like peddlers, and any stranger who had sense enough to come in out of the rain knew to knock on a rancher's front door and state his business. Sneaking around to the back door might be seen in the same light as sneaking up on a man's blind side.

What he couldn't understand was why Hunter and Murray were still on the Bar H at all. They had to know every man on the ranch would be after their blood when they found out what had happened. Of course, Hunter always thought he was a damn sight better than any hired hand, which just proved he was a fool. Looking down on folks had gotten men who were smarter than Hunter killed.

He listened at the door into the front room, his eyes stinging a little from the smoke that lingered in the air, then eased in, his pistol loaded and ready. Both men were sitting on the smoke-blackened sofa with glasses in their hands and a half-empty bottle of Jubilee's Taos Lightning on the floor. Clint Murray had his shirt off and a blood-spotted bandage wrapped around his chest. Mattie must have nicked a vein for him to still be bleeding.

The floor between the sofa and the front door was charred black, Mattie's curtains were ashes, the little round table that used to sit in front of the window was blistered and warped, and most of the south wall of the house was smoke stained. Mattie started herself a mighty fine fire, Tom thought, and wondered if he would have taken such a risk in her place. But it was the only chance she had.

"You two better be thinking about making your peace with God," said Tom.

Samuel jerked his head around, his eyes red veined and tired looking. When he recognized Tom, he sank back against the sofa. "Good afternoon, Miller. I presume you've talked to my wife."

Tom nodded. "You damn near beat her to death, Hunter."

He shrugged. "She probably looks worse than she is. I notice I didn't beat her badly enough to keep her from running off. Where is she, by the way? I still have some business to settle with her."

"I don't think so, Hunter. In fact, you two had better find another neck of the woods."

Hunter looked surprised. "Why should I do that? Because I disciplined my wife for acting unseemly?"

"Mattie may act unseemly sometimes—or a few folks might think she does—but there isn't anybody in the Panhandle who's going to put up with the likes of you two whipping a woman."

Samuel laughed. "People may disapprove, Miller, but that's all they'll do. As long as I don't kill her, nobody will interfere between a husband and a wife. Even you won't or you would have already done it."

"It ain't my place to kill you," said Tom.

Clint sat up, noticeably favoring his left side. "If you're thinking about going to the sheriff, Miller, or Mattie is, I don't advise it. If we're arrested and taken before a grand jury, I doubt Samuel will be indicted and I certainly won't be. I never hit Mattie, and Samuel was within his rights to defend me after she shot me. He may have gotten carried away, but what can a man do when his wife goes crazy and attacks him after shooting his guest? With Mattie's reputation being what it is, the grand jury will let him go. The law, Miller, whether it's the sheriff, or the grand jury, or even a judge, will hesitate to meddle in a man's marital affairs."

"I wasn't thinking about the law, Murray. I was thinking about Jesse McDade. He'll kill you both, and I don't want him doing it here. Mattie doesn't need that kind of aggravation. Now, if I were you, I'd get on those horses and ride like the devil himself is after you—because he is."

CHAPTER

10

Jesse picked up their trail almost immediately as though the land itself had repudiated them. Their horses' hooves left faint prints in the late winter moistness, and the coming spring's first tender blades of green grass caught the occasional splashes of scarlet blood.

He caught up with them at Mattie's old plaza headquarters. Mattie used it as a line shack and supply depot now, and Jesse supposed Samuel and Murray had stopped there to steal provisions.

Or else Murray was dying.

Jesse hoped not.

He left his horse at the bottom of the bluff and darted from cottonwood to cottonwood toward the plaza. The adobe building was in good repair, as though it were still home to that Hunter woman, and Jesse was stunned by the depth of his yearning that it be so. He thought if only he held his breath and hoped, he might see Leon picking tomatoes in the garden behind the kitchen, hear Jubilee banging pots and pans while cooking supper, feel the touch of Mattie's hand on his arm, and smell the scent of wildflowers in her hair. But he saw nothing but dried weeds in the garden, heard nothing but the wind in the cottonwoods, felt nothing but his own cold sweat, smelled nothing but his own violence.

He could not bring back the past nor wish away the present.

Jesse pressed his back against the adobe wall next to the back door and listened. The voices were faint, and he guessed Samuel and Clint were in his old office at the other side of the house. He eased open the door, thankful that the hinges were leather instead of metal, and that the dirt floors wouldn't squeak when a man was trying to walk quietly. He slipped down the wide hall that ran the width of the house, past the old kitchen, past bedrooms still partly furnished for the cowboys who occasionally sheltered there, toward the sound of the voices.

"Quit blubbering and hurry up with that bandage, Samuel," Jesse heard Clint say. "I don't intend to die in a mud hut."

"Better men than you have," said Jesse, stepping into the room with gun drawn.

Clint sat on Jesse's old bed with Samuel struggling to tie up the trailing ends of a strip of torn sheeting wrapped around Murray's waist and chest. No wonder Murray was still bleeding was Jesse's first thought. Samuel's medical skills left a lot to be desired. The bandage was too loose to keep pressure on the wound, and he doubted Clint could walk as far as his horse without blood soaking through the wrapping.

Not that he would have the opportunity.

Samuel leapt up and jerked around, grabbing for his pistol. Jesse shot him—once in the wrist and once in the shoulder—then removed Samuel's pistol from its holster and tossed it in the corner. He ignored the man's screams.

"According to Governor Hogg's proclamation, a man can't wear a gun in the Panhandle anymore. No Indians left to fight, and frontier conditions are improved. We're peaceable now—and civilized. Of course, the governor hasn't seen Mattie or he might just question his own judgment," said Jesse.

"She's still alive, then?" asked Clint.

"Yes," said Jesse.

"Why?" screamed Samuel, writhing on the dirt floor beside the bed and clutching his torn shoulder. "Why kill us over Mattie now? Was it because I beat her? Good God, man, I didn't kill her. I just bruised her a little. You can't kill a man over a few bruises."

Jesse watched the blood trickle between Samuel's fingers and down his arm, then glanced at Clint's gray face. "You're right. I'm not killing two men over a few bruises although that is reason enough."

Samuel's expression of confusion was greater than that of his pain. "Then why? Because you still lust after her? That's it, isn't it, McDade? Kill me, and she'll welcome you back in her bed despite the fact you shamed her in front of the whole Panhandle by marrying someone else. Did she promise you that? Is that your reward—rutting again with Mattie Hunter?"

He pushed himself to a sitting position and scooted back to lean against the wall. He groaned and clenched his jaw before continuing. "Then take her, McDade. Rut with her until your cock rots off. I don't care. She's just another woman, and I have no use for her."

Jesse almost killed him then but held back. He refused to let Samuel Hunter die believing Mattie was his to dispose of like an old rag. "Women are not all alike, Hunter, and a man doesn't have to be inside a woman to know that. He doesn't have to lust after her. He doesn't even have to like her. But he does have to see her as more than a two-legged creature no different from others of her sex. He does have to see her as more than a mare to be traded off when it suits him or whipped like a dog when she disobeys him."

He took a step closer to Samuel's cowering form. "When Mattie cried, you never saw her tears. When she smiled, you never heard her laughter. When she loved, you never felt her heat. When she hurt, you never felt her pain. You never saw her for what she was, Hunter—a woman to walk in no man's shadow nor to be trod beneath his feet. Mattie's rare—like the white buffalo. We may never see her like again in our lifetimes and you offer her to me like a common whore!"

"All right!" cried Samuel. "Mattie's different, and I'm lacking in my regard for her, but you can't shoot a man because he doesn't respect his wife. You didn't respect her either. You rutted with a married woman, McDade! Killing me won't change what you did. My blood won't wash away your sin!"

Jesse choked back his rage at Samuel's words. Sins varied according to the blackness of a man's heart, and he'd be damned if he'd let Samuel use another man's sins to excuse his own. "I know what I did and I expect a reckoning. But not now and not from you. I also know what I did not do. I did not try to destroy Mattie by stealing what she values most."

"Ah, Samuel," said Murray, lying back to rest against the head of the narrow bed. "I believe McDade is finally going to read us the indictment.

This is a rude sort of courtroom, not at all where I would prefer to stand trial. But then there isn't to be a trial, is there, McDade? Only a reading of the verdict and immediate execution of the sentence—both done by the judge. Most irregular, but I suppose any objections will be overruled."

"For God's sake, Clint, don't bait him!" exclaimed Samuel.

"Be quiet, Samuel." He stopped to draw a breath, then continued. "Go on, McDade. Explain the charge. Men—even such men as Samuel and I—deserve to know exactly why we must die. Otherwise, how can we feel remorse?"

"You tried to steal Mattie's land," said Jesse.

"Her land! Her land!" repeated Samuel. "You're going to kill us because I tried to *sell* this miserable ranch?"

Jesse nodded. "This miserable ranch, as you call it, is hers no matter what other name is on the deed. It's hers because she worked for it. She may have had my help building it, but she stands alone in caring for it, in loving it, and in holding it against greedy bastards like you who don't give a damn for what the land means. So you and Murray will die not because you don't respect Mattie, or even because you beat her, but because you tried to steal away her land."

"But I didn't sell it, McDade!" cried Samuel. "You can't kill me for what I didn't do."

"We hang horse thieves in this country, Hunter, even if we recover the horse." He gestured with his gun. "Get up, you miserable bastard, and go look out the window. You, too, Murray."

"So you can shoot us in the back?" asked Samuel, remaining where he was, leaning against the adobe wall with legs outstretched.

Murray struggled up, his bandage turning crimson in the effort. "I don't think that's what McDade has in mind, Samuel. He's never struck me as that kind of man. Besides, would you rather die crouching in the dirt like an animal? Come now, get up. Our judge is about to pronounce sentence, and we as the condemned can at least stand on our feet like men."

As Jesse watched them stagger to the window, he wondered what his own sentence would be for this afternoon's work. He thought of Mattie as he had last seen her—battered and unconscious—and resigned himself. He owed her this. He had brought her to this end. He had taught her how to survive like a man. But she was not a man, and he had never warned her against matching a woman's courage against a man's violent strength. Whatever God demanded as a reckoning, he would pay—but he would not let these two live to threaten her again.

Samuel glanced out the window into the gathering twilight, then turned around, his right arm dangling uselessly at his side. "I've looked, McDade. What was I supposed to see besides dirt and dead grass?"

Jesse almost felt sympathy for any man so blind. Only seconds from dying and Hunter still couldn't respect any life but his own. "In another two months the prairie will be green, the wind soft and warm, and the Canadian running bank to bank with snow melt. The cottonwoods will put forth leaves to make music in the wind and the wild plum trees will bloom. Calves and wolf cubs and rabbits and fawns will play in the grass, and the cowboys will lift their faces to the gentle breeze. Wildflowers will dot the plains with pinks and yellows and blues and Mattie's roses will bloom. But you'll never see any of it, Hunter, because you'll be dead."

He shot Samuel through the chest—where his heart would have been if he had possessed one.

He turned his Colt toward Clint Murray, expecting

to see rage and grief. He saw nothing in those muddy green eyes. "No tears for your paramour, Murray?"

Murray leaned against the wall and shivered, and Jesse knew that his body's heat was seeping away with his blood. "Poor Samuel was always more enamored of me than I was of him, and I found his demands unwelcome much of the time. He lacked imagination and subtlety. For example, despite his literary pretensions, I doubt that he appreciated your very eloquent speech. However, I did. You were very impressive, McDade, but then I expected you to be. You are not an ordinary, uncouth cowboy or Mattie Hunter would never have chosen you to share her bed."

He coughed, pressing his hand over his wound as he did so, then continued, his voice weak and raspy. "The white buffalo only mates with the strongest and most worthy of the herd."

Jesse felt his mouth go dry. "What are you saying?"

"I saw Mattie for what she was."

"Then why did you torment her? Why did you encourage Samuel to torment her?"

Murray closed his eyes for a moment, then opened them to reveal an expression of shocked amusement. "Unlike Samuel, who I believe denied the possibility to the last, I can imagine my own death and I find myself compelled to confess my sins against Mattie. I am as surprised by this as you are, McDade. Perhaps I am not so evil a man as I believed. Or perhaps it is because I am a gambler used to betting on the turn of a card. Perhaps I am only wagering that a confession will gain me a measure of divine mercy."

"Your view of theology is as twisted as your nature, Murray."

"Not twisted—entwined. Good and evil, McDade. I am not so evil as I believed, and you are not as good as you believe. You are going to murder me, and as the only charitable act of my life, I will give you a reason."

"I have a reason," began Jesse.

Murray shook his head. "Without Samuel, I have no power to steal Mattie's land, and without a doctor I will die—very soon, I think. You have only to wait, McDade, and our white buffalo will be free without your shooting another unarmed man. But I choose not to wait, and I don't believe you will choose to let me in any case, so I'll absolve you of guilt in advance."

"I don't need absolution from you."

"If you didn't feel a little guilty, we wouldn't be having this conversation. You would have killed me when you killed Samuel." Murray laughed and more blood seeped through his bandage. "A conscience is a terrible thing, McDade. It interferes at the most unexpected times—or so I'm told."

"Get on with it, Murray," said Jesse, wary of the other man. Clint's words held enough truth to trouble his mind, and he had no desire to measure the blackness of his own heart.

"A man responds to a woman according to his nature. Had I been a different man—a man who loved women—I would not have tormented her. I would have been her champion instead of you. If Mattie had been an ordinary woman, I would have become quickly bored. But that was not the case. I was what I still am, and Mattie was rare and beautiful. And worthy—very, very worthy. First I tormented her for revenge, then for amusement, and finally . . ." He stopped to cough, his whole body shivering uncontrollably.

"And finally what, you bastard? Don't quit now or you'll lose your wager with God."

Murray drew a breath, then continued. "Sport. What greater sport could there be than to stalk and finally trap the white buffalo?"

Jesse shot him then—and wondered if he had killed a man or a beast. He wondered, too, if that last expression in Clint Murray's eyes was one of amusement—or regret.

He let his arm dangle by his side, his Colt hanging loosely from a suddenly weak hand. It was over; now he was free to go to Mattie.

Jesse circled around and rode up to Mattie's house from the south rather than the east. No need for some cowboy after the bodies were found to wonder why Jesse McDade just happened to ride in from the direction of the old plaza. Not that he didn't expect every man who worked for Mattie to keep his suspicions to himself if he had any, but Jesse hadn't survived all these years by trusting men always to do what he expected. There was always one who couldn't resist sharing every damn thing he knew or suspected while under the influence of hard liquor and hot women. There would be enough gossip when the bodies were found—which would be the first time a cowboy rode up to the plaza to pick up supplies or spend the night. No need to add to it.

He was crossing the little creek at the bottom of the pasture in front of Mattie's headquarters, his instincts dulled by the smell of Samuel's blood that still lingered in his nostrils, when he heard the click of a hammer pulled back.

"That's far enough! Get your hands up over your head where I can see them."

Jesse raised his hands even as he recognized the voice. "Hank Wilson, put your gun up. It's Jesse."

A horseman rode out of the shadows cast by a

grove of bare cottonwoods. "Take off your hat and turn your face up to the moonlight so I can get a good gander at it." When Jesse obeyed, he heard Hank exhale. "Figured it was you, Jesse, but I couldn't be sure. Had to draw down on you till I knew for certain. Ride out of that creek before your horse freezes solid, and I'll ride shotgun for you until we get to the house."

"I know the way, Hank."

Hank rested his Winchester across his saddle. "Damn near every cowboy on the place is up at the house, Jesse—the ones who aren't riding guard—and they've all got their guns strapped on and ready to shoot at anything that moves, Governor Hogg be damned. You ain't been ramrod of this outfit in nearly three years. There's some cowboys you ain't acquainted with might be surprised to see you riding up in the dark like a cow with heel flies after her."

Hank leaned over and spat on the ground. "I ain't, though. Soon as I seen your black gelding in the corral and a Bar H horse missing I knew you'd already come and gone. Seeing as how Miss Mattie's in a bad way, I knew you'd be hightailing it back here as soon as you got your business took care of. We best be getting up to the big house. Tom's waiting."

Tom Miller met him at the front door. "Are they dead?" he asked quietly.

"You think I'd quit before they were?" asked Jesse. "I left them where they'd be found quick. Mattie won't feel safe until she sees dirt shoveled on top their coffins and I want her to be safe. And free." He rubbed his hand over his face and felt lines of exhaustion etched around his mouth. "That's all you need to know. The best way to act innocent when the law comes is to be innocent."

Tom grasped his shoulder and Jesse felt how

warm and strong his grip was. "You look like you could use a good meal."

Jesse felt his belly cramp. "I don't feel like eating right now. Maybe later."

Tom nodded. "I reckon in your place I'd feel the same. Killing always gave me a sour stomach even when the killing had to be done." He squeezed Jesse's shoulder. "There's no liquor in the house. What Samuel and Murray didn't drink, I used on Mattie's cuts. But there's coffee if you want some."

"I don't want anything but to see Mattie." He hesitated when he saw Tom's face tighten. "How is she?"

"She's alive, but she hasn't come to yet. I've bound her ribs and put a fresh splint on her wrist. I don't know if she's busted up inside. I sent Danny for a doctor since he's the best rider, but it'll be hours before he gets back from Mobeetie with one. I didn't want to send for the one at Tascosa. Too close. It would cause too much talk." Tom took a breath. "I told Danny to telegraph her pa and Leon and Miss Patty. She'll want her family around her, and a woman to take care of her personal needs."

"The Colonel!" said Jesse, feeling bitterness knot his belly. "That bastard is one of the reasons she's beat to hell. If he'd signed over this place to Mattie as a gift, there wouldn't have been a thing Samuel could do about it."

"If a man starts looking down a trail he's already traveled, he can see all kind of turns he should have taken. Doesn't change where he's already been," said Tom, his eyes looking steadily into Jesse's.

"And it doesn't change the fact that she doesn't need the Colonel. She's already got family. Jubilee and I will take care of her. We've done it before."

Tom stepped back to block the door. "Aren't you forgetting something, McDade?"

"No, but you are," said Jesse, trying to shoulder

past the older man. "You're forgetting who she is and who I am. I just killed two men. Do you think I'd hesitate to kill another if I thought he was standing between me and Mattie?"

Tom caught his arm, his unblinking eyes filled with sympathy. "You're a married man, Jesse. It's not your place to sit with Mattie. Go home to your wife."

Jesse doubled over and caught the door frame to keep himself from falling. "No, I can't," he whispered, looking up at Tom.

Tom's face was implacable. "It's time to let the old scandals die, Jesse."

Jesse straightened, wondering how he could hurt so badly without a single bleeding wound on his body. And how he could hate a decent man like Tom Miller so much for being right. "I won't ride out without telling her good-bye."

"She's unconscious. She won't know you're there," said Tom.

Jesse shook his head, as sure of what he was about to say as he had ever been in his life. "She'll know—and she'll hear me."

Tom hesitated a moment like a man who knows the truth but hates to admit it, then stepped aside. "I reckon she will at that."

Jesse stepped through the door into Mattie's front room. The smell of charred wood and smoke still hung in the air, but the blistered table, the damaged sofa, and singed rugs he'd seen before he'd ridden out to track down Hunter and Murray were gone. Someone had nailed boards over the broken window and scrubbed the smoke stains from the mural on the wall by the front door. The mural was of him, Jesse noticed, and its colors had blurred and faded from the cleaning, leaving his painted face indistinct. There were other murals of him on other walls. Perhaps those, too, should be scrubbed away. Jesse McDade had no place in Mattie's life. Maybe he should have no place on her walls either.

Jesse pushed through the cowboys crowded into the front room. Most he knew. Most he had hired. Others were strangers. But all knew him by reputation or rumor, and all fell back to let him pass. He felt calloused hands clap him on the back or squeeze his arm; heard low voices, hoarse from years of calling cattle in the cold and dust, greeting him; saw eyes questioning him. Did you catch them, Jesse, those bastards who hurt Miss Mattie? Did you kill them for her and us and for yourself?

Red stopped him at the bottom of the stairs. "Anything I can do, Jesse?"

Red's voice was low, and Jesse saw Hank and Squinty, the wooden-legged old hand, backing the other cowboys out of hearing range. "It's been done, Red. Nothing to do now but wait."

Red nodded, his bright blue eyes narrowed. "Reckon I can put the men back to work, then. I noticed the tracks of three horses headed east from the house. I believe I'll drive a herd that way in the morning. No point leaving a trail for other folks to follow."

Hank stepped up. "Might be a good idea to run a herd south across the creek, too, Red. What do you think, Jesse? The grazing any good to the south?"

Jesse swallowed before he could speak. "Might turn east after you cross the creek, Hank, then north just before you reach the river."

"Sounds like good advice to me, Hank," agreed Red. "Let's head them out at dawn."

Jesse shook Red's hand. "Thank you."

Red shrugged. "Just moving a few cows, that's all. Doing what needs to be done—just like you."

Jesse looked at the young man who had been his

top hand and nodded. Red was doing more than that. He was covering Jesse's tracks because he didn't believe a man ought to be hanged for doing what needed to be done.

Jesse turned and walked up the stairs, conscious of the silence behind him. Nothing else would ever be said.

Jubilee rose from Mattie's rocker when Jesse entered her bedroom. His eyes were red, his skin more gunmetal gray than black, and his face had that look of age about it that comes when grief and worry leeches out in a few hours all that is left of youth.

"Jesse! I knowed you'd come back and I been waiting." Like the cowboys downstairs, Jubilee's eyes questioned. Is it done?

Jubilee held a young boy in his arms, and Jesse choked back a gasp when he saw Mattie's golden eyes repeated in her son's face. There was nothing else of Mattie in his features or of Samuel either. Mattie would never look at her son's face and see his father.

"It's over, Jubilee." His voice sounded hollow to his own ears as though echoing through the empty places once filled with dreams.

Jubilee studied him with eyes long familiar with empty places and lost dreams and no choices but unhappy ones. "I guess you'll be saying good-bye now."

"I guess I will."

Jubilee's mouth twisted and he looked away for a moment. "It's best, Jesse."

Jesse felt a last spasm of rebellion against the future. "Is it?"

Tom's voice came from behind him. "Let her go, Jesse. She's free of Samuel and Murray. Let her be free of you, too."

Jesse stared down at Mattie's battered, unconscious face through blurring eyes. "Get out, both of you. I'll take my last leave of her in private."

He waited until the heard the door close, then dropped to his knees beside the bed and raised a trembling hand to stroke Mattie's hair. He remembered how the moonlight always turned it a thousand shades of gleaming silver. He remembered watching her brush it at night after he started sharing her bed at the old plaza headquarters; remembered its scent of sunshine and wildflowers. It smelled of dust and fever now.

His glance traveled to her lips and he remembered her smile and the sound of her laughter, the hint of the South in her voice like the faintest scent of honeysuckle. Her lips were swollen and split and she made no sound but an occasional faint moan as though unconsciousness could not hold back the pain.

He touched her bare shoulder and remembered the way she used to square her shoulders when she argued with him. He remembered her courage, her tears when he kissed her the last time before he married; remembered the self-respect that not even the wedding guests hungry to feed on her pride could take from her.

He remembered it all.

"You're safe now, Mattie. I killed Samuel and Murray. The land is yours alone like it always should have been." She sighed, and he knew she had heard him in whatever place in her mind she was hiding. "I've come to say good-bye. You're free, but I'm not, and we still don't have a future together."

He gently stroked her throat and felt a tiny gold chain. He swallowed, then pulled down the sheet that covered her, gasping at the bruises so vivid against her skin, until the heart-shaped locket lay revealed between her breasts. He touched it lightly, felt the golden shape warm from her body, watched his own hot tears splash on its surface. He pressed his lips against her breast over her heart and thought he heard her sigh again.

He stood up and pulled the sheet over the locket and her nakedness. Picking up her limp hand, he turned it over and traced the callouses and faint scars on its palm. He kissed each fingertip, then pressed her palm against his cheek, needing to feel her touch on his skin once more, and whispered the words he had never spoken to her before and never would again.

"I love you, Mattie."

He left her then, rode away toward his own place beside a woman with no charity in her heart; rode toward a future where any fondness he felt toward Caroline had turned to ashes, and duty stood in place of love.

CHAPTER

11

The sheriff came on the third day.

"I guess trouble in the name of Samuel has been resurrected," remarked Tom as he glanced out of Mattie's window at the lone horseman riding toward the house. "Best we meet him outside. Wouldn't do for him to see the state the front room's still in. Or to see Mattie either—even if she was awake. Jim East has seen enough beatings to know she didn't get those black eyes falling down the stairs. No need to put any suspicions in his mind that aren't already there."

Jubilee nodded. "I 'pect you're right. Besides, with Miss Mattie being out of her head most of the last three days, no telling what's she'd say if he was to talk to her. She ain't never been any great shakes as a liar."

"Can't say that I'm real comfortable at it myself, Jubilee, but I'm a good poker player. I know when to bluff and when to stand pat."

With a last look at an unconscious Mattie, Tom

led the way downstairs and securely closed the front door behind him. Followed by Jubilee he stepped off the porch into the windy morning.

"'Light and hitch, Sheriff," he called, walking toward the hitching rail where the tall lawman was already dismounting.

"Morning, Tom—Jubilee," he said, tying his horse to the hitching rail and walking to meet them.

"One of our boys been misbehaving in Tascosa, Sheriff, to bring you all the way out here?" asked Tom, hooking his thumbs in his front pockets.

"It's a little more than that, Tom. A Scotsman by the name of George Faulkner found Samuel Hunter and that friend of his in that old plaza down by the river. Both of them shot to hell. It's murder, and I'll need to talk to Mrs. Hunter."

A tall, lean man with thick wavy hair and a mustache that did nothing to soften his square chin and features, Jim East had been sheriff of Oldham County and several other counties adjoining it since 1883, and Tom had known him longer than that. He was hard, tough, good with a gun, and a little too close to W.M.D. Lee to Tom's way of thinking. He was not a man to be easily fooled. He wasn't a man to easily change his mind either. If he decided to question Mattie, it would take an act of God to stop him.

Or an act of nature with which no man would argue.

"I'm certain Mattie will be real disturbed to hear that, but the fact is you can't talk to her. She took a fall and banged herself up pretty good—brought on some female trouble, too, I guess, because she's been lying in bed hugging herself and about half out of her mind with pain. You know how women get sometimes. When she's feeling more like herself, Jubilee and I will tell her she's a widow."

He heard Jubilee shuffle his feet and figured the old man was near speechless. Tom could never understand why men always reacted to mention of a woman's monthlies with such red-faced embarrassment, or why they naturally assumed a woman in that condition was slightly mad and ought to be avoided like a loco horse. But they did, and Sheriff Jim East was no different. As he watched the lawman flush and clear his throat as though he had a knot as big as a fist caught in it, Tom decided Mattie was safe from answering questions for the time being. Better yet, East had been distracted from being too curious about what kind of fall Mattie took. Tom didn't like to lie when he could help it. Lying for even a good cause had tripped up better men than him. Besides, when the Lord demanded a man turn over his cards and show his final hand, Tom wasn't sure the Almighty would agree that murder was a good cause.

"I'll have to come back then, Tom."

"I don't know what she could tell you, Sheriff. Hunter and Murray haven't been around here since early last fall, and Hunter wasn't much of a man for writing letters. Half the time Mattie didn't rightly know where he was. She sure as hell didn't know what he was doing that might give somebody the notion to kill him."

"Mr. Faulkner says he was right here at this house with Hunter and Murray at noon on the fifteenth. Says he met Mrs. Hunter."

Tom rubbed his jaws in a slow, thoughtful way that he had learned made a poker opponent doubt his own hand. "That so?"

East hesitated only for a moment, and Tom remembered the sheriff was a pretty fair poker player himself. "You know anything about this, Tom?"

Tom kept his face expressionless. "I didn't shoot

Hunter, if that's what you're asking. I rode back to the house in the late afternoon and found Mattie. Jubilee and I haven't left the place since then."

" 'Pears to me like you barking up the wrong tree, Sheriff," said Jubilee, and Tom felt an instant's worth of concern, then relaxed. Being a slave probably taught a man as much about fooling an opponent as poker did—and a slave damn sure played for higher stakes than a few dollars. The threat of being whipped tended to sharpen a man's wits.

"You oughts to be asking this Mr. Faulkner his business," Jubilee continued. "First he jaws with Mr. Hunter, then he finds Mr. Hunter's body. What was he doing messing around down by that old plaza anyhow? That's on Miss Mattie's property and she don't like folks making themselves to home without asking first."

Tom barely kept himself from flinching. Jubilee had just played a wild card that he had to cover. Tom didn't intend anybody to hang for Samuel's murder—even a Scotsman who was probably as worthless as a milk bucket under a bull—and Jubilee had just tossed Faulkner to the law without a qualm.

Before Tom could speak, Sheriff East chuckled. "Faulkner was lost. According to him, he and that pinch-faced man he calls his valet left here heading toward Tascosa after Mrs. Hunter refused to agree to sell the Bar H to some syndicate his daddy runs. Since neither one of them knew exactly where Tascosa was and we ain't exactly got roads of any description, they got themselves lost in the breaks down on the Canadian. Heard gunshots long about dark and rode up to Mrs. Hunter's old plaza headquarters. They found Hunter and his partner with the blood not dried yet."

"Strikes me you took your time riding out to tell Mattie," said Tom.

"I didn't know about it till late last night. Faulkner and his valet" —Tom heard a note of derision in East's voice— "made camp outside the plaza after they found the bodies. 'Riding around in circles in unfamiliar territory in the dark didn't seem sensible, Constable,' is what Faulkner said. He kept calling me constable. I guess that's what they call the sheriff where he comes from. Anyhow, yesterday morning they packed the bodies over the two men's horses they found hitched behind the plaza, and started for Tascosa. They still didn't know where the hell they were going, and if they hadn't run across a couple of cowboys on their way back to the LS from Mobeetie, those two greenhorns would probably still be wandering around the Panhandle. I don't believe Faulkner killed Hunter and Murray 'cause I can't see as how he's got a reason to. Last I saw of him, he was cozying up to W. S. Mabry, the land surveyor, talking to him about what other places were for sale. He ain't got no need to shoot Hunter over the Bar H. If he had, he would have been more likely to shoot Mrs. Hunter. She was the one who didn't want to sell."

East's lip curled up in the kind of sneer Texans reserved for fools, greenhorns, and sissies. "Besides, Faulkner strikes me as the kind that wouldn't shoot a man close up because it might dirty his hands or splash blood on them fancy riding boots of his. Made his valet drag the bodies out and sling them over the horses' backs. Man like that don't do his own dirty work."

East shook his head. "These murders are personal, Tom. Somebody was real put out with those boys. Hunter was shot three times, and Murray had been wounded sometime before he was killed. Somebody tracked them to that plaza and killed them. Not that there's any tracks left. You folks must have half your cattle milling around that plaza and south and west of there. You got a reason for that?"

Tom shrugged. "Seemed like a good idea."

Jim East made a snorting sound. "That's what all your men said, too. That's about all they said. Know what else they didn't say, Tom? Not a damn one of them from Red down to the newest hand said he was sorry to hear Hunter was dead."

Tom rubbed his chin again and slowed his words even more. "Hunter didn't have a lot to do with the men."

East took off his hat and slapped it against his thigh. "This is me you're talking to, Tom. I've worn out a couple pairs of boots in the Panhandle same as you. And I've listened to the same gossip as you. Hunter didn't have nothing to do with running this ranch except when he wanted to spite his wife—like that drift fence and trying to force the men into quitting during the cowboy strike. Mrs. Hunter ruled the roost out here and these are her men. I reckon if she told them to go jump in the quicksand in the Canadian, they'd do it."

"It's a big jump from quicksand to murder," said Tom.

"If you is saying Miss Mattie told one of her hands to shoot Mr. Hunter, then you just gets yourself off her property. I don't care if you is the law, ain't no man gonna talk about my chile like that," said Jubilee, clenching his fists and crowding Jim East backward.

Tom caught Jubilee's arm. The former slave had been part of Mattie's life so long that she mostly forgot he was not her family by blood and didn't even share her race, and he figured the men on the ranch felt the same. Tom didn't think it was a good idea for Jubilee to threaten a white lawman even if Jim East and most of the folks in the Panhandle didn't hold his race against him. What they did hold against him was the fact that he was Mattie Hunter's man, and Jim East was part of the legal establishment that Mattie Hunter thwarted by refusing to support the actions of Garrett and the Home Rangers.

Tom stepped between the two men. "You're not thinking straight, Sheriff. Mattie would never order one of her cowboys to kill her husband. That Hunter woman does her own dirty work, and she didn't do this. She was in bed and unconscious at twilight three days ago, and every man on this place will swear to it." He didn't add that the men would swear to it even if it had been a lie.

"I'm not accusing her, for God's sake, but Mrs. Hunter and her husband weren't on real affectionate terms and everybody knew it. Maybe somebody who's soft on her decided she'd be happier as a widow. Maybe somebody who wasn't real fond of Hunter in any case—somebody the cowboys like nearly as much as they like Mrs. Hunter—somebody they'd lie for even if they seen him shoot Samuel Hunter down in cold blood with their own eyes. Somebody like Jesse McDade."

Tom heard a sound so faint that afterwards he couldn't explain to himself how he had managed to hear it when the other two men didn't—except maybe Mattie Hunter was inside his heart the same way she was inside Jesse McDade's. Under the guise of rubbing his neck, he stretched his head back and saw her bruised face peering down at him from her bedroom window. Although swollen, both her eyes were open and pleading for him to save Jesse. Tom had known for years that he loved her, but not until that moment did he realize that he'd already made her a part of himself. He knew also that the time was forever past that he could shrug and walk away if he failed to win her. But that didn't mean he was going to trail along in her shadow either. He would walk on her left side—by her heart—and there wasn't room there for Jesse McDade too.

But he still had to save Jesse for her, and there was no gentle way to do it.

"You're still stretching, Sheriff," Tom said.

"There was bad blood between them. McDade nearly beat Hunter to death a couple of years ago in front of half the folks in Tascosa. He told Hunter if he interfered again with how Mattie ran this ranch, he'd kill him. Must have been fifty people who heard him. I'd say Hunter trying to sell this ranch against his wife's wishes just might add up to interference in McDade's books."

"Men say a lot of foolish things when they're fighting," said Tom. "Most of the time it's all hot air that don't mean nothing except their blood's up and they're not thinking any clearer than you are."

Jim East didn't look convinced. "I've known Jesse McDade longer than you have, Tom," he said. "I've never heard him say a foolish thing or make a threat he didn't intend to carry out."

Maybe Jim East was just stubborn, or maybe the fact that Jesse, like Mattie, was on the opposite side of the fence from him on the maverick brand business rubbed him the wrong way. Tom couldn't decide—and he didn't dare take a chance. "Jesse ain't seen Mattie but once in the last three years, and that was at his wedding to another woman. I'm not arguing that he didn't once feel more for her than was proper, but that was a while back. He's got his own place, a wife, and a young'un on the way. Mattie's a mighty fetching woman, but I can't see Jesse risking his family and everything he's built up just to carry out a threat he made because his blood was running to his pecker instead of his head."

Tom could almost see Jubilee swelling up like a toad at this kind of talk about Mattie but hoped the Negro would save his mad until after the sheriff left. "You know how a man can make a damn fool of himself over a woman, Sheriff. You probably done it once or twice yourself. Jesse is no exception. But a man as heated up over a woman as you claim Jesse is over Mattie doesn't go without for three years when all he's got to do to pleasure himself is ride ten miles and knock on her door." *Not unless he loves her more than he wants his own pleasure.*

Jim East's chin jutted out in exasperation. "Maybe she wouldn't let him in. You ever think of that, Tom?"

Tom raised his eyebrows. "Then why the hell would he throw away everything he's got for a woman who won't open her legs?"

Jubilee's fist hit him squarely in the jaw and made his ears ring until he could hardly hear the old man's words. "You just hush your mouth or I'll hit you again. Talking about Miss Mattie like she's a loose woman and making Jesse out to be so low he can't think of nothing except what's in his britches. And after Miss Mattie give you a job when nobody else would. You oughts to be ashamed of yourself."

Jubilee whirled on the sheriff who Tom noticed was backing up and looking less than proud of himself. "You ain't no better even if you is the law. More folks than Jesse didn't like Hunter and you knows it. Fact is, you can't hardly find nobody who did like him. Jesse's just easiest to pick on 'cause of all that gossip by folks no better than they should be—that, and some men just like rolling around in the mud like hogs. Makes you feel big to be talking about what folks do together when the lights go out."

Tom rubbed his jaw and decided he'd have a bruise the size of a saucer. "Don't get in such an uproar, Jubilee. I didn't mean anything against Mattie. I was just trying to tell the sheriff that Jesse ain't likely to still be hankering after her."

"Next time you best figure out a more respectable way to tell him," warned Jubilee, his face as hard as ebony.

Sheriff East pulled a bandanna out of his pocket and wiped his face. "Maybe I was riding off on the wrong horse, Tom, but I'm still gonna have a word with Jesse."

Tom nodded. "Suit yourself, but maybe you best catch Jesse out on the range and talk to him there. That wife of his is due to have her baby real soon. Might not be good to upset her by bringing up Mattie's name in her hearing. You know somebody's probably told her the gossip about her husband and Mattie. I'd sure hate to see her deliver early because of something you said."

The sheriff appeared to be trying to swallow another knot in his throat. "I'll surely do that. No point in making the lady uncomfortable for something probably doesn't amount to a hill of beans."

Like a woman's monthlies, a lady in the family way was a subject with which most men didn't feel at ease despite their responsibility for the condition. Tom thought it a damn shame men couldn't treat pregnancy like the natural occurrence it was instead of a half-shameful, half-mystical experience they had no part in except the obvious. Seemed to him a prospective father who believed that missed sharing something important with his wife. But for the moment he was glad Jim East shared his sex's discomfort. He would stay away from Caroline McDade. Tom trusted Jesse to protect his own hindquarters—and Mattie's, but he didn't trust Caroline McDade worth a damn.

Sheriff East tugged his gun belt up and nodded to Tom and Jubilee. "Guess I'll be heading back to Tascosa. Things are lively what with the troubles over the maverick brands."

Tom stuck his hands in his back pockets. "Not going over to see Jesse?"

East shook his head, a resigned expression in his eyes. "I'll catch him next time he comes to town. Ain't worth a ride over to his place because he's not gonna tell me a damn thing more than anybody else has. Be seeing you, Tom. Been an interesting visit."

Tom watched the sheriff ride away, then leaned over and spat on the ground. "Have a bad taste in my mouth."

Jubilee glared at him. "Talking filth allus leaves a bad taste. Can't hardly believe you done it."

Tom wiped his hand across his mouth. "Throwing dirt in a man's eyes is one way to blind him. In this case it was the only way."

"How's that?" asked Jubilee.

"By making him believe that Jesse's heat stopped short of his heart and settled in his loins, and that Jesse is too smart a man to kill over a three-year-old fit of lust."

"You think he believed it?"

Tom felt his jaw again. "He's smarter than that. When he blinks his eyes clear of the dirt, he won't take my word and he won't take Jesse's word. Then he'll be back to talk to the only person who can convince him. He'll be back to talk to Mattie."

The wind blew across the bluff above the old plaza, whistled around the small weathered cross of wood that marked the grave of Mattie's stillborn daughter, and chilled the spectators gathered to watch Samuel Hunter buried.

There had been no funeral. Outside of Mobeetie and Clarendon, public health rather than religious custom dictated funeral ritual, and after six days above ground, the bodies needed burying more than they needed the services of a minister, even had there been one nearer than a hundred miles. Those who knew the two men best doubted that even prayers by a man trained to the task would alter Samuel's and Clint's final destination in any case. A last-minute plea was unlikely to undo the unkind deeds of a lifetime.

There were no mourners among those gathered despite the solemn faces. Samuel and Clint had done no one a good turn while alive so there was no one to grieve at their death. Grief, like mercy, must be earned. Respect for the dead did not convey spiritual worth nor forgiveness for the lack of it. It was a hard philosophy that matched a hard land.

It was a philosophy that Mattie accepted only at Tom's insistence. Her own was much harsher.

"Let the folks in Tascosa bury them," she had said when Tom had broached the subject yesterday morning. "I'll pay the grave diggers whatever they want."

"Samuel was your husband no matter how sorry a specimen he turned out to be. You owe him a decent burial," replied Tom.

To Mattie, his hazel eyes appeared darker than usual as though fatigue had stolen away the lighter blues and greens that ordinarily swirled through the brown. Or perhaps Samuel's marks upon her body had so darkened her own life that she only saw shades of brown.

"I owe him nothing! Let him and Clint Murray, too, rot on the prairie until their bodies swell up and burst like the carcasses of dead cattle! Let the vultures and the maggots feed on their flesh, and the scavengers can gnaw their bones! I don't care!" she cried.

Tom leaned against the wall next to the window, one foot crossed over the other, a half-smoked cigarette in his hand. He stared back at her impassively. "You can't afford to give folks something else to gossip about, not while Sheriff East is still sniffing around like a lobo trailing a crippled cow. Besides, what you said isn't right."

"Why isn't it right, Tom? Because Samuel was a man and men are worth more than cattle? That depends on whether you want a kind word or a pair of cowhide boots. Samuel couldn't provide either one."

"It's the duty of the living to bury the dead. Best to do it and put it behind you."

Mattie laughed and kept laughing as she struggled out of bed, pain streaking up and down her legs the moment her feet touched the floor. Knowing she could never undo tiny buttons with her awkward left hand, she hooked her fingers in the neck of her nightgown and ripped it open. Turning her back, she shrugged the voluminous garment off her shoulders until it slid to her waist, clutching only enough of its ripped bodice to cover her breasts.

She glanced over her shoulder at Tom. "Look at my back. Jubilee tells me it is bruised black as his skin. I wouldn't know. I haven't looked at myself in a mirror. I don't need one to see my bruised legs or my broken wrist. I don't need one to feel my broken ribs with every breath I take or to know my face frightens children. Should I put this behind me and do my duty? Do I owe the husband who nearly kicked me to death a decent funeral?"

She turned toward him. "If I weep over his coffin will the sheriff believe I'm sorry? Will folks stop talking about that Hunter woman and Jesse McDade?"

"No," answered Tom.

She flinched away from the pity she saw in his eyes. "You want him buried, Tom, do it yourself."

Tom uncrossed his feet and pushed himself away from the wall. He ground out his cigarette in a candy dish sitting on the windowsill, then crossed the room toward her with that loose-limbed grace common to all working cowboys of Mattie's acquaintance. She smelled his scent of tobacco and leather and maleness, so like yet unlike that of other men, felt the heat from his lean body as he reached around her to gently pull the gown back over her shoulders.

"Are you trying to cover up what he did? Are you trying to forget it, or hope I will?" she asked, still feeling undone by Tom's words to the sheriff. She understood his intent, even agreed with him, but to deny Jesse and pay homage to Samuel sickened her.

He shook his head, that terrible pity still in his eyes. "I did my best when I sewed up those cuts on your face, but I reckon you'll still have scars. I'm not so handy with a needle and thread and I was afraid to wait for a doctor. Not that you won't heal up so beautiful that men will catch their breath when you walk in a room. Even black and blue you're mighty distracting, Mattie Hunter. But you'll remember what Samuel did every time you look in the mirror— and I'll remember every time I look into your eyes and see hurt inside you."

He laid his hand on her breast over her heart. "Inside here, Mattie, where a young girl weeps and wounds can bleed forever."

She interrupted him, fearing his slow deep voice would weaken her resolve. She would not let that happen. She owed it to herself—and to Jesse. "Don't think you can talk me into changing my mind, Tom Miller. I meant what I said. I won't do it."

"Sometimes we have to put a good face on things and this is one of those times. Samuel was Leon's daddy and nothing will change that. You might not care what happens to your husband's carcass, but you don't know how Leon feels. You can't ask a son to hate his father just because you do. It isn't right to share your wounds with him. So you go pay your respects to the dead for Leon's sake."

"I won't wring my hands and weep over his grave, Tom." Her voice choked on a sob.

Tom put his arms around her and gently pulled her against his chest. "Then how about I just hold you while you do your weeping now."

She let fall her tears then, tears of pain, of bitterness, of disillusionment, of hatred, but mostly of grief. She grieved for the young girl she had been who believed in happiness ever after; she grieved for the young man who saw in her a chance to sweeten his own unkind nature; she grieved for her young son deprived of even so unworthy a father as Samuel; she grieved for love found too late, for love betrayed, for love forbidden. She wept until she had no more tears to give.

And now she stood dry-eyed under the heavy black veil and watched the cowboys lower Samuel's coffin into the grave. Custom dictated that a father should lie beside his daughter, but Mattie had forbidden it and no one saw fit to argue. Custom be damned. Samuel had no right to lie by the innocent.

And neither did she.

Yesterday she had shed the last of her innocence along with her tears. Yesterday the young girl who left Pueblo in 1877 had finally been laid to rest by Mattie Jo Hunter. Yesterday that young girl had believed she was free, her reckoning was paid, and her vengeance earned.

Today Mattie knew that she was not free, that

reckonings carried usurious interest, that vengeance was never an even trade. At best it bloodied him who took it; at worst it endangered his life.

Yesterday that young girl had believed that the fangs of dead rattlesnakes held no venom, that the pieces of her life that were Samuel and Clint could be trampled underfoot without regard to danger to oneself.

Today Mattie knew that Clint and Samuel dead could still strike the living and inflict a mortal wound.

Yesterday that young girl had believed the cost of sinning for love was self-denial and self-sacrifice.

Today Mattie knew it was self-respect.

Jesse had killed for her. She would lie for him.

When the first shovelful of dirt fell on Samuel's coffin, Mattie turned away from the grave, clenching her teeth against the pain of walking. With each step, each beat of her heart, blood surged through her bruised and swollen muscles in succeeding waves of agony. The bandage that held her broken ribs in place choked her like a corset laced too tightly and she could only breathe in quick, shallow pants. She clung to Tom's arm, tempted to sink again into the darkness where she had hidden for three days after her beating. Instead, she faced the lanky, hard-eyed man who stood waiting by her wagon.

"Sheriff East," she said. "I understand you wished to talk to me about my husband's death."

"About his murder," replied the sheriff, tipping his hat. "I don't want to intrude during a time of grief, Mrs. Hunter."

Mattie allowed Tom to lift her onto the high wagon seat, biting back a moan at even his gentle effort. She drew a shallow breath. "Tom repeated your conversation of a few days ago, Sheriff. I am aware of your opinion of my marriage. As you can see, I'm still suffering from the effects of my fall and wish to return home as quickly as possible, so please don't waste my time or yours on false condolences."

"I thought you might be feeling a little sorry, Mrs. Hunter. He was your husband," replied the sheriff. Mattie could see the disapproval on his face even through her veil—a veil thick enough to hide her rice-powdered features from even a man as sharp-eyed as Jim East.

"What did you want to ask me, Sheriff?"

"You have any idea who might have killed your husband?"

"He was not a likable man. I imagine he must have had a good many enemies I knew nothing about. I believe you arrested him for some unpleasantness in the Equity Bar."

East shifted his weight. "Just doing my duty, Mrs. Hunter. Have any idea what he was doing at your old plaza?"

"None."

"You think Jesse McDade might know something about this?"

Mattie was glad she wore a veil or else the sheriff would see the loss in her eyes. "I can't imagine why he would."

"He might have been trying to please you, Mrs. Hunter," said East.

She was shivering and it wasn't cold. The wind was blowing, but the sun was warm, almost hot. The grass was greening with faint color as though a paint pot had spilled and been wiped up, leaving behind not color but tint. The land was caught between winter and spring as she was caught truth and falsehood. She heard the wagon seat creak as Tom shifted uneasily, and she shivered again. Poor

Tom. She had warned him not to take her hand.

"I wish you had listened to Tom. I wish you had believed him instead of the gossip. Then I wouldn't have to shame myself like this." She took another shallow breath. "I never rejected Jesse McDade, Sheriff. He rejected me. I was his whore and now I'm a woman scorned."

Sheriff East seemed too shocked to speak and Mattie was uninterested in any case. She knew he believed her without questioning how she knew or the strength of her certainty. The how didn't matter and she knew the why. It was because she was telling the truth. Jesse had betrayed her by marrying another woman. That he had not forsaken her, that the bond was too strong, was also a truth—but one that must remain always unspoken.

CHAPTER

12

November 1885

In July, amidst the bawling of animals, the shouts of men, and the smell of burning hide and hair, Mattie's giant awoke. The three-million-acre kingdom owned by the Capitol Freehold Land Investment Company, Ltd. received its first subjects, a herd of two thousand five hundred longhorns from the Fort Concho country far to the south. Ab Blocker, the trail boss of the herd, designed the coat of arms for the giant by scratching three letters—XIT—with his bootheel in the corral dust, or so Tom heard. He suspected it was only the first of what would be many legends about the XIT. Whether it was true or not didn't matter. Legend was always stronger than truth.

Tom supposed folks created legends because they needed them. Sometimes truth was a miserable thing that a man would rather not face head on. Truth also depended on where a man stood when he faced it. One man's hero was another man's villain. Legend split the difference and wove together truth and lies to create a ranch or a land or a man more wonderful than reality and stronger than falsehood. Tom reckoned being a legend didn't hurt the XIT or the Panhandle any, but it was hell on mortal man. Or woman.

Particularly when the legends were mostly true.

Legend was liable to put Jesse McDade's neck in a noose and shame Mattie Hunter past bearing.

Tom didn't intend to see that happen, but changing the course of a legend was like changing the course of a river. A man could do it given sufficient time and luck and determination and the right materials, but the next spring flood would likely as not wipe out his puny efforts.

Still, he had to try.

Buffeted by the warm November wind, Tom reined in his horse next to the silent man who watched from Hunter property while an XIT crew plowed furrows on either side of a strip of land two hundred feet wide inside their fence line. When the wind died down, the men would burn the grass between the furrows to create a fireguard.

"I reckon Abner Taylor plans on plowing fireguards around every pasture on the XIT," remarked Tom, observing the other rider out of the corner of his eye.

"I don't imagine either one of us rode out here to watch a bunch of cowboys wrestle plows," said the rider, turning his head toward Tom. "I sure as hell didn't."

Jesse McDade looked more like a desperado than a legend: older, harder, and less accepting of what had to be. Tom discarded his hopes of settling their business peaceably. "You got another reason to be on Hunter property, McDade?"

Jesse lifted his hat and settled it more firmly on his head, and Tom caught a glimpse of a white strand or two in the wavy hair that had always been black as a crow's wing. "I knew you couldn't avoid me if I planted my feet on Mattie's land. I want to know how she is, Miller. It's been damn near eight months, and all I hear are rumors."

Tom nodded as he studied the other man. Jesse McDade looked to be as eaten up inside as Mattie did. "I figured it was something like that."

"I've got a right to know."

Tom rested his hands on the saddle horn and looked toward the XIT fence line where the warm, dry November wind whipped up clouds of dirt from the newly plowed furrows. "Rumor is a lot like that dust. When the wind dies down, the dust settles and a woman can sweep it up and her floor is as clean as ever. But if the wind keeps stirring up the dust, a woman never can sweep it all out. She tracks it into every room in her house. I figure you're the wind, McDade. Every time you see Mattie or ask after her, you're spreading dirt same as the wind."

"Is that the only reason everybody from the Hunter ranch rides in the other direction when they see me coming, Miller? Is that why they all drink up and leave the Equity Bar when I walk in the door? They don't want to encourage the gossips? Or is it because somebody gave the hands orders not to talk to me? Are you interfering where you've got no right to?"

"The hands are smarter than you, McDade. Rumor says you killed Hunter and Murray. Nobody on this ranch wants to add to that rumor, maybe risk stirring the sheriff up again, by seeming too friendly with you. Red and I had a word with a couple of the boys too thick between the ears to see that, so I guess you could accuse me of interfering."

"So you're keeping me ignorant of Mattie for my own good?"

Tom pulled out his tobacco pouch and rolled himself a cigarette to give himself time to think. Not until he blew out his match, broke it in two, and dropped it in his vest pocket did he answer. "More like for Mattie's good. She called herself your whore to the sheriff's face. Said you spurned her and wouldn't have killed for her. I don't want you making her out to be a liar by asking after her welfare. I don't want Mattie Jo Hunter having to defend you by calling herself a whore again."

Jesse bent over his horse's neck as though Tom's words had slugged him in the belly. "God Almighty," he whispered. "Why didn't you stop her?"

Tom took a quick puff of his cigarette. There were two answers to the question and he didn't much like either one of them. He didn't figure McDade would either. The truth was he didn't know what Mattie would tell the sheriff. On the other hand, he had laid the groundwork so there wasn't much else Mattie could say.

"Why didn't you stop her?" Jesse repeated, straightening up and leaning over to grab Tom's arm.

Tom didn't try to free himself. He figured he owed McDade one. "Because the sheriff didn't believe me."

Jesse backhanded him. "You son of a bitch! You called Mattie a whore?"

Tom grabbed the saddle horn before he could topple from his horse and wiped a trickle of blood from the corner of his mouth. "No. I called you a coldhearted bastard who wouldn't risk what he had to help a woman whose reputation he ruined."

"Damn you, Miller!"

"I reckon we all are, McDade, one way or another.

Nobody lives to be any age at all without earning some damnation along the way. Only thing to do is try to work it off and hope we come out even or a little ahead by the time we die. Why don't you work some of yours off by going home to your wife and baby? Leave Mattie's welfare to me."

For a moment Tom thought the sun had gone behind a cloud. But there were no clouds—hadn't been for months. It was the light going out in Jesse's eyes. "You'd like that, wouldn't you, Miller? Mattie's free and you'd like to hang your pants on her bedpost. You'd like to prop your feet on her porch railing in the evenings and look over her spread and congratulate yourself on landing jam side up. A pretty woman, a fine house, and seven hundred thousand acres. Not bad for a drifter with a lot of hard riding behind him and not much to show for it."

Tom wrapped the reins around one hand and rested the other on his saddle horn. "I let you smite one cheek, McDade, but I'm not about to turn the other. Only reason you're not sitting in the dirt spitting out loose teeth is that I don't care to kick a man when he's already down. You're hurting mighty near as much as Mattie, and you're looking for somebody to fight, same as her. But don't pick me. I've always hankered after Mattie and it doesn't have a damn thing to do with how many acres she owns or whether she lives in a fine house or a dugout. You've always known that, too, or you wouldn't have sent me to work for her in the first place."

Tom saw the red stain Jesse's cheekbones and knew it was shame. Legend said Jesse McDade never hit below the belt or accused a man unjustly. "I apologize for the insult, Miller."

"I reckon I might say the same in your place."

Jesse clenched his jaw and swallowed before he spoke. "I can do without your understanding of my mood. In fact, it's best if you don't say anything more about being in my place. I haven't got but a minute's worth of patience left so why don't you answer my question. How is she, Miller?"

Tom gazed over Jesse's shoulder toward the north where acres of brown grama grass spread unbroken to the horizon. Mattie's land—land she loved above all else. Maybe above the man who stared at him from silver eyes.

"Her bones are healed and her bruises have faded but anger still festers inside her strong as ever."

"She's got a right to hate, for God's sake!" exclaimed Jesse. "How else is she supposed to feel after that bastard beat her half to death?"

"That's not why she hates so much, McDade. She lost her land, or half of it anyhow."

Jesse paled. "What are you talking about?"

"Not coming from a wealthy family I hadn't given much time to worrying about inheritance laws and wills and such, but Mattie barely waited for her swollen face to heal before she wrote a note to her lawyer, Temple Houston, asking about settling Samuel's estate."

Tom wiped his sleeve across his forehead. Just talking about Mattie's reaction made him sweat. "I was there the day Houston rode up to the house to explain to Mattie what her rights were. I reckon she would rather have taken another beating than hear what he had to say. His answer set her rage to burning like a lighted match dropped on the dry prairie. I've watched it burn hotter and brighter with every passing day since last spring."

"What was his answer, Miller?"

"Hunter didn't leave a will and according to the laws of Texas, his property is divided between his wife and his kids. Mattie gets a half interest or three hundred and fifty thousand acres of the Bar H. The other half, or three hundred and fifty thousand acres, is divided between Leon and Robert."

"My God!" exclaimed Jesse.

Tom looked at him. "There's more. Mattie doesn't have any authority over her own children unless the court appoints her legal guardian. She has no authority over half the land she worked so hard for unless the court appoints her administrator of Leon's and Robert's share until both boys reach their majority."

Tom took and deep breath. "Where I come from, among the poor dirt farmers in East Texas, everybody understood that a widow claimed her husband's property and held it for whichever son was best suited to have it. Nobody in my neck of the woods owned a farm big enough to divide without every heir ending up with a piece of land no bigger than a garden patch. And for damn sure folks wouldn't given a moment's thought to a law that said if a man died without a will, the court had the right to appoint a guardian for his children. Children belong to their parents, and if one parent died, then the other took over. That was God's way, and the law had no business messing in family affairs. As long as taxes were paid on a man's miserable piece of property, the law overlooked the widow."

"But Mattie's no East Texas dirt farmer," said Jesse bitterly. "She owns too damn much for the law to overlook her even if she wasn't a woman who likes things down on paper and filed at the courthouse."

"That's about the size of it, McDade. Nobody will overlook Mattie Hunter, and there's nothing to say that the judge has to appoint her guardian of her own children and administrator of her own land—if he decides she's unsuitable. So it's best if you stay away from her—and stay away from Tascosa tomorrow. She goes to court in the morning and she doesn't need you in town at the same time, reminding folks of what's best forgotten."

Tom gathered his reins and turned his horse east toward headquarters. "You can't help her, McDade. Don't back her into a corner so she has to choose between taking up with you or holding fast to her land as best she can."

He rode away, holding his horse to a gentle canter. He couldn't ride fast enough to escape his last glimpse of Jesse McDade's face so there was no sense in running his horse into the ground. He wished he hadn't taken that last look. Witnessing another's man recognition of his own helplessness was a little too much like seeing him chained and naked in a cage with no way out.

Jesse watched Tom Miller gallop off toward the east and Mattie, then leaned over to spit out the bile of jealousy. Miller was a decent man—an honorable man—and Jesse admitted he hated him about as much as he hated anyone. The admission only made him feel sicker. He was like a kid who couldn't play with a particular toy so he didn't want anyone else playing with it either. But he wasn't a kid, and Mattie damn sure wasn't a toy, and he ought to act more like the man he pretended to be. He couldn't help Mattie—except by denying her. He couldn't even pray for her because he doubted God had much use for the prayers of adulterers, especially when the adulterer wasn't asking forgiveness.

He doubted the Almighty had much more use for a murderer and Jesse wasn't asking forgiveness for that either. A man sinned, regretted what he would not repeat if he had his life to live over, and accepted his punishment for the rest.

Jesse regretted neither his time with Mattie nor his killing Hunter and Murray.

He shifted and heard his saddle creak under his weight and thought his heart must sound much the same each time it beat. It too was hard as dry leather. Sometimes he wondered if it would bleed if he was shot or if a man truly could die from the heart out and still continue to live.

He guessed so.

He was proof.

"I would die for you, Mattie, but I cannot live for you."

He stared unseeing toward the sky and the God to whom he could not pray. He had named his own damnation when he denied Mattie with those words. God let him live without her.

It was the worst punishment Jesse could imagine.

Tom watched Mattie stumble through the door of Tascosa's fine new stone courthouse. Her face was as flushed as though a prairie fire burned just under her skin, and the scar under her chin was a fine white streak against the pink. He had done what he could to put off Mattie's going to court to settle up Samuel's estate until her anger had time to burn itself out before she faced the district judge. If her expression was any indication, he had wasted his time.

Tom ground out his cigarette under his bootheel while he watched Mattie's slim fingers trace the thin scar beneath her chin. Samuel's mark. The bastard didn't haunt her sleep anymore, but he sure as hell still troubled her waking hours, and every time he did, she rubbed that scar.

"All done?" he asked.

"Yes," she said, pinching her lips closed on the word until white lines bracketed her mouth.

He waited for her to say more, but didn't press her when she remained silent. She'd tell him what passed between her and the district judge in her own time when she didn't feel so ill-used. Meanwhile, he needed to get Mattie home before any more folks found an excuse to ride by the courthouse steps in hopes of seeing her. She was touchy these days and it wouldn't take more than a hard look or a whispered comment she didn't quite hear to set her off. Then there was no telling what she might say or do.

"I stopped by McMasters's store and picked up the mail while you were talking to the judge," he said, taking her elbow to help her down the courthouse steps. She was still a mite frail and the dry wind was strong enough to whip her navy skirts around her legs and trip her.

She glanced up at him, an expression of bitterness in her eyes. "Were you afraid folks would stare at me if I picked up my own mail?"

"Some folks don't have nothing better to do."

Her smile held no humor. "I should have worn my dark red dress with the English turban and really given them something to talk about."

He grimaced. He'd had the devil's own time talking her out of wearing that dress. "No point in cutting off your nose to spite your face, Mattie."

"Since I branded myself a whore I thought it was an appropriate choice."

He helped her into the buggy, noticing that the color had faded from her face, leaving it pale as cloudy ice with no sign of the rage that burned inside. "You don't know that the sheriff repeated what you said, and even if he did, there was no need to remind folks. There was for certain no need to get the judge's back up by not dressing to fit your station as a widow. You've been downright reckless since we buried Hunter. What with fencing off his and Murray's graves outside the rest of that little cemetery, and ordering me to burn down the plaza, not to mention locking yourself in your bedroom for three days when you heard Jesse McDade had a daughter."

She looked straight ahead. "I don't want to hear it."

"I don't know what you're likely to do next," he continued.

She laughed, then abruptly stopped and drew a shuddering breath. "What would you have me do, Tom? Ride out on the prairie and scream hate at the wind? I've done that. I've screamed until my voice is gone, but more screams well up in my throat. The hate is still there. The anger is still there."

He unwrapped the reins from the hitching post and climbed into the buggy while he considered how to answer her. "You got a lot of hurt and mad stored up inside you," he finally said.

"Yes!" cried Mattie. "Being beaten either makes you afraid or it makes you angry. I'm angry."

"It's not the beating you took from Samuel's fists that's making you angry as much as it is the blow he landed just by dying. It's the insult as much as the injury."

Her hand stole up to rub the scar beneath her chin. "Alive, he couldn't defeat me, Tom. I was stronger than he was. Alive, Samuel couldn't sell the ranch, but dead, he divided it."

Her eyes looked huge and yellow and desperate. Tom had seen that same expression in the eyes of a cornered wolf: knowledge that it was trapped and determination to fight to the death regardless. But there was no one Mattie could fight.

"You best find some way to vent your spleen besides taking it out on everybody around you or by making a spectacle of yourself, Mattie," he said gently.

Her body went rigid and Tom saw her cheeks turn red again. When she spoke, her voice was deep and ragged. "I can't, Tom, unless I resurrect Samuel and kill him all over again, only this time with my own finger on the trigger. But first I'd make sure he left a will."

He felt Mattie shiver. "You want your shawl or the lap robe I got folded up next to me?"

She shook her head and he wasn't surprised. It wasn't Mattie's body that was cold; it was her spirit, and all the shawls in the world wouldn't warm her. And neither would her rage. Someone had to reach inside and warm her heart.

Someone who loved her.

Someone she trusted.

She clenched her fists. "Damn Samuel! Damn him to hell!"

"I figure he already is, Mattie," said Tom.

Her head jerked up and she stared blankly at him a few seconds as though she hadn't realized she had spoken aloud, then her eyes shifted to focus on something only she could see. "I hope so, Tom."

She laughed, and Tom shivered as the tinkling sound reminded him of the wind blowing through the bare, frozen limbs of a cottonwood tree. "For every second I held back bitter words this morning as I listened to the judge appoint me guardian of my own flesh and blood, I hoped Samuel Hunter was screaming in hell. I hope he's at the devil's mercy like I'm at the court's mercy." She turned to stare at Tom again. "I was ordered to submit a report of my stewardship of Robert's and Leon's property each year. I'll be subjected to the court's scrutiny. I'll have to defend my decisions."

"Leastways it'll be you watching out for the land and not some stranger, Mattie."

She leaned closer to him. "That's not the point,

Tom. In a few short years the Bar H won't answer to a single will, but to a trinity. In a few short years its plains and breaks and creeks and line shacks and cattle and horses, its cedar and cottonwood and plum thickets and hay meadows will be divided and diminished. The court will split my land asunder!"

"It would go to your boys in any account, Mattie. They'll just hold title sooner."

She clutched his arm. "I didn't want that. I wanted to leave the land to the son who loved it the most, who would hold it against greed and speculation and pass it along intact to his own heir. I wanted the Bar H to always speak with a single voice."

She didn't want any more than the East Texas widows of his boyhood wanted, but none of them saw the land as anything more than a means of making a living. Mattie saw the land differently. Tom spat over the side of the buggy. "Which son will that be, Mattie? Which son do you favor?"

She released his arm and sank back against the seat, and he felt ice forming again as the heat of her rage receded. "I don't know. Robert is still a baby. I won't know his worth as a man until he's grown. And Leon" — she hesitated, and Tom saw a wistful expression cross her face— "Leon I don't know at all. Those years without me—when he lived with my father—changed him."

"He's still your boy, Mattie."

She turned her head to meet Tom's eyes. "Leon keeps his own counsel now."

"He's nine years old, closer to ten, Mattie. Boys turn to men fast in this country, and men keep their own counsel. It's the way we are. Don't shut him out on that account."

He saw her rage flicker at his flat tone. "I'm not shutting him out."

She flexed her right hand, then rubbed her wrist.

The broken bone had mended, but Tom knew the wrist still ached on occasion. Sometimes he hurt for her, but he didn't let her know it. Mattie didn't appreciate pity; in fact, she got downright mean if she suspected anybody was feeling sorry for her. She was like a dog that had been whipped until it snapped at everybody and forgot how to let itself be petted. Tom Miller had been nipped a few times by dogs. He figured he'd survive a bite or two from Mattie.

"You got plenty of land, Mattie. You can be fair to both your boys."

"A kingdom too often divided is a kingdom lost," she stated coldly.

"And setting brother against brother is the best way to lose it, Mattie. You'll start a blood feud between your sons that they'll pass along to their sons."

"No, I won't! I'll give one son land and the other son money. That will be fair."

He looked into her eyes so filled with blind earnestness and sighed. "You don't know that, Mattie, 'cause you don't know what those boys will feel when they're grown. They might not see fair the same way you do. They might wonder if maybe you think more of the land than you think of them."

She turned her head away and clasped her hands in her lap, a lady coated in ice. "I heard enough from the judge this morning on how to manage my own affairs. I don't need you telling me what to do."

"You've never been mine to order about, Mattie," he said, reaching over to squeeze her clasped hands. "But I've always been yours when you have had need of me."

She didn't move or speak or turn toward him, but he saw a single tear glisten in the sunlight like a single drop of water from an icicle.

It was enough for now.

CHAPTER

13

"Prairie's burning!"

Mattie heard Hank Wilson shouting long before she stepped out on the porch to see him yank back on the reins so hard that his horse skidded in a half circle on the dried grass in front of the house. She had time to assume the calm, icy mask that had become so familiar to all who saw her, had time to control her trembling hands that revealed more fear than she cared to admit.

"Prairie's burning, Miss Mattie!" repeated Hank.

"Where, Hank?" she asked, stepping off the porch. She could smell the burning grass now, but only faintly, more a promise of fire than fire itself.

Hank pointed. "Northwest and coming this way. Wind's high, Miss Mattie. Could burn all the way to the Canadian if we don't get it stopped."

Mattie hurried down the porch steps and around the side of the house. Dismissing any concern for modesty, she lifted her skirts and ran toward the small mesa behind the house, stumbling to her hands and knees in her scramble to its top for an unrestricted view. She shaded her eyes and looked to the northwest. The horizon was lost in a faint gray cloud with streamers of smoke spiraling upward to meet the sun in the early afternoon sky. Even if she had not smelled the fire, seen its smoke, the birds would have told her of its presence. Like a giant fall migration, flocks of birds flew overhead, fleeing before the cloud of smoke.

The birds were not alone in foretelling the coming fire. As Mattie stumbled back down the mesa toward the house, a family of rabbits darted in front of her, closely followed by a coyote. She watched as the coyote overtook the rabbits and passed them by. It was a scene she knew would be repeated endlessly as long as the fire burned: prey and predator racing side by side, their natural roles forgotten in the instinct to survive.

As she reached the house, she heard the thunder of hooves over the drumming of her own blood. "The cattle are running."

Hank nodded. "Reckon it's the herds in the north pastures. I wouldn't worry none, Miss Mattie. A few of the boys will trail the cattle to the river, try to keep them from trampling each other, and the rest of the hands will ride out to fight the fire. We all know what to do. We've done it before. Damn near every year, as a matter of fact."

"We haven't fought one like this in years, Hank. Maybe never. That damn XIT looks to be on fire. The smoke covers a twenty-mile front already. The fire wagon's ready except for filling the water cans. Tie your horse on the back and head out. All the hands close are likely already there. They'll need the axes and gunny sacks."

Hank didn't argue with her orders, just turned his

horse toward the barn where a wagon sat all year, every year, loaded with all the equipment to fight a prairie fire. At first some of the men had snickered at her idea of a fire wagon, but no one laughed now. While men from the other ranches survived on water from their canteens and whatever kind of cold food their chuck wagon carried, provided they had a chuck wagon handy, Bar H cowboys drank from five- gallon water cans and ate dried peaches and apples, canned tomatoes and jerky, until Jubilee arrived with cold beef or bacon sandwiches. While other cowboys fought fires with whatever they could carry on horseback, Bar H men had axes, shovels, rope, bales of gunny sacks dropped in a stock tank and loaded wet, extra slickers and saddle blankets to beat out flames. Mattie, like all ranchers, expected her men to fight a fire until it was extinguished whether it took one hour or three days, but she didn't intend that they should go hungry or thirsty while they did it—or to be without what they needed when they needed it.

But Mattie's wagon didn't carry the principal piece of fire-fighting equipment. There was no need. Any cow would do. Or rather two cows—or more—depending on how wide a front the fire burned and how many tongues of flames licked out from its voracious mouth. Each tongue shot forward in a V, with the sides burning more slowly than the point. The first cowboys to arrive would promptly shoot two cows, cut off the heads, and split each carcass lengthwise. Working in pairs the cowboys then tied ropes to a fore and hind leg, dally the other end of their ropes to the saddle horn, and drag a carcass, bloody side down, over the burning grass with one man riding on the outside and the other on the inside of the fire line. Two other cowboys, a dead cow similarly tied to their saddle horns, rode the fire line in the opposite direction. Men on foot followed them, beating out flames with slickers and blankets and gunny sacks.

In a land without water—or very little water—man used what weapons were at hand to fight a fire. He had no choice. Burned pastures meant whole herds could starve. Mattie taught herself to think of the slaughter of two head of cattle or a dozen head as sacrifices to appease a god of fire. The necessity sickened her, a womanish softness she carefully hid from her men, not because they would think less of her, but because she would think less of herself.

The land had no use for a soft woman.

The wind whipped her skirt about her legs, and she turned and ran into the house to change clothes. She served no purpose standing in her front yard bellowing orders to men who already knew what to do.

Jubilee caught her descending the stairs from her bedroom. "Where you think you be going in them britches?"

"To fight the fire. You keep Robert with you in the chuck wagon. He'll be safer there than riding with me."

Jubilee shook his head and folded his arms across his chest. "You ain't gonna fight no fire so long as I gots breath in my body, Miss Mattie. You gonna stay right here and mind your own chile."

She felt rage warming her skin. "I have no intention of cowering in this house or on top of the windmill or sitting freezing in a stock tank while the fire sweeps by me."

Jubilee scratched his head. "Now that I thinks about it, you is right. You take Robert and ride for Tascosa. Settin' on the Canadian the way it does, it oughts to be safe. I been watching the smoke from the back door while you been upstairs. It pert' near covers the sky from north to west. Worst fire I ever seen since we gots to this country. Worse than '77 or '79. Them years the Canadian River was between our place and the fires. Ain't nothing between us and it this time but barbed-wire fence."

"And the barbed wire belongs to the XIT. I think the fire started there, damn that syndicate to hell."

Jubilee's brow wrinkled in a frown. "You don't be using language like that, Miss Mattie. It ain't becoming for a lady. 'Sides, you don't know for certain where that fire started and it don't make no difference nohow."

Mattie took a deep breath. "It does make a difference, Jubilee. The XIT can lose a hundred thousand acres—two hundred thousand acres—and absorb the loss. Their stock tanks and division headquarters can burn to ashes and the Scots and English investors will cover the losses. I can't. But mark my words. If that fire started on the XIT for any reason other than lightning, I'll demand Abner Taylor and his damnable Capitol company make good on every cow, every acre of grass, every fence post I lose."

"I reckon you'll be butting your head against a brick wall, Miss Mattie. Mr. Taylor didn't start that fire on a purpose, and I don't think you gonna find a judge what will say he did. You just looking for a fight same as you been doing since that Mr. Temple Houston told you what kind of fix that worthless Hunter left you in."

Mattie rubbed the scar beneath her chin. "Do you blame me?"

She flinched at his piercing look, feeling as though he were weighing her question against some ancient wisdom only the persecuted possessed. Finally, he sighed. "I reckon you better get on to that fire."

"Why did you change your mind?" she asked.

He met her eyes. "I stopped fooling myself that you is all well. You ain't well, Miss Mattie, and you ain't gonna get better so long as you hold your hate inside. You needs to fight more than you needs to be safe. You can't fight no dead man and you can't fight what the judge done yesterday in Tascosa, but you can fight that fire. Maybe it'll burn out that mad that's living in you. Maybe what you need to heal is to win against something bigger and meaner than you are, and a prairie fire is about the biggest, meanest thing there is."

Jubilee clasped her shoulders. "Ain't nobody died in a prairie fire that I've heared about anyhow, so maybe you won't either. But if you does, leastways it'll be faster than the way you're dying now—shriveling up inside till there ain't hardly nothing left of you that anybody knows."

She swallowed. "And you'd rather see me dead than for me to live like that?"

Jubilee released her shoulders and turned away. "On your way to the fire you best stop by Jesse's and see about his wife. Likely she's by herself with that young'un."

"Jesse was so bent on marrying her. Let him see to her."

Jubilee turned around. "Jesse probably seen to her as best he could, but men can't sit around comforting their womenfolk while the prairie's burning. You knows that as well as me. Men fights fire and women see to their own selves. Just stop by there— see that she knows what's best to do if that fire reaches her house. Or put her in a wagon and point her toward Tascosa."

"Jesse probably already did."

"Maybe. Maybe not. Maybe he's depending on her to have good sense and do for herself if needs be."

"It's a good gamble on Jesse's part. I never met anyone who knows how to look after her own interests any better than Caroline McDade—even if it means turning away a woman who needs help," said Mattie, her bitterness nearly choking her.

Jubilee shook his head. "I ain't forgot what she done to you, Miss Mattie, but that ain't no excuse to lower yourself to acting like her. She ain't been through a bad fire before, and you can be spared to look in on her better than a man."

"She wouldn't appreciate my offering her a cup of water if she was burning in hell. And I wouldn't offer her one!" shouted Mattie, pushing by Jubilee and rushing toward the front door.

"Jesse's baby ain't done nothing to you, Miss Mattie."

His words jerked her up short. Slowly she turned to face him. "Damn you, Jubilee."

He folded his arms across his chest, his ebony black face impassive. His judgment on her resided in his eyes and they were merciless. "You don't look in on Jesse's wife and that young'un, then I reckons my answer's yes. You best off dead."

The smell of smoke was stronger at Jesse's place. To the northwest Mattie could see a faint red-orange tint to the sky and she shivered. There was danger in front of a fire and disaster behind it and how much of either depended on the dryness of the prairie and the strength of the wind. In her judgment the fire would miss the Flying MJ, but the wind could veer and blow a wall of flame that would burn Jesse's headquarters to ash. And anyone in it.

Mattie tied her reins to the hitching post in front of Jesse's porch. She felt as if she were the only living thing on the place other than two horses in the otherwise deserted corral. Ranchers always sent most of their remuda to a fire since riders had to change horses every twenty or thirty minutes. Any longer than that and the horse's feet were injured by the heat and his hooves would slough off. Days after a fire shots rang out in corrals as cowboys put down horses that had lost one or more hooves in spite of all the care taken to rotate mounts. That Jesse had left two horses behind, horses he might desperately need, meant that Caroline must still be on the place.

Mattie felt rage licking at her self-control like the flames licking the grass. Why hadn't Jesse sent Caroline to safety? Why hadn't Caroline left of her own accord when the danger became clear. Even a greenhorn knew to run from a fire. Why must it be up to Mattie Jo Hunter to look after a woman who despised her? Damn Jubilee and damn her own decency.

Mattie knocked on the front door several times before finally opening it and stepping inside Jesse's house for the second time in her life. The first time, before Jesse had quit as her range manager, he had been carrying her in his arms and she had been blind to all but the passion burning in his eyes. This time her eyes were open and she did not like what she saw: a horsehair sofa with starched white doilies on the back and arms; a small round table covered with a scarf; an upright piano with no sheet music visible and the keyboard closed and covered with a long, white runner that matched the doilies on the sofa; a delicate secretary with closed inkwell and untouched blotter; a grandfather clock that measured lives passing with each swing of its pendulum.

Jesse did not live in this room.

No one did.

Shivering, Mattie rubbed her arms and called out. "Hello?"

Only the slow ticking of the clock answered her.

Unable to stand the chill silence any longer, she hurriedly searched the rest of the house, leaving the large bedroom for last. Drawing a deep breath and steeling herself to bear the sight of the room Jesse shared with another woman, she pushed open the door.

Caroline McDade stood by the bed, her face as cold and unwelcoming as her parlor, and a queer expression of satisfaction, almost of smugness, in her eyes. But it was the sight of Caroline's hand pressed firmly over the mouth of the scarlet-faced infant in her arms that took away Mattie's breath as though she had fallen into an icy stream.

Stunned, she watched the baby's tiny chest jerk in its effort to breathe for a few seconds before she cried out. "Dear God, you're choking her!"

Caroline lifted her hand from the infant's mouth and smoothed its sweat-soaked hair—hair as black as Jesse's. "I had to keep Louisa from crying. I watched you ride up and I didn't want her crying to warn you before I knew for certain."

"I don't understand," began Mattie, then stopped abruptly when Louisa sucked in a breath and wailed, a thin, rattling sound that spoke of an infant suffering from more than exhaustion and fear. The sound terrified Mattie and she started toward the other woman. "She has a weak chest, doesn't she, Caroline? A chill wind or dirt blowing in the wind and she chokes up. And this smoke— my God—soon she won't be able to breathe at all. She can't stay here. You'll have to take her to Tascosa. Let me hold her while you gather your things."

Caroline twisted away from Mattie's outstretched arms. "Don't touch her! I'll not have your filthy hands on her!"

Mattie held up her hands and backed away. Caroline hated her too much to accept such personal help, and Mattie didn't have time to argue. The air inside the house already seemed thicker, drier, and more overheated than a few minutes ago. "I won't touch her, Caroline. I'll go hitch up your wagon and lash the cradle in the back and cover it with a wet sheet. That should keep out the worst of the smoke and cinders until you get to Tascosa. When you get there, go to Grandma Cartwright's. She'll help you. She's such a charitable, tolerant woman she even allows my son Leon to board with her so he can attend school." Mattie heard the hint of bitterness in her own voice but didn't dwell on it. This wasn't the time to think on her own resentments.

"I knew it! I knew it! Condemned out of your own mouth," said Caroline, a self-satisfied expression on her face that stirred uneasiness in Mattie.

"What are you talking about, Caroline?" demanded Mattie.

"Don't pretend you are concerned with my daughter's delicate health! That's not why you're here. You thought I was gone," she said, raising her voice over Louisa's hiccuping sobs. "When Jesse tried to force me to go to Tascosa I knew there was more to it than he was telling me. It was your idea, wasn't it? You thought wild tales about a fire would chase me away and you could wait for Jesse. You brazen hussy! Walking into my bedroom bold as you please. Were you planning to strip yourself naked and wait for him in my bed?"

She looked over Mattie's shoulder, her eyes darting around the room. "Where is he? Jesse! I didn't go to Tascosa. I circled around and came back. I knew you were lying to me about the danger." She brushed by Mattie and walked to the door. "Jesse!

I've found you out! Come face me!"

Mattie took a step back. "You are mad, Caroline. Worse than that, you are a fool. You're risking your baby's life because of a jealous notion."

Caroline tilted her chin up. "You're here, aren't you? Standing in my bedroom? I'm not so easy to fool as you and Jesse think."

Mattie clenched her hands to keep from grabbing Caroline and shaking her. "I came to see about you. You're new to the Panhandle, and we haven't had a bad fire near our ranches since you came here. I was afraid you might not know how to protect yourself."

Caroline's face turned a mottled red. "So you say! But I don't believe you. Or Jesse. Talking about a grass fire as though it was Armageddon."

Mattie stared at her in growing disbelief. "A grass fire! God in heaven, I'm not talking about a *grass* fire. I'm talking about hell on earth—hell that can burn for days if the wind stays high, and sucks every bit of moisture from man and beast and soil. I'm talking about flames sixty feet high—flames that race across the prairie as fast as a man can ride on a good horse. I'm talking about heat so intense in the heart of the fire line that it will kill a man if he gets too close. I *am* talking about Armageddon, you ignorant fool!"

For the first time Mattie saw fear in Caroline's eyes—but not enough, and it came and went too fast. "I don't believe you," she said, turning and laying red-faced, sobbing Louisa in her cradle.

Mattie always thought later it was that single, heartless action—Caroline's refusing to hold and comfort and reassure a frightened, sobbing infant—that burned away the last of her self-control and set free her rage. Seizing Caroline by the arm, Mattie yanked her toward the window, shoving her face against the glass.

"Look at the smoke, Caroline! Do you see it? Black like the worst thunderhead. But thunderheads don't touch the ground, and their hearts aren't red. It's a prairie fire. The worst of all disasters in a land without water. If it comes this way, it will swallow you up in its red heart, and I don't care!" She leaned over the shorter woman and put her lips close to Caroline's ear. "Do you hear me? I don't care if your hair turns to fire and the blood boils away in your veins and your flesh melts until you are nothing but bone and grinning skull, but I won't let your foolishness kill Jesse's baby."

She grabbed Caroline's shoulders and shook her. "Do you understand me? You may wait for Jesse since you're so sure he's dishonorable enough to frighten you with lies just so he can bed me, but I'm taking Louisa to Tascosa where the air will at least be cleaner than here. I won't let her choke for the sake of your mistrust. But think of this, Caroline. If you are wrong, if you wait and the wind shifts this way, you will die. Then Jesse will be free to claim me. I'll have your husband and your daughter."

Caroline slapped her. "No!"

Mattie's cheek stung and she knew she'd wear a bruise tomorrow, but she didn't dare let go of Caroline's shoulders. If her hands were free she might strike Caroline back, and Mattie wasn't certain she could live with the burden of hitting another woman—even Jesse's wife. "No, you won't go to Tascosa, or no, you won't let me have your husband and daughter? Which is it, Caroline?"

Caroline licked her lips, fear and desperation finally wiping her face clear of its certainty and smugness. "How dare you threaten me in such a manner? You are a hard, cold woman."

"Which will it be, Caroline? Will you go to Tascosa, or will I?"

Caroline glanced out the window at the black smoke, then back at Mattie. "I'll go. I wouldn't trust a woman like you with Louisa."

Mattie released the other woman's shoulders and stepped away. "I'll go hitch up your wagon."

She turned toward the door when Caroline's voice stopped her. "I won't forget what you did, Mattie Hunter, and one day I'll get my own back."

Mattie pressed her suddenly trembling hands against her thighs as she glanced over her shoulder at the other woman. "I doubt it, Caroline. Given the opportunity, you would never save my life."

CHAPTER

14

A prairie fire smelled of smoke and flame, sweat and blood, singed hair and the burning flesh of animals and men, but by the evening of the second day Mattie no longer noticed. The sound of crackling flames towering ten times her height, shrill screams of frightened horses barely controlled by their wranglers, the soft explosions as burning buffalo chips blown by the wind burst apart, or the hoarse curses of men too exhausted to care that their language might offend no longer deafened her. Nor did she flinch at the slapping sounds of blankets and slickers, the dull thuds of shovels and brooms beating out smoldering clumps of grass, the harsh grunts of men whose parched throats and tongues forbade them more articulate speech. The sight of suppurating blisters or bloody patches of skin seared raw by sparks that burned through shirts and trousers or landed on exposed faces no longer caused her tears.

She had no more tears to fall.

She could no more heal the wounds of man and prairie than she could change the past. Samuel was dead, the land divided, and Jesse was married. All she had were her sons, her cowboys, and a ranch she had built. Her rage against what she could not change was gone—replaced by a determination to save what she could of what she had. As she retreated before the fire, tripping over the barbed-wire fence battered down by fleeing XIT cattle, her determination grew. She was now standing on Bar H land. Her land was burning.

She shook her fist at the advancing flames. "No! I won't let your red heart swallow up my land!"

She felt someone grab her arm and pull her out of the line of men beating at the flames. "Miss Mattie!"

She recognized Jubilee only by his voice. With a bandanna tied over his mouth and nose his exposed skin looked no blacker than the sooty faces of the white men and his eyes were no more bloodshot. "Let me go, damn it! I have to fight this fire."

Jubilee didn't loosen his grip. "You been fighting it for nearly two days, Miss Mattie, and there ain't no man could have done no better. But you is talking crazy and you weaving around like a willow tree in a high wind. You is gonna fall down and not get up again like Squinty done."

She froze. "Squinty?"

Jubilee nodded his head. "The smoke got him is what Tom thinks. His wooden leg weren't even burned when Hank Wilson found him. We put him in the fire wagon."

Mattie dropped her sodden blanket and wiped her eyes on her sleeve. "Squinty's dead?"

"That's what I been telling you, Miss Mattie," he said patiently. "And you is going to be, too, iffen you don't quit and let the menfolks take up the slack. Man or woman just got so much strength and so much time, and Squinty used his up. I ain't intending that you use up yours."

Mattie bit her lip to stop its quivering. "But he rode from Pueblo with us. I tended him when the rustlers shot him. He's one of our kind, Jubilee, one of our folks. He can't be dead!"

Jubilee patted her shoulder. "Folks dying is something else you can't fight, Miss Mattie."

She tried to pull free. "I know that, Jubilee. That's why I have to fight the fire. It's like you said. I can fight a prairie fire—and I can win. I *will* win. I'm using up my mad on something that can be beaten." She touched the hand he had wrapped around her arm. "Let me go. This is my land and I'm responsible. I have to defend it."

He shook his head. "It ain't the land, Miss Mattie. The land don't care who defends it, just like the river don't care who dies in its quicksand. It's the belonging you're fighting to save. You belongs to this land a lot more than the land belongs to you, and your folks is all part of that belonging. A man who rode for you is dead. You needs to tend to him."

"But I can't resurrect him!" she cried.

"You can pack his body back to the house and lay him out proper. When the fire's out, we'll bury him."

"But I'm needed here!"

"You ain't needed here—not anymore. The wind's dropping and every man for a hundred miles around is beating at that fire. They'll lick it as sure the sun rises in the morning. Besides, you ain't got no more strength and you starting to get in the way. How many times you fallen down since the sun set? How many times has somebody stopped what they was doing and hoisted you up? How bad are your legs shaking? How much longer they gonna hold you ?"

He rubbed his thumb over her cheek. "I swear you is as black as me and ten times as tired and only 'bout half as smart. You done all you could—just like you allus have—but you can't do no more here. You poured out your mad on the fire and now you is empty. You needs to fill yourself up again with feelings what don't eat you up. You fill yourself up with caring for your folks again, Miss Mattie. They is fighting this fire 'cause it has to be done, but they fighting it for you, too. They belongs to you more than this land—more than I ever belonged to the Colonel 'cause they always been free to choose."

Mattie looked at the ragged line of men beating out the flames—tired men, wounded men, men who earned only a bare living as cowhands, men who worked for no rancher but came to fight anyway. They belonged, the living and the dead, and someone must tend to them—someone with gentle hands and a soft voice—and tears.

A woman.

Perhaps her woman's tears would heal her wounded men after all. She looked at Jubilee. "I'll take Squinty back, Jubilee. He's one of our folks and we take care of our own."

She thought for a second that Jubilee might hug her, but he caught himself and squeezed her hands instead. They might be in the middle of a prairie fire in a wilderness few people knew, but Jubilee remembered his place—or what he saw as his place. Mattie smiled. She wondered what the ex-slave would say if she told him he was more her kind than Caroline McDade. Probably nothing. He wouldn't believe it.

"You go on over to the wagon, Miss Mattie, and I'll find a horse that's won't be too skitterish to carry Squinty's body."

Jubilee released her and started across the unburned prairie toward the remuda. He stopped before he had taken more than a few steps and glanced back at her. "I is glad your heart ain't burning up like it was, Miss Mattie. You gave off a powerful heat, but a man couldn't warm himself by it. You reckon maybe it's different now?"

Mattie swallowed and felt her lip tremble again. "I reckon so, Jubilee."

He nodded and walked on toward the horses while Mattie turned toward the wagon. When the burning buffalo chip exploded against her back, her knees buckled and she fell face first. The grass was not on fire this close to the wagon, but the ground was hot as a furnace. Now the singed hair and burning flesh she smelled was her own as her shirt caught fire.

"Dear God, not now!" she screamed as she shoved herself to her knees, arching backward and brushing at her shoulders, then ripping at the buttons on her shirt. "I can't die now! My folks need me!"

Jesse saw the flaming buffalo chip hit Mattie and burst into a thousand sparks. He jerked his bowie knife from its sheath and sliced through the rope that anchored his horse to the dead steer he and Hank Wilson had been dragging over the fire. Cursing himself for bowing to Tom Miller's demands that he fight the fire at least a hundred yards from Mattie to "avoid talk," he spurred his horse into a run. He shouldn't have listened to Tom. He should have fought beside Mattie and to hell with the talk. Only a damn fool would think he would take liberties with Mattie during a goddamn prairie fire. Or that she would welcome them. Tom Miller's sense of propriety just might kill Mattie—or maim her so badly she might wish she was dead—and if that happened, Jesse planned to kill that sorry son of a bitch. Tom Miller had interfered for the last time with his talk of what was right and fitting and honorable. When a man—or woman—was about to die, honorable didn't comfort like being held and knowing someone cared.

As Jesse rode his exhausted, laboring horse toward Mattie, a smoke-blackened man in sooty clothes darted out of the fire-lit darkness and ripped off her burning shirt and a white undergarmet, then in almost the same motion jerked her waist length braid over her head and sliced it in half, throwing its flaming end down on the ground and stamping on it.

Jesse threw his leg over the saddle, jumped off his horse, and staggered toward the kneeling, half-naked woman. He dropped to his knees and reached for her. "Mattie! Dear God, Mattie!"

She cupped her hands over her bare breasts and raised her head. "Jesse," she whispered.

Even by the fire's smoky light he could see the joy beneath the pain in her red-rimmed, golden eyes. Like a frightened child in search of comfort she burrowed against his chest. He caught his breath at the sight of the crimson skin across her shoulders swelling into a mass of blisters, some as large as his palm. He had seen worse burns—burns where the skin cracked and sloughed off to leave raw bloody flesh beneath—but to see these ugly blisters on skin he had once caressed sickened him. He wished he had been burned in her stead—his skin was not so tender, so fragile as hers. He wished he could take away her pain. But he could not. He could only gently wrap his arms around her waist, and pull her more tightly against him. Feeling their bodies mold one against the other like two halves of a perfect whole, he closed his eyes and rested his cheek against hers. For however long this moment lasted, it belonged to them.

Like all their moments, this one also was too short.

"You best let go of her, McDade," said Tom Miller in the calm, steady way of a man suggesting the wisest course.

Wisdom had its place, Jesse supposed, but not here where the world burned, and not now when he felt his heart soften and fill up with life again. He lifted his hand and stripped off his glove with his teeth. He laid his fingertips against the tiny pulse in Mattie's throat and felt its rhythm slow to match the beat of his heart. It had always been so with them—almost from the time they first touched—as if they shared a single heart.

He lifted his head and glanced over his shoulder at Tom Miller. "Not this time, Miller. This time I'll hold her while she's hurting."

"It ain't your place, Jesse," said Jubilee. "It's ours. We is her folks."

Jesse didn't argue. There wasn't time and nothing he could say would change anyone's mind—least of all his own. He looked at the soot-darkened man who had saved Mattie's life, then had the decency to turn his back and not gawk while Jesse held her. "Take off your shirt and hand it here."

The man turned around, carefully keeping his eyes on Jesse. "I beg your pardon."

Jesse arched one eyebrow at the thick Scots burr, and felt Mattie draw back slightly to look at the stranger. "Mattie—Mrs. Hunter—needs a shirt, and mine is wool. Too damn scratchy for her to wear over those blisters. The same is true for every other man's shirt—except yours. If it isn't silk, it's the closest thing to it. At least it won't rub Mattie's back raw."

The stranger unbuttoned his shirt and peeled it over his head. "It would be my pleasure to provide Mrs. Hunter whatever assistance is within my power to compensate for any unpleasantness I may have caused her upon the occasion of our first meeting." He bowed to Mattie as he held out his shirt. "Would that it were silk, madam, but it is only linen, although very finely woven linen. Even an eccentric Scot such as I'm rumored to be hesitates to wear silk to a prairie fire."

Jesse plucked the shirt out of the man's hand and dropped it over Mattie's head, gently pulling it down and buttoning it to cover her nudity. "You must be George Faulkner."

Faulkner pulled down the once white linen handkerchief that covered his nose and mouth. "Actually, it's George Henry Edward Faulkner, Esquire—my mother was English and named me in honor of several kings—but the shorter form of address will do. I assume my reputation precedes me."

"I've heard rumors of you. I'm Jesse McDade."

"I assumed as much."

Jesse heard a faint hint of irony beneath the Scot's bland tones, and suddenly realized what a revealing tableau he and Mattie presented. "Then my reputation must have preceded me."

The Scot picked up a singed blanket and wrapped it around his shoulders, covering a chest dusted with red-gold body hair—a chest too broad and muscular in Jesse's opinion to belong to a pampered aristocrat. "I've heard rumors of you, m'lad."

Jesse gently guided Mattie's right arm through an overlarge sleeve, then glanced up at the Scot, wondering how much the man knew of the "unpleasantness" Mattie had suffered following his offer to buy the Bar H. "I hope you have the good sense not to believe everything you hear—nor everything you see."

Faulkner's eyes flickered between Jesse and Mattie. "It's a foolish man who makes his final judgment on the basis of a rumor. I'm not foolish, Mr. McDade."

No, he wasn't, Jesse decided. And he wasn't the fop he pretended to be either. But exactly what or who George Faulkner was ceased to matter when Jesse rolled up the sleeve of the Scotsman's shirt and saw that Mattie's left wrist was swollen nearly double its size. "My God! That bastard left you maimed!"

Mattie frowned and touched her wrist. "It swells sometimes. I don't notice it anymore."

Jesse sprang up and whirled around to confront Tom Miller. "You told me Mattie was healed. You lied to me. Then you let her fight this goddamn fire like she was a man with two good arms when all the time you knew better!"

"A man doesn't *let* Mattie Jo Hunter do anything. I do as I please," Mattie interrupted, staggering to her feet. Her voice was hoarse and barely carried over the sounds of the fire, but only a deaf man would call it weak. It was hard as granite. "Otherwise, I wouldn't last a minute. Every smooth-talking swindler or worthless ruffian would take advantage of me any way they could."

"Not when a man knows that I'll back you up," said Jesse.

"I can't hang back and let men do my fighting."

"And it's nearly gotten you killed twice, Mattie!"

"That's no reason to quit and no reason to hide behind a man's britches."

Her gaze was steady as a man's. But then it always had been, Jesse remembered. She had never fluttered her lashes or dropped her eyes in a coy fashion, never used her femininity to sway a man's judgment. But her smile still tore at his heart.

"Besides, isn't it only the good who die young, Jesse? In the opinion of most folks I fall short of goodness."

CHAPTER

15

January 7, 1886

Tom Miller slung his saddle over one of the wooden beams that rested like a fence rail on cedar posts, then savored the masculine smell of leather that filled the tack room. Well-cured cowhide was a cowboy's scent and in Tom's opinion any man who didn't smell as much of leather as he did of horses and cattle and honest sweat wasn't a man to be trusted around women and children, not to mention expensive livestock. He closed the tack-room door and walked toward Mattie's kitchen door. He might be a mite prejudiced in favor of leather, but these days any smell that didn't carry a taint of smoke was worth a second sniff. After every prairie fire a half-blind man would notice the hands sniffing like a pack of hounds after anything—or anyone—whose odor might clean out the smell of smoke in their nostrils: fresh green grass, coffee boiling over a campfire, clothes dried in the sunshine, a sweat-stained deck of old cards, a well-oiled gun, and a clean-smelling woman. Tom grinned. If the truth be told, a man wasn't too particular whether the woman smelled clean as much as he was that she smelled of woman. There was nothing like fighting a fire to make a man want to rub up against soft tender places on a woman's body—and do a lot more than just rub. Mattie must have sensed her men's needs because as soon the fire was out, Squinty buried, and the men rested, she handed out what she called a "bonus" and gave everybody in turn two days off to spend in Tascosa. The bartender at the Equity Bar allowed to Tom that if that Hunter woman was as generous after the next fire, he'd be a rich man, and the whores down in the Hogtown section of Tascosa wouldn't be bad off either.

Mattie understood about smells, too. She decorated her house and the bunkhouse with cedar boughs tied with ribbons, then ordered Hank Wilson to chop down the tallest cedar for a Christmas tree. Any hand not riding herd was welcome in the house every evening and fed spicy cookies and cakes. Tom figured those cookies and the Christmas tree did more to win Mattie her men's total loyalty than even her bonus had. Any jackass could hand out a couple of extra dollars for a job well done, but a woman didn't use up every sack of flour and sugar on the place and spend hours baking cookies for a bunch of ugly, awkward men unless she cared.

A man couldn't put a price on caring.

Tom stopped by the woodpile where Jubilee, wrapped up in what looked like two blanket coats and three mufflers, busily chopped up the Christmas tree.

"I guess this means Christmas is really over," he remarked to the Negro.

Jubilee leaned on the ax handle and wiped a gloved hand over his sweating face. His breath formed little white clouds quickly ripped apart by the wind. "Aunt Patty allowed as how she's mighty tired of sweeping up cedar drippings off a dried-up old tree and for me to haul it out and chop it up for kindling. Aunt Patty don't believe in wasting much." He blew out another breath. "I tells you what, Tom, I'm mighty fond of that woman but she worse than an overseer about handing out orders. A couple of cowboys didn't get their horses saddled fast enough to ride out of her sight this morning, and she's got them in the house waxing the floor. She says she gonna leave Miss Mattie with a clean house before she and the Colonel pack up to go back to Pueblo. It's getting so the cowboys are hiding under their bunks or in the hayloft just so Aunt Patty can't find them. You know them boys don't want to do nothing that can't be done from horseback if they can help it. But there ain't no way to help it with Miss Patty around. If she'd been a general for the South, I'd still be a slave. 'Course if she'd had her say, probably wouldn't have been no war. Wars make too much mess and Aunt Patty don't like messes."

"She is a managing kind of woman," agreed Tom.

Jubilee nodded as he glanced toward the back door. "Just as well sometimes. Leastwise she got Miss Mattie's two boys straightened up so they ain't picking at each other like two roosters over the same hen."

"Mattie being the hen," said Tom.

Jubilee looked somber. "Ain't right for brothers to act like them two when they both come from the same nest and all. You remember what little Robert did first time he seen Leon when the Colonel brought him home after Miss Mattie was beat?"

Tom rubbed his chin. He remembered all right.

Two-year-old Robert had screamed and torn into Leon with both fists and his feet. And Leon, well, Leon had pushed him away and called him a bastard. "I always figured the Colonel made a mistake whipping Leon for calling his brother a name. Might have been wiser to let the boys work it out themselves even if there was seven years difference between them. I doubt Leon would have hurt Robert. From what I've seen of him, he appears to be a kind lad."

"Oh, he allus was," said Jubilee eagerly. "He was the finest boy you ever seen, Tom, and good company. Why, everybody used to fight over him. He rode along with the hands soon as he was old enough to stay on a horse by hisself, and before that he rode with Miss Mattie. She didn't hardly leave the house less that boy was riding in the saddle in front of her."

"Then she sent him off to Pueblo, and the first time he comes back, his mother is nursing another baby—a baby I'll bet he didn't know his mother was expecting," said Tom.

"Womenfolk don't go around talking about things like that to young'uns," objected Jubilee delicately. "It just ain't done."

"Then when Leon finally comes home to stay, he finds his mother beaten, his father murdered, and a young brother he doesn't know who hates him. Mighty confusing for a youngster."

"Miss Mattie didn't have no choice, Tom. She had to keep Leon safe."

Tom sighed. "I suspect Mattie has never had any choices but bad ones."

Jubilee picked up his ax and chopped a branch off the bedraggled Christmas tree. "Them young'uns need a pa. They need somebody to tan their hides when they needs it, and lets them tag along behind him when they don't."

"I think a pa is what is at the bottom of the hard feelings between those two, Jubilee. I think Leon looks too much like Samuel to Robert's eyes."

Jubilee dropped his ax and whirled around to face Tom. "He don't look nothing like him. He looks like Miss Mattie."

Tom shook his head. "His hair is closer to Samuel's color than Mattie's and he's such a stubborn little cuss. To a two-year-old with no good memories of his pa, that's enough."

"You done lost your wits, Tom," said Jubilee firmly.

"No, but I think Robert did the day Mattie was beaten. He was in the house, probably heard it. He damn sure heard what Mattie told Caroline McDade, and we weren't thinking too hard about what we said in front of him about Samuel that night. Guess we thought he was too young to understand, but he did, and now he's got Leon and Samuel all tangled up in his head. He's such a hardheaded little cuss it's going to be harder than pulling teeth to put him straight."

"Takes after his mama in that way," said Jubilee.

Tom wasn't sure that all of Robert's stubbornness came from Mattie. Now that the youngster was growing from baby to young boy and his face was thinning down, there was a look about Robert that didn't resemble Mattie or her father or Samuel—a way of narrowing his eyes and clenching his jaw that set Tom to imagining what he'd rather not.

"Mattie in the house, Jubilee?"

Jubilee caught his arm. "You ain't gonna talk to her about none of this, are you, Tom? We can't undo nothing of what's been done and she can't neither. We just gots to make them boys treat each other like they was brothers and maybe it'll get to be a habit. But I don't think Miss Mattie can help. I don't think she can talk about Samuel to them boys without the hate spilling out. Maybe when they is older. Maybe then."

Tom hoped the secrets all of them held in their hearts would stay buried that long. "I won't say anything, Jubilee. I just want to share a cup of coffee with her."

"Well, she ain't here. Her and the Colonel rode out this morning toward the burn. She was all gussied up in that red riding habit her pa brung her for Christmas. She even throwed a sidesaddle over her horse, and you know she ain't rode on no sidesaddle on the ranch since Hector was a pup. One reason folks don't think she's a real lady. Nobody but Indian squaws and white trash rides astride. I allus tell her that, and she ain't never listened till now. I don't know what she's got in mind, but she's softening up her pa. Wouldn't dress in no riding habit if she weren't."

Tom looked up toward the sky and sucked in a deep breath. He coughed and spat. He noticed he wasn't coughing up black phlegm anymore. Three days of breathing smoke while fighting a fire left a man's lungs blacker than charcoal. He guessed his were up to snuff again. He hoped so. Anybody with a chest still full of smoke was liable to catch pneumonia sure as hell now that winter had settled in. And settle in it had. After a long dry fall of unseasonably warm weather, "almost as pleasant as May" one newspaper called it, the weather changed abruptly on New Year's Eve. One snow barely had time to melt before another hit. Tom hadn't classified any of the snows as blizzards, but it was early yet. The blizzards would come and his bones told him they would be worse than last winter's. It would be an old rip snorter of a winter, the worst since Washington crossed the Delaware according to

Hank Wilson. Tom wouldn't argue with Hank. The old cowboy's bones were as reliable as his own.

"She and the Colonel better not stay long. Look at those clouds, Jubilee," said Tom. "They're nearly touching the prairie and they're full of snow. Liable to start falling anytime now and no way in hell to know when it will stop. The wind's picking up every minute, too. It's a blue norther for sure, and a man caught in it can freeze to death between one breath and the next and not know it until he finds himself trying to explain to the Lord how come he was so stupid."

Tom turned back toward the barn with its attached tack room. "I'd best saddle a horse and go find them."

"There'll be a worse storm than that if you bothers Miss Mattie 'fore she finishes her business with the Colonel, Tom." The old man clasped Tom's shoulders. "Leave her be. She gots good sense about the land and the weather. She'll turn tail and run for the house 'fore it gets too bad. And you don't be worrying no more 'bout little Robert and Leon, and trust the Lord to see they gets along better."

Tom nodded without agreeing. No point in reminding Jubilee that the sins of the fathers were visited on the sons. He figured that went for the sins of the mother, too. When God called for a reckoning, more than one generation had to pay.

Mattie reined in her horse next to her father's at the edge of what she called the great burn—charred black land that stretched as far to the west and north and east as she could see. The *Dallas Morning News* reported that the burn was 175 miles long and 125 miles wide. Mattie would not argue with those figures.

She could still smell the fire after several weeks and the intervening snows. The land gave off an odor of death as though it suffered from a gangrenous wound. The very ground had cracked from the heat, but she avoided looking in the deep fissures. She could only stand to see so much hurt, and she already had seen her limit: cattle burned brown and crisp, horses shot when their hooves sloughed off, the corpses of all manner of wild creatures who couldn't creep or fly or crawl or run fast enough to escape, men whose arms and faces and bodies bore fresh scars. She could not bear to also look into the cracked heart of her land and see its pain.

"Rumor says that the XIT lost nearly a million acres in the fire," she said to her father. She carefully kept her voice as matter-of-fact as possible—an assessment of damage, not a litany of grief. "The number of cattle they lost varies according to who you talk to, but the best estimate is between four and five thousand. Likely no one outside of Abner Taylor and the Capitol Land Company will ever really know the true figures, but they were hurt worse than they let on. Sharp-eyed cowboys riding across XIT land on their way from New Mexico report seeing cattle burned so badly that their hides hang in strips and their eyesight is gone."

Mattie heard her voice break and saw her father glance sharply at her. She drew a deep breath to calm herself. This was no time to shed tears over another's maimed cattle. "Charlie Goodnight claims he lost two hundred sections of good grazing land. I estimate my own losses at nearly a hundred fifty thousand acres burned and five hundred head lost. I had planned to hold the XIT accountable but that came to naught just as Jubilee predicted. Mr. Reynolds of the LE, whose ranch is even more devastated than the Bar H, accused an XIT fencing crew of starting the blaze, but Billy Dixon, whose word is held in as high esteem as Goodnight's, claims he saw the fire burn south from the Oklahoma Strip and jump the Cimarron River. From there it raced a hundred miles to burn itself out in the Canadian breaks. The XIT refuses to honor my claims or those of Mr. Reynolds."

Mattie's voice broke again, and she hoped her father assumed it was from anger. On no account must he know she was afraid. But she was. She faced a winter short of the dried buffalo grass she needed to nurture her cattle. She must spend precious cash on supplementary hay and grain. She must rebuild burned line shacks and stock tanks and repair what few windmills she had. Thanks to Samuel's draining of the ranch's accounts before his death, the Bar H's cash reserve's were less than Mattie wished—less than she needed. Another natural disaster or a depressed cattle market in the spring and summer, and she might very well have to sell off some of her land to survive.

She would rather sell her soul to the devil.

Or borrow money from her father—which in her experience was the same thing.

She wondered when daughters became equals, or if in their fathers's eyes they ever did.

"I've seen worse, Mattie," said the Colonel abruptly. "Sherman on his march to the sea burned a sizable piece of real estate and left women and children and old folks to fend for themselves as best they could without shelter and crops. The Lord only knows how many couldn't manage and laid down and died of the fire without a mark on them. At least only one man died in this fire."

Mattie felt her eyes sting and blinked away the tears. Grief must wait for another time. "But Squinty Smith was one of my men," she said.

The Colonel reached over and patted her shoulder. "And you did right by him, Mattie, although I can't agree that burying him right next to your daughter's grave was the proper thing to do. It doesn't look right—burying a common ranch hand next to family and fencing off your own husband's grave."

He raised his hand to hush her before she could argue. "Mind you, I'm not defending Samuel. Lord knows I would like to spit on his grave."

"So would I," snapped Mattie.

The Colonel rubbed his chin. "I imagine you would. The difference between us is that I have sense enough to do it without the neighbors watching. You don't. Burying that cowboy next to your daughter is spitting on Samuel's grave in public, and it was a foolish thing to do. It isn't what folks know for a fact that can hurt you. It's what they suspect—and want to believe. You would have made a poor general, Mattie. You don't look to your defenses."

Mattie thought of Caroline McDade and shivered. "I can't change the past and no one would believe me if I suddenly started acting the grieving widow."

The Colonel nodded, his eyes on the black desolation of the prairie. "I agree. Hypocrisy requires a sincerity of a sort which you lack."

He turned his head to look at her, and Mattie suddenly noticed how lined and slack his face was—as though muscle and tendon had shrunk away from his skull, allowing his skin to wrinkle like an ill-fitted garment. She was certain her father did not accept encroaching age with grace and she was equally certain that his distress over her behavior was in part responsible for his sudden deterioration. She felt a stirring of pity and guilt and hoped her father sensed neither. He might consider her a poor general but she knew better than to place such weapons in his hands.

She smiled instead. "I don't believe my inability to be a successful hypocrite is a flaw in my character."

Her father waved away her words. "Of course it is, Mattie. Without hypocrisy and polite lies masquerading as manners and diplomacy, men would rend one another like wild beasts."

"Men do that anyway," remarked Mattie.

Her father ignored her. "However, thanks to your prairie fire, we don't have to depend on crocodile tears and widows' weeds to extricate you from your difficulties." He slapped his thigh with glee. "By God, I would have set that fire myself if I had thought of it." The Colonel leaned toward her. "Don't you see, Mattie? You've been burned out, your husband foully murdered, your sons in need of decent schooling, and you in need of male protection."

She straightened her back, feeling the tender new skin across her shoulders pull uncomfortably. "What I *need* is a loan, Papa, money to rebuild. I still have over a half million acres—or rather, my sons and I together do," she corrected herself. "That is sufficient collateral, I believe. As for male protection, I have over a hundred men riding for my brand. Surely that's enough for any woman."

"A loan? Is that why you dragged me out in this miserable icy weather to look at the damage? So you could ask me for a loan? You want me to pour additional money down this rat hole of a country?"

"As I recall, Papa, you made a handsome profit the last time you loaned money to the Bar H."

He nodded. "That's true enough—but Jesse McDade was manager then, not you."

"Jesse hasn't managed this ranch for nearly four years, Papa. I have, and I've made a profit every one of those years. Without Samuel to siphon off money and with a small loan to tide me over, I'll continue to make a profit. With a strong cattle market and a little luck, I'll be able to repay you by next fall."

"Luck is poor collateral, Mattie, and there are other considerations," said the Colonel, his faded blue eyes studying her as though she were a rampart he was about to charge. "I think it would be best for all concerned if you moved back to Pueblo."

"No!"

The Colonel continued as though she had not interrupted. "No one would question your reasons for selling up and fleeing this godforsaken country. If by chance any gossip about your behavior reaches so far, I shall stop it by whatever means necessary." He smiled at her. "Having one's finger in several different financial pies does have its advantages, Mattie. In Pueblo, I'm in a position to ruin whoever dares to treat you less than I expect."

"In other words, you would buy me respectability."

"Short of locking you in a nunnery, I see no other way for you to regain it. A suitable marriage would suffice, I suppose, provided I could find a man so besotted with you that he would overlook the nature of your friendship with McDade."

Mattie clenched her jaw before answering. "Why don't you say what you really mean? That the man who marries me marries Jesse McDade's leavings!"

"Honesty need not be expressed in such indelicate terms, Mattie," said the Colonel, frowning in disapproval.

"On the plains I can see what's coming because there's no place to hide, Papa. I feel the same way about talk. I want to hear what a man feels and intends. I don't want his meaning hidden behind words."

The Colonel sighed and folded his hands over his saddle horn. "In spite of my harsh words when I first suspected your relationship with McDade, I have never thought of you as his whore, Mattie. Sometimes a woman bestows her heart unwisely."

"And doesn't a man?" she asked.

"Perhaps less often, my dear, and he does not pay so heavily for his foolishness as a woman—except in this case."

Not even the icy wind that promised snow later in the day could account for how cold she suddenly felt. "I don't know what you mean, Papa."

He clicked his tongue at her. "I'm not a fool. Before you even woke up after your beating, I knew McDade had murdered Samuel and that worthless gambler. Oh, no one told me, and I had sense enough not to ask. No point in stirring up trouble when there is a representative of the law lurking about. But I knew the truth all the same. This ranch stinks of secrets, Mattie, and if I smell them, then others can, too."

Mattie traced the scar under her chin and swallowed back her fear. "Please, Papa, please don't speculate about Samuel's death."

"Then come home to Pueblo, Mattie," the Colonel urged. "You'll be safe there."

"I'm safe here."

The Colonel turned to stare at the blackened prairie again, and Mattie sensed that he was gathering his weapons and planning his tactics. Finally, he turned back and she saw the merciless expression in his eyes. "But Jesse is only safe until the first person talks out of turn."

She clenched her hands into fists to hide their trembling. "Are you threatening Jesse?"

The Colonel's face took on a wounded expression. "Mattie! How could you think such a thing of me? I do have some feelings of gratitude toward the young man. I'd also like to horsewhip him. Sometimes I don't know which feeling is stronger."

"Then what did you mean?" she whispered.

"Strike a lighted match to dry kindling and you always have a fire, Mattie, and you're that lighted match. Without you, the kindling won't burn. There'll be no flames for the gossips to fan, and Jesse will be safe. It's not his misdeeds that endanger him. It's yours."

"Why is it my fault? Why can't I be left alone?" she cried. "Why can't Jesse be left alone?"

The Colonel shook his head in frustration. "Because you're not ashamed, girl! That's why folks can't forget."

"If a beating and a prairie fire can't break me, vicious talk from folks who ought to look to their own sins can't either. I'm not going to Pueblo. I'm not leaving my land."

The Colonel grabbed her reins as she turned her horse toward headquarters. "Not even for a loan, Mattie?" His blue eyes pierced her. "Turn the ranch over to Tom Miller to manage, and I'll loan you however much money is needed to keep this damnable place going and I'll loan it at no interest. In exchange, you come home to Pueblo and swear you will never set foot in Texas again."

"No!"

The Colonel released her reins and slumped in his saddle, a look of grief on his face. "Then I won't loan you money, and I'll use my influence to block a loan from another bank. I owe it to McDade to see to his safety and that means forcing you to leave."

She fought to draw a breath against a sickness that churned in her belly. "What have you done, Papa? What kind of devil's bargain did you make with Jesse?"

"I've not seen nor talked to McDade since he walked off this property four years ago, but I'm indebted to him nevertheless. He rid me of Samuel. I just wish he had been less open about his intentions and shot the bastard from ambush like any intelligent man would have."

"I don't believe you! Jesse would never want to see me lose my land—not if he had a choice."

"I am aware of that, so it is not to him that I am offering a choice. It is to you. What is your answer, Mattie?"

"Jesse and I have survived gossip before. We will survive it again. I'm not accepting your offer. I'm not leaving my land."

The Colonel was silent for a moment and when he spoke again his voice held a note of anguish that Mattie had never heard before. "Then McDade is a fool, Mattie, for trusting his life to you. But it is more honorable to be a fool than to be a whore, and only a whore would risk a man's life for this ugly, waterless, charred piece of dirt."

"You're wrong, Papa."

His eyes held a mixture of expressions: regret, grief, hope, but overpowering these was resignation. "I wish to God I were, Mattie, but if the time ever comes that you have to choose between McDade and this land, I don't give McDade more than even odds."

He spurred his horse into a gallop as though he couldn't ride away from her fast enough.

Mattie licked her lips and tasted icy tears. Until that moment she hadn't known she was crying.

CHAPTER

16

The blizzard hit before Mattie reached home and within seconds its fierce wind stole her breath and numbed her face. She bowed her head and drifted before its blinding veil of wind-blown flakes, trusting her horse's sense of direction more than her own. She would survive or she would die. Either way she feared the blizzard less than she feared her own thoughts. A blizzard presented no puzzling motives to those caught in its maelstrom of whirling snow and freezing wind. A blizzard was neither good nor evil; it neither judged nor condemned; it simply existed, and Mattie found its indifference comforting. There were no choices to be made, no doubts to face, no guilt to shoulder, no loss to mourn, no secrets to hide, no lies to be told.

A blizzard didn't care why she cried.

She clung to her horse's mane, her right leg nearly paralyzed from being hooked around the horn of her sidesaddle while her left hung stiff and numb from hip to toes. She assumed her foot still rested in its stirrup but she couldn't be sure. Her fancy ladies' riding boots were never meant to be worn in a blizzard any more than the red velvet habit and she had no feeling left in her feet. She had worn both boots and habit to please her father and proved nothing but that she was a fool. Colonel Andrew J. Corley cared nothing for modest attire—only for modest behavior.

And that Hunter woman cared more for the land than she cared for a man.

"No, Jesse! That's not true!" she cried.

"Mattie!"

She peered through the blowing snow at the muffled figure on horseback riding out of the curtain of snow. "Jesse, it that you?"

"Reckon not this time, Mattie," said Tom, reining in so close to her that his leg brushed hers as he threw a blanket around her shoulders.

She could hear the relief in his voice, feel it in the hands that lingered on her shoulders before he released her to slip the reins from between her numb fingers. Dear, sweet Tom, she thought as she lifted her hand to clumsily touch his cheek.

Before she could speak—before she could smile—as though her touch had cut some restraint, Tom dropped the reins and clasped his hand around the back of her neck and pulled her toward him until his warm breath made her lips tingle. "When your pa rode back without you, I damn near lost my wits. All I could think of was you lost in the snow, riding in circles until you froze solid. Don't ever scare me like this again, or by God I'll lock you up in a room and keep the only key. Do you hear me, Mattie Jo Hunter? I'll keep you safe whether you like it or not."

Reluctantly freeing her, he nudged his gelding into a trot, leading Mattie's horse by its reins. "I best get you to the house. Aunt Patty plans to duck you in a tub of hot water until you turn pink again while Jubilee is determined to fill you up with beef stew and Taos Lightning. As soon as you're warm inside and out, Mattie Hunter, I'm gonna talk to you. I'm a patient man, but I've waited long enough."

Tom's words warmed her heart. At least somebody cared. She opened her lips to reply, but forgot the words before she could speak. She forgot everything at the sight of cattle streaming past them, some so close she felt their heat. Cattle drifting south before the storm—drifting south into the fences Samuel had ordered built against her will. Fences she had traded for peace from Samuel's interfering during the cowboy strike. Fences that in her anguish after her beating she had failed to order torn down. She had failed to order her section of the drift fence on her northern boundary torn down either, but that didn't concern her. Cattle drifting from the north would die against that fence, but she couldn't worry about her neighbors' animals now—not when her own were in danger.

"Dear God, Tom!" she screamed against the wind. "The cattle are drifting! We've got to cut the southern fences!"

He glanced over his shoulder at her and shook his head without speaking, pointing instead at Mattie's house that loomed out of the snow. Impatiently she kicked her gelding, but he sensed home and his trot turned into a gallop. Only Tom's grip on the reins turned the horse toward the back porch where Jubilee waited instead of to the barn.

Jubilee dragged Mattie off her horse and carried her into the house. "Lordy, but I was scared Tom couldn't find you, and your pa—well, your pa took on something awful 'bout running off and leaving you. Finally dosed him up on Taos Lightning till he passed out. Good thing, too. He was running around like a chicken with its head cut off. Wasn't doing nobody no good. Me and Miss Patty will get you dried out and warmed up and you can go soothe his mind."

Mattie struggled out of his arms and collapsed on the floor as her stiff and numb legs gave way under her weight. Never again, so help her God, would she ride sidesaddle, she thought grimly as she crawled to the table and pulled herself upright. The devil with being a lady and the devil with what the neighbors thought.

"Jubilee, send somebody out to saddle me a horse and call the men together. We've got to cut the south fences."

Jubilee folded his arms. "I ain't gonna do no such thing."

"Then I'll do it myself," she said, staggering across the floor toward the back door.

Jubilee grabbed her arms and whirled her around. "You ain't gonna do it neither."

She felt a blast of icy wind as the back door opened, then slammed shut, but she was too angry to wonder who came in. She jerked loose and slapped Jubilee. "You'll do as I tell you! My cattle will die against that fence! I won't let that happen!"

"Nothing you can do about it, Mattie."

She whirled around. "Don't tell me what to do, Tom!"

"Reckon I will this time, Mattie, and slapping me won't do you any more good than slapping Jubilee did. I'm not sending men out to die in that storm."

Jesse smelled the storm coming long before it hit. He was like the cattle and horses in that respect, he thought. He always sensed bad weather. And this might be the worst weather in his memory—certainly the worst since he'd been in the Panhandle. The snow clouds pressed down on the land until he could hardly see space between land and sky, and the wind blew with the ferocity of a wild beast. Drifts would be over a man's head before the storm blew itself out, and any man caught outside would freeze if he couldn't find shelter. The cattle would drift south before the storm, staying alive as long as they moved. Jesse would be weeks gathering his cattle back onto his own range, but he was damn glad he hadn't strung barbed wire around his property like most of the other ranchers had. Sure, he had fences, but none to the south. His land was open-ended. His fences would funnel his cattle toward open range—all but the few who grazed in the west pasture next to Mattie's land. There was no barbed wire along that few miles of property line—not because it would have cut off his direct route to Tascosa, but because he hadn't wanted to fence himself off from Mattie.

He shrugged out of his coat and poured himself a cup of coffee as he calculated how many head of cattle his sentiment would cost him. Not more than a hundred, he thought. After Mattie lost so much grazing to the fire, he had tried to keep his animals on his side of the property line. Mattie didn't need another man's cattle foraging on what grass she had left. Not that it mattered in the long run. Before the storm was over, most of Mattie's herds would bunch up against her south fence and freeze where they stood. Sometimes cattle had no more goddamn sense than a chicken, and in Jesse's opinion God had never made a dumber animal than the domestic fowl.

"Jesse, you're dripping melted snow all over my floor. Please take off your boots and set them by the stove."

Jesse turned toward his wife, his greeting dying

on his lips as he saw what she held. "What are you doing with that book?"

Caroline arched her eyebrows. "I'm reading it, of course. Sometimes Shakespeare is not proper, but some of his plays are exciting."

"You never read anything but the ladies' magazines," he said, his eyes riveted on the pressed leaf she held in one hand.

She smiled but her eyes held a watchful expression as though she were weighing his reactions. "I see you reading Shakespeare so often that I was curious. You must even carry it with you sometimes." She held out her hand. "I found this leaf between the pages of *Romeo and Juliet*. Is it a bookmark, Jesse?"

Jesse closed his eyes against the memories, but he could not close his mind. He remembered breaking that leaf off Mattie's cottonwood tree the night he left the Bar H forever after promising the Colonel he wouldn't see Mattie again. He remembered the moonlight, the faint breeze, his own shame. That leaf was the only tangible thing he had of Mattie's— the only memory he could touch.

"Put it back, Caroline," he said hoarsely, opening his eyes.

"Is it a bookmark, Jesse?" she repeated.

He looked at the leaf laying on her palm. "Yes," he whispered.

"Did *she* give it to you?"

Jesse didn't ask who Caroline meant. He knew. "No, Mattie didn't give it to me."

Caroline cocked her head to one side, and Jesse wondered if her smile had always been so cold and he had never noticed, or if it was a reflection of her own frozen heart—or of his.

She closed her hand on the dried leaf and crushed it. "Then it doesn't matter if I throw it away, does it? I've never liked pressed leaves and flowers. They crumble and make such a mess."

He watched her dust her hands off and noticed her smile was no longer cold and her eyes no longer watchful. Both expressed a triumph that if he had the means to test its temperature would be hotter than the sun.

He glanced at the bits of leaf scattered at her feet.

"You look so stricken, Jesse. Did your *bookmark* hold some other meaning for you?"

He met her eyes. "No," he said, then fell silent as he realized he had condemned himself by his answer. He felt a grudging respect for Caroline's clever phrasing of her question. Whichever way he answered, he was wrong. He had no defense—and no right to feel the rage that tightened his chest. He was a married man with a keepsake that reminded him of another woman.

Her gaze sharpened until he felt cut by it. "I won't be scorned, Jesse, not by you and not by the likes of that Hunter woman."

"Then leave the past alone," he replied, feeling an aching exhaustion that had nothing to do with physical exertion. "I told you before that I'm done with Mattie, and she with me. She is a neighbor with whom I shared hardship. Whatever else there was is past and none of your concern. If there is any hope of our living together amiably, Caroline, we must start from this moment."

"Then keep her away from me!" she cried, her mouth twisting with ugliness as she spat out the words. "I won't have her putting her hands on me again. I won't have her walking into my home without a welcome and threatening me."

Jesse stiffened. "When did Mattie ever set foot in this house since I married you? When did she ever threaten you? Not when she came to you after

Hunter beat her. You closed the door in her face and sent her away." He grasped her arm when she tried to walk away. "When, Caroline? When did you see Mattie?"

She slapped at his hand. "Let me go!"

He grabbed her other arm, holding her fast. "Tell me, Caroline."

She struggled, her hatred a palpable thing. "Don't lie to me, Jesse. She told you. She wouldn't be able to resist putting me in a bad light just because I didn't believe the fire was dangerous."

"The fire? Mattie was here the day the prairie fire started?"

"You know she was. And she threatened to leave me in this house to die if I didn't take Louisa to Tascosa." Caroline nodded her head. "She didn't tell you that, did she? Didn't tell you how she bruised my arms pulling me this way and that in the name of saving me?"

Jesse drew a deep breath and let go of her arms, unsure that he wouldn't strangle Caroline if he didn't step away. "You didn't go to Tascosa when I told you to. You didn't believe me. You didn't *trust* me." He saw a flicker of guilt in her eyes. "If Mattie hadn't been neighborly, Louisa would have sickened and died from the smoke."

"Where are you going, Jesse?" Caroline asked hysterically as he picked up his coat and slipped it on, buttoning it tight and wrapping a muffler around his neck.

He put his hat on and began stuffing jerky and coffee and flour into a bag. "I helped Mattie before when you refused to act like a Christian woman and give her protection when she was in need. I'll help her again, Caroline, because she saved my daughter's life if for no other reason. I'll ride out and cut her damn fences so she doesn't lose her cattle to the storm. It's the least I can do."

She threw herself against him, clutching his shoulders. "You'll leave me here alone? In this terrible storm?"

He pushed her away. "You have food, water, enough buffalo chips and wood to last a month, and cowboys in the bunkhouse a few yards away."

She clenched her fists, her whole body stiff with anger. "Let Mattie Hunter take care of herself."

He walked to the door before turning back to face her. "You don't understand, Caroline. Mattie Hunter would see us all in hell before she would fail to answer the call of her land, but when her range was in danger of burning, she took the time to come see to you and Louisa. You can't begin to know what a sacrifice that must have been for Mattie. Even if I hated her, I would still owe her."

"But you don't hate her, do you?" screamed Caroline.

"No, I don't," he said quietly.

She stood panting, her fingers opening and closing, her whole face crimson. "I won't be beholden to that slut!"

He clenched his teeth at her epithet, but didn't raise his voice. "Then don't put yourself in her debt again, Caroline." He stepped into the screaming wind and closed the door behind him.

CHAPTER

17

Shivering, Mattie huddled deeper into Jubilee's coat and clenched her jaw to keep her teeth from chattering. She had one muffler wrapped around her neck, another covered her head and ears, while a third masked her face from the numbing wind. She wore no hat, seeing no way to fit one over her wrapped-up head. Jubilee wouldn't approve, believing as he did that a hat promoted good health. "Keeps a man from getting his brain boiled in the summer and froze in the winter" was his unfailing pronouncement on the subject, and like most of Jubilee's pronouncements, held more than a grain of truth.

It wasn't a truth Mattie bothered with at the moment any more than she had bothered with soaking in Aunt Patty's tub of hot water or sipping Jubilee's Taos Lightning. Instead she had stripped off her wet clothes, donned dry ones, and slipped down the back stairs and out of the house without anyone seeing her. The price of such urgency was a body already chilled before she rode out into the storm. She was cold—colder than she ever remembered being—and alone in a swirling, stinging snowstorm whose voice was the howling wind. It was a price Mattie was willing to pay, however, but not one she could ask of others. Tom, as wise in his own way as Jubilee was in his, was right as usual. She could not order men out into this blizzard. She would risk her own life to save her cattle, but she hadn't the right to ask it of someone else.

She would cut her own fence.

She nudged her horse into a faster walk. The snow was already deep and she couldn't ask more of the animal than she already had. Gripping the reins tighter, she prayed that she might survive this freezing cold night. Whatever it took for however long, she would do. But she would save her cattle—or as many of them as possible.

There was a line cabin—a tiny shack of cottonwood logs barely eight by ten—near the west end of the fence. No one slept there regularly since Tom judged it was too close to headquarters. A cowboy riding that section of the fence might as well sleep in the bunkhouse. Still, the shack was provisioned. All the line cabins were. No telling when a rider might need food and shelter for the night. Mattie decided she would cut fence until she reached the cabin—a distance of eight to ten miles—then sit out the rest of the storm. With luck—and God owed her some of that, she thought grimly—the herds would find the gap and drift through it to the south. With luck—and grit—she would weather this storm, and so would her cattle.

She gave the better odds to the cattle.

Even with God's help, she would never survive this weather long enough to cut ten miles of fence. She doubted she would live to cut five miles.

"Damn you, Samuel," she cried to the wind. "And damn my own frailty."

Scarcely had the words left her mouth when her horse shied and she clamped her legs tight against its sides. Dear God, if she were thrown, she would die. Not that she didn't expect to die, but be damned if she'd do it before she cut the fence. She stood up in the stirrups and peered through the snow, dimly seeing the milling, shoving bodies of her cattle. Over the wind's shriek, she heard their panicked lowing. It was the herd that had passed Tom and her as they had ridden for the house. It was the first of several herds that would be drifting down from what was left of her northern pastures after the fire.

Quickly she turned her horse and kicked it into a floundering gallop along the edge of the herd for a half mile, until she could swerve around it and reach the fence. Leaning over, she dropped a loop of rope over one fence post, dallied the other end round her saddle horn, and turned her horse into the storm. She barely nudged the gelding before he eagerly broke into another awkward gallop. Mattie spared a moment of pity for the animal's misunderstanding. He thought his rider was heading for the barn and was willing to do his part to get there. When the gelding reached the end of the rope, he reared in protest, then dug his hooves in and pulled. Mattie heard the post snap off at ground level, the sing of barbed wire as staples gave way on other posts, and the pounding of hooves as the herd leaders poured through the narrow gap. As more and more cattle pushed through, their massive bodies trampled down more fence. Their hooves churned the fallen snow to blood red slush as the animals climbed over the bodies of cattle already dead.

Mattie rode into the face of the wind, pulling

barbed wire and fence posts behind her, until her horse stumbled to its knees. Quickly, she pulled the gelding up and forced him around to follow the rope back to its end. Loosening her noose from around the first post, she rode along the fence line, chose another post, dropped her loop, then used her horse's strength to pull down another long section of barbed wire. Over and over she repeated the pattern until she felt her gelding's sides heaving beneath her legs. She knew without feeling his coat that the animal was white with lather rather than snow and would likely die. Sweat and a blizzard was a deadly combination for both woman and animal.

Coiling the rope, she looped it around the saddle horn, then dismounted, gripping the reins in one hand and a fence cutter in the other. Her feet sank into the snow past her boot tops where the wind had sculptured a drift along the fence and she fell, dropping the reins as she attempted to catch herself. On her hands and knees, she watched the gelding whirl round and head north toward headquarters as though fleeing from the devil himself. Mattie didn't blame the horse. Even a dumb animal knew when a man—or a woman—was intent on killing it in the name of some higher purpose.

Wearily, she pushed herself up onto feet so numb with cold they felt like blocks of wood, picked up the fence cutters, and staggered toward the barbed wire. Shaking from the cold, panting from exhaustion, she barely found the strength to manipulate the long-handled tool and cut through the five strands of wire. Then she trudged on to the next section, and the next, racing against the storm and knowing she had very little time left before the cold overtook her. It was an unequal race at best and she knew it—had known it from the beginning—and had chosen to run it anyway. A strong woman lived with her choices—or in this instance, died with them—but she did not cry foul. She would die—she accepted that—but she would not die a weak woman.

How long Mattie stumbled from section to section, she had no way of knowing. How far she had struggled, she had no way of knowing either, but finally, too weak to lift the fence cutters, she sank to her knees. She no longer felt cold and knew then the race was over and she had lost. She thought how merciful death by freezing was. Before the cold killed one, it first warmed the body and freed the mind to dream of other places, other times. She stretched out in the snow, unlocked the doors of her mind, and let free the memories. Examining them one by one, she chose those of Jesse. Life had forbidden them to be together, but Death was more charitable. He would carry her away with Jesse's face clear in her mind and his name on her lips.

Of her sins, she only regretted one.

She was sorry she had slapped Jubilee.

The shack had a dirt floor, a few shelves lined with canned goods on one log wall, a potbellied stove in the corner next to a box overflowing with buffalo chips, a tiny shuttered window, a splintery table and two chairs, and a narrow metal cot. Its other appointments were scarcely less homey: a coal-oil lamp, a soiled deck of cards, tin plates and cups on the table, and a few pages torn from the Montgomery Ward catalogue tacked to the walls, pages that mostly pictured ladies in their corsets.

Mattie had expected heaven to be more of an improvement over the world she knew, and hell to be a lot warmer. She shivered violently, and wondered what was the point of dying tragically and bravely if nothing changed.

A tall figure rose from the foot of the bed and spread another blanket over her—a horse blanket, judging from the smell, thought Mattie vaguely, peering through the gloomy light cast by the coal-oil lamp. When the man lifted his head and silver eyes glittered in the feeble light, the question of heaven or hell no longer mattered.

"Jesse! Did you die, too?"

Jesse knelt beside the cot. Eyes sunken with exhaustion beyond imagining and face ravaged with grief beyond bearing, he looked years older than his age. Looking at him, Mattie knew she was alive after all. Even in hell no man could look as tortured as Jesse.

"I found your body before the snow had time to drift over it. Otherwise, I wouldn't have seen you at all. I carried you back here—it's your line shack on the Bar H—and did what I could for you. Stripped off your wet clothes, dried you off with my union suit— it being the only dry cloth that wasn't scratchy— covered you up, rubbed your hands and feet."

He looked away and swallowed. "And I rubbed your body, too. Touching your skin was like touching cold, cold satin. Nothing like I remembered. That's when I despaired. I've seen too many strong men die without waking once the cold seduced them into sleep to believe you had much of a chance to live."

He rose and tucked the blankets around her shoulders. "I'll stoke up the fire a bit now that you're awake and shivering. I knew better than to overheat the air at first. Anybody who nearly dies by freezing needs to warm up slowly. Heat up a body too quickly and the flesh dies—like searing a steak—and gangrene sets in, particularly in the extremities."

She watched him add buffalo chips to the stove and thought his shoulders were too rigid, his body too tense, as if he were uneasy in her presence.

"Thank you, Jesse," she said, and flinched as he whirled around and stalked back to lean over her.

"Don't get ahead of yourself thanking me, Mattie. When I stripped off your boots and gloves, they were filled with snow. Your fingers and toes were so cold and stiff, it's a wonder they didn't crack off like icicles."

"Well, they didn't, and it's nothing you did, anyway."

He sank to his knees, his face looking even more strained than before. "The cold burns just like fire, Mattie. Your hands will swell up with blisters and the skin will slough off. If you're lucky, the scars won't be bad."

Outside of Jesse's finding her before she froze to death, Mattie hadn't noticed luck favoring her lately, but she saw no point in saying so. Jesse looked burdened enough without her crying over spilled milk—or scars. "I can always wear gloves in polite company, Jesse, and nobody ever sees a lady's feet but her husband—and I have no husband."

"Mattie "—he swallowed again— "Mattie, I think you'll lose some toes. The little one on your left foot for sure, and maybe more. I can't be certain."

Mattie turned her head and closed her eyes. She thought she might like to sleep again. Maybe she would wake up to find that Jesse was wrong. Odd how she found losing a toe so much more frightening than losing her life. Perhaps because she would have died whole, while living with part of herself missing—even such an insignificant part—seemed so terrible.

She heard him calling her name, then felt his fingers pressing against the side of her throat. He had done the same thing at the fire—searched for her heartbeat and gave her his own strength. She wished he wouldn't. She wished he would let her go to whatever the darkness held.

"Don't let her die now. Don't let her die wrapped in a horse blanket in a stinking, dirt-floored line cabin with no one to hold her hand but the bastard who dishonored her."

She took a deep breath and opened her eyes. Her tears felt scalding hot against her cheeks. Jesse had killed for her; she could at least live for him.

She could also ease his mind of foolish guilt. "We sinned together, Jesse," she whispered.

He caught her hand and kissed its palm, then carefully released it. "That's what I told myself and that's what I told you the day I married Caroline. We're both good at believing my lies. When I first met you in your father's office, you were so young, so fragile, so beautiful, and so damn unhappy you made my heart ache. I told myself I was taking you along on the cattle drive to the Panhandle because you needed to be respected as a woman, not treated like an idiot girl child good for nothing but pouring tea and wearing pretty dresses. I told myself I'd rid you of the foolish notion that you must live your life to please others. I told myself you would be a happier woman in Texas."

"I am a happier woman," she said and felt anger begin to stir when he ignored her.

"I lied, Mattie. It wasn't just my heart that ached. It was my body, too. I brought you along because I wanted you and I wasn't strong enough or honorable enough to leave you behind. Once the drive started there was no one to protect you against me but an old Negro and a worthless husband, and you couldn't protect yourself. You didn't know how. You were an innocent young girl for all that you were a wife, and sheltered like a hothouse rose by your reprobate of a father. You had no defenses against a man as hard as me."

"I was such a weak-minded, addlepated female, so helpless in the face of your masculine wiles."

He heard her then, and his eyebrows drew together in displeasure at her interruption. "I touched you when I had no call to. I kissed you when I had no right."

"As I remember, I kissed you first—when you threw me in the Canadian to rid me of lice. My first step down the road to perdition."

"You kissed me on the hand in gratitude!" he yelled. "That didn't give me any excuse to take your mouth and kiss you like I was starving for your taste!"

She licked her lips and smiled. "And I knelt there in the river and let you."

He clenched his jaw. He always did that when they argued and he was losing, she thought. "Don't you understand what I said? The fault was mine. The sin was mine. My time as your trail boss and ranch manager was one long seduction, Mattie Jo Hunter."

"It was certainly long enough. It took you four years to finally seduce me. The average man would have given up, but you always were uncommonly stubborn, Jesse."

Jesse looked like a cornered man with no idea how it had come about. "Goddamn it, Mattie, if it weren't for me you wouldn't be in this filthy cabin half frozen to death."

She nodded thoughtfully. "That's true. I'd be dead."

"That's not what I meant!" he exclaimed.

"I know what you meant. If it wasn't for you, I'd still be in Pueblo."

"Yes! And you'd be safe," he added.

"And completely frozen to death."

"What are you saying?" he asked, staring at her as if he was afraid the cold had addled her wits.

"I was dying in Pueblo—or at least the part of me that mattered. I was turning to ice, freezing to death in the cold of others' expectations. Even a hothouse rose needs the sun to live, Jesse."

He shook his head. "Not my kind of sun, Mattie."

"Whose then? Samuel's? My father's?"

"You would have found your own sun, Mattie, if I hadn't interfered. You'd be warm and safe and respected and living a gentle life that didn't grind you down like a mill does corn."

"I wouldn't know, Jesse. I can't judge a life I haven't lived. I can only judge this one."

He sank back on his heels and let his head drop to his chest. "I'm sorry, Mattie."

"Jesse?"

He lifted his head and she slapped him. Her hand burned and tingled so from returning circulation, she judged that the blow really did hurt her more than him. "You should be sorry, Jesse. I don't allow any man to call me foolish anymore."

"I didn't call you foolish!"

"I'm not a spineless female to be seduced into a man's bed either—particularly the bed of a man who took nearly four years to accomplish his ends. If I was as weak as you say, I would have given up when you left me—or found another man's bed to share. But I didn't. You saved my spirit from freezing in Pueblo and you saved my body from freezing tonight. You taught me to survive and you taught me to manage my own affairs, but you did not seduce me. I lay with you of my own free will, so take that hangdog look off your face, Jesse McDade. Your wife may need a guilt-ridden man, but I don't."

"You damn sure need a man of some kind, Mattie Jo Hunter! What in God's name were you doing out in this blizzard?"

"I was cutting my fence so my cattle wouldn't die!" she shouted, raising herself up to lean on one elbow. "What were you doing?"

"I was cutting your fence!"

She felt her nipples tighten under the blankets and heat that had nothing to do with the warming air that flushed her skin. Her womb contracted as though his body was already filling hers. Other women were wooed with flowers and soft words. That Hunter woman was wooed through her land.

Mattie touched his arm. It was rigid as iron beneath her fingers. "Why, Jesse?"

He drew a shaky breath and raised his eyes to meet hers. "I owed you my daughter's life, and" —he licked his lips while she waited expectantly— "and I couldn't let you lose your cattle if I could help it. I can't stand by and let you suffer—ever. I can't stay out of your life even if I have to beg outside your door like a poor relation. When I found you asleep in the snow and so white and cold, I blamed myself for bringing you to this pass. While I waited to see if you would waken, I nearly promised God that I would leave Texas—that I would never see you or take your side again—if only He would let you live."

He reached out to stroke her cheek, then let his hand trail down to rest between her breasts, over the golden locket she still wore. "I never made that promise to God because I knew I'd never keep it. I can't give you up if it costs me everything I have. I'm weaker than you, Mattie. You could smile at my wedding to another woman. I'd shoot the man you tried to marry. You're so deep inside me that our hearts beat with the same rhythm when we touch. When your heart stops, so will mine. But the reverse isn't true. If I die first, you'll grieve—maybe even for the rest of your life—but you'll go on living without me because that's the kind of woman you are. A whole woman in and of yourself. I'm a whole man only when you make me so."

He shifted his hand until it covered her breast. "You called me the sun, but it is you who warms me. And I've been so cold since I left you, Mattie."

She saw his need in his eyes, felt it in his calloused fingertips that brushed her nipple, and in his helpless trembling when she stroked his aroused body. But need was as far as he would go unless she deemed otherwise. For all his talk of seduction, Jesse McDade would not take what she did not offer. She knew that as surely as she knew they would lie together this night as they had so many other nights, but this time Jesse's would be the greater sin. She was free but he was not. He was vulnerable to her as he had never been before. She could claim him openly, drive Caroline from the Panhandle in complete humiliation, and Mattie Jo Hunter would have it all: the land *and* the man.

And she could not do it.

"Come warm yourself, Jesse, for as long as the storm lasts."

She saw first the angry denial in his eyes, then the dawning acknowledgment of what she already knew: He might not be able to give her up, but he couldn't live with her either. He had no right to destroy Caroline McDade, and Mattie Hunter had no right to ask it of him.

"For as long as the storm lasts," he agreed.

CHAPTER

18

The storm raged for three days and three nights.

On the fourth day the sun rose on a pure white prairie on which the only discernible landmarks were a few windmills poking their blades out of snowdrifts twice as tall as a man's head. Tree branches, snapped off by the weight of the ice and snow, littered the banks of the Canadian and its tributary creeks. Cowboys caught in line shacks that dotted the boundaries of the large ranches burned first the meager furnishings, then tore shelves off the walls, when they ran out of buffalo chips and firewood. They ate jerky and canned tomatoes when they could no longer cook beans and biscuits for lack of a fire. Those men fortunate enough to be at the various headquarters when the blizzard hit fared better. At least they had plenty of food and firewood and one another's company. But no one was really warm. The ferocious wind blew snow through cracks around ill-fitting windows and doors and the cold seeped through walls and up from floors. Cowboys and their bosses alike huddled in heavy clothing close to potbellied stoves and waited out the storm. When the weather finally cleared, the snow was so deep and the drifts so high a man could scarcely dig his way from bunkhouse to barn without losing his way. If he did manage to saddle a horse, he might still lose his way before he rode a mile. Staring into the light reflecting off the snow would blind a man as quickly as staring into the sun.

Tom Miller disregarded such obstacles. He would blind every horse and man on the place and kill them too if that's what it took to find Mattie. He would have ridden out in the blizzard itself the minute he discovered Mattie missing if Jubilee hadn't laid the barrel of his Winchester across the side of Tom's head, then tied him up hand and foot like a calf ready for branding.

No amount of cursing changed Jubilee's mind. "Miss Mattie's either daid, and there ain't no sense in killing yourself looking for her body, or she's holed up somewhere waiting to be rescued. Whichever way it is, she gonna have to wait and so is you."

"Goddamn it, Jubilee, don't you care that she's out there alone?"

Jubilee's face didn't soften in spite of the tears running down his cheeks. "I cares, Tom. I probably cares more than anybody on this place. I been watching over her since she was borned. If she daid, I'll be watching over her grave. But that don't change nothing. You white men don't take to the idea of waiting, but I was a slave. I knows there's times a man's gots to wait 'cause there's nothing else he can do. You gots to take things as they come, do what you can, and wait out the rest."

Tom mulled over Jubilee's words as he had done

again and again since the afternoon he had burst through that line shack door and found Mattie feverish and unconscious and missing the little toe on her left foot. Mostly it was good advice. Tom had taken things as they came and followed the sound of Jesse McDade's gunshots to the shack, so he hadn't blinded any horses or men searching for Mattie. He had done what he could—loaning McDade a horse, wrapping Mattie up and holding her in his arms as he rode back to headquarters—and he had waited as days turned to weeks while she lay in a feverish stupor brought on by pneumonia and calling him by Jesse's name.

Mattie was well now, and the long winter looked to be over. The snow had melted, mud was thick underfoot, the pastures were greening up, a spring breeze was blowing, and Tom no longer intended to take things as they came. He had waited long enough.

He turned away from Mattie's window and studied her as she sat up in bed sipping a cup of coffee. Her hands were streaked with shiny pink skin to replace that which frostbite had killed, and her hair was a little thinner from the fever. Not that anyone would notice, thought Tom. Mattie still had more hair than the prairie had new grass, and it was still the color of newly minted gold coins. Freshly washed, it rippled over her shoulders and breasts like golden waves and smelled of rose water—which was a damn sight better than smelling of sickness and Jesse McDade.

Mattie set her coffee cup down. "What's the matter, Tom? You've been staring at me this morning as though you'd never seen me before. You did the same thing yesterday and the day before and every day since I woke up and started getting well. I know I'm skinny as a broomstick, as Jubilee would say, but have I changed so much? Or has some catastrophe happened that you don't want to tell me about? That's it, isn't it? My cattle died after all. I didn't cut enough of the fence. Is that it? Tell me, damn it. I'm perfectly well now if still a little weak. I won't fall into a faint at bad news, and I want to know."

"Your cattle are fine, Mattie. I've told you that every day since you came to your senses and knew me. I don't rightly know how many head you may have lost yet, and won't until Hank and the boys gather them up and drive them back to Bar H pastures, but you're in a damn sight better shape than anybody else in the Panhandle—you and Jesse McDade—so stop fretting about it."

"How bad were the losses for the other ranchers, Tom?" she asked.

Tom hesitated. He hadn't talked much to her about what folks were already calling the Big Die Up because he hadn't wanted her bothered until she was well. Tears had come to her too easily while she was sick. But she looked stronger today.

"The nester ranchers are wiped out, Mattie. Lost every head each of them had. They're selling up and moving on. The big ranchers aren't in much better shape. If the LX can round up a thousand head, I'll be surprised. The XIT, the LIT, the Frying Pan—all of them are hit hard. I heard some men estimating losses between twenty and ninety percent of their herds—maybe two hundred thousand head in the whole Panhandle. Lee over at the LS looks to be all right. He didn't have as much of his pasture fenced and his cattle drifted into the breaks and sheltered there."

Mattie smiled. "You might know W.M.D. Lee would land jam side up. What about the drift fence, Tom? How many cattle died?"

Tom wiped his face with his hand. He wished he

could wipe out his memory, too. "It was a deathtrap just like you predicted, Mattie. A man could walk for miles across the Panhandle on the frozen bodies of dead animals without touching the ground with his feet. Frozen cattle are stacked up in piles four hundred yards wide in some places—some of them frozen standing up. I heard the LX boys have been skinning two hundred and fifty cattle to the mile and they'd done nearly thirty-five miles. Gossip says a merchant over in Mobeetie has already bought forty-five thousand cowhides from various ranchers. That's damn near all some of them have to sell."

Mattie turned pale and closed her eyes. "Dear God," she whispered. "Why wouldn't the other ranchers listen to me?"

Tom sat down of the edge of the bed and rested his arms on his thighs, his hands dangling loosely between his knees. "A man don't like to take advice from a woman, Mattie—particularly about business."

"I've noticed men are fools sometimes," she said tartly. "They cut off their noses to spite their faces this time."

He glanced over his shoulder at her. "That's not the only reason. Remember, a bunch of these ranches are owned by the syndicates, and most boards of directors weren't fixing to listen to a bunch of cowboys or pioneer ranchers with cow dung on their boots who tried to warn them not to trust the weather. But all those foreigners saw was free grass and high prices and mostly easy winters the last eight years. They didn't take notice when last winter was so bad up north. They never thought it could happen here, but it has. They didn't know this country and they didn't listen to the folks who did and now they're ruined. They'll be selling up, too,

Mattie, if not this year, then the next or the one after. I see it coming."

"When they do, I'll buy some of their holdings." She rubbed the scar under her chin, and her eyes held a look that reminded him of the Colonel. She had inherited some of her daddy's scavenger instincts.

Tom clasped his hands together. "You best look to repairing what the fire and the blizzard did instead of biting off more than you can chew, Mattie. The beef bonanza in the Panhandle—and everywhere else—is over whether you or anybody else wants to believe it or not. By the time it's said and done, I believe the losses on the plains—from the Panhandle north to Canada—will run more than a million head. Maybe a lot more than that."

"But I didn't lose my cattle, Tom. I saved mine. I'll have cattle to sell this spring and fall and they ought to bring high prices. I'll have money to buy more land if anyone's interested in selling."

"You can't buy up enough land to hold back change, Mattie, and that's what you're trying to do whether you admit it or not. You want to keep things the way they were when you and Jesse first built up this range."

"'Dwell in a time too late,'" murmured Mattie, her eyes looking backward into a past that Tom knew he had no part of. She blinked and focused on him once more. "That's what the sheepherder who sold us the plaza headquarters said he planned to do—live in a time he chose for as long as he could."

"That ain't gonna be long for you, Mattie," said Tom bluntly. "With no cows on their land and banks leery to loan them money for new herds, the syndicates will break up the big ranches. Most of them have been fencing in school lands they don't own anyway. The land commissioner down in Austin is under fire not to sell big blocks of free land to a single man—and the railroads won't do it anymore either. The railroads want people living on the land—lots of people. There's no money to be made running trains across prairies empty of people, and shipping cattle back east is seasonal work. The railroad men will sell the land the state granted them— what's left that you and Jesse and Charlie Goodnight didn't buy—to as many people as they can. The more people, the more money. That means men with plows. The farmers and small ranchers will move into this country—and soon. It's all coming together at the same time—barbed wire, the storm wiping out the big cattlemen, the railroad due next year, pressure from Austin, the farmers coming."

"That all has nothing to do with me, Tom."

"It means the final end to open range, Mattie. It means you won't control the ballot box by telling your men to vote as a block. You'll be outnumbered. You'll be surrounded by more folks, each one owning less land than you but together having more influence."

She shook her head impatiently. "I've always gotten along with the nester ranchers and other folks who only own a section or two. God knows, I get along better with them than I do most of the big ranchers. I don't see any reason for newcomers to resent me."

He saw she really didn't understand. Or maybe she didn't want to. "There'll be towns springing up, Mattie. Churches, schools, ladies' reading circles. Law and order won't be a hit-or-miss proposition anymore. I guess you might say the Panhandle is about to be civilized, and that means folks will be expected to mind their manners a little better." He leaned over to touch the golden locket she wore round her neck. "And you and McDade can no longer live like nobody else's opinion matters."

She closed her hand around the locket. "What is between Jesse and me is none of your business, Tom."

He couldn't remember the last time he'd lost his temper, but he was damn close to losing it now. "What do you aim to do about Jesse McDade?"

Her eyes narrowed and a telltale blush colored her pale cheeks. "I'm sure I don't know what you're talking about."

"Jesse made you a whore again in your neighbors' eyes. What do you intend to do about it? What does *he* intend to do about it?"

"I don't hear anyone calling me a whore but you, Tom Miller! Jesse saved my life! He was the only man with grit enough to ride out in the storm and cut my fences. Something *you* didn't do."

Tom felt like somebody had slapped a cinch around his chest and was pulling it tight. He ought to tell her that Jubilee kept him hog-tied for most of two days, but be damned if he would. If she could believe he was a coward after all the years she'd known him, then to hell with her. He was a patient man, but he wasn't much good at groveling—not even for Mattie Hunter.

She leaned toward him. "I saved my cows and Jesse saved me. That's all anybody needs to know."

"But that's not all everybody's saying, Mattie."

"I don't care what the neighbors are saying. I lost my reputation. I also lost my toe, if you recall. But I saved my cows. I'd make the same trade again."

"That's not all you traded, Mattie. You smelled of Jesse McDade's scent and seed. No woman smells like that if she hasn't been loved long and hard."

Her blush deepened at his words. "And you wish it had been you!" she cried.

Tom drew a breath and let it out slowly. "I reckon I do."

"Jesse would put a bullet through your jealous heart before he'd let you touch me in that way."

"He was a Texas Ranger, I heard somewhere. And an Indian fighter. Between the two professions I figure he's killed men who galled him a lot less than I do. But that's not what stopped me from drawing down on him in the shack after I smelled him all over you. It was your sickness—and something Jubilee said. Sometimes a man has to wait because there's nothing else he can do. What was wrong with you couldn't be put right by my getting riled up and shooting Jesse McDade. Not right then, anyway. I left it for later. Now is later."

Mattie clutched his arm, her eyes as huge in her thin face. "Leave Jesse be."

Tom freed his arm from her grip. "He wronged two women by marrying, and he wronged both women again by lying with you. The way I see it, he's got to set things right. One way is for him to get shed of his wife and take up with you legally since it appears he's going to do it every chance he gets, anyway. The other way is for me to shoot him. I figure that would put three people out of their misery. Four—if you count me."

Mattie's body went rigid. Tom figured she'd pull out that .45 she always kept under her pillow, and he'd end up gut shot on the floor. He wasn't real sure he cared one way or the other. He certainly couldn't hurt any worse than he was hurting now. All the years he had drifted looking for a land to claim and a woman to love and he had found both too late.

Suddenly Mattie sagged back against the pillows. "He can't make it right. I won't let him."

Tom felt sweat trickle down his back. "That didn't stop him from crawling into bed with you."

Mattie closed her eyes. "I judged adultery was a lesser wrong than husband stealing."

Tom thought he would rather Mattie had shot him after all. He had always laid most of the blame for Mattie's indiscretions on Jesse. He was a fool. Mattie Hunter made her own choices, and if he felt betrayed, it was his own fault.

"I don't think your distinction is one other folks are likely to hold in high regard," Tom said. "Jesse's wife, for instance. I don't think she's going to appreciate another woman saving her marriage."

Mattie opened her eyes. "Caroline would believe the worst if Jesse had never touched me. Just the fact that he rode out to help me is enough. And I wasn't strong or noble or honorable enough to turn him away. I may never be that strong. You might as well try to put out a prairie fire with spit as to dampen the heat between Jesse and me."

Her features took on a brooding expression. "But I didn't take anything from Caroline that she really wanted, Tom. She has Jesse's name, Jesse's money, and Jesse's child. And everyone's sympathy as the wronged woman. Don't forget that. She won't. As for me, I'm the woman Jesse McDade scorned—again— for Caroline. That ought to set the tongues wagging. That Hunter woman had a second chance to trap Jesse McDade—and she failed again. No one will ever know I chose to fail because as much as I hate Caroline McDade, she is innocent. She did not deliberately set herself against me by marrying Jesse, and I cannot allow Jesse to divorce her."

She hesitated, and Tom hoped never to see another such expression on her face. It was the look of a woman bleeding deep inside who knew she was beyond help. Worse, she was beyond hope.

"There is no setting right what is wrong."

Tom leaned over and cupped her face between his hands. "Maybe not, Mattie, but I can stop the talk. I can marry you."

CHAPTER

19

March 1886

They called it the Big Fight when four men were shot down in Tascosa on March 21. Ostensibly, it was a long-standing quarrel that got out of hand between Lem Woodruff and LS cowboy Ed King over the favors of a saloon girl named Sally Emory. But Mattie knew the roots of the trouble had little to do with a woman and a lot to do with leftover bitterness between nester ranchers and those who still did a spot of mavericking, and the big ranchers. Nobody had forgotten the cowboy strike and Pat Garrett and his Home Rangers. Ed King and the two other LS cowboys killed had been Home Rangers, while Lem Woodruff and three other men charged with the murders were members of the nester faction. The fourth body found dead in the street when the sun rose was that of Jesse Sheets, a café owner who belonged to neither camp, but had the misfortune to get in the way of a bullet.

Red had the bad luck to be playing cards in the back room of Jenkins's saloon when three LS cowboys burst in to find the man who had just killed Ed King. Red was definitely more sympathetic to the nester faction, but he swore to Mattie before he died that he hadn't drawn a gun—just stood up at the wrong time and been gut shot by Frank Valley. In the resulting gunfight Red had crawled out the saloon's back door and lived long enough to ride back to the Bar H and die on Mattie's front porch.

Mattie sent Tom and thirty Bar H men to Tascosa the next morning with orders to find Frank Valley and have him arrested or shoot him—whichever was most convenient. Tom hadn't argued with her, but he hadn't followed orders either. In fact, she could hardly believe what he had done.

"Frank Valley was already dead, Mattie, and nobody has mentioned seeing Red shot. Everybody that wasn't already shooting emptied out of that saloon like hornets out of a nest, and I don't think a soul knows that Red is the fifth victim. He was just another cowboy anxious to get out the best way he could."

Mattie clenched her fists, conscious of Red's body, bathed and laid out in her dining room. "He got out, but not the best way. I want Mr. Lee and Mr. Scott to know that the next time any of the LS men look crosswise at one of my men, I'll carry the fight onto their doorstep. We'll settle this quarrel between the little men and the big ranchers once and for all."

"I heard in town that some of the LS boys were in favor of settling things, too. There's wild rumors that some of the cowboys want to hang all the opposition, then burn Tascosa down to the ground to make sure they didn't miss anybody, but I talked to McAllister, the LS ranch manager, and he's not going to let his men carry on the fight. There's too many folks in Tascosa that just want both sides to make peace. Everyone's fed up, Mattie, and this fight just about finished off any sympathy no matter which side of the fence a person's standing on."

"Is that some of your civilization, Tom? Shake hands and forget what happened?"

Tom looked at her with that guarded expression he had worn since she refused his proposal. "I never knew you to be so bloodthirsty, Mattie."

She sat down behind her desk. She still tired easily, but her weariness had more to do with mind than body. Tom talked to her, was polite enough, but he wasn't her companion any longer. And she wasn't easy with him. She kept thinking of him as a man who longed to touch her in all the ways Jesse did, and she grew flustered. She did not love Tom, but she respected him, depended on him, and liked him as well as anyone she had ever known. She did not like this distance between them.

She felt lonely.

She looked up at Tom, standing in front of her desk with his Stetson in his hands and appearing as calm as always. She felt as if she were stepping onto quicksand and didn't know which patch would suck her under every time she talked to him now. She just didn't know Tom Miller anymore.

"I don't want a range war, Tom, but I can't allow anyone to take advantage of me—or to think they can. I can't allow Red's killing to go unavenged. I have to do something."

Tom sat down in his favorite chair in front of her desk and stretched his long legs out. "I never talked to the sheriff. Nobody knows Red died because of the fight. I put it out that he got throwed from his horse and broke his neck while hurrying on back to tell you what was happening. I said we were burying him in the Hunter cemetery tomorrow so the Bar H wouldn't be sending anybody to Tascosa to attend the four funerals there. I didn't think it was a good idea to let our men mix with the LS boys."

Mattie rose and leaned over her desk to shout at him. "How dare you make my decisions for me! How dare you expect me to bury Red like I was ashamed of him!"

"I figured you'd see it that way. That's why I just went ahead and did it without saying anything to you beforehand. Keeping your name out of this mess was the last thing I could do for you, Mattie. In the first place, there's no way to win a feud. One wrong just leads to another. In the second place, I didn't want to remind Sheriff East that there was another woman besides Sally Emory who might have sparked off murder. The sheriff is a stubborn cuss and he still don't rest easy about Samuel's murder. Won't do to stir him up. You did enough of that when you and McDade got stranded during the storm. Right now he's got his hands full tracking down and arresting Woodruff and his friends. Don't sidetrack him."

Tom stood up, put on his Stetson, and rested his thumbs in his gun belt. He looked dangerous—and sad. Mattie had never thought of him before as dangerous. "I'll go tell the boys that we'll have Red's burial tomorrow. Closed casket at the grave in case some of his friends who ride for other brands come to pay their respects. His new suit hides the hole in his belly well enough, but there's not much we can do to cover up his face. That bullet went in one cheek and out the other and nobody's going to believe a horse is responsible."

Mattie swallowed back bile. "Please, Tom."

A look of pity flickered briefly across his face but disappeared between one heartbeat and the next. "If

you talk range war, Mattie, you best get used to seeing shot-up men. Get used to soaking the blood out
of your dresses, because you'll have more men die
with their heads in your lap."

She put her hands over her ears and bowed her
head, but she couldn't stop the funeral procession
of memories: Squinty Smith, one cheek swelled out
with tobacco, riding off to the fire; Red, never without a grin except when confronting her during the
cowboy strike; Samuel in the days before they left
for Texas, flicking dust off his coat with a graceful,
languid gesture; even Clint Murray strolled across
her mind.

Dead. All dead.

"Mattie?"

She lowered her hands and lifted her head. She
hesitated, rubbing the slick new skin on the back of
her hand. Jubilee had assured her that the scars
would fade with time until no one noticed them.
Perhaps. Perhaps not. Like her scars, perhaps the bitterness between the nester and the big rancher would
fade. Then again, perhaps it would only fade until hot
tempers and cold anger brought it to the fore.

But it would not be Mattie Hunter's temper that
set off a war.

"I will not carry on the fight. Red's murderer is dead.
A life for a life. Tell the men to hold their tongues. I will
not bring in the law for no good purpose."

Tom nodded. "I'll have Hank tell the men."

Uneasiness tightened her throat. "No. You do it.
I'm making you manager of the Bar H."

Want shadowed his eyes for a moment, then he
shook his head. "Give the job to Hank. He's a good
man and has no need to leave. I'll be moving on after
Red's burying tomorrow."

Mattie sprang up, knocking her chair to the floor.
"Leave? But you can't. I need you."

"I'm past forty, Mattie, and I've been looking for a home place all my life. I thought I found what I was looking for on the Bar H but I was wrong. I gambled and I lost. No point in staying in the game any longer. I knew from the first hand I was playing against a stacked deck, but like a fool I thought I could still win."

She came around the desk to grip his hands. "This is because I refused you, isn't it, Tom? I hurt you and I didn't mean to. I'm sorry. I knew you were fond of me, but so are many of my other men. You never touched me in any way but that of a friend. You never asked anything of me as a woman. You never looked at me with heat in your eyes."

He squeezed her hands. "I decided a long time ago I wouldn't dishonor you by taking liberties with you. As for asking anything of you as a woman, I did, and you gave it to me. A woman has more to offer than just her body, Mattie. Loyalty, easy conversation after supper, sharing her thoughts, giving comfort to a man when he's downhearted, crying in a man's arms when she's the one feeling low. And trust. That's the hardest thing for a woman to give a man, and you gave yours to me."

He smiled at her. "And heat, Mattie? I looked at you with heat, but you didn't notice. There is fire that warms you and fire that makes you burn. I'm one, but Jesse McDade is the other. You can't feel my warmth for his fire, so I reckon I better hunt for a woman who can."

"But she won't be me," said Mattie involuntarily.

Tom smiled again. "No, she won't be you. But I won't forget the prettiest woman in Texas, Mattie." He gently freed his hands. "We'll not talk alone again. We've said what needs to be said and any further conversation would be uncomfortable for both of us."

She grabbed hold of his loose vest with both hands. "No. You can't leave. You own six sections inside my south pasture."

"I'll sell them to you for a fair price, Mattie."

"I don't want to buy them! I want you to stay here. There are respectable women in the Panhandle. Marry one and build a house on your land. You can still be my manager and live with your wife and family instead of here."

His eyes turned stern. "I won't wrong a woman by making her live in your backyard, Mattie."

He loosened her hands, then stood looking down at her face, his expression bringing a blush to her cheeks. "I will do one thing, Mattie, and I won't ask your permission first. This is one time you don't have to make a choice."

He cupped the back of her head in one hand and, leaning down, covered her mouth with his own. He smelled of crisp Panhandle air and warm sunshine, leather and the musky scent of a man. She parted her lips under the pressure of his and felt the gentle stroking of his tongue. He tasted of coffee and the sweet molasses he had poured over Jubilee's flapjacks at breakfast. She swayed against him and clutched his vest again while the kiss went on and on until she had no breath but what he gave her of his own.

He lifted his head and stepped back, gently freeing himself of her clutching hands. "Good-bye, Mattie."

She watched him walk to the door before he turned one last time to look at her. She felt herself being memorized and knew that wherever he was and for as long as time lasted, he would remember her as she was this moment. She wished she had worn something more elegant than a plain white waist and brown wool skirt.

She stretched her hand toward him as though to hold him back as she thought of all the years past when he had always walked by her side and all the lonely years ahead when she would walk alone. He was as much a part of herself as Jesse, and she was suddenly terrified. "Tom, if I need you, will you come?"

He smiled, that gentle smile that had always reassured her. "You'll do all right, Mattie Jo Hunter."

True to his word, Tom Miller left the Bar H the morning after Red's funeral without further conversation with Mattie. He rode out the same way he had ridden in: on a sorrel gelding with a bedroll and slicker tied behind his saddle. He took nothing with him he had not brought except Mattie's tears and the cowboys' somber faces. He left nothing behind but an empty cot in the bunkhouse, an empty chair at the dining room table, and an empty place in Mattie's life.

He hired on as temporary manager for George Faulkner's Four F ranch, which the Scotsman had bought from his father's syndicate after the Big Die Up left the operation with less than ten percent of its cattle and massive losses posted in its ledger books. Mattie pinched her lips together when she heard of Tom's new job and said nothing. She would not hold it against Tom that he now rode for Faulkner's brand. It was not Tom's fault—or the Scotsman's either—that Faulkner and the pain and humiliation of her beating would be forever tangled together in her mind. She had stolen three years of Tom's life. Let him now build a future as best he could without her displaying hurt feelings at his choices. She owed him that much—and he owed her nothing.

Mattie squared her shoulders and prepared to live without Tom as she had learned to live without Red and Squinty and even Jesse. If she was lonely and sometimes woke up in the middle of the night with her heart pounding with fear, she never mentioned it. She would survive.

She would do all right.

On April 1, with three of the men charged with murder for their part in the Big Fight in the Tascosa jail, and the fourth, Lem Woodruff, lying between life and death from bullet wounds, Sheriff Jim East turned his attention back to Mattie. Backed by twelve hastily appointed and heavily armed deputies, many of them LS boys, he rode up to the Bar H, arriving at midmorning when most of Mattie's cowboys were scattered hither and yon on the ranch.

Mattie met him on the porch. She was backed by her three-year-old son and an ex-slave.

She surveyed the men spread out in a semicircle in front of her house, recognizing several. "Well, boys, work must be slack on the LS if Mr. Lee and Mr. Scott can afford to loan you out to the sheriff for a day."

The men stared back at her with no expression save excited curiosity. They knew her and she knew them—there were too few people in the Panhandle for any to remain strangers—but for all the easy talk they had done about her, most had never passed the time of day with that Hunter woman.

Mattie didn't mind the curiosity, but the air of excitement about the men tightened her throat until it was an effort to keep her voice firm and unemotional when she spoke to East. "Sheriff, I presume you have not ridden all the way from Tascosa for the exercise. Suppose you state your business, but I'll warn you ahead of time that I won't allow you to bother my men about the Big Fight. Although the Bar

H has always been sympathetic toward the little men, no one on my place had any part in that shootout."

Sheriff East rested his hand on his hip within comfortable drawing distance of his gun. "Right interesting that you brought that up, Mrs. Hunter. Witnesses are all kind of confused and telling different stories about what went on, depending on which opinion they hold about the men involved, but one man did mention he saw your ranch manager in Jenkins's saloon."

Mattie lifted her head a little higher. "Several of my men were in Tascosa that night, Sheriff. There was a baile, a dance, at Casimiro Romero's home and as I've always enjoyed cordial relations with Mr. Romero, my men were invited. But they all cut for home when the fight started. They all know better than to do any shooting except at lobos and rattlesnakes and rustlers without my permission, and while I might argue that Ed King and his partners fall into one of those catagories, my men did not draw their guns."

"That brings up another interesting point, Mrs. Hunter. If nobody does any shooting on the Bar H without orders from you, then you still claim none of your men shot your husband and Murray?"

Mattie felt her hands began to shake and clasped them together. She heard Jubilee shift his feet beside her and threw him a warning glance. It wasn't necessary. As a slave, Jubilee had learned early to hide his feelings behind a mask.

Mattie moistened her lips. "None of my men shot Samuel or Murray."

Sheriff East nodded. "I just wanted to hear you say it again in front of witnesses. I don't want to arrest a prominent rancher and have it turn out some cowboy did the actual killing."

Mattie felt her heart began to pound. Jesse! Dear God, he was going to arrest Jesse! "I don't recall Samuel having a serious difference of opinion with another rancher. How could he have? I ran this ranch and everyone knew it. I was the one the other ranchers found disagreeable. Shooting Samuel would not change that."

"You're quite a talker, Mrs. Hunter. Your problem is you talked too much. My witness feels bad about holding back the truth so long, but she feels worse about turning in another woman. She said she might never have done it if she hadn't begun to worry that her own life was in danger."

Mattie swayed and grabbed Jubilee's arm. The blood pounded in her ears until she was nearly deafened by it. "She? Who are you talking about?"

Sheriff East moved his hand to rest it on the grip of his revolver. "Mrs. Caroline McDade swore to me yesterday that you rode to her place a few hours before your husband was murdered. She swore that you were a little bruised and a lot furious. You told her that you planned to return home and shoot Samuel Hunter and Clint Murray down like dogs. She further swore that you told her you would no longer permit Samuel Hunter to stand between you and what you wanted. You wanted the Bar H free and clear of Hunter's interference."

"That's a lie, Sheriff! I told her Samuel had beat me. I never told her I intended to kill him. Never! She's lying because she's a jealous woman."

"I don't doubt that, Mrs. Hunter. But she's also a frightened woman. She said you tried to lure her husband away during the blizzard, but he refused. Now she's afraid you'll murder her so you can claim Jesse McDade."

"That woman hates Miss Mattie so bad, she make up any kind of lies to hurt her. And her lies don't make no sense nohow. You think Miss Mattie can't get any man she takes a fancy to just by snapping her fingers? And just what does Jesse say 'bout all this? 'Pears to me that if two hens is fighting over a rooster, the rooster ought to be crowing, but I ain't heard you say nothing about hearing him."

"Mrs. McDade came alone," said Sheriff East without looking away from Mattie. "Jesse ain't back from gathering up his herds that drifted during the winter, but there's nothing he could say if he was here. Mrs. McDade never told him what Mrs. Hunter said. Now that's where that particular rooster stands unless you know something that needs to be told."

Mattie shuddered at the inquisitory expression in his eyes. East might take Caroline McDade's story at face value, but he was reluctant to give up his suspicions of Jesse.

"Hush up, Jubilee!" Mattie snapped, digging her nails into his arm. She had to think, had to refute Caroline's story and protect Jesse at the same time, and she would fail at both if Jubilee didn't hold his tongue.

"The blizzard was in January, Sheriff," she said, raising her voice. "Why did Mrs. McDade wait so long to decide I was planning to kill her? For that matter, why did she wait over a year to tell the truth about a woman she suspected was after her husband?"

"She felt sorry for you, Mrs. Hunter," said East. "And she felt some loyalty toward you as a member of her sex. Then, too, she was in the family way and ladies like her don't seek out public attention at such a time. But when Jesse McDade saved your life and you tried to tempt him into divorcing his wife, Mrs. McDade knew she was in danger. She waited until the weather warmed up and the mud dried to ride into Tascosa."

Of all Caroline's lies, Mattie believed the last one without reservation. Caroline wouldn't risk muddy shoes and skirts when a few weeks' wait didn't matter one way or the other.

"I don't believe you can convict me on such evidence, Sheriff. A jury would recognize Caroline's story as the ravings of a jealous woman."

"That's up to the jury, Mrs. Hunter. For myself, I've got a warrant for your arrest for the murder of Samuel Hunter and Clint Murray on or about the fifteeth of March, 1885."

Jesse rode into Tascosa at noon five days after Mattie's arrest. A hundred heavily armed cowboys from the Bar H and his own Flying MJ surrounded him. Jubilee followed in Mattie's buggy, his Winchester out of sight on the floorboard under his feet. Respected as Jubilee was in Tascosa and elsewhere, Jesse didn't want to take a chance on resurrecting any buried prejudice against Negroes carrying guns. Feelings were running too high as it was, and his army of men constituted enough of a spark to ignite another gunfight without giving some drunken ignoramus with nothing to commend him but his white skin an excuse to voice a foolish belief. Jubilee resented the necessity of Jesse's order but obeyed anyway. He was too old and too wise to believe resentment ever changed anything and more often than not got a man killed.

Jesse's first stop was the Exchange Hotel where Mattie was held under house arrest, the jail being already occupied by Lem Woodruff's partners in the Big Fight. Lem himself still languished at Theodore Briggs's house and was something of a hero to many of the local citizens. They figured anyone who lived through an appendectomy performed by a .45-caliber bullet, then rode three miles leaking blood must have right on his side.

Mattie's case was more ambiguous. While everyone agreed that Samuel was no decent man to strike a woman, no one was willing to go so far as to say that it justified Mattie's killing him. At least, no man was willing to go that far. Many women, particularly those who lived in Hogtown under the dubious protection of whatever man they managed to persuade to pay their expenses in exchange for female companionship of an intimate nature, were conspicuously reluctant to condemn Mattie on the issue.

Unfortunately, women didn't serve on juries.

On the other hand, the women soundly condemned Mattie for playing up to another woman's husband. Had she been a whore, such loose behavior would have been overlooked as expected of a woman engaged in such a profession. But Mattie claimed to be a respectable woman—though many had doubted it for years—and a respectable woman did not tempt another's husband.

Fortunately, women didn't serve on juries.

But everyone agreed that no woman should be locked up in the same jail as murderers—even if the woman in question had killed two men all by herself. The four murderers charged as a result of the Big Fight had only managed to down one man each. One trail hand, a stranger from Fort Worth who ought to have known not to mix in local affairs, had stated that made Mattie Hunter twice as dangerous as any of the four men. Danny Boone, Mattie's horse wrangler, loosened most of the trail hand's teeth before the other occupants of the Equity Bar broke up the fight. No one called the sheriff. The trail hand was clearly out of line, and Danny was within his rights to straighten him out. No self-respecting cowboy let a stranger insult the brand he rode for.

Jesse handed his reins to Hank Wilson. "Don't stable the horses, and tell the men to spread out and block both ends of the street. But no shooting unless someone else shoots first, which I doubt they will. Nobody wants any more dead bodies littering the real estate, and the boys who ride for the big ranchers aren't in town."

Hank caught Jesse's arm. "Hadn't I better go in with you? There's a deputy with her all the time. He might feel obliged to draw down on you."

Jesse settled his gun belt more comfortably on his hips, took off his right glove, and flexed his fingers. "He's not going to be any more anxious to start a shooting match than I am. I only brought you men along in case the sheriff doesn't prove reasonable about releasing Mattie. I don't think it will come to that." He clasped Hank's shoulder. "When East comes hotfooting over from the courthouse, let him through."

With a last look up and down the street, Jesse entered the hotel and came face to face with the deputy. "I'm here to see Mattie Hunter."

The deputy's eyes darted past Jesse to see the armed cowboys. "Don't start anything, McDade. Mrs. Hunter is a legal prisoner of Oldham County and the sheriff don't want her having any visitors except her lawyer and such of her men as she needs to give orders to about her ranch."

"I'm one of her men," said Jesse, resting his hand on his gun.

Tom Miller stepped out of the shadows behind the deputy, easing a door closed behind him. "Better make an exception and let McDade see her."

Jesse spared a glance at Tom. "I thought you were riding for George Faulkner these days."

Tom shrugged. "Watching out for Mattie is a hard habit to break, and Faulkner allowed as how she needed me more right now than the few scraggly cows the storm left him. I reckon he feels a mite guilty about riding off and leaving her to face Samuel that day." He put on his Stetson, tilting its brim forward so his eyes were shadowed. "Now that you're here, I'll ride on back to the Four F. Mattie won't need me anymore."

Jesse wished he could see Tom's eyes. "Stay awhile, Tom. She'll need you worse than you think."

Jesse felt Tom studying him before the other man finally spoke. "Like that, is it?"

"Yes," Jesse answered, as he turned to the fidgeting deputy. "Unlock the door," he ordered.

With an uneasy glance at both men, the deputy stepped away from the door. "Hell, it ain't locked. Miller here is always running in and out, and besides, Mrs. Hunter gave her word she wouldn't run."

Jesse cast an ironic glance at the deputy as he opened the door and stepped inside the room. Jim East would take Mattie's word she wouldn't escape, but wouldn't believe her when she denied killing Samuel. It was another example of men treating her as an equal on the one hand and an untrustworthy woman on the other.

Mattie was facing the door when he walked in. Her face was pale and her eyes held the first expression of fear Jesse had seen her show in years.

"Jesse!" She swayed and caught the back of a wooden rocker. "Jesse, go home. There's nothing you can do. My lawyer, Temple Houston, feels certain he can obtain bail for me as soon as he catches up with Judge Willis who is holding court at Clarendon. Or is he at Mobeetie?" She tried to smile, but her lips quivered too much. "I can't remember at present where the judge is, but I'm sure Mr. Houston will find him. I never imagined a misunderstanding between two women could kick up such a fuss, but Mr. Houston is certain the grand jury will not indict me. I have so many witnesses to the fact that I was too badly beaten to have tracked Samuel down. Tom has already sworn that I was unconscious when Samuel and Clint left headquarters and didn't wake up for several days."

Jesse kicked the rocker aside and caught Mattie

in his arms. "The sheriff doesn't believe Tom. He thinks Miller is too besotted with you to tell the truth."

Mattie tilted her head back, and Jesse caught his breath as he realized her expression of fear was not for herself but for him.

"But the jury will believe him. Temple Houston is certain of it. And besides, it will be my word against Caroline's, and it isn't honorable to doubt a lady's word, so with all my witnesses and none for Caroline, I'll be acquitted."

"It won't come to a trial, Mattie," he said, lowering his head. "Now kiss me while you can."

She opened her mouth to protest but he covered it with his own. He pulled her more tightly into his arms and closed his mind to everything but the feel of her lips, the taste of her. He had so little time and so many memories to store against the coming years.

"McDade, I reckon you best let go of Mrs. Hunter and explain what you got in mind—you and that army of cowboys outside."

Jesse heard the sheriff's voice and wanted to scream out in protest. He hadn't held Mattie long enough—hadn't kissed her enough. God, would they ever have time together? Reluctantly he ended the kiss and turned around. "I brought them along to make sure Mrs. Hunter got home all right after you released her."

Jim East narrowed his eyes. "And just why would I be releasing her, McDade?"

Jesse unbuckled his gun belt and handed it to the sheriff. "Because I shot Samuel Hunter and Clint Murray, and I'd do the same thing again."

He heard Mattie screaming his name all the way to the jail.

CHAPTER

20

The Exchange Hotel wasn't so far from Tascosa's schoolhouse that Leon couldn't hear his mother screaming. He dropped his head and squirmed with embarrassment. It was bad enough that his mother was under arrest, but that she would holler like that was almost beyond bearing. It wasn't a hurt cry, he knew that; it was more a lost cry like a lobo made when a cowboy killed her mate. It rolled down Tascosa's streets and echoed through the breaks on either side of the Canadian River and finally faded away on the prairies far to the north. She sounded like a woman who had lost her wits, and Leon wondered if he would have to defend her against a charge of craziness along with everything else the town said about her.

He could feel the other children staring at him, could hear a few snickers before the teacher rapped his ruler for attention. Glancing up quickly, Leon marked the boys who laughed. He'd bust their mouths after school and maybe they wouldn't be so quick to call his mother names. He wasn't sure what he would do to the girls. His mother and Jubilee always told him never to hit a girl. Leon didn't think that was fair. Maybe later, when he was full grown and strong, it wouldn't be right, but for now the girls were his same size and some of them were tough as shoe leather. Particularly the ones whose mothers lived in those little houses behind the saloons. Those mothers were whores. He knew that from overhearing men talk both at the Bar H and when he wandered down the streets in Tascosa. Leon wasn't sure exactly what men did with whores but he knew it had something to do with a man's pecker. He had asked Jubilee and Red about it, but both men had told him he was too young to be thinking about such things.

He wished his father wasn't dead. He bet his father would tell him the straight of it. He pushed out of his mind the niggling memory that Samuel Hunter had seldom taken notice of his son except to yell at him. Fathers were supposed to explain men's business to their sons, and Samuel would have if his mother hadn't killed him.

Leon wiped his nose on his sleeve. No, that wasn't right. His mother hadn't killed his father. Jubilee had told him so, and Tom had, too. Jubilee sometimes exaggerated if he thought he had a good enough reason, but Leon had never known Tom to lie. Of course, he didn't know Tom too well. Certainly not as well as he knew Jesse.

Leon shifted restlessly. He wished he could ask Jesse about whores and men and his mother. He wished he could ask Jesse who killed his father. Jesse had always told him the truth. Jesse had always taken time to talk to him about any number of things, like how you could tell the rain was coming just by smelling the wind. His mother used to talk to him a lot, too, but not since she sent him to Pueblo. Now her time was spent with Robert.

Leon hated Robert. All the bad things that had gone wrong with his life started when his mother got fat with Robert. Aunt Patty and Jubilee could talk all they wanted about how Robert was his brother and smaller than he was and how he ought to love him. Leon didn't believe it, and he didn't think his grandfather believed it either. He had caught a funny expression on the Colonel's face every time he looked at Robert.

"Leon Hunter!"

Leon jerked at the sound of his name and knocked his *McGuffey's Reader* on the floor. The other children laughed and he felt his face turn hot. He knew it was turning red, too, including his ears and the back of his neck. He looked toward the front of the schoolroom and saw Tom Miller standing next to his teacher. Seeing Tom made his stomach hurt at the same time that he wanted to run up and hide behind the man. Tom was the one who told him the sheriff had arrested his mother and why. Tom was the one who walked him from Grandma Cartwright's to the hotel to visit his mother every night. Tom was the one who never mentioned that Leon's sniffles were from tears instead of a cold. Tom always made him feel good and bad at the same time.

"Get your books and coat, son," said Tom. "Your mother's waiting."

Leon picked up his reader, managing to elbow the boy who sat next to him in the process. That would teach the misbegotten little son of a one-legged whore not to laugh at Leon Hunter. Leon wasn't sure what misbegotten meant, but he had heard Danny call a particularly sly mustang by that moniker so he figured it must be something really bad—worse even than merely being the son of a one-legged whore.

He walked outside with Tom and climbed in the buggy between his mother and Jubilee. Immediately Jubilee slapped the reins and drove away with Tom and Hank riding on either side and most of the Bar H boys following behind. Feeling uneasy, Leon glanced up at his mother. She looked brittle, like one of the molasses lace cookies Jubilee made that were thin as paper and shattered like glass if you dropped them. Maybe his mother really was crazy. Maybe that's why the sheriff had let her go. Leon felt responsibility fall on his shoulders like a harness. He supposed he'd have to look after the ranch and her if that was the case. He wouldn't let anybody lock up his mother in a madhouse though, or let his grandfather take her back to Pueblo. Mattie Hunter surely would lose her wits, if she hadn't already, if she had to leave the Bar H. Leon knew that without knowing how he knew.

Suddenly Mattie hugged him tightly and Leon first thought to squirm away. It was embarrassing to be hugged like a baby in front of everybody, particularly all the Bar H boys. How could he give orders to men if they saw him treated like a baby? But when he felt his mother shaking all over like she had a fever, he stopped trying to pull away. She was scared. He tried to remember the last time he had seen his mother scared of anything. He couldn't.

Mattie drew back and touched Leon's swollen eye and split lip. "You've been fighting, Leon. Why?"

Leon hunched his shoulders. "Nothing."

He saw Mattie exchange glances with Tom and clenched his jaw. His mother wasn't dumb and neither was Tom. He figured they both guessed why he was fighting, but that didn't mean he intended to admit it. He didn't intend to repeat all the bad names the other children had called Mattie. Repeating them would be like admitting they were true.

Leon saw his mother's eyes start to brighten like there were flames in back of them. She stopped shaking, too, and clenched her hands into fists. She wasn't afraid anymore; she was angry, angrier than he had ever seen her. He guessed angry was better than scared, and both were better than crazy, but neither one made a boy comfortable.

"Jubilee, take Leon home and pack up his and Robert's clothes. Take both boys to Pueblo and tell my father to watch out for them until after the trial. He might not be too pleased with me, but he won't turn the boys away," said Mattie.

"No!" shouted Leon. "I won't go to Grandpa's with Robert. I'm not a little baby like him."

Mattie grasped his shoulders. "You'll do as I say. I won't have you and Robert stay here to be taunted. This is my business and I'll tend to it, but I can't be worrying about you and your brother at the same time."

"It's my business, too," said Leon. "And families hold fast in time of trouble. Jubilee says so."

Mattie bit her lip, and Leon thought he had won the argument. His mother had a lot of respect for Jubilee's sayings.

"And Jubilee is right, Leon," Mattie finally said. "And that's why your grandpa needs you more than I do. He needs to know that no matter what happens to me, he still has family."

Leon's stomach hurt worse. "What's going to happen to you? Is the sheriff going to hang you? But you didn't kill my papa. Someone else did. Why doesn't the sheriff find him? I'll do it if he can't. I'll hang the bastard from a cottonwood tree!" He stopped abruptly. He'd never said a bad word in front of his mother, but he wasn't sorry he'd said one now. He meant it.

Mattie turned pale and her hands started to shake again. "Jubilee, take him home."

Leon threw his arms around his mother's neck and hung on. "I'm not going home! The sheriff won't hang you if I'm along. It wouldn't be seemly."

Mattie laughed hysterically, and Jubilee pulled Leon away from his mother. "You hush up. You is making a scene and your mama don't need no scene. Nobody's gonna hang your mama. The sheriff done released her."

Leon wiped his eyes on his shirt sleeve. "Then who did he arrest? He wouldn't let Mama go unless he caught somebody else. I heard Tom say so."

Tom cleared his throat. "Tell him the truth, Mattie. It's past time and there's no way to keep him from hearing even if you sent him to Canada to live with Eskimos."

Mattie turned even paler, right down to her hands, and Leon could clearly see the scars from her frostbite. If her hands got too cold or too hot, the scars always showed. He wondered which she was now and guessed cold. He saw her lift one hand to rub the scar under her chin, the scar left from the beating that everyone spoke about in whispers when he was around. Leon felt even sicker looking at that scar. It was a sign of all the things that had happened to his life that he didn't understand. For just a second he wondered if he wasn't better off not understanding.

Mattie rubbed the scar once more, then folded her hands. She faced Leon squarely, and he found he couldn't lower his eyes. "The sheriff arrested Jesse and I have to help him."

Leon felt his world crumble. He swallowed, then forced out his question. "Did Jesse shoot my pa?"

Mattie closed her eyes briefly, then opened them. "Your" —she hesitated— "father nearly beat me to death. He would have tried again, Leon, and I would not have allowed myself to be a victim. No one has the right to ask that of me—including a husband. I am not a dog to be beaten nor a piece of property to be disposed of at a man's whim. Every person has more than one face, and each of us must address the face we see. Samuel was your father, but to me he was my would-be murderer. Not even for you will I say I'm sorry he's dead."

Leon saw his mother's face through a veil of tears. "Did Jesse shoot my pa?" he asked again.

"Jesse saved my life and I won't see him hang for it." She stroked his cheek once more, then turned to Tom. "Get me a horse. I'm riding to Jesse's place."

Leon clenched his fists and lowered his head. He had lost his mother and his father and Jesse. He couldn't remember ever feeling so lonely.

Mattie rode across the prairie toward her reckoning with Caroline, leaving behind a son with empty eyes and no one to trust. Yet she could have answered Leon in no other way. Painting Samuel's character in tones of loving kindness created a false image. Leon needed to know *why* his father had died. Otherwise, he would never forgive her trying to save Jesse. He might not anyway. Yet she could not let Jesse die to keep Leon's good opinion. Whichever way she turned, she lost.

She dismounted in front of Jesse's headquarters and wiped away her tears. She had lost her son to disillusionment and Tom to a more peaceful life. She would not lose Jesse to the hangman.

So help her God.

With a mocking smile and a pistol, Caroline

stepped outside the house as Mattie reached the porch. "I've been expecting you."

Mattie glanced at the gun, then at Caroline. "If you are planning to kill me, then make the first shot count because otherwise I'll take that gun away from you and put a bullet through your lying mouth before I die."

Caroline's lips twisted in disapproval. "You speak as plainly and coarsely as a man, Mrs. Hunter."

"I've lived alone in a world of men much of my life and I've grown used to plain talk. I've lost that soft veneer of feminine tact the world judges a woman should possess."

"I wonder that Jesse finds you so attractive, but of course, men have always used women such as you for the pleasures that they can't decently demand of their wives."

Mattie wondered what pleasures those might be. A little warmth to thaw a man frozen by a 'proper' wife taught to separate her mind from her body? "While I may not be a 'good woman' as other people define the term, I'll be damned if I'm any worse than you. You deliberately lied for revenge and condemned your own husband. Or are you going to claim you didn't know Jesse killed Samuel?"

"Of course I knew it. Jesse came home that night somber as a judge and smelling of gunpowder. When your husband's body was found the next day, I had no doubts at all that Jesse killed him."

"Then why did you tell the sheriff such a story? Did you believe that Jesse would keep quiet and hide behind your lies because that's what you would have done in his position?"

Caroline's pale skin flushed and she raised her pistol to point it at Mattie's heart. "Don't speak to me with such contempt!"

Mattie clenched her fists. "Then put away that

gun before you misjudge my actions as badly as you misjudged Jesse's."

Caroline smiled, an expression so full of malice and triumph that Mattie took a step backward as if a rattlesnake had suddenly appeared in her path.

"I didn't misjudge Jesse. I knew he would never let you hang. I knew it before he told me this morning he was planning to confess."

"You knew, and you still refused to take back your lies?"

"Jesse didn't scorn me. You did."

Mattie felt cold all over as if Caroline had sucked all the heat from the day. "This isn't about Jesse at all, is it? You don't care if Jesse killed ten men for me. You don't even care if he laid with me in that line shack. What galls you is that I sent him back to you. What galls you is *not* that I tried to steal your husband, but that I *didn't.* To soothe your hurt pride and to punish me, you'll let Jesse hang."

Ignoring the pistol, Mattie stepped closer to the other woman. "Your evil revenge won't work, Caroline, not if I have to kill you and buy the perjured testimony of ten thousand others, I'll never let Jesse hang."

"You seem determined to misjudge me, Mattie Hunter. Your punishment is not to see Jesse hang. Your punishment is to save him."

"Jesse is only a pawn, isn't he?" asked Mattie slowly, finally understanding Caroline's strategy. Her father was right after all. Her own misdeeds had brought Jesse down. "You knew a threat to him would put me at your mercy, and that's what you want. You want to humble me."

Caroline nodded. "Yes! I am tired of hearing tales of how smart you are, how much grit you have. I am tired of hearing men condemn your behavior out of one side of their mouths and praise your abilities out of the other. I want to humble that Hunter woman."

Mattie's shoulders sagged. "I am humbled. What more do you want? Do you want me to confess to the murders?"

Caroline laughed. "The sheriff would never believe you."

"Then for God's sake, what must I do to save Jesse?"

Caroline tucked a loose strand of chestnut hair behind her ear. "Agree to my terms and I'll save my husband and you at the same time. I'll swear that Jesse and I kept vigil at your bedside all afternoon and evening. I'll swear my jealousy overcame my judgment and I made up that terrible story about you. My husband was so horrified that he tried to save you with that false confession. He hoped to shock me back into my senses—and he did. I'll act so ashamed and remorseful that the sheriff—and the jury if it comes to that—will believe me. I'll be an innocent wife trying to fight as best I can against the scarlet woman who is trying to take my husband."

Maggie leaned back against one of the cottonwood logs that held up the porch roof. Caroline was right. The jury would believe her. She, unlike that Hunter woman, had an unblemished reputation. Caroline McDade had plotted Mattie Hunter's defeat as skillfully as any general. It only remained for Mattie to surrender.

"What are your terms, Caroline?" she asked.

"Your land, Mattie Hunter. You lust after your land more than you lust for any man. Depriving you of your land in exchange for Jesse's life will hurt you like nothing else. It might even hurt you more than watching Jesse hang. What is you answer, Mrs. Hunter, the land or the man?"

And that Hunter woman cares more for the land than for the man.

"No!" cried Mattie.

"I think yes. Jesse said I put myself in your debt the day of the fire. Now, you are in my debt—and so is he. He will pay by coming back to me and being my husband because *I* demand it, not because you order him to. You will pay by signing over the Bar H to me and leaving the Panhandle. You'll lose both your land and Jesse. It's a fitting punishment."

Mattie turned around and looked to the east where her headquarters lay. The land. Her land— land for which she had fought drought and snow, rustlers and fire, Texas fever and the dictates of the Stock Association—and she must give it up to Caroline McDade or Jesse would die.

And she could not.

She turned around to face Caroline. "I can't sign over the Bar H. I only own half of it. My two sons own the other half and I cannot sell it without going to court for permission. If I did that, everyone would know I was buying your testimony."

Caroline frowned, studying Mattie's face as though looking for a lie, then smiled. "Sign over your half, hire a manager for your sons' portion, and leave. Do you agree to that? Do you give me your word?"

Mattie gasped. "You'd take my word as though this was an honorable contract instead of an instrument of theft? After all you've accused me of?"

"Of course. Other than breaking marriage vows to commit sins of the flesh, I haven't ever heard of you or Jesse failing to keep your word. Besides, you are in my debt for Jesse's life and you always pay your debts."

What Samuel had failed to do, Caroline McDade had accomplished. Mattie Hunter felt her self-respect vanish like rainwater into the thirsty prairie.

"You have my word, Caroline. I'll sign the deed over to you. I hope that will satisfy you because I can't promise that I'll leave the Panhandle. The court holds me responsible for my sons' inheritance. I can't turn it over to a manager as if I was a British syndicate. You've seen what too often happens in those cases? Overgrazing, heavy losses from rustling because no one respects absentee landlords, and sometimes outright theft. I wronged you, and you have a right to hate me for it, but I did save your daughter's life. You owe me the right to protect my sons' land."

Mattie, so sick with defeat she could hardly stand up, looked at Caroline. "Please, Caroline, I'm begging you. Don't force me to forfeit my sons' inheritance. Don't let our feud touch our children, and I give you my word that I will never see Jesse again, and that if he approaches me, I'll walk away."

Caroline studied Mattie's face for several minutes while only the loud ticking of the grandfather clock inside the house broke the silence. Mattie felt the muscles in her thighs and calves begin to cramp from tension before the other woman finally spoke.

"Your word's not good enough."

"You'll take my word on everything else. Why not about this?"

An expression of distaste crossed Caroline's face. "Because neither you or Jesse can be trusted when it comes to the sins of the flesh. Of course, no man is to be trusted when it comes to a loose woman, but you especially have the heart of a trollop to seek out a man for such a purpose. No, I shall require something more. I shall require a guard against your loose behavior."

She smiled, and this time the smile held genuine amusement. "You must marry again, Mattie Hunter."

* * *

The next day Mattie sat facing Tom Miller in George Faulkner's tiny office on the Four F. Faulkner's headquarters was a cottonwood dogtrot cabin: two rooms on one side and two rooms on the other side of an open breezeway. It was not elegant, and Mattie wondered that a Scots aristocrat would live there. But then there had always been a hidden side to George Faulkner. Whether he was more or less than the soft greenhorn he appeared was something Mattie had never been able to decide. That he had bought the bankrupt Four F from his father's syndicate, spending almost all of his inheritance to do so according to gossip, only added to the Scotsman's mystery. Still, he seemed straightforward enough when he offered her tea in a thin china cup more appropriate to a manor house drawing room in Scotland than a dogtrot cabin in the Texas Panhandle.

"May I offer you something to eat while you and Tom settle your business?" he asked, the odd gray-green color of his eyes again reminding Mattie of sagebrush leaves. "My man, Douglass, makes a respectable crumpet given the primitive kitchen."

Mattie shook her head. "No, thank you. I'm not hungry." And she wasn't. Her meeting with Caroline Hunter yesterday had Mattie's stomach too tied in knots to consider food. The prospect of talking alone with Tom only worsened the pain in her belly.

Faulkner bowed his head at her refusal. "Then I'll leave the two of you alone."

He closed the door behind him, and Mattie resolutely rose from the wooden rocker Faulkner had insisted was the more comfortable of the office's two chairs. Tom sat in the other, his fingers laced together, his eyes curious.

"Tom," Mattie began, only to hear her voice crack. She cleared her throat and began again. "I talked to Caroline yesterday."

"Judging from the black circles under your eyes, I reckon whatever she said kept you awake last night." His voice was deep and slow, and Mattie remembered the many occasions his masculine tones had soothed her. "You best tell me what happened, Mattie. You didn't ride over here to have tea and crumpets. You came because you're in need of a man you can trust."

Mattie flinched at his words. Dear God, but she wished she weren't so desperate that she had to misuse this man. She drew a deep breath and recounted her conversation with Caroline—or most of it, anyway.

Tom rubbed his chin, a sign he was weighing each word she spoke. "So Caroline McDade set a bear trap and you and Jesse stepped in it."

Mattie paced the tiny office, then stopped in front of Tom. "She knew the only way to hurt me was by threatening Jesse. She manipulated us both just so I would be in her debt. She held a knife to my throat and I tilted my head back and let her slice me until I bled away my life."

Tom reached out and caught her hands. "What did you give her, Mattie?"

Mattie tried to answer but too many tears unshed blocked her throat. She swallowed and drew a shallow breath. "I gave her the Bar H."

For the first time in all the years she had known him, Tom Miller lost his composure and uttered a foul curse in her presence. Mattie smiled bitterly. "I couldn't sign over the deed to the boys' half so Caroline generously gave up her claim on my sons' inheritance."

"That's a mighty hard and shrewd woman."

There was an odd note in his voice that Mattie didn't like. She jerked out of his grip. "You sound like you admire her!"

Tom shook his head. "I don't admire her putting a man's head in a noose to get back at you, and I damn sure don't admire her taking away your land, but I don't blame her for fighting you. You were poaching."

Unable to meet the truth in Tom's eyes, she turned away. "I know."

"Don't hang your head in shame, Mattie. You didn't poach out of meanness or because you're a loose woman, and you've paid the piper—paid more than is right. Caroline McDade should have been satisfied with humbling you."

"Oh, she did that, Tom." She carefully kept her back to him. Recounting the next part of her conversation with Caroline while looking at Tom was beyond her meager resources. "She first wanted me to hire a manager for the boys' property and then leave the Panhandle forever, but after I begged" — she stuttered over the word— "she agreed I could stay on to watch over the boys' land. I promised her I would never see or talk to Jesse again."

Mattie lowered her head and stared at the dirt floor of the cabin. "It wasn't enough, Tom."

She heard his chair creak as he rose, then felt his calloused hands rest on her slumped shoulders. "What more does she want, Mattie?"

"She wants me to marry again."

She heard Tom catch his breath, then heard nothing else as time stretched out thin as the gossamer thread spun by a spider for her web. He lifted his hands from her shoulders and finally spoke. "Turn around, Mattie, and look at me while you talk. I'd not be guessing what feelings your eyes hold."

Slowly Mattie turned and licked her lips before

she spoke. She had never seen a hanging but she visualized Jesse, his hands and feet tied, twisting at the end of a rope until his tongue protruded and his silver eyes tarnished and he breathed no more.

The vision was stronger than her shame at once more preying on Tom's good nature and his feelings for her. "I can only ask you straight out, Tom, if your offer to marry me is still good?"

He studied her face, his hazel eyes seeming to pierce through her skull to all the guilt hidden within. He said nothing, and she burst out with more words, hardly knowing what she was saying. "I called for your company when I was arrested and you came. Dear God, you came, and I used you as a shield against my own fear. I took advantage of your feelings, and I consider that a more heinous sin than my adultery with Jesse. Turning you away after my release was probably the only decent thing I've done in a long, long time—and the hardest. I had lost my son, Jesse was in danger, and I didn't want to lose you, too. But I couldn't hold you by me while promising you nothing."

"What are you promising me now, Mattie?" Tom asked, clasping her waist loosely with his hands.

She searched his eyes for some hint of what answer he might desire, but found only calm watchfulness. "Less than I could have given you last week. I have no land, no house—it goes with my half of the ranch—some capital but not much. I have a reputation no decent woman would envy, and must squat upon my sons' land like a charity case. It's no good hand you've won, Tom Miller."

"It's not the property that concerns me, Mattie. It is the woman. What do you promise me of the woman?"

Her chest felt constricted as though she wore a corset. "What do you ask of the woman?"

He tightened his hands about her waist and lowered his face toward hers until she could feel his breath. "I'll be taking my wedding vows to heart, Mattie, and I'll expect you to do the same."

She nodded. She would sell her soul for Jesse, but all Tom wanted was loyalty from her body and seemly behavior. That she could do—would do in any case. She respected Tom too much to cheat him.

Tom brushed his lips against hers, then raised his head to gaze down at her. "I'll marry you, but I won't lie with you until after the charges against Jesse are settled. Until then your mind will be torn, and I won't bed half a woman. But afterwards, Mattie Jo Hunter, is our time together, and one day your mind will find as much joy in being my wife as I intend that your body shall."

"But what of my heart, Tom?" she whispered.

He smiled, and now she saw the heat in his eyes. "A sensible man woos that Hunter woman's mind if he hopes to win her heart. Nobody ever said I was less than a sensible man."

CHAPTER

21

The Oldham County Courthouse was the pride of Tascosa. Built of sandstone and granite and two stories tall, it was a symbol of permanence in a town of adobe. Stone did not melt away like mud brick if the Canadian should overflow or a gully-washing rain fall. When the railroad came to Tascosa, and everyone was certain it would, then the citizens could point to the courthouse as proof the town was built upon stone rather than the shifting sands of the Canadian. None of Tascosa's nearly six hundred residents were much given to philosophical musing so no one remarked on the incongruity of a stone courthouse in a town built of mud. No one considered that the courthouse might well outlast the town and serve as its tombstone.

Tascosa had other irons in the fire besides philosophy in May of 1886—one being the upcoming trial of the murderers from the Big Fight who were presently locked up in the old adobe jail next to the courthouse.

Another was Mattie Hunter's wedding.

Mattie Hunter married Tom Miller in a civil ceremony held in Tascosa's schoolhouse. Caroline McDade witnessed the ceremony and hosted a reception for the couple at the Exchange Hotel to which everyone in Tascosa and the surrounding countryside was invited. Somber as always, Charlie Goodnight gave away the bride and later stood by her in the receiving line. His presence quieted the rowdier guests who might have been tempted to speculate on the bride's future performance in the marriage bed in view of her past behavior. Anyone foolish enough to buck Goodnight's view of propriety reconsidered when they saw Tom Miller's forbidding expression and the heavily armed Bar H cowboys. It was less painful to swallow lewd remarks than to dig a bullet out of one's hide.

Even Tom Miller and Charlie Goodnight couldn't altogether quiet the gossip about Mattie's hasty wedding to which, so went the rumors, she had not invited her father and sons. That no one called it a shotgun wedding was due more to Tom's reputation than to Mattie's. No one believed that Tom would jump the gun on his wedding vows. No one doubted that Mattie would. All agreed that there was more to her marriage than a sudden overwhelming affection for Tom Miller.

Few guests remarked on the bride's stiff white face and shadowed eyes, and those who did, mostly women, felt a sadness within themselves they couldn't explain. Neither could they explain why they hugged the bride as if she was a hurt child no one could heal. Imagine feeling pity for that Hunter woman.

* * *

Jesse spent the day of Mattie's wedding as he had all of his days since his arrest: caged up behind a mesh door woven of long narrow pieces of iron, in the twelve-by-five-foot jail cell in the sheriff's office on the first floor of the Tascosa courthouse. He had promised himself he wouldn't look out his cell's tiny window toward the schoolhouse and watch Mattie leave the little adobe building with her new husband. Watching her would amount to self-torture and add to his already unbearable pain.

He watched anyway.

He watched until Mattie in her lace-trimmed yellow dress passed out of his range of vision, and he could no longer see her even by standing on his toes and twisting his head to get a better angle of sight. Then he sank face down onto the straw-filled mattress that was the cell's only furnishing, every muscle rigid as he fought his own desire to weep. Soul-deep wounds did not bleed or else the white plaster walls and oak floor of his cell would be splattered with red stains. Nonetheless Jesse knew he was dying. By marrying on the eve of his trial, Mattie had severed the bond between them.

And left a wound that bled away hope.

"Jesse?"

Jesse raised his head off the straw mattress as the sound of his name penetrated the self-imposed shell behind which he hid with his pain and grief. He shook his head in denial. He didn't want to talk to anyone, didn't want to see anyone, didn't want to acknowledge that a world existed beyond this cell. A man had a right to suffer alone if he chose, and in Jesse's circumstances, that was the only choice left to him.

"Jesse, I knows you is in there—can't be no place else—and I needs to talk to you."

The voice tugged at Jesse's mind, stirring up memories of other times, other places, when his visitor had also called to him in desperation and pleading. Wearily, he pushed himself first to his knees, then to his feet, and stepped to the window to look out. The window was six feet from his cell's floor with a twenty-two-inch-deep sill, but was more than seven and a half feet from level ground outside so even by stretching Jesse could hardly see the figure standing outside.

"Jubilee! Is that you?"

Jubilee's voice floated through the iron mesh screen. "I is here, Jesse, and I gots to tell you something quick afore Miss Mattie starts looking around wondering where I got to."

"Miss Mattie is probably busy with her new husband," said Jesse bitterly, awkwardly peering down at Jubilee. "She won't have you on her mind."

"I reckon she's got something on her mind, but it ain't Tom Miller."

The bleak tone in Jubilee's voice caught Jesse's attention and he tried to decipher what he could see of the other man's expression in the deepening twilight. He felt the hair on the back of his neck prickle as it used to when he was fighting the Comanches and knew an ambush waited over the next rise.

"Tell me, Jubilee!" he ordered.

Jubilee hesitated, then the words burst out. "It's your wife, Jesse! I 'spect it was her dirty work that made Miss Mattie marry Tom. I ain't got nothing against Tom Miller, you understand. He's one of the finest white men I ever knowed, but Miss Mattie ain't never been het up over him before now."

"Mattie has never been accused of murder, then ruined by gossip before either. Up until now all the talk about her has been about how disrespectful of a woman's place she's been. No one knew for sure how close we kept company. Now they do. Maybe she figured Tom's reputation would redeem her

own," said Jesse even while everything in him rejected that suggestion. "There's nothing to say that
Caroline had a hand in Mattie's decision."

"I don't think you is thinking clear, Jesse. Them
two women hate each other. There ain't no reason
why you wife would be giving a wedding party for
Miss Mattie, and no reason for Miss Mattie to
let her."

Jesse rested his face against the cool strap-iron
screen. Jubilee was right. He was not thinking clearly. In fact, he had not been thinking at all—not since
he had seen Mattie walk through the schoolhouse
door. He had been so wounded that he had shut
down his mind to any thoughts about her lest he
imagine seeing her in Miller's arms. Imagined sights
often murdered sanity.

He lifted his head when Jubilee spoke again.
"That ain't all, Jesse. Right after Miss Mattie talked
to your wife the day you was jailed, she come home
and ordered up a crew of Mexicans to rebuild the
old plaza headquarters that she had Tom burn
down. Then she ordered me to pack up everything
that weren't nailed down, but she wasn't fixing to
tell me why. Just looked at me out of them yeller
eyes of hers and told me to mind my own business
instead of hers. Well, her business is my business,
and I wasn't fixing to do nothing till I knew what she
was planning. When she come riding home with
Tom and tells me they is getting married, I knowed
for sure something was bad wrong. I took to listening at her office door in the evening when her and
Tom was talking. She don't know that I know what
she's done, and she sure don't know I'm over here
talking to you, 'cause best I can figure, she promised
your wife she wouldn't say nothing to you—ever."

Jesse heard Jubilee spit on the ground as if to
clean his mouth of a nasty taste before he contin-

ued. "I ain't promised your wife nothing, Jesse, and I wouldn't keep it if I had. I don't keep my word to thieves and Miss Mattie hadn't ought to neither."

"What did Caroline do?" demanded Jesse.

"She plucked Miss Mattie clean, Jesse. Miss Mattie done gave the ranch to your wife to save your hide."

Jubilee's words exploded in his mind and when the dust cleared from his thoughts, Jesse saw clearly the altered landscape of recent events and the visible footprints of his wife's deceit and it was infinitely worse than Jubilee envisioned. Like any successful villain, Caroline had used others to achieve her ends. Sheriff East had refused to release him, declaring he didn't have the authority to dismiss charges once a man had been indicted by a grand jury. Jesse knew now that if East hadn't used that excuse, he would have used another. The sheriff knew how to flush game as well as the next man. He didn't believe Caroline's first set of lies any more than he believed the sun rose in the west, but he knew a threat to Mattie Hunter would flush out Jesse. The sheriff disregarded Caroline's second set of lies as a wife's effort to save her husband's life. Jesse knew better. For a woman, Caroline herself knew a little about flushing game, but the game she was interested in was Mattie, and Mattie had allowed herself to be caught. Caroline's changed story was the result of a successful hunt. Her testimony might save Jesse from the gallows, but the heart of her lies remained unchanged: Mattie Hunter was a slut who drove a decent woman to lie. Caroline would parade Mattie's behavior before the jury and the town like a Comanche brave showing off a scalp.

Marrying Tom Miller wouldn't save Mattie.

But Jesse McDade could.

"What we going to do, Jesse?" asked Jubilee plaintively.

"Jubilee, you go on back to Mattie before she notices you're gone, and not a word to her about seeing me. I can't do anything about her marriage, but I can damn sure save her land."

He heard Jubilee shuffling his feet in the bare dirt. "I reckon I didn't want you stopping the wedding, Jesse, or I'd been over here 'fore now. Iffen they hang you, then Miss Mattie needs a good man who can hold her tight without any other kind of carrying on while she's grieving. Iffen they lets you go, then she still needs a good man, one you respects too much to be going behind his back to get to his wife, and I reckon Tom Miller fits the bill on both counts."

Jesse gripped the strap-iron bars. "Damn you, Jubilee! Damn you to hell! You condemned her to a marriage against her will."

"You can cuss me all you wants, Jesse, but I knowed what I was doing. Being a slave till Mr. Lincoln freed me, I understands better than you how it feels to be forced into doing something you don't want to do. While it don't set right with me that Miss Mattie was forced into marrying Tom, I sees some good that might come out of it. If it wasn't for what's between you and her, she might have taken up with him a lot sooner. He'll do right by her, and maybe one day she'll stop seeing your face everywhere she looks and see his instead."

"Don't bet on it, Jubilee. I tried marriage as a way to free my life from Mattie's and look where it got me," said Jesse grimly.

"You figured if you couldn't have Miss Mattie, then anybody would do. You was a fool. Miss Mattie is a mite smarter. She picked somebody she liked. But that don't change the fact she tied herself to another man when she wasn't aiming to, and gave up her ranch to boot to save your hide. I don't reckon she can make her feelings for you any plainer. You be satisfied with that and let her be after this trial."

Jesse reared his head back and stared at the domed stone ceiling above his head. He had always known he and Mattie faced a reckoning, but his very flesh shrank from its cost. Still, he would pay his debts, but be damned if he would allow Mattie to pay more than what was fair—particularly not to a woman who charged usurious interest.

"Jubilee, I give my word that Mattie won't be bothered again by me after this trial."

CHAPTER

22

The long, narrow room on the second floor of Tascosa's courthouse had plaster walls, high ceilings, open windows on the north and east to let out the heat and let in whatever bugs and noise chose to enter, two ordinary doors set in one wall, a few rough benches for the spectators and jury, a couple of tables and straight chairs for the lawyers and judge, and woodwork painted the same bilious dark green as that downstairs. The color reminded Tom of a horsefly's wings, but without the shine. But the county commissioners's choice of paint wasn't the only peculiar thing about the courthouse. While the first floor looked to be built by craftsmen, the second floor looked to be built by drunken cowboys. Not a wall was plumb, a window or door square, a floor level.

It wasn't the kind of courtroom where a man would expect to find the youngest son of the revered Sam Houston. Of course, Tom admitted to himself, Temple Houston was a little peculiar himself in his personal habits, so maybe the two were suited.

The Panhandle's first district attorney and now its first state senator, Temple Houston wore his wavy auburn hair to his shoulders and was clean shaven when most men wore their hair short and generally sported a mustache. His eyes were as gray as Jesse McDade's, but more luminous, as though Houston's life held light where Jesse's only held shadows. Today, as most days, the young lawyer wore a long frock coat, and a pearl-handled revolver named Betsy strapped around his waist. Tom had never heard of Houston losing a shooting match with either Betsy or a rifle.

He didn't lose many cases either. Temple Houston quoted from the Bible and from Shakespeare and lesser known literary giants during closing arguments in a slow, deep voice that tugged at the heartstrings and won acquittal for his clients. Houston argued for justice and sometimes that wasn't the same thing as the law. Tom guessed that was the real job of a jury: to decide between justice and law, and nobody could make that difference clearer than Temple Houston.

But Temple Houston couldn't perform miracles even if he was larger than life and on his way to becoming a legend. In Tom's opinion, God himself couldn't sway the jury lined up to try Jesse McDade. Stalwart Texas cowboys might respect women and disapprove of Samuel Hunter's nearly beating his wife to death, but Tom didn't think that would stop this particular jury of cowboys from finding Jesse guilty.

Tom smoothed his mustache with the knuckle of one finger while he studied the men ready to judge Jesse McDade. To a man they all rode for the big brands. They remembered that Mattie and Jesse supported the cowboy strike. They remembered both refused to support Pat Garrett and the Home Rangers when they arrested nester ranchers indicted for running maverick brands. Blood was running high and hot at present between the men who worked for the syndicates and the big brands, and the one-horse outfits and the nesters. The Big Fight hadn't helped soothe hard feelings either; just made them worse. No one straddled the fence in this feud. A man walked on one side or the other, and Jesse McDade walked on the opposite side from his prospective jury.

Tom sighed as he glanced at Mattie's bloodless face. The odds were against Jesse McDade, and Tom didn't want to think about what that would do to Mattie. One thing was certain. The woman who had walked into that courtroom hanging on to his arm like he was the only person standing between her and hell wouldn't be the same woman who walked out. Whatever happened, Mattie Hunter would never be the same again. Her reckoning had cost her what she valued the most: her land and Jesse McDade. Caroline McDade's testimony would cost her what she valued least but was most irreplaceable: the tattered remains of her reputation.

Tom sneaked a look at Caroline McDade's face and grimaced at the sight of her pleased expression. No, pleased wasn't the right word; gloating better described it. He shivered. He fell victim to a chill every time he looked at that woman. There was no heat to her—not even to her anger. Her vengeance wouldn't burn up Mattie and Jesse; it would destroy them with a killing frost.

He noticed Jesse arguing with Temple Houston and wondered what the fight was about. Tom didn't think this was the time for Jesse to have a falling out with his lawyer. Much as it went against the grain for a man like McDade to trust his life to another, Tom didn't see that Jesse had a choice. He had to trust someone to defend him, and Temple Houston was the best damn lawyer in Texas.

Jesse didn't hire Temple Houston for his competence, but for a lesser known trait of Houston's.

Temple Houston was rumored to be sympathetic to soiled doves.

In a goodly number of minds, Mattie Hunter was the Panhandle's most notorious soiled dove.

"I would die for you, Mattie, but I can't live for you."

Jesse drew a deep breath and let it out slowly, then repeated his statement that had so dismayed Houston. "Tell the judge that I want to plead guilty and ask him to decide the punishment."

"Are you asking to be hanged, Jesse?" demanded Houston.

Jesse couldn't suppress a shudder and felt sweat bead his forehead. No, he didn't want to hang, but he damn well wasn't going to live at Mattie's expense.

He managed a crooked grin at Houston. "Maybe I expect you to pull one of those famous heartrending arguments out of that white Stetson of yours, one that will bring tears to the judge's eyes and inspire the women in the courtroom to rend their garments in sorrow."

Houston rubbed his smooth-shaven face. "You grant me greater oratorical gifts than even I possess. I'm not certain when Judge Willis last cried, but it wasn't recently, and it wasn't at anything I said. As for the ladies in the courtroom, I doubt your wife would willingly ruin on your behalf what I suspect is a new dress. Mattie Hunter, however, is a woman from a Greek tragedy. Tears from her eyes are as precious pearls."

Pain lanced through Jesse at the mention of her name, and he resisted the urge to turn and look at her. Their eyes had met when Sheriff East had escorted him into the courtroom and Mattie's look of desperation had nearly unmanned him. Besides, Tom Miller was sitting beside her, and Jesse didn't want to look at him. He couldn't fault Tom for marrying Mattie. He was keeping his word to look after her as best he could, and Jesse knew he ought to be grateful.

He wasn't.

If he hadn't been locked up in jail, jealousy might have tempted him to shoot Tom Miller before the wedding. It didn't make him feel any better to admit such a dishonorable thought, but any man liable to be hanged ought to be honest at least with himself.

Caroline he couldn't bear to look at without bile rising in his throat.

Finally he answered Houston. "I'm not as well read in the classics as you, Temple, but as I recall, the women in the Greek tragedies mostly fared ill. I don't want Mattie called as a witness, and I forbid you to call Caroline. I won't have Mattie further savaged by public opinion, and I'll not hide behind my wife's lies."

"Then at least let me argue punishment in front of the jury," urged Houston. "I'll have twelve chances to save you instead of one. They'll go easier on you than the judge might."

Jesse wondered what the jury might do if they knew Samuel was a sodomist. Most folks would regard sodomy as a greater sin than wife beating, but Jesse didn't kill Samuel because he was a sodomist. He killed him because Samuel Hunter was a vicious bastard, and that was all anyone, especial-

ly Mattie, needed to know. She was the subject of
enough gossip as it was without folks knowing of her
dead husband's peculiar nature.

"I'll take my chances with the judge, Temple, and
if he sentences me to hang, I'll at least be hanging
for the truth."

Houston clasped Jesse's shoulder. "Without your
wife's and Mattie Hunter's testimony, I couldn't
defend Christ against a charge of blasphemy, much
less you against a charge of murder."

Jesse smiled. "You're not defending me, Temple.
You're defending Mattie Hunter against public opinion. I'm the one in the dock, but Mattie is the one
being tried."

"No! Jesse! No!"

Mattie's cries had shattered the silence that followed Jesse's guilty plea, and Jesse had whipped
around, his face gaunt and harsh. His eyes had held
no mercy as he looked at Mattie, or at least none
that Tom saw—just the expression of a man exerting
his will over that of another. Ordinarily, Tom figured
it would have been a draw between those two, but
Jesse's choosing the time of his death gave him an
edge.

At any rate Tom suspected it was Jesse's fierce
look and not Judge Willis's threat to remove her
from the court that accounted for Mattie's silence
the last hour or so while witnesses were called to
prove Jesse's confession. Still, he figured her temper
was like a stick of dynamite whose fuse was burning.
God knew, he figured she wanted to explode, wanted to rain fire and rage upon Judge Willis, upon W.
H. Woodman, the district attorney—even upon
Jesse. Maybe most of all on Jesse.

To Mattie's way of thinking, Jesse was throwing

his life away rather than allow women to lie for him. He would choke to death on a man's pride. Tom didn't see it that way. He figured Jesse McDade just chose to hang for a better reason than killing Samuel Hunter and Clint Murray. Protecting Mattie Hunter was that better reason.

He glanced at Mattie, saw the tears that welled endlessly from her eyes, and clasped her hand as Temple Houston turned to look at her over the crowded courtroom.

Houston paced back and forth with quick, nervous steps. Abruptly he stopped, whirled toward the spectators, and pointed his finger.

"Your Honor, Mrs. Hunter is the first to call my client a damnable liar."

Judge Willis, nearly three hundred pounds of shocked jurisprudence, sat as stunned as Mattie before he finally collected himself and pounded his gavel. "Mr. Houston, sir, you cannot use such language in my court."

Houston waited a few seconds until the eyes of every cowboy and merchant, wife and fancy woman, gambler and freighter gawked at Mattie. Then he gracefully turned to Judge Willis. "I apologize if I gave offense, Your Honor, but I do not apologize for my words. Jesse McDade is a liar and Mattie Jo Hunter knows it better than anyone. We have heard his confession as read into the court record by my opponent, Mr. Woodman. Jesse McDade confesses to riding to Mattie Hunter's house and finding her near unto death from a vicious beating administered by her husband. He further confesses to tracking down Samuel Hunter and Clint Murray and shooting them."

Houston whirled away again and faced the packed courtroom. "We know his confession is the truth because we heard not only Mattie Hunter's employees testify to her condition, but also the doctor who tended her and who has no reason to lie. We also know that Samuel Hunter and Clint Murray were shot because Mr. Faulkner discovered the bodies and both are now moldering in the ground."

Houston paused, letting the silence build until only the buzzing of flies disturbed the hot, still air. "While Jesse McDade's confession is true, he is still a liar. He pled guilty to murder, *but he did not commit murder!* The laws of Texas do not decree that a man must hang for defending the helpless. And Mattie Jo Hunter was helpless—unconscious, with broken ribs and arm, so beaten about the face that she even now bares the scars."

Unconsciously Mattie touched the fine white line under her chin while a multitude of eyes watched her. When she realized what she was doing, she flushed and jerked her hand down. Tom ached for her. Even with head bowed, he knew she could feel the stares.

"You've heard the prosecution refer to the cold cruelty of Jesse McDade's acts, but I did not hear his voice raised to condemn the cruelty of Samuel Hunter who beat his wife until her blood flowed and her flesh turned black with the marks of his fists and boots. The prosecution has painted a picture of Jesse McDade as a man with too close an interest in another man's wife, but nowhere in that picture do I see Jesse McDade claiming Mattie Hunter as the reward for his actions. On the contrary, he rode back to his own wife. Do you think that Jesse McDade would risk his own marriage by committing murder if he had a choice? Do you think Mattie Hunter would have asked him to if *she* had had a choice?"

Houston shook his head. "Of course, Mattie Hunter had no chance to make a choice. She was unconscious, possibly dying, so Jesse McDade chose for her because he knew—as does Your Honor and every man in this room—that his way was the only way to save her life! She had no other champion save the law, and when has the law saved a woman from the excesses of her own husband? Seldom, Your Honor, seldom. Our sex make the laws, we administer the laws, and we conduct trials by those laws. *And a wife cannot testify against her husband!*"

He pointed again at Mattie. "What could be more pathetic than the spectacle Mattie Hunter presented that night in March of 1885? Unaware of her surroundings, in pain, and helpless, at the mercy of her husband and of the law. She had no witnesses to testify on her behalf except her two-year-old son, and only her abused body as evidence. Would that have been enough to send Samuel Hunter to prison for attempted murder? Unlikely, Your Honor. Very unlikely. At most he might—*might*—have served a few days in jail. What of Mattie Hunter then?"

Houston hesitated a few seconds, and Tom saw everyone leaning forward so they might not miss a word, then the attorney raised one clenched fist. "I promise you that Mattie Hunter would have died at the hands of her husband within hours of his release from jail. But that did not come to pass because Jesse McDade came to her defense."

Houston dropped his fist. "And what, you may ask, did Mattie Hunter do to so enrage her husband? What can we say in Samuel Hunter's defense? That his wife was disrespectful and thus violated biblical authority? Should not a husband have to earn a wife's respect? That she refused to sell her land—*as is her right under Texas law?* That she conducted ranch business in violation of society's belief that a woman leave such matters to her husband? In

Mattie Hunter's case, her husband would have gambled away all that she possessed. Neither the law of Texas nor the law of God say that a woman need impoverish herself and her children for the sake of a husband who lacks the sense to manage his financial affairs."

Houston walked into the crowd of spectators, his eyes on Mattie. "What other sins might Mattie Hunter have committed that justified her husband's attempt to murder her? That she admired Jesse McDade more than propriety allowed?"

Tom watched Mattie turn white, then crimson, and he started to rise. If Temple Houston planned to strip Mattie and Jesse naked before the judge and all these people, then he could damn well do it without Mattie present. No one in this courtroom would understand the bond between her and Jesse, or understand the strength of it. To most folks any bond she and Jesse shared began in their loins and ended there. Mattie Hunter was nothing more than a woman taken in adultery, and Jesse a man caught in a fix.

He jerked in surprise when he saw strong hands clasp Mattie's shoulders, and looked up to see Temple Houston. Almost imperceptibly the lawyer shook his head, and Tom sank back down.

Houston raised his head, his glance sweeping the courtroom. "You know the story of the prodigal son, but he was a son. He was one of us, Your Honor, like Samuel Hunter. He flouted his father's wishes, squandered his inheritance, no doubt gambled and drank and caroused. Yet he was forgiven and welcomed home with a great feast."

He squeezed Mattie's shoulders. "For the prodigal daughter there is no forgiveness. Were she, with her wasted form and bleeding feet, fallen and lost, to drag herself back home, what would be her welcome? A feast—or a locked and barred door? You know as well as I that she would be cast out. Men judge themselves by one standard and women by another. Let a woman, locked in the cage of a brutal marriage with no decent way out, reach through the bars to clasp in innocent friendship the hand of a man not her husband, and all gather stones to slay her as though she was Mary Magdalene rather than a wife forced by the profligate behavior of her own husband to seek help from another."

Houston drew in a deep breath. "Jesse McDade did not turn her away although the pious among us believe he should have lectured her on the role of a dutiful wife instead of encouraging her to think for herself. If he had, Jesse McDade would not be in the dock today. Once a woman begins to think for herself instead of pandering to her husband's opinions, however foolish they may be, then she becomes a man's equal. Your Honor, Mattie Hunter's belief in her equality was the sin Samuel Hunter could not forgive, and it was the sin she would not give up. So he used the one weapon man possesses that is superior to a woman's. He used his physical strength against her."

Houston abruptly released Mattie and walked back to the front of the courtroom. "When Jesse McDade defended Mattie Hunter against the brutality of her husband, he proclaimed that a wife is not a man's to do with as he pleases. She is neither chattel nor child. She is *equal!*"

He bowed his head before the judge. "Your Honor, I beseech you to be merciful to Jesse McDade. He defended the women of Texas against the callous and uncaring laws and conventions which fail so miserably to protect them against the assaults and frauds of their own husbands. In this instance, Mattie Jo Hunter just happens to be the name they call themselves."

Only the buzzing of flies broke the silence of the courtroom after Temple Houston sat down, then one by one the women rose, all but Caroline McDade, and applauded the young lawyer.

Judge Willis sentenced Jesse to ten years in prison.

Tom guessed a woman's equality would have to wait for another day.

CHAPTER

23

What ought to be and what is are two different things, thought Tom four days after Jesse's trial. And sometimes right is wrong. Mattie and Jesse ought to be together. Instead Jesse was bound for prison, and Mattie was married to an aging cowboy from what Tom was sure the Colonel would consider "common stock." That is, he would when Mattie got around to telling her pa she'd married again. She hadn't even invited him to the wedding. Tom didn't think her decision had anything to do with her being ashamed of who she was marrying. It was more likely the fact that the Colonel got under Mattie's skin worse than a sand flea, and she hadn't had the time or energy to spend scratching. Then, too, she hadn't wanted her boys under foot during the trial—or while she was moving to the newly built plaza headquarters on the Canadian.

In Tom's opinion, giving up the Bar H was something right that was for damn certain wrong.

He watched Mattie folding up a dress and packing it away in a trunk and figured he'd try arguing with her one more time.

"Jesse confessed, Mattie, so you didn't get value for your trade. Caroline McDade didn't testify. If one party doesn't live up to his end of the bargain, then the bargain's off."

Mattie straightened up, her face as somber as it had been since the day of Jesse's arrest. He wondered if she would ever smile again, or if Caroline McDade had stolen Mattie's laughter along with her land.

"A bargain is a bargain, Tom. Caroline didn't break it. She told the sheriff exactly what she promised me she would say. That she didn't testify, and that her story didn't change the outcome is a risk I took. I won't go back on my word."

"Damn it, Mattie, she cheated you!"

Mattie smiled then, but Tom wished she hadn't. Some smiles hurt a man worse to look at than a sad face. "I cheated her first, though. You said so yourself. I poached on her property, and she took mine in retribution. I always knew I'd face a reckoning for my sins, Tom, and I'll pay it." She paused, and her face took on a bleak look he was beginning to hate. "I never thought it would cost me everything I hold dear, but it has—everything but you and Jubilee and the men. You all stood by me. I expected it of Jubilee. He's loved me like I was his daughter. In fact, I may have cheated him of a daughter of his own blood. If his life hadn't been so twisted up with mine, maybe he would have left after the war and sought out a woman of his own race to marry."

She reached for another dress and began to fold it. "As for the men—well, most of them have ridden for the Bar H brand since Jesse and I founded it, and cowboys are loyal to the bone. Besides, no one else pays as well as I do, or treats them like equals. That means more to a cowboy than money."

She tucked the folded dress in the trunk and turned to him. "But you, Tom, you didn't work for me anymore. I had turned you away. Yet you came when I needed you—even married me when you knew I would not have asked you if I'd had a choice."

"You did have a choice, Mattie. You could have married any man on this ranch and probably on any other. George Faulkner would have married you if you'd asked him, and he's from a good family. Of all the men I figure were ready, willing, and able, why did you ask me?"

She looked surprised, then her eyes went blank and he knew she had disappeared inside herself like she did when she was looking for answers to her own behavior. He imagined her sorting her reasons just as she was sorting through her clothes, discarding those too worn from hard use, and keeping those still fresh enough to be truth.

Finally, she looked up at him, her eyes as transparent as spring water so he could see clear to the bottom of her soul. "I wanted a man who was honest enough to forgive my sins and weaknesses without pretending to overlook them. I wanted a man who appreciated my strengths without feeling I threatened his own. I wanted a man who saw me as his equal." She hesitated, then spoke again. "Most of all I wanted a man who loved me, not just admired me for my looks or lusted after me for the same reason. Samuel never loved me, and I couldn't stand being married again to a man who didn't. You've never said the words, Tom, but I think you love me."

Tom took her in his arms, holding her against his body, and looking down at her uplifted face. "The words come harder for a man than for a woman, but I've never said anything that came easier to me. I love you, Mattie Jo Hunter, and I'll do right by you."

She closed her eyes, but not before he saw the relief in them. It shocked him to see it until he thought about it. Then he felt his gut knot with pity. So many men loved parts of Mattie, but only he and Jesse had ever loved her as a woman all of one piece.

He stroked her cheek and marveled again at how soft her skin was. This country dried out a woman before her time, but it treated Mattie kindly. "And you, Mattie? What words do you have for me?"

She opened her eyes, and this time he saw hope—and sorrow. "You are dear to me, Tom Miller. When you left me, I knew you were as much a part of me as Jesse, and I'm happy to claim you again."

He pressed her head against his shoulder so she couldn't see what he was afraid his eyes might reveal despite his years of keeping his thoughts private. He might be a part of Mattie as she claimed, but Jesse was the biggest part. She still belonged more to Jesse McDade than she did to him.

"I'll take those words and press for different ones when the right time comes."

She lifted her head again. "When will that be and what if it never comes, Tom?"

He smiled. "It'll come, Mattie, and I'll wait. I'm a patient man."

He gathered her closer and kissed her, tracing the seam of her lips with his tongue until she opened her mouth to him. He felt his male part stiffen and knew she felt him because she flinched ever so slightly.

He ended the kiss and grinned. "I guess some parts of me aren't as patient as others."

Her laughter warmed him all over, and he was

lowering his head again when Jubilee knocked on the bedroom door.

"Tom! Jesse's done come here and he wants to talk to you."

Mattie's face went white, and she looked at him as if she hated him. Tom reckoned that she just might at that particular minute. She'd just been reminded that Tom Miller wasn't Jesse McDade, and Tom figured she was feeling unfaithful. He wished to hell it was him she felt unfaithful to.

God damn Jesse McDade to hell.

Jesse was waiting for him under the big cottonwood tree. "I thought you'd be on your way to prison in Huntsville instead of showing up here just when Mattie's settling down," said Tom.

Jesse's eyes turned dark like night falling, and Tom felt ashamed that he hadn't choked back his words. Jealousy made a horse's ass out of a well-meaning man. "I'm sorry, Jesse. What I said was uncalled for. After what you did for Mattie, the least I could be is grateful."

Jesse nodded but Tom was certain it wasn't in response to his apology. Jesse had the look of a burdened man who couldn't spare the time to react to careless words. "I don't mean to be pushing my way in where I don't belong, Tom." He glanced toward the house. "Where I never did belong."

He directed his eyes back toward Tom. "The judge gave me a week's parole and trusted me not to interfere again in the sanctity of another man's marriage long enough to take care of my business affairs. You can trust me, too."

Tom relaxed. "You got a raw deal, Jesse."

Jesse looked toward the house again. "Did I, Tom? I killed two men. The judge couldn't overlook that. The law doesn't care *why* I killed, just *who* I killed."

"I don't recall hearing Judge Willis mentioning Hunter's and Murray's names when he sentenced you."

"Maybe he thought Temple Houston mentioned them often enough while he was defending me."

"Temple Houston didn't defend you as much as he defended Mattie, and the judge didn't sentence you for murder as much as he sentenced you for adultery," said Tom bluntly.

Jesse nodded thoughtfully. "I'm guilty of that, too, and maybe the judge was saying something after all about women being equal to men. It's usually women who pay for adultery while men get off scot-free. Maybe the judge was balancing the scale the only way he could."

"I reckon he overbalanced it, then. Mattie was just as guilty."

Jesse smiled. "Not in the eyes of the world. Remember Temple's story of the prodigal daughter. But I didn't come out here to talk about my trial. I came out to ask you if you would take over management of the Flying MJ while I'm in prison. My land joins Mattie's, so you can run cattle jointly. And I trust you. Things are changing, Tom, faster than maybe I would like, and I need a good man to hold things together for me. I'll have Temple draw up the necessary papers for you if you agree. I'm not good at groveling, but I will if that's what you want."

"Mattie doesn't own this land anymore, Jesse."

"Yes, she does, Tom. I've got her deed in my pocket. Caroline is a smart woman, smarter than I gave her credit for, but she lacks Mattie's business sense. Caroline didn't know she had to file the deed at the courthouse, so the transaction is no good. She can go to court if she wants, but she won't risk it. Unlike Mattie, she cares about what the neighbors think, and the neighbors won't think highly of a woman ready to let her husband hang if Mattie hadn't met her price."

"I'll watch out for your land, Jesse. Here's my hand on it."

Mattie watched Tom and Jesse shake hands from her bedroom window. She wondered if they had talked about her, her husband and her lover, and what each had said to the other. She crumpled the curtains in her fists and rested her head against the glass. Dear God, but she felt so guilty for kissing Tom, and guilty for feeling guilt. Tom was her husband and a better man could not be found. She owed him loyalty. More than that, she owed him love. She had promised him that when she spoke her marriage vows. She must lock Jesse away in her mind with her other memories. And she must never, never pretend Tom was Jesse when he finally took her to bed.

"Mattie?"

She whirled around to see Tom standing in the bedroom door. "What did Jesse want?"

Tom walked over and took her hand. "I'm to manage his ranch while he's in prison."

She looked away to hide her disappointment. How vain to think he had come to say good-bye. She had already cost him enough. "He needs a man he can trust."

He led her toward the door. "He asked to see you, Mattie."

She hung back. "I can't, Tom. I made a bargain with you and I intend to keep it."

He turned toward her. "Don't talk of bargains between us, Mattie. Marriage is more than trading pieces of lives back and forth. It's starting fresh and grafting lives together and hoping they'll grow. I think ours will, but not until you say good-bye to Jesse."

"Tom," she began.

He put his hand over her mouth, holding back her words. "You don't have to tell me that Jesse will always have a little bit of your life and you'll own part of his. I know that already, but I'd rather not hear you say it."

He led her downstairs. "He's waiting, Mattie, and he bought these few minutes alone with you with his freedom." He smoothed a tendril of hair behind her ear. "When you walk back through this door, we'll start fresh."

He closed the front door behind her.

Jesse waited under the cottonwood tree that had witnessed their first joining and now must witness their final parting.

She walked toward him on trembling legs. "Jesse."

"Mattie."

His voice was deep and slow but hoarse—as if his throat hurt. His eyes were darker than she had ever seen them: dulled silver that no one cared enough to polish.

He held out a rolled document. "Here's your deed, Mattie. Tom said I needed to give to you, not him, since he had no part in your bargain."

Mattie looked at the document. "How did you know?"

"Jubilee told me."

"Dear God, that's why you pled guilty!" Mattie swallowed, then swallowed again, and finally bent over, holding her hands over her mouth, but she couldn't stop the sobs that erupted from her throat. She sank to her knees and rocked back and forth like a primitive mourner lamenting the dead.

She felt Jesse gather her into his arms and they knelt together. She cried until her chest hurt and her tears soaked through his shirt to his heart. She felt one convulsive sob rip loose his control, then he held her away from his body.

"Mattie, listen to me. I can't trespass on Tom's good nature much longer, but I can't leave this matter unsettled between us."

The urgency in Jesse's voice and his reminder that they were sharing borrowed time—again—pulled her back from the grief that tore at her mind. She took several shallow breaths and wiped her eyes.

He cupped his hands around her face. "Mattie, I will not allow Caroline to take your land."

"I made a bargain. I gave her my word," said Mattie.

"You made no bargain. You paid her a ransom for my life, and I'm returning it. You can't make choices for other people, Mattie. It was my life, my choice, and I chose not to reward Caroline for lying. Now, take the deed."

"Your sacrifice!" she cried.

He nodded. "Don't refuse it, Mattie. Not only did I kill him because Samuel beat you, I killed him because he tried to steal your land from you. If you keep your bargain with Caroline, then I killed Samuel for nothing and I'll go to prison for nothing. I have to know something good came out of this, and knowing that you're safe on your own land and married to a good man will help me hold back despair."

She leaned against him, her hands resting on his shoulders. "You bought me a fresh chance at life at the price of your own. Oh, God, Jesse, I'm so sorry."

He studied her, his expression guarded. "Do you wish you'd never met me?"

She hesitated, remembering entering her father's office and meeting Jesse for the first time. She remembered feeling that the room and everyone else in it had disappeared, stranding Jesse and her alone in a time and in a world that existed only in their minds. She remembered thinking that if she didn't turn away from him at that very moment, she would never have another chance.

"Yes!" she said fiercely. "If it would save you from going to prison, then yes, I wish it!"

He got to his feet, pulling her up with him, and held her tightly against him. She felt his chest rise and fall as he sucked in a breath and let it out slowly. "If I had known before we ever met the final cost of knowing you, of lying with you, I still would have sought you out. I have no regrets, Mattie."

He lowered his head. "I have a need of memories. Will you kiss me one last time, Mattie Jo Hunter?"

With a cry she kissed him, taking his tongue into her mouth as she wished to take his body into hers, tasting passion suppressed and love unspoken.

He finally broke the kiss and raised his head. He stroked her hair, then her face—tracing her features and rubbing his thumb over her lips. He released her and stepped back, holding her away when she would have followed. "No, Mattie. I have to leave now, and I want to remember you just like this, standing under your cottonwood tree."

He snapped off a leaf and carefully tucked it in his pocket. "A bookmark," he said. He smiled, then turned and walked toward the hitching post where his black gelding waited.

Mattie watched until he rode out of sight, then walked back to the house and to Tom, to give him what part of her heart she was able.

C H A P T E R

THE RECKONING

Summer 1889

Mattie brought forth her third son into a world unimagined when she gave birth to her second son a mere six years before.

Gone were the huge herds and limitless horizons.

The summer of 1886 had blistered the Panhandle as a merciless sun destroyed grazing, dried up water holes, and melted weight off herds still struggling to recover from the effects of the prairie fire followed by the Big Die Up. The fierce storms of the winter of 1886-87 further weakened the ranchers and the cattle market finally collapsed. The price of beef per hundredweight dropped to a dollar ninety, and what few cattle were driven to market were of such poor quality that most sold for less than that. The legislature in Austin revised the lease law to encourage more settlers by classifying public land as either farm land or grazing land and limiting the number of sections an individual could buy to four. Large ranchers evaded the law by having their cowboys file on the land, then sell it to their employers for a small profit. Smaller stockmen, bankrupted by the blizzard and falling prices, sold their land piecemeal and closed out their brands. The syndicates, reeling from losses caused by severe weather, ignorance of both the country and cattle, prairie fires and brand changing, and poor management, saw the sale of land as the only way to recoup their investment, and began to sell up just as Tom had predicted.

With the notable exception of the XIT, the domination of ranching in the Panhandle by foreign investors was over, but Mattie's era of ranching kingdoms was also fading as settlers, lured by cheap land, poured into the region.

Joseph Stryker Miller, Mattie's and Tom's infant son, would never know the freedom of open range, would never ride a full day without seeing another man, would never enjoy a cattle drive to Dodge City.

Ranchers, finally admitting what Mattie and Jesse had known, pulled down the drift fence, and strung barbed wire around individual pastures and provided feed and shelter for their herds. Cowboys rode fence instead of open range, and drove their herds to the new shipping point where railroads crossed just a few miles southeast of Tascosa at a town called Amarillo.

By the fall of 1889 civilization seemed poised to descend upon the Panhandle.

Leon was less concerned about civilization than about his mother. It seemed forever since she'd clutched her belly and Tom had carried her upstairs. Tom had wanted to stay, but Aunt Patty had told him that "birthing was women's business and he'd already done his part." Leon shied away from thinking about his mother and Tom making a baby, and he wished he hadn't heard Aunt Patty's words. They reminded him of what he wanted to forget: that his mother was more than a mother; she was a woman. He wasn't comfortable thinking of her that way because it brought to mind the kids in school calling her a whore. Mothers weren't whores, but sometimes women were.

He squirmed on the couch, uncomfortable in mind and body. His thoughts crawled around inside his head and devoured peace; his skin felt too tight and squeezed his chest. Tom, leaning against the wall by the fireplace, didn't look too comfortable, either. He kept watching the staircase for Aunt Patty, and Leon wondered if he was scared, too.

Suddenly the waiting and the thinking and the listening for muffled cries became too much, and Leon bounded off the sofa. "Tom, is Ma going to die?"

He heard his voice break and hoped he wouldn't cry. He'd learned when he was six years old and his mother sent him away with his grandfather that crying didn't change anything and made adults uncomfortable.

"Mothers don't die till they get real old, older than Jubilee and Grandpa," said Robert.

Leon whirled around to confront his younger brother. "You don't know nothing about it, so shut up. Women die all the time birthing babies."

Robert leapt off the sofa, chin trust forward and fists clenched. At six years old, he was only a head shorter than Leon at thirteen. Robert was going to be a "big man" in Jubilee's words, and he was already a lot stronger than he ought to be. With a good mad on, he could leave bruises everywhere he hit Leon.

"Ma ain't no woman!" Robert yelled as he

attacked Leon, butting and kicking like a frenzied calf.

Leon met the attack with his own, grabbing Robert around the waist and tumbling him to the floor. Suddenly he felt himself jerked up by his collar, and saw Jubilee pull his brother off the floor by his suspenders.

Tom shifted his grip to Leon's arm. "I won't have you boys fighting while your mama's working and worrying at this birthing."

"He needs to be taken to the woodshed," said the Colonel in an outraged voice.

Leon didn't need to look at his grandfather to know he was glaring at Robert. The Colonel always seemed to expect the worst from his second grandson and was seldom disappointed. Leon felt an unaccustomed twinge of protectiveness for his brother.

"That might straighten up their bodies," said Tom calmly, "but it wouldn't do a thing about what's inside their heads."

He sat Leon down on one end of the sofa, and motioned Jubilee to sit Robert on the other end. He knelt on the floor between them. "Leon, your mama's not going to die. I talked to Miss Patty less than an hour ago, and she said everything was coming along fine. Having a baby just takes a long time."

"Does it hurt a lot?" asked Robert, his yellow brown eyes so much like Mattie's that Leon felt another twinge of conscience. "I heard Ma yell."

Tom nodded. "I reckon it hurts a lot."

"Tom," interrupted the Colonel. "I don't think this a proper subject for young boys to be thinking about."

Tom glanced up at him. "There's nothing unnatural about a woman giving birth, and there's nothing unnatural about men being scared about it." He looked back at Leon, then at Robert. "We're helpless, you see, and men don't like feeling helpless. We can't stop birth from happening and we can't speed it up. We wait, and most men aren't too good at waiting, either."

"What do women feel, do you reckon?" asked Leon curiously.

Tom smiled and ruffled his hair. "I guess they feel helpless, too, son, but they do what they have to do—just like women have always done. God gave men greater strength, but he gave women more heart. Birthing takes stamina and grit, and your mama has both, but I reckon it would make her chore easier if you two boys buried the hatchet while she was about it."

Tom's voice was deep and slow the way it always was and his eyes held the same expression of tolerance and patience and what looked to be affection that Leon had noticed the first time he'd met him. Leon swallowed hard. He tried to remember his own father looking at him like that and couldn't.

Leon suddenly wished that Tom was his real father, and just as suddenly felt guilty. He owed loyalty to Samuel's memory. His guilt shifted as he heard his mother give a long shriek. But he owed loyalty to Mattie, too, and his father had tried to kill her.

Leon felt the familiar loneliness wrap itself around his heart and wished he was five years old again—before Jesse had left the Bar H and his mother was still a mother and not a woman.

Tom noticed Leon's face take on that somber look that closed everybody out. Mattie's older son carried a wound inside that wouldn't heal. Robert had lost a father he didn't remember—if Samuel *was* his father, which was something that troubled Tom's sleep more than he admitted. Leon had lost not only the father of his blood, but the father of his spirit. Tom had no doubt that Jesse's bullet had killed more than Samuel that day; it killed a boy's belief that there was more goodness than evil in the world and left him with nobody to trust.

Robert accepted his mother's marrying without reservations. Tom knew it didn't have so much to do with his own worth as a stepfather as with the fact that Robert couldn't remember a time that Tom Miller wasn't part and parcel of his world. It was only natural that his mother marry him.

Leon didn't altogether accept him, and Tom judged the odds were about even as to whether he ever would. The boy was skittish as a young colt about trusting anyone. Then, too, because of the scandal over Jesse and Mattie, Leon had learned too early that his mother was a woman, and maybe more woman than mother. That always disturbed a youngster—especially a son. From what he'd observed in his years, Tom figured daughters always knew there was a woman inside their mothers. Sons didn't generally recognize that fact unless their mothers did something they considered unseemly or embarrassing—like sleeping with a man and having his baby.

The thin wail of an angry infant wiped out Tom's worry over Mattie's two sons. Jubilee and the Colonel could take care of the boys. He'd waited nearly forty-three years to hear the cry of his own child, and he didn't intend to waste another minute. He ran up the stairs, bursting into the bedroom.

Aunt Patty turned around. Behind her Tom saw Mattie holding a naked baby. "You come up too soon, Tom. I ain't got her and the baby cleaned up yet."

Tom leaned over the bed, examining the crimson squalling infant. A son! He had a son! He kissed Mattie's dry, cracked lips. "Thank you, sweetheart," he whispered softly, then picked up the baby with trembling hands. "I'll wash up the young'un, Aunt Patty. A boy ought to know his daddy as soon as he's out of the chute. That way he don't ever doubt that he was welcome."

Aunt Patty gave him an approving look before she turned back to Mattie. "You be careful with that young'un. Something that small can slip out of a man's grip if he ain't careful."

Tom carried the baby over to a basin of water sitting on the table by the window. "Not this man's grip, Aunt Patty."

He washed the tiny body, marveling over each feature as he did so: a cap of gold curls darker than Mattie's; blue eyes he figured might turn to his own hazel color; his nose and mouth, but handsomer somehow, as though Mattie's blood had refined the coarseness of the face he willed to his son.

"He's a mighty fine-looking boy, isn't he, Aunt Patty?" Tom asked.

"Reckon he's gonna be," she replied, turning toward him. "Give him to me now while you help Miss Mattie to the rocking chair. Then she can put that baby to the breast while I get the bed changed. The sooner she suckles him, the sooner her milk will come in."

Tom gave up his son to the old woman and gathered his wife into his arms. One felt as good to carry as the other, he thought, but in different ways.

Mattie touched his cheek as he gently sat her in the rocker. "Thank you," she whispered. "I never had a husband before who was proud of his son."

He noticed she said son, not sons. Truth had a habit of slipping out without a person being aware of it, but Tom hoped Mattie didn't realize she'd given herself away. His knowing wouldn't change the past, and it just might make Mattie uncomfortable. He didn't want that.

"I'm the first real husband you've had, Mattie. Samuel gave you his name, that's all."

"And children," she said softly, looking at him with guarded eyes. "Even if one didn't live."

Tom nodded, thinking that she had caught on to what she revealed, and was covering her tracks as best she could without lying to him. Samuel had given her children—Leon and a stillborn daughter buried in the cemetery overlooking the Canadian.

"It takes more than begetting offspring to be a husband, Mattie. That's no more than any bull on the place can do."

Mattie closed her eyes and swallowed. "Thank you, Tom, for being my only husband."

He figured she was thanking him for more than that, but some things are best left unsaid.

CHAPTER

The Canadian River has reached the condition where it is not now running at all, and in this condition it has not previously been for a half dozen years—since April and May of '83, at which time it ceased to run for some six weeks, following a rainless and snowless winter. It is certainly a dry stream now—as dry as a Tascosa citizen would get if starting on a fifty-mile journey with no more than a quart. It is dry, truly—as dry as we are at this very moment. Not a spoonful of water can be found in the neighborhood of the big bridge without digging, and even the sandy bed shows no particular degree of dampness as indicating water at a shallow depth. It is rarely that it goes so completely dry, but we've written it up this time with perfect veracity—if we don't use the same again for a long, long time.

—The Tascosa Pioneer, September 21, 1889

Mattie didn't need to read Mr. Rudolph's newspaper to know that a drought threatened the Panhandle. After good rains in April, the blistering sun dried out the prairie worse than the summer of '86. Still, she believed the picture was not as bleak as Rudolph painted it. He was a relative newcomer, after all, arriving in Tascosa in June of 1886. He hadn't lived through the dry years of '80 and '81 as she had. Mattie remembered the Canadian drying up in '83 as Rudolph mentioned in his paper, but the rains had come. They would come again. It was only a matter of surviving until they did.

She switched Joe from one breast to the other. Other than a grunt the baby didn't protest the temporary interruption of his meal. He was so different from Robert. Her second son had always let out a wail of displeasure, and even Leon had fussed more. Joe was as patient as his father.

She stroked his soft cheek and he opened his eyes to gaze up at her. She felt his mouth ease its suckling for a second, and was certain he had smiled at her. Aunt Patty swore Joe was too young to smile, that his expression came from gas in his belly, not love in his heart. Mattie knew better. Joe was like his father—loving.

She glanced at Tom, who lay stretched out on the bed watching her nurse his son. She supposed most women would be embarrassed to be the subject of such regard. Certainly she doubted that most women would nurse their children in front of their husbands with their nightgowns stripped to their waists. Of course, she thought most men would be at least a little embarrassed, too. Not Tom. He thought she was beautiful when she nursed Joe. He had told her so. She thought Tom Miller must be the only man in the world besides Jesse who accepted all functions of a woman's body as completely natural and beautiful.

Tom rubbed his finger across her forehead. "What are you frowning about, sweetheart?"

"Did you read Rudolph's article in *The Pioneer*?" she asked quickly, anxious to deflect Tom's attention. Her husband always sensed when she allowed Jesse's name to enter her thoughts, and she had no wish to hurt Tom. Yet Jesse sat in a prison cell because of her. Sometimes she pictured herself slowly choking to death, strangled by two nooses: one her bond with Jesse, and the other her growing bond with Tom.

Tom sighed and sat up. "I read it."

"I think Mr. Rudolph is exaggerating as usual."

"You sound like W.M.D. Lee, Mattie. He doesn't appreciate Rudolph either."

"I'm not as bad as Lee, but I don't approve of Tascosa's only newspaper being so hostile to the ranchers. Did you read what Rudolph said last week? He called Charlie Goodnight "the greatest living obstacle to the settlement of the Panhandle." My God, Tom, Goodnight opened up this country for settlement. He started the Stock Association. He started the subscription funds for the first school and talked the other ranchers into donating."

She saw that Joe had gone to sleep and lifted him to her shoulder, patting his back until she heard him belch. "Rudolph just doesn't understand this country. The land's not suitable for farming. There's not enough rain. This drought proves it. We ranchers can survive it—we've done it before—and these farmers can't. Their crops will burn up in the fields and leave the land naked to the wind."

Tom chuckled and leaned over to lift the sleeping baby off her shoulder. "You're the only woman I know who can argue business and mother a baby at the same time. Wash yourself off and I'll put this little feller to bed."

Mattie went to the washstand and wiped the milky film off her breasts. "If more women were like me, men like Lee and Rudolph wouldn't be at loggerheads with each other."

She started to pull her nightgown up when she felt Tom's hands clasp her waist, then stroke upwards to cup her breasts. "How are you at arguing and loving at the same time?"

She caught her breath and leaned back against his chest, letting her gown slip from her hands and down her legs to pool at her feet. "I prefer to do them one at a time."

"I'm glad you've got a one-track mind about some things, Mattie," he whispered as he swept her hair out of his way and kissed the side of her throat.

She glanced in the mirror over the washstand and watched him kiss her, occasionally touching his tongue to her skin as if he thought she was good enough to eat.

He was always so careful to avoid touching the thin gold chain she wore around her neck. Her only remaining link with Jesse.

She closed her eyes, but the tears ran down her cheeks anyway.

"Mattie? Did I hurt you? Are your breasts too tender for my rough hands?"

She opened her eyes and watched him in the mirror. But that was just a reflection, and his concern was real.

She freed herself and stepped away, turning to face him as she did. "Why have you never asked me to take off this locket, Tom?"

He met her eyes. "It wouldn't mean anything if I had to ask you, Mattie."

She lifted her arms and unfastened the tiny catch.

Tom didn't move to embrace her as she thought he would. "Are you certain, Mattie? Taking it off just to please me won't mean much of anything either."

She walked to her dresser and dropped the locket into her jewelry box and closed the lid. "I'm doing it to please myself."

"Does it grieve you?"

The cold edge of the dresser pressed against her bare hips, reminding her that she was naked and vulnerable from her uncovered head to her feet with the one missing toe. "Yes," she admitted.

He nodded. "Only a cold woman would not grieve, Mattie, and you're not cold."

She rubbed her bare arms. "Then why am I shivering?"

He moved then, gathering her into his arms. "Because you finally stripped yourself bare in front of me and you're afraid." He stroked her back. "Put your gown back on and go to bed, Mattie. I won't ask you to share your body with me tonight. I don't begrudge you time to grieve, and I don't begrudge your memories of Jesse so don't be afraid to say his name to me. I wish I owned all your heart, but I'm content with what you've offered. You would be less than you are if you denied Jesse any part of you."

Her tears wet his chest and turned the silky brown hair into damp ringlets. She held him tighter and lifted her head. "Love me, Tom. My heart's like an empty room now and I need you to fill it with shared memories." She rose up on her toes to reach his mouth. "Make a memory with me tonight," she said against his lips.

The rains did come as Mattie predicted, but they were too scant to fill the small creeks, much less the Canadian. By November, Tom was seriously worried and knew he couldn't put off telling Mattie any longer.

After supper one night, he held his son in his lap and faced his wife across the kitchen table where they had gotten in the habit of joining Hank Wilson and Danny Boone for a last cup of coffee before bed.

"Mattie," Tom said without beating around the bush. "The cattle are dying from lack of water."

She went white, and he feared she might faint. Then she straightened her shoulders. "But we had rain, Tom."

"It weren't enough, Miss Mattie," said Hank Wilson, looking little older and more grizzled than when he'd signed on with the Bar H eleven years before. "Tom and me been checking the water holes and creeks the past couple weeks. Everything is dry as a bone."

"But the windmills, Hank. Aren't the windmills keeping the stock tanks filled?"

"We don't have near enough windmills, Mattie, and the cattle are so maddened from the smell of water that they kick them in the wooden slats of the stock tanks and knock over the watering troughs," answered Tom. "The clay ponds fare little better. The herds trample down the sides."

"Can't you water a few head at a time?" asked Mattie. Tom heard the quiver in her voice and felt sorry for her.

"We've been trying, Miss Mattie," said Danny Boone. The former horse wrangler for the Bar H, Danny was now a top hand, and along with a few others, one of the remaining cowboys who had trailed the first herd of Mattie's cattle down from Pueblo.

"But it's not working out too well," continued Danny. "Them cattle been knocking down fences to get to the water. It's worse than a stampede some days. And we have to keep moving them from one pasture to another 'cause the forage is so bad. You're death on overgrazing, Miss Mattie, and you ain't wrong about that, but there ain't hardly any help for it. There just ain't no grazing or water to be had."

Tom saw Mattie take a deep breath and slowly let it out. "I see."

Tom rocked his sleeping son in his arms, and wished he didn't have to upset the baby's mother, but there was no way around it. "We're going to have to sell off some cattle, Mattie. We're going to have to sell off a lot."

"But the market's bad!" she protested.

"Reckon we'll have to take what we can get, Mattie. We got too many cattle for the grazing and the water. We pulled through the last few years by the skin of our teeth, but we won't make it another year. And we need more windmills."

"We're barely meeting expenses now," said Mattie slowly.

Hank Wilson cleared his throat. "Miss Mattie, I never been a drinker or a gambler, and buying a woman's company for an evening never was something I did any more than I had to, so I got some money saved up. You been paying us men what amounts to a rich man's wages for a cowboy for a lot of years now, and some of us figure you might be a good investment. For sure a better gamble than them poker games down in Tascosa."

Mattie's chin quivered before Tom saw her clench her jaw to regain control. She cried sometimes in front of him, but she tried never to do it in front of the men.

"I can't take your money, Hank. Or any of the other men's either."

Hank scratched his head. "We ain't giving it to

you, Miss Mattie. We're *loaning* it. We expect to get it back with interest."

"And if you don't, Hank?" she asked.

Hank grinned. "Hell's bells, Miss Mattie. Ain't no cowboy I ever knowed who died with money in the bank anyway. Tell you what. Most of us don't have no families—or none we've seen for years—and no matter what happens, we'd kind of like to stick around. If you'll keep us fed and watered and promise us a spot to rest in your cemetery when the time comes, then I guess we got a fair deal even if we don't get a dime back."

Mattie knocked her chair over in her hurry to run out of the kitchen. The baby let out a frightened wail when the chair crashed to the oak-plank floor, and Tom cuddled him against his shoulder.

Hank rubbed his hand over his balding head. "Damn it, Tom, I never meant to set her off like that."

"I reckon she's more used to folks criticizing her than approving of her. It caught her unawares." He pushed back his chair. "I'll go see about her."

"I reckons you best let her be, Tom," said Jubilee. "She gots to do her crying by herself, then make up her mind by herself. She needs you too bad for me to be letting you chance giving her advice. She might take it and maybe later decide she was wrong and hold it against you."

The old man met Tom's eyes without flinching, and Tom sat back down. He recognized wisdom when he heard it.

"Hank, Danny."

Mattie walked back into the kitchen, and Tom recognized her at once—but not as his wife. There were no tear tracks on her pale cheeks and her eyes, though red, were not wet. That Hunter woman was done with crying—and it was she who stood at the head of the table, not the wife of Tom Miller who nursed his son and slept softly in his arms at night. This woman accepted no pity, tolerated no authority but her own, and met adversity with bared teeth.

Much as Tom admired her, he was sorry she was back. That Hunter woman wouldn't thank him for protecting her.

Hank and Danny recognized her, too, and pushed back their chairs and awkwardly stood up. "Yes, ma'am," they chorused.

Mattie kicked her fallen chair out of her way as if it had nothing to do with her. The sound of it sliding across the room seeming deafening in the quiet room. "I thank you both for your generosity, but I will not take advantage of it. I am not so poor yet that I must borrow from friends." She cleared her throat. "Hank, please round up as many of the weaker cattle as need be to save the others. Drive them to Amarillo and make the best bargain you can."

"Begging your pardon, Miss Mattie, but the weak ones won't make it, and if they do, nobody'll buy them. Some of them cows are so skinny, you can count every rib. There's no meat on them anywhere—just hide and bone. You want to sell cattle, you're going to have to send your best, and they ain't none too good."

Mattie nodded, accepting his judgment. Tom thought he saw grief flicker behind her glittering yellow eyes, but it vanished as quickly as water vanished into the dry prairie, leaving behind not even a hint to suggest that Hunter woman was anything but hard as the land itself.

"Then shoot the worst, Hank, because they will die anyway and a quick death is more merciful than letting them suffer a slow one. Divide up the best of what remains. Keep some to rebuild the herd and sell the rest. You and Danny get the men out tomorrow and tend to it. Leave the carcasses on the prairie to give food to the wild animals. Maybe if we feed the lobos, they won't be so quick to bring down my healthy cows and calves."

"Tom," she said, shifting her eyes to look at him. "Pay off some of the men, beginning with the ones who signed on last. Keep on the ones with families, and the ones who offered to loan me money. I would rather I had another choice, but I don't."

"Don't take on about it, Miss Mattie. It's happening on all the other ranches, too. Dead cattle don't need cowboys," said Danny.

She smiled, accepting the young cowhand's reassurance even though Tom knew she didn't need it. That Hunter woman did what was necessary. "Thank you, Danny—Hank. That will be all for tonight."

Hank swallowed the last of his coffee. He was wise enough to know a dismissal when he heard it. "Come on, Danny. Time to turn in. Gonna be a long, bad day tomorrow. We best get what sleep we can." He nodded at Tom and Mattie. "Good night, folks."

Mattie waited until the door closed, then looked at Tom. "Why didn't you tell me how desperate things were before my cattle started dying?"

"I didn't want you worried before you birthed, Mattie, and then I didn't want you bothered while you healed."

"Judging by your actions at night I've been *healed* for several months."

"You don't be jumping on Tom like that, Miss Mattie. You had this young'un to feed—ain't nobody can do that 'cepting you—and there wasn't nothing you could do nohow," said Jubilee.

"Leave it, Jubilee," said Tom. "There's no point in you catching hell when it's me she's angry at. I did what I judged best, Mattie, for you and our son, and I won't apologize for it. You couldn't have done any more than I did. Not even that Hunter woman can call down the rains."

Her lips thinned. "Don't stand between me and my land again, Tom."

"Then don't ever put your land between you and me, Mattie," said Tom softly, rising to face her across the length of the table. "I won't risk you for the sake of this hard country."

"Don't threaten me! The last man who did is dead!"

Jubilee grabbed her arm and whirled her to face him. "You listen to yourself, Miss Mattie. You talking like what Tom did and what that no-'count Hunter did was one and the same. You talking like you wants to break Jesse out of prison and ask him to shoot Tom. I ain't gonna have it, you hear? And don't give me that ugly look neither. I knowed you since you was born, and I ain't scared of that Hunter woman. She ain't nobody but a woman who had to be hard 'cause she never had no husband worth his salt till now."

"I did what I had to do," said Mattie.

"But Lordy, Miss Mattie, you don't have to do it no more," said Jubilee.

"You don't understand, Jubilee. There's no turning back for me. It's too late. I'm a woman grown into my ways and they suit me now. I can't be a helpless young woman of no business sense or judgment again any more than Leon can return to being an infant. Or you could return to being Papa's valet. No one grows backward."

Two tears ran down the deep grooves on either side of Jubilee's nose. Tom supposed every man grieved for the loss of a child—and Mattie the child was truly dead—grown into a woman of her own.

"Growing up don't mean spitting on a decent man's kindness, Miss Mattie, and that's what you just done to Tom. I'm ashamed of you and you ought to be ashamed of yourself."

"I reckon you better stop while you're ahead, Jubilee, or else we'll both find ourselves out of favor. Mattie," he called softly to the woman standing rigidly in the old man's grip. When she finally turned her head toward him, he continued. "According to your lights, you figure you got a right to take a strip off me for not telling you sooner that things were bad. I won't argue with that. But I didn't do it because I thought I was better or smarter than you, or because I thought you were less than me. Like you, I did what I had to do until the time came for hard choices and you were up to making them. I judged that time was now."

Jubilee let go of Mattie's arm, and Tom watched her turn away and walk to the window next to the back door. She flipped aside the curtain and stared out. She was renewing herself, Tom knew, gaining strength from the sight of her land.

He waited.

Finally, she turned. Her face was still pale, and her eyes still those of that Hunter woman, but the bitter anger was gone.

"I'm sorry for my wicked tongue," she said.

Tom felt his own fear ease. She wouldn't throw him off the place, but he didn't fool himself that he'd escaped by much. He wasn't Jesse. If Mattie had to choose between him and her land, he wasn't certain but what Tom Miller wouldn't end up with the short end of the stick. "I expected a few harsh words. You don't take to being coddled."

He heard Jubilee clear his throat. "If you two is through with your fussing, I has got a dried-apple pie hid away. I'll just cut us each a piece. This evening started off bad. We needs to finish it up good."

Mattie remained where she was. "The bad part isn't done, Jubilee. Tom and I will be going to Mobeetie tomorrow."

"What for you going there, Miss Mattie?" asked Jubilee.

"To borrow money from the bank for windmills."

"You're mortgaging part of your land?" asked Tom.

She shook her head. "I'm using my jewelry as collateral."

"Jewelry," said Jubilee, his brow wrinkling in puzzlement. "You ain't got enough to get no money out of no bankers. You was too little 'fore you got married to have much but a few pearls. Wasn't fitting for a young girl to wear much of anything else. And that worthless piece of trash you married for certain never bought you anything. So just where you getting all this jewels?"

"That's none of your business, Jubilee," replied Mattie, looking away.

"They your mama's, ain't they, Miss Mattie? What do you mean by trading off your mama's jewels?" demanded Jubilee.

"I own two things of value. My land and my mother's jewels. I won't mortgage my land. That leaves the jewels."

Jubilee leaned over the table as upset as Tom had ever seen him. "Your mama kept them things through the whole war, Miss Mattie. She finally sewed them into the hem of her skirt to keep them safe from the Yankees. She made me promise that if she was kilt before the Colonel came home, that I was to keep them jewels for you. They was handed down from mama to daughter in her family for as long as she knew, and she was gonna pass them along to you. Now you're telling me you're giving them to some banker so you can build windmills."

"Yes, that's what I'm telling you."

Jubilee looked desperate. "It ain't right, Miss Mattie. You don't own them jewels. Your mama and your grandmama and your daughter and her daughter owns them just as much as you do."

Mattie closed her eyes for a moment, then opened them to look at the old man. "Please, don't torture me with what once was or what might be. My mother is dead and I have no daughter. The jewels are mine and I *will* save my land."

CHAPTER

26

Wednesday was a windy enough day, but it was about midnight or a little after that things went to shaking and nodding in the breezes and getting a move on themselves about right. From that until daylight was the hardest windstorm the oldest inhabitant knows anything of. It just naturally blew and blew and blew, and blowed and blowed and blowed, and swept the country all up in one great big continuous sweep. In that latter half of the night it piled dust heaps everywhere, and sent it through and into the tightest buildings, and rattled the roofs and shook the fences and scattered the loose boards and boxes and barrels and bent the trees and roared and howled and shrieked and hissed till nothing else could be heard. It was frightful. It filled the river with sand till it went temporarily dry. It kept up that lick all of Thursday. It made us tired and several others reported on the same line.

—*The Tascosa Pioneer*, March 29, 1890

There was no escaping the dust as the parched land gave up its soil to the wind.

What rain fell—and Mattie's rain gauge had measured less than a quarter inch for five different months—disappeared into the blistered ground without leaving enough dampness behind to muddy a man's boot. Even in the wettest month—and there was only one and it was none too wet—dust particles danced in the wind and wiggled under doorjambs and around window frames.

It was the worst drought—and the dirtiest—Tom could remember and by his estimation was in its fourth summer. A man never felt clean even indoors. No one walked across a hardwood floor without his footsteps sounding gritty, and no one slept without waking up covered with a fine powder. Everyone suffered, but perhaps none suffered more than the new settlers who believed the false promises of an ungentle land.

Tom watched those who had come to the Panhandle with dreams leave with defeat as the farmers and small ranchers who filed on their four sections after the lease law was revised by the legislature in 1887 saw their hopes shrivel along with their crops under the hot sun and the dry winds. The most desperate ones—or the most determined, depending on how one looked at it—gathered up buffalo and cattle bones and sold them for eight to ten dollars a ton to agents of Eastern fertilizer plants. Tom guessed nothing was so bad that something good didn't come out of it. The great buffalo slaughter of the 1870s that deprived the Plains Indians of their principle source of food, and the Big Die Up that ruined so many ranchers provided the bones the settlers gathered. What hurt one group of folks gave another group their only source of survival. Everything evened out at the end.

What Tom saw as a cruel kind of fairness, Mattie saw as an inadvertent weapon against ranching. The cattle bones left by the Big Die Up were being turned into the fertilizer to enrich farm land. A disaster for the rancher would one day become a bonanza for the farmer—when the drought broke.

If it ever broke.

Until it did, Mattie, along with other big ranchers, reduced her herds still further and paid off more of her men. As each man rode off with his final pay from the Bar H, he carried away that Hunter woman's promise that when times got better, his job would be waiting. Tom didn't doubt Mattie's sincerity, but damn sure doubted her foresight. Times got no better and Tom watched Mattie's remaining cattle grow more gaunt as 1890 wore on.

But her cattle weren't the only gaunt creatures on the Bar H. The sun burned away a man's spare flesh and left him whipcord lean and brown as cured leather. Tom figured his appearance was no worse than that of any other man on the place who rode out each day into the wind, but he knew it was no better. The cowboys looked like scarecrows riding bundles of bones and so did he. Lately he had trouble remembering a time when exhaustion didn't weight him down, a time when a troubled mind didn't keep him awake at night.

Tom slapped his hat against his clothes to rid himself of the layer of fine grit that covered him from hat to boots, then stepped up on the porch where Mattie stood waiting for him as she did every evening. She was thinner, as everyone else was. The heat stole appetite as well as moisture, and a man or woman ate when hunger drove him to it. Mostly what a man wanted more than food was water. Tom dreamed of lying buck naked in a rainstorm. He dreamed of swimming in a Canadian River that ran bank to bank. He dreamed of drinking one cup of cold spring water after another until his stringy frame swelled up like leather left in the rain.

He wiped his face on his sleeve and looked over the pastureland that stretched south from the house to the small creek a mile away.

"If you're looking for signs of life, you needn't bother," said Mattie, her voice as flat and dry as the land as she stepped up beside him. "The pasture is dead and the creek is dry. There's no hope in that direction."

"There's not much hope in any direction, Mattie."

"The windmills?" she asked.

"The windmills won't do it. Too few and too late," answered Tom, his own voice sounding nearly as flat as hers. "Reckon you got to make some more hard choices."

"Then I lost my mother's heritage for nothing." She laughed as she held out an official-looking document, but Tom figured it was only because she lacked the moisture to shed tears.

He looked at her. Her eyes had lost the shimmering gleam of gold coins and taken on the bleak, yellow-brown color of the land. Tom didn't consider himself a superstitious man, but sometimes he wondered if Mattie was mortal at all, or if she was the land made flesh. When it suffered, so did she.

"From the bank?" he asked without taking the document.

She nodded, then frowned. "Ever since our disagreement last year, you've been standoffish in some respects." She held up her hand when he started to protest. "Oh, you still take me to bed every night except during my monthlies, and you don't hesitate to kiss or caress me at other times, but you hold yourself back when it comes to my land. You act like you married the woman, but only work for the rancher."

"I reckon that's so," he admitted. "Seems you wanted it that way and I obliged you."

She clutched his sleeve, standing so close he could smell her skin. "I *don't* want it that way. You are part of me and I'm part of you, and we share responsibility for this land. I didn't think so last year when I said such hateful things to you, but I know it's true now."

He covered her hand with his. "I love this place, Mattie. It calls to me same as it does to you, but I never earned the right to claim it as home like you did. You bought it with grit and determination and your neighbors' good opinion—you and Jesse McDade. I forgot that last year. That doesn't mean I wouldn't do the same thing over again—protecting you and Joe—but I damn certain wouldn't be so cocksure about it. Guess I was feeling like a wild mustang stallion with a mare in heat. All I had to do was mount you and I had the right to choose where you'd graze and what water holes you'd drink from. Well, I still mount you since it appears from the sounds you make and the way you buck that you like it nearly as much as I do, but I damn sure think twice now about nipping you if you head for a different pasture than I have in mind."

"Why didn't you tell me this sooner?"

"I reckon you riled me, Mattie, thinking the worst of me like you did. Thought I'd let you make the first move."

She shivered and stepped closer to him. "You hold a grudge a long time."

He thought about it. He wouldn't call his holding back a grudge exactly; it was more like acting to save his self-respect, but he wasn't sure even a woman like Mattie would understand that. Men and women saw things differently, and he didn't think that would ever change.

"I'm a man, Mattie, and I don't find it any easier to admit I was partly in the wrong than the next man would." He tipped her face up. "Mind you, I said partly wrong. I won't take the whole blame just to buy my way back into your good graces. You're a strong-willed, hardheaded woman, and you'd ride roughshod over a man if he let you. I won't let you, so don't dig your spurs in me again, sweetheart."

It wasn't a threat; it wasn't even a warning, although he supposed Mattie might take it that way. It was a simple declaration that he wouldn't give up more ground than she was entitled to.

She smiled—the first real smile he'd seen on her face for a long time—and he had a gut feeling he'd misjudged Mattie Jo Hunter again. "I'm glad," she said. "Equality works both ways, and I never had any use for a man who would lie down and let himself be stepped on."

Tom tilted his head back and laughed, then wrapped her up in his arms and kissed her. She tasted of woman and dust, but damned if a man couldn't learn to enjoy a little grit with his meal—if it was served up on Mattie Hunter's lips.

He lifted his head and set her away. He'd never gotten over losing his wits every time he rubbed up against her, and he figured he might have need of a clear head in the next minute or two.

"Now, tell me what the bank said, Mattie, so I can share your worries."

"The bank will auction the jewels if I don't pay off the loan by Friday," she said.

He wiped his sweaty face on his bandanna. "And I take it there's no money?"

She shook her head. "Not unless I sell some land in the next three days."

"I wouldn't count on that if I were you, Mattie.

Nobody wants this land anymore. Folks called this country the Great American Desert when they didn't know any better, but now it looks more and more like they were right and the rest of us were wrong. The ground's too dry to hold the grass, which is dead anyway, and the wind is blowing away both. Places on this ranch—and every other ranch for that matter—look like a desert. We're down to bare dirt in some spots."

She looked up at him, her eyes losing whatever light they held a minute before. "Then I gambled and lost anyway. There's no hope."

He laid his hands on her shoulders, sensing somewhere inside that if he didn't think of some way of saving the land, Mattie would perish along with it.

"Sometimes hard work means the same thing as hope, Mattie"

Mattie wiped her face on her sleeve and dropped to the sandy ground beside the Canadian. Up and down the riverbed for as far as she could see were deep holes laboriously dug with scrapers hitched to teams. Although there was nothing but bone-dry sand along vast stretches of the river itself, underneath the riverbed was water—or so Tom hoped. The hard work was in trying to dig far enough below the bed to find it. With any luck, the water would seep into the holes overnight and each morning the men could water the cattle. The trick was to control the thirst-mad cattle and to keep away the wild animals who also scented water. Tom had already ordered a few men to stand guard with rifles and shoot any four-legged beast that didn't wear the Bar H brand. Mattie hardened her heart against thoughts of the graceful antelope, the deer and prairie hen, the quail and wild turkeys, that would die beside the water holes. In a drought there was no room for pity. The wild animals could migrate to wetter climates—and would—but her cattle could not.

Tom squatted down beside her and jerked off his hat. His hair was plastered to his head and sand filled the lines and grooves of his face. Mattie felt her heart twist inside her chest. The drought had aged them all—she had noticed a few silver strands in her hair, a faint tracing of lines at the corners of her eyes—but Tom seemed to have aged most of all. His hair was mostly that yellow-white color that once had only been a halo about his face, and he no longer seemed to stand so straight and tall as he had in the past as cares and worries almost imperceptibly rounded his shoulders. His face was craggy now, with seams and lines and grooves like weathered granite. Only his eyes remained the same: patient, calm, and loving or hard, depending on whom he was looking at.

At the moment they were loving as he stripped off a glove and brushed his hand along her jaw. "You feeling all right, sweetheart?" he asked.

His smile hadn't changed either, thought Mattie. It was still the sweetest smile she had ever seen on a man. Dear God, but she had done nothing to deserve such a good man.

She caught his hand and pressed it against her cheek. "I'm fine, Tom. Just a little tired and hot, but I'd feel so even if I had stayed at the house. Carrying babies always makes me tired the first few months."

He freed his hand from her grasp and gently stroked her belly, just barely rounded with new life. "I should've been more careful to spill my seed outside your body, Mattie. Joe isn't two yet, and you're so thinned down from this drought."

She cupped his sand-coated face in her hands. "I'll be all right, Tom. Women have had babies in worse times than these and survived. I will, too. I'm a hard woman, or have you forgotten?"

He smiled at her teasing. "I guess it will take more than a drought to do you in, Mattie Hunter."

She frowned. "Why do you always call me Mattie Hunter? My name is Mattie Miller, or have you forgotten that, too?"

He sat down beside her. "I haven't forgotten. I haven't forgotten either that you made your mark in this country as Mattie Hunter. Marrying me and taking my name legally doesn't change that. I suspect you'll always be that Hunter woman to folks. Being my wife doesn't wipe out who you were before and will be again since I'm a lot older than you, and barring accidents, you'll likely outlive me by a considerable number of years."

She clapped her hands over his mouth, shivering in the heat as a sense of foreboding touched her with an icy finger. "Don't say that, Tom. You'll be around until we're old and gray and Joe's children sit at your feet."

He gently lifted her hands away. "I'll damn sure try, Mattie, but nothing's ever certain. I guess that's as much why I never leave you unloved at night as the fact you're still the prettiest woman in Texas and just looking at you gets me stirred up. I want to fill every day with as much of you as I can because everything comes to an end—good times and bad."

To the end of her days Mattie remembered that moment with Tom more clearly than any other. She remembered the sunlight pouring through the wilted leaves of the cottonwood tree underneath which she sat; the strong wind whipping up the sand piled beside the holes dug in the riverbed; the smell of sweat and the sound of murmurs from tired men.

Most of all, she remembered the expression of contentment in Tom's eyes. Whatever happened in the future, Tom Miller lived with no regrets for his past choices.

She reached out for Tom, but Jubilee stumbled up the river's shallow banks, waving his hat in the air and shouting—and her moment passed and left words unsaid.

"Lordy, Lordy, Tom! Miss Mattie! There's water seeping in them holes. Praise the Lord, we is saved!"

CHAPTER

27

It is useless to make a long to-do about it, or to magnify a thing of no great moment, but this, kind friends, is the closing chapter in the history of The Pioneer. *For nearly five years it has gone forth proclaiming to the world that we had here a country and a town; has tooted his horn as faithfully as it knew how for the spot on which it hoped to grow up, has kept the best foot forward and a smiling face under every condition, but has battled with difficulties and hoped against hope—but today we lay down the saber and give up the fight; and* The Pioneer *is an institution of the past, a back number, a remembrance, a reminiscence and a dream.*

It might have different with The Pioneer— *but it wasn't. Had Tascosa fared well at fortune's hands, that would have meant permanency for the paper; the citizens have been uniformly liberal in their support of it, and it acknowledges its deep debt of gratitude. But business has gone down to where profit is an unknown and undiscoverable quantity, and the near future holds no promise—and which one of you would do aught but give it up at that? Sentiment is creditable and the home feeling may be hard to stifle, but after all, duty points to go wherever labor hath a sure reward.*

So we quit to seek a new field—it would be childish to hesitate about it longer. We surrender the whole question—we feel that we have done all our duty—and we go with a clear conscience, a heavy heart and a light pocketbook. Friends will be remembered for their friendship, and the years of pleasant association with place and people will never fade from memory. The warmest spot in our heart will long be for this little gem of a city on the turbid Canadian, sandy, sheltered, quaint Tascosa.

No more will The Pioneer *crack its ancient chestnuts in your tired ears—no more sing of the glories of Rockislandville—no more picture in wearisome detail the coming country—no more importune the young man to come west—no more chronicle the return of fly time—no more wage relentless war on the poor bachelors. We have had our say and now you can have yours—but as the pall of eternal silence settles down about us we are troubled with the thought: will they cuss us when we are gone?*
—The Tascosa Pioneer, *spring 1891*

Mattie folded the last issue of *The Pioneer* and laid it on the ground beside her. Tascosa's first and only newspaper had gone the way of prosperity. She wondered if Rudolph realized his last editorial chronicled more than the death of his paper. More than *The Pioneer* was a remembrance, a reminiscence, and a dream. So were the vast herds, the plentiful grazing, the feeling that just beyond the horizon was a glorious future. And so was Tascosa.

Rudolph was also right that it might have been different. Had his newspaper not driven the wedge deeper between the big rancher and the nester, perhaps men like Lee and the stockholders of the XIT might have thrown their support behind the Rock Island Railroad's early plans to build a line from Liberal, Kansas, to El Paso with a major shipping point being Tascosa. Perhaps, had Rudolph been more of a peacemaker, the XIT would not have moved its headquarters from Tascosa to a new town, and forbidden any travel across its holdings. Had the Big Die Up not happened, the big ranches that surrounded Tascosa might not have enclosed their land behind unfriendly barbed wire that barred transient cattle drives and travelers from the town. Had the drought not struck, the small landholders would not have fled and might have done their buying in Tascosa. As it was, Rudolph might hold Tascosa close to his heart, but too many others did not and took their commerce elsewhere.

It might have been different—but it wasn't.

Sandy, sheltered, quaint Tascosa was a cow town, and its only reason for existence were now skeletal beasts bawling weakly in dusty pastures as the drought tightened its grip for the fifth year.

"Miss Mattie, you best come in the house now."

Jubilee was past seventy now, gray and stooped, but his voice had lost none of its authority, thought Mattie. He still tried to order her about as though she were still a young girl with little sense.

"In a minute, Jubilee. I've been confined for so long, I just had to get out in the fresh air."

"There ain't no fresh air out here. Ain't nothing but wind and dirt—ain't been nothing else for years. And your sitting on the ground beside this pond ain't gonna make the springs run again. Can't you see, Miss Mattie, this pond is done bone dry? Its bottom is cracked like God took a hammer to the ground."

Mattie looked sadly at the dust-filled depression that once was a spring-fed pond at the foot of the mesa behind headquarters. In happier times she had often sat in a tiny grove of cottonwood trees on its north bank.

The trees had died in the drought's third year.

"The pond is a remembrance and a reminiscence—like Mr. Rudolph's newspaper. Like all of us, Jubilee." She glanced up at him. "We're a dying breed—the last of our kind. It's as if the land is demanding a reckoning from those who failed to love it. But those men are gone—or soon will be. The syndicates, the absentee owners, the foolish, and the greedy—all gone. It's the pioneers like Bugbee and Cresswell and Goodnight and Jesse and me who are bearing the brunt of the land's fury. We cherished this land—husbanded it—yet it's us it demands as sacrifice." She pounded her fist against ground. "Damn you! Damn you!"

"The land don't know the difference between who treated it right and who didn't," said Jubilee, hunkering down and catching her hands. "We just happens to be the only ones left to be tormented. There ain't nothing deliberate 'cause the land ain't human, Miss Mattie. You ain't had too good a grip on yourself anyhow since you birthed that young'un last month. You didn't have no business getting out of bed so quick. It has done addled your wits."

Mattie resented his look of sympathy as much as she resented his assumption that she was delicate and that childbirth was a life-threatening illness. If she lived to be a hundred she would never understand why most men couldn't accept childbirth as naturally as they accepted a cow dropping a calf—or why most women encouraged such awe. Unless, of course, it was because having a baby was the only time women held the upper hand.

Thank God Tom wasn't most men and she wasn't most women. The only awe-inspiring thing about childbirth was the result—not the process.

Obviously Jubilee didn't feel that way.

"I'm not addlepated, Jubilee. I know the land's not human like me or you, but it's alive in its own way, and it's dying the same as my cattle or my horses—or us."

Jubilee's look of sympathy turned to one of alarm, and he pulled her to feet and slipped an arm about her waist. "You come in the house now," he crooned. "That baby needs to be fed, and you needs to rest your thinking. You're talking wild. Anybody else heared what you're saying would think Tom had best lock you up before you do harm to yourself."

Mattie pulled away. "I'm not mad, Jubilee, except after the fashion that all of us who stay are mad. Perhaps we all should take Mr. Rudolph's advice and 'go wherever labor hath a sure reward.'"

"You ain't never thought enough of Mr. Rudolph before to do more than cuss him. Don't know why you'd take anything he said for gospel now 'cept you're feeling down."

She clutched his arm, digging her nails into his flesh until he flinched. "How can I not, Jubilee? Look around you. My land is nothing but dusty earth with the grass fighting to survive. It is repudiating me. I gave it my youth—endured marriage with Samuel rather than divorce him and lose half of it. I sold my mother's jewelry. And for what? Why am I holding on? To see the last of my cattle die of thirst or be ravaged by the wolves? To watch my life blow away with the wind?"

She looked into the black eyes that had always held a wisdom only given to those whose fate had rested in the careless hands of others. "Why won't I give up, Jubilee?"

"I reckon you figure if you walk far enough down a road, it's closer to go on than to turn back."

"Closer to what, Jubilee?"

"To the end," he said, lifting his head to look west over the dusty plains. "To whatever is in store for you. Most folks drop out along the way. They sit by the side of the road with their lives wrapped up in bundles and wait for somebody to come along and give them a ride. Only nobody ever does 'cause you gots to walk down that road on your own two feet or you don't walk down it at all. But a few folks—like you—just kept walking even if their feet bleed and they have to pay toll with pieces of their lives—or other people's lives. You see, Miss Mattie, you just gots to see what's at the end of that road."

"And what if there's nothing waiting, Jubilee?"

He shook his head as he looked back at her. "Don't matter none. You still gots to know, Miss Mattie."

"No, I don't," she said, releasing his arm and letting her shoulders slump. She was tired—too tired to walk farther. Too tired to struggle longer. "I know enough as it is. I know I threw away lives on that road. Samuel died—and Clint Murray—because I wouldn't give up this land."

"Weren't neither one of them any great loss. They got what was coming to them."

"And what of all the others I've buried in that Hunter woman's cemetery?" she asked, meeting his eyes. "Did they get what was coming to them, or did they die because their lives got too tangled up with mine? Squinty died so my pastures wouldn't burn. Red died because he got caught in the middle of a fight over this land. And Jesse" —she took a breath— "Jesse went to prison because I loved this land too much."

"You think a powerful lot of yourself, Miss Mattie, believing you is the only reason men die. You didn't make Hunter mean as a snake, you didn't set that prairie fire, and you didn't have no say in why Red got caught in the middle of a fight I suspect had as much to with liquor as with hard feelings. Wringing your hands and carrying a load of guilt and pride on your back ain't gonna change what happened yesterday and ain't gonna stop what happens tomorrow."

She shook her head. "It's over, Jubilee. I'm turning back. I'll watch no more cattle die. I'll bury no more of my folks in this hard, dry earth."

"Them cattle gonna die anyway, and somebody gots to lay out the dead. Somebody gotta stay on the land, Miss Mattie."

"Let it be someone else. Leaving the land is my reckoning, Jubilee. Samuel's death and Jesse's going to prison only delayed what was meant to be." She raised her arms toward the cloudless sky. "Did you hear me? That Hunter woman surrenders."

"Ain't nobody listening, Miss Mattie. You is talking to yourself."

She tilted her head back farther to the sky and the sun. "I'm talking to the wind, Jubilee. The wind will carry my words over the prairies and the dry creek beds and watering holes and springs. You see, there is no one else to listen—no one else to pass the word. Mr. Rudolph was wrong. No one will cuss us when we're gone because no one is left but us."

She let her arms fall and turned toward the house. Even it showed the effects of the drought. Windblown dirt had scoured away paint until it bared the wood on the south and west sides of the house. Boards shrank in the dry heat until cracks appeared in the plaster walls and the hardwood floors squeaked at every step. And always there was the dust—on the window sills, the tables, in the curtains, and the rugs.

She had been mad not to surrender before.

As she stepped through the front door, she heard her infant daughter fussing and the deep, melodious voice of Tom as he tried to soothe her. "Your mama is coming, little sweetheart. Just hold on and she'll feed you."

Mattie let the screen door close behind her, but didn't move toward Tom. She watched him instead as he cradled the baby in one arm and stroked its tiny head with his other hand. His daughter, Rachel. Her daughter.

Her second daughter.

Mattie felt her eyes burn and blur from tears as she remembered that other baby girl, buried on the bluff high above the Canadian one blustery January day in 1878. Dead before birth, that other daughter had never been held by her father—nor her mother. Only Jesse had ever touched her as he wrapped his buffalo robe around her as a shroud. She had died without knowing laughter or sorrow, hope or love. Conceived by rape, she had died without seeing the flat plains in all their shades of green and brown.

Mattie closed her eyes as she remembered the vow she had made on her daughter's grave—that she would survive and flourish, and that no man would shame her.

No man had—not even Samuel.

She had survived and flourished for a time.

Mattie opened her eyes to see Tom watching her and holding Rachel, her second daughter, conceived by a gentle man's love and born on the very plains that held her sister's bones. The quick and the dead—and to each she owed a debt.

"Tom," she said slowly. "Be my witness. I swear by the name of my living daughter that I will not leave this land. I will survive this reckoning, and the land will not defeat me."

CHAPTER

Late summer 1893

"Jubilee says this drought is like the one Joseph foretold to the Egyptian king," said Robert, nudging his skinny horse down the bluff toward the Canadian. "It's gonna last seven years."

Leon glanced at his younger brother. At ten years old, Robert was nearly as tall as he, but blessed with a broad-shouldered frame that Leon lacked. It was just one more reason for Leon to resent him. At seventeen, he should be head and shoulders taller than Robert.

"The Egyptians had a pharaoh, not a king," said Leon, trying to keep his voice from sounding snappish. Since the night Joe was born, Leon had tried to make peace with his younger brother. It wasn't easy. Robert was too strong willed to compromise; too single-minded to see any point of view but his own; and he possessed a violent nature that only lately had he learned to leash.

Arching one eyebrow, Robert glanced at him. "Doesn't make any difference what you call him—pharaoh or king—he was still the fellow in charge."

The sight of that one raised eyebrow stirred a swift, uneasy spasm in Leon's chest. Its familiarity taunted him. Somewhere, sometime, he had known another man with that same physical quirk.

"It does matter what title you give folks, Robert. Otherwise, somebody might think you're too ignorant to know the difference."

Robert reined in his horse next to Leon's. "Are you calling me ignorant?"

Leon shook his head, suddenly weary of arguing. "No, I'm not. I'm telling you what other folks might think. It's for your own good."

Robert studied his older brother's face with eyes the color of his mother's and not one whit less hard than Mattie's when she was feeling distrustful. "You never bothered about my good before."

Leon wiped his face on his sleeve. "I can change my mind, can't I?"

Robert hesitated, then nodded. "I suppose—but I don't generally trust folks who change their minds too often."

"Damn it all, but you're hard to like!"

Robert glanced quickly away but not before Leon saw his chin quiver. "I reckon I must be. You and the colonel think so, anyhow."

Leon tried to fight back guilt. "Why don't you call him Grandpa like I do and Joe and Rachel?"

"Seems better if I don't."

Leon didn't reply. Robert might be right at that. Grandpa Corley never seemed at ease around Robert.

Leon nudged his horse and started down the bluff again. "Best we check on the water holes in the riverbed. See if they filled up again overnight. God knows, they're nearly the only source of water for the herd. What's left of it," he added bitterly.

Robert followed him. "I'll check the ones downriver. You take the ones close to the plaza."

Leon felt a stab of irritation at being ordered about by a ten-year-old. "How come we don't swap? I'll go downriver and you go to the plaza."

There was a flash of something like uneasiness in Robert's eyes. "You're the one always talking about living there. I figured you must like to ride that way."

"I didn't live in that plaza! Ma ordered the old one burned down after our pa was murdered there. This is a new one she had built later. It's not even in the same spot. It's farther upriver."

Robert was silent for a long moment. "It doesn't matter. It doesn't welcome me."

Leon frowned in confusion. "You're talking crazy, Robert. It's just an adobe building. It's got no feelings."

"It's too close to the ruins of the first one—not more than a hundred feet."

"But the ruins are where they found our pa's body. They're like a cemetery."

"I don't like that place, and I'm not riding that way," said Robert.

"Are you saying it's haunted?" Leon started to laugh until he saw Robert's eyes flash with anger and humiliation and swallowed back his mirth. He kept forgetting Robert was just a kid, and kids still sometimes believed in ghosts.

"I'm not saying anything of the kind, but I feel things just like Ma. She doesn't visit the ruins either."

"But if there's a spirit there, Robert, it's the spirit of our father. It won't hurt you."

Robert threw him a quick glance he couldn't read. "My pa is Tom Miller. Always has been."

"No, he isn't," insisted Leon. "Samuel Hunter was your father. Don't you remember him at all?"

Robert's eyes darkened until they were a pale brown, and his lean face suddenly looked hard and old. "No—and I don't want to either."

"Surely you don't believe those stories about his nearly killing Ma. . . ." began Leon.

"Yes!" cried Robert. "And you ought to believe them, too, and stop talking about him around Ma. It's bad enough you look like him."

"Is that why you don't like me? Then you must remember him if you think I look like him."

"I ain't going to talk about *him* anymore, and you're ignorant as dirt if you think what folks said about him isn't true! That's the same as calling everybody you know liars."

Leon felt his heart twist painfully as he tried to sort out his feelings once more—and once more failed. If his father was innocent, then his mother was a liar. If his father was guilty, then Jesse was innocent of murder—unless his mother was keeping company with Jesse the way some folks said. Leon rubbed his forehead where an ache was beginning. His doubts circled around inside his head like a mule tied to a treadmill. There was no beginning and no ending.

"I'll ride upriver by the plaza, Robert," he said wearily. "I'm not scared of it."

Robert hit him—a powerful blow to his shoulder that nearly sent Leon tumbling off his horse. The younger boy's eyes were a glittering yellow, as if firelight was trapped in their depths. "I'm not scared! I just don't go where I'm not welcome unless there's a reason."

Before Leon could answer a voice hailed them from the other side of the river.

"Ho! Robert! Leon!"

Robert spurred his horse down the bluff in a cloud of dust. "Mr. Faulkner!"

Leon rubbed his aching shoulder that he knew would carry a purple bruise tomorrow, and followed his brother to the river.

The Canadian was mostly sandbars and limp-leafed trees. A tiny narrow stream meandered its way down the very center of its bed. Leon remembered the river when it had been a raging torrent during the spring runoff, its waters blood red. But that had been in his childhood—and he hadn't been a child for a long time.

He reined in his horse in the middle of the riverbed, next to Robert's and Faulkner's. "Mr. Faulkner, what can we do for you?"

Faulkner still dressed like a British aristocrat and spoke like one, but Leon noticed his fine lawn shirt was frayed around the cuffs and his riding boots were worn down at the heels. Folks were saying he was having a hard time holding on to his ranch, and Leon guessed it must be true because the Scotsman didn't look like he had two nickels to rub together anymore than Mattie and Tom did.

George Faulkner pulled a linen handkerchief from his pocket and blotted his face. "A bit warm today," he said, then grinned. "Of course, it's a bit warm every day. Still, I prefer it to the British Isles with their interminable rains—although, to be honest, I do wish we could engage in a mutual trade in weather futures. A little of their rain for a little of our sun."

He tucked his handkerchief away and adjusted his hat. He did wear a Stetson now, Leon noticed.

"Your stepfather agreed to allow me to water my cattle with yours. My stretch of the river is completely dry and I haven't the men to dig these clever holes. A bit of a financial bind forced me to let all of my hands but Douglass go. No openings for trained personal valets, you know. Besides, he's been with the family for years. I doubt if I could kick him out if I tried—and I haven't tried. Fortunately, he's become quite a competent cowboy—and he does have a deft hand with crumpets. With his help and that of my son and wife, we have managed. My father, of course, is horror-struck that I have allotted a man's job to a boy."

Leon nodded. George Faulkner had married shortly after Mattie's wedding and his son was a year older than Joe, which made him somewhere around six. Leon had ridden out with the hands at that age. Maybe other folks in other places thought it was too young, but then they didn't grow up in a hard land.

"My father doesn't see my wife's herding cattle as equally unsuitable since he considered her as sturdy yeoman stock." Faulkner smiled wryly. "My father and I disagree on the precise definition of wellborn. In his eyes I am, but my wife isn't. She finds his attitude amusing while I find it abhorrent."

He flushed as if suddenly realizing he was committing a breach of etiquette by speaking of private matters. Leon decided Faulkner's mind must be badly troubled to reveal himself so nakedly.

"How many head are we talking about?" asked Robert, his yellow eyes narrowed. If he noticed Faulkner's lapse of reserve, he didn't show it.

Faulkner shrugged. "A little over two thousand. My windmills can take care of the rest."

"You don't have but five windmills," said Robert.

"I don't have many cattle either. Between the drought and the wolves, my losses have been heavy."

Leon interrupted. "Stop questioning the man, Robert. If Tom gave permission, then that's the end of it. It doesn't matter if he's got two thousand or ten thousand."

Robert swung his head toward Leon. "It's my land and my water we're talking about, too. And yours—but you don't seem to care much."

"Listen, you little varmint!" Leon spat out the words, furious at his brother's accusation. "I was working this ranch before you were born, so you keep your insults to yourself or I'll shove them down your throat until you choke on them."

"Silence!" shouted Faulkner, his voice echoing against the bluffs along the river. Leon jerked around in the saddle to stare at the Scotsman and saw Robert do the same.

Faulkner stood up in his stirrups and pointed toward the north. "There are clouds coming up."

Leon shaded his eyes and peered down the broad river valley. A great white cloud did seem to be rolling in from the north—an immense cloud that extended from horizon to horizon as he could see it hiding the newly risen sun in the east and rising toward the heavens above the bluffs to the west. At first he thought the cloud must hold ice crystals within its heart for it reflected back the sun in a thousand glittering spots.

"It's a strange cloud—like white vapor," he said, feeling uneasy without knowing why.

"It's not a rain cloud," Robert whispered.

"Of course, it is," began Leon, turning to look at his brother, then swallowing the rest of his words. Robert's eyes were fixed in his head as he stared at the cloud filling the sky. His body was rigid and Leon watched as goose bumps erupted on the young boy's arms.

"Robert?" asked Leon, reaching out to shake his younger brother, but Faulkner grabbed his arm before he touched Robert.

"Leave him be," whispered Faulkner. "'Tis the Sight he's having. I've seen it before in Scotland."

Leon didn't know which frightened him more: Robert's odd behavior or Faulkner's look of awe. "What are you talking about?"

"The Sight. Certain Scots have it. He sees things we cannot see."

"We're not Scots. We're English and always have been."

Faulkner shook his head. "You perhaps, but not him."

"He's just showing off," Leon insisted. "He's always been odd. Just before you rode up he was saying that he wasn't welcome around the ruins of the old plaza."

Faulkner's gray-green eyes held a look of pity. "Poor child. To be cursed with sensing too much. It will not make for a happy life."

"You're crazy," said Leon, pulling his arm free of Faulkner's grip and slapping Robert across the face. "Stop it, damn you!"

Robert blinked and shuddered and slumped over clinging to his saddle horn.

"What did you see, boy?" asked Faulkner urgently.

"I saw the land crawling. And wings," answered Robert. "Can't you hear the sound of the wings?"

Leon turned his head toward the north and closed his eyes. He felt the fine hairs on his arms spring erect as he heard a faint whirring sound carried on the wind. "What is it?" he whispered.

Robert's voice rang with certainty. "It is a plague. Just like the plague God sent down on the Egyptians."

Mattie's first inkling of the plague was the sound of Jubilee's agitated voice calling her from downstairs. "Lordy, Lordy, Miss Mattie, come quick!"

Mattie was in no mood to come quickly or any other way for that matter. Her sleep had been restless and she was feeling out of sorts as she sat in her rocker and watched Rachel toddle about the bedroom clutching a rag doll and crooning to it. Even the sight of the huge cottonwood tree in the front yard failed to soothe her. Instead it freed memories she had locked away in her mind, and Jesse's specter beckoned her to visit the past where once more she might hear his deep, teasing voice, feel his touch, lose herself in his arms.

She rubbed her forehead. Such memories were never free of guilt. She could not persuade herself that her past was her own and no business of Tom's. At odd times when she least expected it, Jesse filled her heart and mind as though it had been yesterday she last saw him instead of seven years ago. She rested her head against the back of the rocker and closed her eyes to squeeze back tears. Why, in spite of time and distance and the love of a good man, did her hunger for Jesse sometimes overwhelm her? Dear God in heaven, why did a woman have no choice as to which man bound her spirit to his?

Her eyes snapped open at the sound of pounding against the door. "Miss Mattie! Is you awake? You needs to come see. It's the plague of Egypt."

"I'm coming, Jubilee," she answered as she rose and picked up Rachel. The little girl smiled at her mother, proudly showing off several pearly white teeth. Mattie squeezed back more tears. Rachel's smile was like Tom's: sweet and loving. How could she hold Tom Miller's daughter in her arms and still feel Jesse's presence in her heart?

She opened her door just as Jubilee raised his hand to knock again, and saw Robert standing beside him, his golden eyes so much like hers in color and so much like Jesse's in expression. Robert was her child as much as Rachel, and she would never be free of the father her son would never know. She was doomed to love a man she could not have and a land she could not save.

"What is all this about the plagues of Egypt? Is the Canadian running red with blood?" she teased.

"Robert knew they were coming," announced Leon, his face pale and his voice accusing.

Robert glanced back at his brother. "I did not! I just knew it wasn't a rain cloud 'cause I didn't smell the wet dirt. There's always a wet-dirt smell when rain's coming. Besides, I could hear the sounds. You could have, too, if you'd listened."

"Hear what, Robert?" demanded Mattie impatiently.

The young boy looked at her, and she realized with a start that he was as tall as she. "The grasshoppers, Ma. The sky is full of grasshoppers."

Five-year-old Joe, standing beside his adored idol, Robert, jumped up and down flapping his arms. "It's 'hoppers, Mama. Hundreds and hundreds of 'hoppers.

Mattie felt chills dance over her arms and down her back as she thrust Rachel at Jubilee. "Hold her," she ordered as she gathered up her skirts and rushed downstairs, her heart pounding so hard she could hardly hear the whirring song of a million insects. She pushed open the screen door, knocking several grasshoppers off its mesh as she let it slam behind her, and ran out in the front yard.

"They're coming from the north, Ma," said Leon breathlessly as he followed at her heels.

Mattie stopped abruptly, her breath catching in her throat as she looked toward the mesa behind the house. It was moving! Its steep sides wiggled and flowed as though water were running down them and pouring across the prairie. But it wasn't water. It was grasshoppers—millions of them—so thick they covered the ground without space to stick a straw between the bodies. Every green stem of vegetation disappeared beneath their onslaught as they marched down the mesa and joined the army pouring across the prairie from the north. They piled up waist deep in the dry pond and hopped over its banks toward the vegetable garden Mattie and Jubilee had fought so hard to keep alive by digging an irrigation ditch from the windmill standing by the corral—an irrigation ditch now choked with leaping, twitching insects. Buzzing, clicking, whirring sounds filled the air as the army of grasshoppers engulfed the garden and began to devour it right in front of Mattie's horrified eyes.

"Robert!" she screamed. "Run to the henhouse and drive the chickens out toward the garden! Leon, get shovels out of the barn. We'll beat back the grasshoppers from the garden. Joe, take Rachel and go in the house."

"I want to help kill the 'hoppers, Mama," protested Joe.

Mattie whirled on him. "You get in the house like I told you!"

"Miss Mattie, we can't beat them 'hoppers," said Jubilee, handing a screaming Rachel to her sobbing brother. "They gonna roll over us like the Red Sea over the Egyptians."

"You hush up about the Egyptians, Jubilee!" she shouted. "The blizzard didn't beat me. We're surviving the drought, and I'll be damned to hell if a bunch of grasshoppers will make me give up."

In the far corner of her mind, she noticed that Jubilee didn't chide her for her unladylike language as he ran along beside her to the garden. Even Jubilee recognized when not to waste his breath.

Time stopped—or perhaps hours passed—Mattie

had no way of knowing which. When each hour was exactly like the preceding one, how could she tell one hour from another? She and Jubilee and her two sons beat at the living carpet of insects with shovels until her shoulders and back were one burning ache and her hands blistered. For every grasshopper killed, a thousand took its place. The chickens feasted on the insects until they could eat no more, without diminishing the horde. Hairy tarantulas crawled out of their holes to join flocks of birds—hawks and curlews with six-inch bills—swooping out of the sky to devour grasshoppers.

Still they hopped, flew, leapt, and crawled—an army without end.

Mattie poured kerosene around the perimeters of headquarters and set fire to the liquid. The insects smothered the flames in a suicidal march and continued to ravage. They invaded the barn and ate the hay and grain stored there. They swarmed over the clothes line strung in back of the house and ate the linens, the shirts, Rachel's diapers, and Mattie's dresses. They crawled up the few remaining trees around headquarters and stripped them nude of leaves before beginning to eat the bark.

When they attacked Mattie's giant cottonwood in the front yard, she ran toward it, her mind empty of any thought but to protect the living symbol of all her memories.

"Goddamn you!" she screamed as she beat at the trunk and flailed at the low-hanging branches with her shovel. "You can't have this tree!"

Grasshoppers shaken from the branches dropped on her head, entangling themselves in her hair, clung to her blouse, and crawled up her skirt to nibble at its cotton twill. Skin crawling with revulsion, Mattie dropped her shovel and clawed frantically at her hair, crushing insects with her bare hands.

Distantly she heard herself screaming, felt pain as she ripped out strands of her own hair, but neither the screaming nor the pain meant anything at all as she retreated further and further into her own mind, slamming and locking doors behind her in an effort to keep her terror at bay.

Tom heard Mattie screaming, the wind carrying the sound across the dusty prairie, and he spurred his tired horse into a run. He knew he'd see blood on his spurs come evening when he took them off, but given a choice between treating his horse kindly and reaching Mattie as fast as possible, he knew he had no choice at all. He'd kill every animal on the place if need be.

He rode up to the house and leapt off his bleeding horse, leaving it to buck and whinny in a frenzied attempt to dislodge the grasshoppers that immediately swarmed up its nostrils and in its ears. He saw Jubilee and Leon and Robert fighting over a bundle of rags on the ground beneath the cottonwood tree. The tree itself writhed with grasshoppers while a sea of the insects lapped against its trunk. His boots made a crunching sound as he ran toward the tree. Not until he was nearly on top of the old black man and Mattie's two sons did he see that the bundle of rags alive with grasshoppers was his wife.

"Mattie!" he cried.

Jubilee didn't look up from his frantic brushing of Mattie's clothes. "Lordy, Tom," he moaned. "They is killing her. Gonna eat her alive just like she was a tree."

"No, they won't," said Tom, shouldering aside Jubilee and the two boys and lifting Mattie into his arms. He ran toward the stock tank in the corral, afraid to look at Mattie. He didn't think he could stand another glance only to see that blank stare in her eyes. He felt the grasshoppers crawl from her body to his and swallowed back his nausea. Without hesitation, he leapt into the wooden watering tank with Mattie in his arms. He dunked Mattie until only her face showed above the surface of the water on which hundreds of dead grasshoppers floated.

Tom had never enjoyed seeing the death of any living thing, had never felt the blood lust to kill that he'd seen in other men, but be damned if he didn't rejoice in the sight of those dead grasshoppers. As he ripped off Mattie's skirt and blouse and petticoat, as he combed his fingers through her long hair, he laughed at the feeble efforts of each insect to survive as they struggled free of Mattie's clothes and hair.

"Die, you sons of bitches," he cursed as he ran his hands over Mattie's submerged body and plucked drowned insects from her hair.

"Lordy, Tom, she's done lost her mind," said Jubilee, peering over the edge of the tank.

Tom looked at Mattie's still face and felt a cold spot expand inside his body until he shivered. She was breathing—he could feel her chest rising and falling—but her eyes were staring through him at some memory he did not share. He felt her mind slipping away from him with every passing minute.

"She acting just like she did when she caught lice on the trail drive to the Panhandle," said Jubilee. "She crawling away inside herself 'cause she feels dirty. She never could stand no crawling things even when she was just a young'un."

"How did you bring her back, Jubilee?" asked Tom urgently.

"I didn't. Jesse did. He stripped her down and threw her in the Canadian River and scrubbed her down with lye soap. He just wouldn't let her hide."

Tom threw his head back and laughed. "Damn McDade. He bathed her in a river while I throw her in a stock tank. He outdoes me at every turn."

He looked down at Mattie, at her still, slack face and staring eyes, and did what he had never done before in his life: he slapped a woman.

Mattie blinked, her eyes clearing of one memory only to take on another. "Bastard!" she croaked, and reared up to claw at his face.

Tom felt the flesh rip over his cheekbone as her fingernails gored his face. Grabbing her arms, he pinned them behind her back. "Mattie," he called, repeating himself over and over again. "Mattie, it's Tom. Samuel's dead. You don't have to fight anymore."

Gradually, the rage in her eyes faded, and he saw her return to herself. "Tom," she whispered. "Dear God, Tom, the grasshoppers."

"You're free of them, Mattie. I killed them all."

"You saved the tree?" she asked, trying to struggle up.

Tom didn't need to ask her which tree. He knew. Mattie's attachment for that cottonwood tree was one of the few mysteries about her past he'd never been able to decipher, but he suspected it had something to do with Jesse. All the secrets she held close had to do with him.

"Nobody can save the tree, sweetheart. It will survive or it will die the same as the land."

She didn't say anything, just took a deep breath, but Tom saw a grief so deep in her eyes that he wanted to cry himself.

"All right," she said. "I'll take your word for it because I know you would save it if you could."

Tom felt guilt twist his belly. He wasn't sure of

that at all. He didn't know if his nature was generous enough to save a tree he knew in his heart was a stronger symbol of Jesse McDade than any gold locket.

Thank God he didn't have to make a choice.

CHAPTER

September 1893

The drought broke and Jesse McDade came home on the same day.

Pardoned by the governor for saving the warden's life during a prison riot, Jesse rode the train as far as Clarendon on a ticket Tom Miller had sent him, then met Jubilee at the livery stable.

The former slave slapped him on the shoulder. "Your face is a sight for sore eyes, Jesse."

Jesse would have laughed—if he hadn't lost that particular skill one month into his sentence when he broke another convict's neck for trying to sodomize him. He was never tried for murder since there was no proof against him, but the warden had sent Jesse to solitary confinement for six months.

Laughing was one more thing he would have to relearn—if he could.

"You are a fine liar, Jubilee. I look like warmed-over cow shit and you know it. If a man wants to look old before his time, I can recommend prison."

"You don't look no older than anybody else, Jesse. All of us in these parts gots more gray in their hair than what we want, and ain't nobody lived through the drought without it showing up on their faces. I gots more new wrinkles myself than Miss Mattie's tablecloth before she irons it." He broke off suddenly, but it was too late. He'd mentioned Mattie's name.

Jesse stroked a large bay gelding that Jubilee already had saddled for him. He traced the Bar H brand on its withers. "How is she?" he asked, looking over the horse's back at Jubilee.

Jubilee looked back at him in that direct way Jesse remembered. "She's fine. She and Tom gots two babies now. Joe's near five and Rachel's two. She's happy, or near enough. Times have been hard with the drought and all, but I reckon she's lived through the worst."

Jealousy buffeted Jesse like a strong wind. He grabbed the pommel of the saddle and hung on until he could speak without cursing. "Tom didn't mention anything in his letters about children."

"Reckon he didn't figure it was any of your business."

Jesse heard the warning tone in Jubilee's voice and answered it. "I went to prison for her, Jubilee. Don't you think that entitles me to keep track of her?"

"Not if you plans on starting trouble. Miss Mattie's nearly respectable now. Folks think a lot of her and Tom for how they've fought to stay on the land. I ain't gonna stand by and let you pull her down again—and neither is Tom. He ain't no Samuel Hunter, Jesse. I reckon he'd kill you if you go after his wife."

"Or I'd kill him."

"Don't matter which one of you might kill the other. Miss Mattie would never forgive the man who won. Besides, ain't saving her from gossip the reason you went to prison in the first place? Don't make no sense to throw away seven years for nothing."

Jesse rested his head against the saddle. The scent of leather and horseflesh filled his nostrils, reminding him of time lost and debts owed. He lifted his head. "I owe Tom for looking after my place while I was gone. And I owe him for taking care of Mattie, too." He looked away for a moment. "Hell, I even owe Tom for the train ticket and this horse."

Jubilee took off his hat, revealing almost white hair, and wiped his face on his sleeve before speaking. "Tom never bought that ticket. I did. He don't expect you for another couple of weeks, but I figured to talk to you before he did. It's a fair ride from Clarendon to your place. We oughts to be able to get a lot of talking done."

"You're warning me off, aren't you, Jubilee? That's why you sent me the ticket and that's why you met me. Otherwise, I could have walked home from Huntsville for all you cared. All right, you warned me. Now get the hell out of my way. I figure to make it to Tascosa a little after dark day after tomorrow. I got seven years to make up for and a bottle of whiskey and a willing woman will do for a start."

Jubilee fidgeted a minute with his hat, adjusting it three times before he found just the angle he wanted. "That's ain't the only reason I come to meet you," he finally said. "You one of the best men I ever knowed and you always treated me like I was as good as you and not just a nigger. And what you done for Miss Mattie—well, it was a fine thing. I is grateful to you and so is Tom."

"What about Mattie? Is she grateful, too?" asked Jesse bitterly. "I don't know how she feels because in seven years she never wrote me a letter."

Jubilee clasped Jesse's arm, his face a sorrowful mask. "That's the other thing I come to tell you. Miss Mattie ain't never freed herself of you. She used to stand underneath that cottonwood tree every day when the sun come up and look in the direction of Huntsville. Tom never said nothing about it 'cause I guess he thought taking on about it wouldn't do no good 'cept to make her feel worse. I guess what I'm asking you, Jesse, is to be content with knowing you still owns part of her. You both paid for what you done. Let it go at that."

"Go and sin no more. Is that what you're asking, Jubilee?"

"I reckon so."

Jesse grasped the saddle horn and mounted the bay. He gathered the reins in one fist and sat looking down at Jubilee. "I'll be riding to the Bar H with you. I have business with Tom. And I will see Mattie while I'm there just to satisfy myself that prison didn't kill all my feelings. I have to know I'm not dead inside, Jubilee, and Mattie's the only one who can prove it to me. If I can't feel anything for her besides lust, then Tom Miller might as well shoot me because I'm not fit to live anyway."

Lightning flickered in the towering black clouds that filled the sky and thunder rolled across the prairie as Jesse and Jubilee rode out of Clarendon. The wind that whipped them into leaning over their saddles to avoid being blown off their horses carried the smell of wet earth. Before they were a mile out of town the rain fell down from the skies until Jesse felt he was riding through a never-ending waterfall. Water poured off the brim of his hat and down the back of his neck until his clothes were sodden underneath his slicker. Rain hit the earth with such force it sent geysers of liquid mud to splash against his horse's flanks. His leather saddle grew slick and keeping his seat became a chore.

"Where the hell is all this mud coming from, Jubilee? Even in a drought the buffalo grass keeps its roots in the ground."

"It was the 'hoppers, Jesse. They settled to ground and ate up everything but the bull thistles and yucca plants. They was particularly partial to onions. Miss Mattie had a batch stored in the storm cellar, and them 'hoppers ate every one. I swear I could smell onion on their breath when they hopped out of that cellar. When they run out of anything green and growing to eat, they ate the bark off the fence posts and the clothes off the line. They drove the stock crazy by crawling up their noses and into their ears. They even et up Miss Rachel's rag doll. Miss Mattie didn't find nothing of it left but two black buttons she sewed on for eyes. That 'bout broke her, Jesse, that and the 'hoppers eating her cottonwood tree down to the bare branches. But she endured. That's what she's best at."

Jesse reached out and grabbed Jubilee's arm. "Did the tree die?"

"Don't know yet, Jesse, but I suspects one branch is gone. The 'hoppers chewed the bark up pretty good. I think the rest of it will come back next spring—'bout in time to be et again. The female 'hoppers bored into the prairie and laid eggs before the horde moved on. I reckon them eggs will hatch next summer, and we'll have to live through the misery all over again."

Jesse closed his eyes and offered up his first prayer of thanksgiving since being arrested seven years before. The cottonwood tree survived. Hurt, maybe, like he and Mattie were hurt, by capricious fate, but alive. Of all the images he had held fast during the endless lifetime in prison, loving Mattie under the cottonwood tree was the only one that time and misery had not blurred.

By the time Jesse and Jubilee reached Tascosa, every depression in the prairie, every buffalo wallow, every playa lake, every creek dry for years was flooded with water and the overflow reached the Canadian in record time, filling its riverbed from bank to bank. They crossed the wagon bridge into Tascosa just before a torrent of water rammed into the bridge and carried away one of its spans. The harsh sound of ripping wood might have been the death rattle of the town itself as the inhabitants finally ventured out on the third day after the rains stopped. Seventeen houses washed away or collapsed, mostly in the Hogtown section, as the river flooded its banks.

Jesse held his horse to a walk as he rode down the streets of Tascosa when the sun finally broke through the clouds. No building had escaped the deluge. Windows were broken, adobe brick scoured clean of whitewash and softened by the rain. Business signs were ripped off. The Equity Bar had lost its red-and-white-striped awning.

"God Almighty, Jesse," said Jubilee as he rode along side. "This is plumb awful."

Jesse felt disoriented. The bustling town he had left behind in 1886 was now a drowned derelict. Many of the adobe houses looked abandoned and many of the business establishments were vacant.

"What happened to the town, Jubilee?"

The old man sent him a startled look. "It done been flooded, Jesse."

Jesse shook his head. "It's more than that. Where

are all the people? Why are so many houses empty?"

"Hard times, Jesse. When the XIT moved its headquarters and started a new town called Channing, lots of folks followed. Then Mr. Lee and the other big ranchers got into a fight with the county commissioners over taxes to build that bridge that done washed out, and that didn't help Tascosa none. With towns popping up along the railroad, the ranchers didn't have to buy supplies in Tascosa no more if it didn't suit their fancy—and it sure didn't suit Mr. Lee's fancy. Folks gots to make a living, and there just ain't much of one to be made in Tascosa anymore 'less you're a gambler or a fancy woman. The cowboys still come in to drink and carouse, but not much of anybody else."

Jesse felt a sense of time passing him by—of beginning and end meeting. "Tascosa started as a cow town where a man could buy a bottle or a woman and raise a little hell. It looks like its going to end that way, too. I always felt the earth would swallow it up one day and I guess I was right."

Sadness choked off his words suddenly and he was silent until they rode north past Casimiro Romero's flooded hay meadow, then cut west toward the Bar H. Jesse reined in at the top of a gentle rise and looked back toward Tascosa. "I would save it if I could, Jubilee. Tascosa is bound up with my life—with the lives of all the cowmen, big and little. It was the castle on the hill when we all rode on the open range."

"Times is changed since you been gone, Jesse," said Jubilee with a faraway look in his eyes as if he, too, were looking to the past. "Ain't no more open range nowhere. Ain't nothing but barbed wire and cowboys spending more time fixing fence than herding cattle."

"No more cattle kingdoms," mused Jesse. "No

more knights on horseback. I guess we don't need a castle."

Jesse laid his hat over his heart in a last salute to the lonely, dying town of his past, then turned his face toward his equally lonely and uncertain future.

Mattie sat on the porch swing beside Tom guiltily enjoying the smell of wet dirt and the sight of Rachel and Joe splashing in mud puddles while at the same time she worried over Jubilee's continued absence. It had been a week since he abruptly announced he had "business in Clarendon" and rode off leading another horse without any explanation as to just what kind of business might be involved.

"Where do you suppose he is, Tom?" asked Mattie, breaking the silence.

Tom laid his arm along the back of the swing and stretched out his legs, crossing one foot over the other. He looked so relaxed that Mattie wanted to scream. "I reckon he'll be back when he gets his business finished, sweetheart."

"What business? Jubilee hasn't been to Clarendon more than once in his life that I know of. He said a town that concentrates so hard on being free of sin is unnatural."

Tom grinned. "I think it's changed a little since Jubilee's first visit. The Methodists have lost their grip a mite. I heard tell there's a drinking establishment there now. Or maybe I heard somebody wanted to open one. I can't remember which, but when those folks moved the town six miles so it would be on the railroad, I think they left some of their righteousness behind."

Mattie shifted impatiently. "I don't care what kind of town it is. I want to know where Jubilee is. Dear God, it's been a week, and with all this rain he might have been caught in a flash flood. Or he might be sick. He's an old man, Tom. He doesn't have any business running off like this."

"He's a sly old man, Mattie," said Tom in such a peculiar tone of voice that Mattie looked sharply at him.

"What's that supposed to mean?" asked Mattie.

Tom didn't turn his head to look at her, but continued to watch the south pasture. "He's too clever to let himself get caught out by the weather. Jubilee's a survivor—just like you."

Mattie flounced up. "If you're not going to ride out to check the pastures, I think you ought to go look for him instead of just sitting here."

"Hank and the men are checking the pastures and the cattle. If one or the other needs my attention, Hank will send Robert or Leon back to the house to tell me. For the time being I'm just gonna sit here, look at the muddy land and my pretty wife, and wait."

Mattie paced up and down the porch in front of him. "Wait for what, Tom? Jubilee to come home? Well, I don't have your patience. I'm going to saddle a horse and go look for him."

She turned to leave when Tom rose and seized her arm. "I believe that's Jubilee topping the rise down by the creek now."

Mattie shaded her eyes with her free hand. "You have eyes sharper than a hawk, Tom. I can't make out the faces from here."

She turned to look up at him. "Who's that with Jubilee?"

"I reckon it's the end of my peace or the end of yours. I don't know which yet."

Again Tom's voice sounded peculiar to her, and she turned back to watch the riders. She started to smile as she recognized Jubilee's awkward seat.

Nearly fourteen years in Texas and Jubilee still didn't ride a horse much better than he had when they left Pueblo. His companion though, rode as if he and the animal were one. Not many men were so at home on a horse.

Suddenly Mattie gasped and swayed as the rider's identity struck her in the heart. "It's Jesse!" she whispered.

Without thinking she tried to pull free of Tom's grip. "Let me go! It's Jesse!"

Tom caught her other arm and swung her around to face him. "I reckon it is, Mattie. I knew the governor pardoned him and I suspected Jubilee rode off to meet him. They were friends in the early days in spite of being different colors and Jubilee admires him in spite of disapproving of what Jesse was to you. Question is, what is Jesse McDade to you now."

Mattie stared at her husband. Once again she felt the nooses of conflicting loyalties choking her. Tom was her husband, the father of two of her children, the man who loved her. A patient man.

No, not really patient anymore, she thought as she studied his hard eyes. He demands an answer, a commitment in words. It was not enough that she'd put away Jesse's locket—she knew that now. She must also put away Jesse in the flesh.

She didn't know if she could.

"He was my guide, my friend, and yes, my lover when I was still learning how to be a strong woman. We built the Bar H together. We stood against the Stock Association together when we disagreed with its aims." Her voice dropped to a whisper. "We faced shame and ridicule together, Tom."

"And you bore him a son he doesn't know about, Mattie." He tightened his grip when she tried to shrink away. "Robert is his son. Give him Jesse's coloring instead of yours, and nobody would be fooled."

"No!" she cried.

"You married a man you didn't love to save Jesse," continued Tom.

"And he killed for me," whispered Mattie.

"That's all in the past, and I can't change what you share with him. But that's not what's worrying me. I'll ask you again, Mattie. What is Jesse McDade to you now?"

Mattie had known this confrontation was coming—had always known it—but had put it out of her mind. Now it was here and once more all her choices were bad ones. Deny Jesse—and deny her own past and soul. Deny Tom—and deny her present and future and a portion of her heart. She had to choose. She had to hurt one man or the other—and she shrank from hurting either.

"You are my husband," she said, forcing the words out of a reluctant spirit. "I will not dishonor you."

She knew it was not the answer Tom sought, but it was the only one she could give and not further diminish herself in her own eyes by lying.

She had made her choice. She only hoped she could live with the consequences.

And that Jesse could.

The sun dimmed under the shadow of her grief.

Seven years of prison had not stolen away Jesse's faintly arrogant swagger, nor rounded his broad shoulders. Nor were his eyes any less direct nor his expression less proud. Not that the changes in his appearance were any less shocking to Mattie—his hair was silver at the temples and grooves scored his cheeks where once were attractive dimples—but at least he did not return a broken man. She couldn't have borne that.

Jesse removed his gloves and held out his hand. "Hello, Mattie."

She stared at his outstretched hand, her stomach cold with fear before slowly extending her own. She closed her eyes against the rush of feelings when his fingers closed over hers. It took all her strength to open her eyes and answer.

"Hello, Jesse. We're glad you're home."

Her voice sounded weak to her own ears, and she

watched bitterness settle in Jesse's eyes and his face turn hard. He glanced over her shoulder at Tom. "Are we indeed?"

Tom stepped around Mattie and held out his hand. "I haven't forgotten what you did, McDade."

Those bitter eyes narrowed and an equally bitter smile lifted the corners of Jesse's lips. "I don't doubt it, Tom."

Mattie curled her hands into balls until the pain of her nails gouging into her palms forced her to relax them. She wondered what a stranger would make of this conversation. Would a stranger sense that each spoken word carried more than one meaning? Or was it her own guilty conscience?

"You're welcome to stay in the bunkhouse while we straighten out our affairs," said Tom. "I figure it'll take a few days for you to judge whether I've done right by my responsibilities."

"In the bunkhouse?" echoed Mattie, turning to face her husband.

Tom's eyes were as hard as Jesse's. "Yes, Mattie?"

She was suddenly weary of the games men played—tired of being the chess queen each man wished to capture. She was that Hunter woman and be damned if she would allow either man to make the rules in a game in which she was the trophy.

"Jesse will stay in the house, Tom. He is a neighbor who acted against his own interests to help me." Deliberately she raised her hand and brushed the scar under her chin. "I would not dishonor him either," she added softly.

Tom's expression didn't soften although he reached out and brushed her cheek. "I won't argue with you, Mattie. It is your choice and I accept it."

For the first time since she had met Tom Miller,

Mattie knew he was lying to her. He didn't accept her choice with good grace, but he was a patient man. He would have to tell her so in his own good time.

It was another confrontation she would just as soon not face.

Jesse sank into the leather chair in front of Mattie's desk in her office. For a moment he allowed himself to enjoy the luxury of a comfortable chair, the warmth of the wood-paneled room, and the view through a window without bars. It had been seven years since he had sat on a surface that conformed to his body. In prison it had been the other way around. Every surface was unyielding: bunk, chairs, walls, bars. A man could bruise body and soul on the hardness surrounding him.

With an effort he turned his mind toward the man facing him across the width of Mattie's desk. He kept his face as bland as he had when he used to play poker, as bland as he had in prison when he learned to guard his intentions, but he didn't fool himself into believing that Tom Miller didn't know exactly how weak his hand was, or what his intentions were.

Tom Miller, he recalled, had been a formidable poker player himself.

"I won't sweeten the bad news, McDade," said Tom. "We've had a seven-year drought topped off by a plague of grasshoppers. You're no worse off than Mattie, but that's not saying much. What's left of your herds are gaunt and their numbers are small. Your headquarters looks better—mainly because your log house suits the country a hell of a lot more than Mattie's frame one—but that's not saying much either. The fact is, both of us have our backs to the wall. We're not in debt and neither are you—or at least no debt that threatens your land—but we'll both be years rebuilding our places, and I don't know that we'll ever see the wealth we had before. The cattle market's unsettled, and with what the politicians are calling the Panic of '93, there's no money to be borrowed. None to be stolen either. At least, not around here."

Tom gestured at a stack of ledgers. "You're welcome to go over the books and take a strip off my back if you see anywhere I could have done better."

Jesse shook his head. "I trust you, Tom. Your letters to me in prison were clear enough that I wasn't expecting my place to be in the same shape it was when I left it. The rain falls on the just and the unjust alike. Isn't that what the Good Book says? I guess the same is true of drought. Maybe it's not fair to the good stockgrowers like Mattie and me, but then I haven't found life to be fair—certainly not in the last few years."

"I guess I'd feel the same in your shoes."

Jesse felt a flash of resentment at Tom's remark, and recognized with despair that he would always resent the assumption that a man who had never been to prison could imagine what it was like for the man who had. "But then you're not in my shoes, are you, Tom Miller? You didn't spend seven years locked up in a filthy cage with men you wouldn't say hello to in the street."

Jesse saw resentment surface briefly in Tom's eyes and recognized it for what it was: a dislike of feeling beholden to Jesse McDade. In Tom's position, Jesse knew he would feel the same way.

"Do you begrudge me for those years, McDade?"

Jesse looked past him and out the window at the flat prairie stretching toward the east. Tom's question was one he'd asked himself the past seven years and he had clung to his answer as the only hint of decency left to him. "I'd spend those years again for Mattie's sake. Don't ever doubt that I would. But yes, Tom Miller, I do begrudge you those years of loving Mattie, of giving her children, of keeping her safe. It was the memory of her face that kept me from going mad in that cage. It was the memory of her holding me in her arms that drove me to survive one more day when it would have been easier to give up living. Mattie and that" —he waved his hand toward the window— "the land that goes on forever and urges a man to be greater than he is. I hungered every day of that seven years for the woman and the land. And I still hunger."

"The woman is mine, McDade. Your hunger won't change that," said Tom.

Jesse noticed the glint of sunlight on a playa lake near the eastern horizon, and contemplated the image of a faint depression filled with life-giving rain. In a few days the lake would vanish, its water evaporating in the hot sun or soaking into the thirsty earth. No man could hold back the progression.

"That's where you're wrong, Miller. Mattie belongs to herself. She always has. What she offers, neither one of us can coerce. I was her man because she wanted it that way. I'm still her man."

"I'll fight you to keep her, McDade, and I'll kill you if I have to."

Jesse's gaze drifted away from the window to focus on Tom. "Then you'll lose her because the only way to hold Mattie Jo Hunter is to let her go free."

"I guess that cage must have killed what honor you took with you, McDade."

Jesse closed his eyes and rested his head against the back of his chair as he admitted to himself that Tom's accusation held some truth. He opened his eyes, and saw Tom flinch at the bleak self-knowledge Jesse knew he revealed. "When I went to prison, I discovered soft places in myself I didn't know I possessed. I don't have them anymore. I learned to stand aside while two men killed each other. I learned to take what I needed to survive and to hell with anybody who got in my way. I learned to kill and I didn't care whether it was a fair fight or not. I took my honor off like it was a ragged coat and threw it over the wall to be put on again if I walked through those prison gates alive."

Jesse rose and leaned over the desk. "You know what I found when I got out, Miller? I found that honor doesn't fit me well anymore. I shrank while I was inside those walls. The best part of me died and turned to dust and leaked away."

"Mattie's the best part of you, McDade, and she's still alive."

Jesse felt anger and hunger and despair twine themselves around his heart and he fell back in his chair like a wounded man. "Goddamn you, Tom Miller. Don't push me."

Tom slammed his fist on the desk and stood up. "Then stop talking around the subject and tell me your intentions. Do you have enough honor left to let Mattie be or not?"

Jesse stood up also, and for the first time since he rode in, for the first time in seven years, he bared his soul to another man. "I don't know, Tom. I'm not the man I was. I may never be that man again. So much of me died that I don't know for certain what's left. A man needs to hold fast to a standard of conduct—one against which he measures himself every day to see if he grows or shrinks in moral stature. In prison, the only conduct that counts is that which allows a man to survive. If he wants to—and plenty of men didn't. Some were buried and some walked out free men, but the ones who lived were no more alive than the ones who died. I told Jubilee and I'll tell you. I have to see Mattie. She's my standard. I have to see if I measure up to the man she remembered all these years. If there's any unselfish decency left in me, Mattie will bring it out."

His chest heaved as he took a deep breath. "If there's not, Tom, then I'll take her any way I can—now or later. If I find I'm alive after all, instead of one of the walking dead, then we'll get our business done and I'll ride away. I'll leave her and you both in peace. I don't imagine you've really had much of that lately."

"It's been peaceful off and on, McDade. There were sometimes weeks at a stretch when I didn't dread this day," said Tom.

"You've never been in prison, Miller. The first thing we learn to guard against is frankness. It's a weapon in another man's hand."

"Or it's an honest man's last defense," replied Tom, sitting down again. "And I believe you are still an honest man beneath your anger. You were frank with me about your intentions toward Mattie, and I take it as a sign you're not so dead inside as you claim. You're like the Canadian during the drought—hard and cracked on the surface, but still with water to be had if a man digs down far enough. How deep will you dig to find your honor, McDade? Deep enough to ride back to the Flying MJ and live with your wife again?"

Jesse slowly sat down again, his mind momentarily stunned by Tom's question. "My wife?"

Tom nodded, his face expressionless, but his eyes watchful. "Your wife is living on your spread again. I rode to Mobeetie to tell her you were coming home."

Jesse felt consumed with rage. "I have no home

with that woman. If she had any sense, she'd run as far away from me as fear would take her."

"She seems anxious to make amends."

"God Almighty! And you believed her after she did her best to see Mattie hanged?"

"I don't recall hanging Mattie being what she was after. She wanted to humble her—and that's what she did. It was a damn humble Mattie Hunter who asked me to marry her. Your wife's a lucky woman that things worked out the way they did. It just as easily could have gone the other way."

"Do you mean you might have turned Mattie down? I don't believe that, Miller. You waited too long for her."

Tom sighed. "Did you ever think that Mattie might have refused to give up her land for you?"

Jesse shifted uneasily, suddenly feeling pity awake from a seven years' sleep. "Since I didn't know she had until the day before my trial, I can't answer that question."

"Did you ever think she would have refused, McDade? Answer me, damn it!"

Jesse leaned forward. "Goddamn it, man! I don't want to hurt you."

"Answer me, McDade," insisted Tom.

Jess slumped back in his chair. "No. I never doubted Mattie would give up the land for me."

Tom nodded. "If she hadn't thought enough of you to sign away this land, she never would have married me. I owe my marriage to Mattie's feelings for you, and sometimes that fact eats away at me. Like now."

Jesse felt pity and guilt begin to overwhelm his anger and fought back. He had lived so long with anger, he wasn't sure he could survive without it. "You're being frank again, Miller. Don't trust me with that weapon." Jesse cringed inwardly at the quiet anguish he saw in the other man's eyes.

"I don't reckon I have a choice. I can either tell the truth or kill you, and I never was fond of killing. But mind, it's not you I'm trusting. It's Mattie. I knew when I married her that I was sitting in on a poker game with the cards marked in your favor, but I have to place my bet anyway or throw in my hand— and I'm not about to do that. I'll gamble on Mattie."

Jesse felt admiration and respect for Mattie's husband begin to unfurl, and knew he wasn't one of the walking dead after all.

If the resurrection of his own decency cost him Mattie, he wasn't sure but what he wouldn't rather be dead.

"Where are you going with that quilt and pillow, Tom?"

Tom hesitated, then turned toward the bed. Still flushed from loving, Mattie sat leaning against the headboard. He supposed most women would be grabbing for the sheet to cover their breasts from view. Of course, modesty would hold most women back from stripping off their nightgowns in the first place, or at least the women Tom had bedded before he married Mattie—mostly widows uninterested in tying up with a man for any longer than it took to get the crops out of the fields. Some folks might not see the difference between those widows and whores since both traded their company for gain, but Tom never held to such a judgment. The widows weighed a man's decency and a whore weighed a man's coin. There were exceptions, he guessed, but probably not many.

Mattie was different still. She weighed a man's love and her own, then gave herself generously without thought of gain. Tom was gambling his heart that Mattie Hunter had chosen to marry him because she held him in loving regard even if she didn't realize it at the time. Surely to God she realized it now.

Surely to God.

The question was, did Mattie's regard for Tom Miller outweigh her bond with Jesse McDade?

Tom never remembered being so scared before.

"Tom, aren't you going to answer me?" asked Mattie, scrambling to her knees.

He swallowed hard. A man would have to be dead not to be moved by the sight of Mattie Hunter naked and on her knees in the middle of a disordered bed with all her golden hair swirling around her face and down her back. A man would have to be a fool to do what he intended.

He cleared his throat. "I'm going to sleep in the bunkhouse."

Her eyes lost their sleepy, satisfied look for one of hesitation. "Why?"

Tom knew he could still draw back from the course he had set for himself. He also knew he wouldn't. This hand fate had dealt them had already gone on far too long. It was time for him to call.

"I don't care to sleep under the same roof with Jesse McDade."

Her look of hesitation changed to one of confusion and anger, and for a moment he doubted himself again. But to turn back now would be a sign of weakness, and while a man could show Mattie Hunter kindness or tenderness, only a fool showed her weakness. The only fit mate for that Hunter woman was a hard man with a will as strong as hers.

"You said you would abide by my choice," she said.

"I am. You made your choice and I've made mine. You can't have it both ways, Mattie. You can't honor me and honor Jesse at the same time."

She scrambled off the bed to clutch his arm. The gentle scent of rose water and woman enveloped him, and he came close to dropping the quilt and pillow and loving her again. But he didn't.

"But he killed Samuel to save me! He went to prison to save me! Do you expect me to repay him by refusing him hospitality?"

"He made his choices and you made yours and now I've made mine. I want to be your husband, Mattie. I want to walk by your side to wherever the road leads, but I'm not having Jesse McDade walk along with us."

"But you *are* my husband, Tom, and I took off Jesse's locket to prove it!"

Tom raised his hand and traced the outline of a heart between Mattie's breasts. "But you didn't throw away the locket, did you, Mattie. You hoard it in your jewel box like a keepsake."

She twisted away from him but not before he saw her nipples pucker into rosy crowns and felt a man's triumph at knowing his touch pleased his woman in spite of herself. It was one more thing in his favor.

She whirled around and raked her long hair over her bare breasts to hide them from his view. "That's all it is, Tom. A keepsake of my life before I married you. You never asked me to deny my past. You said you were content with what I gave you."

"That was before Jesse McDade came back, and I discovered I was a man like any other. I waited for seven years to marry you, and I've waited another seven years for you to put away all your memories and love me. Even Jacob only waited fourteen years for his Rachel. How many more years must I wait for my own Rachel, Mattie? How many more years do I have to share you with Jesse McDade?"

"You don't share me, Tom! Do you believe I would

walk down the hall to lie with Jesse while I'm married to you?"

"I reckon not. Regardless of how high and hot your blood might run, you won't go to Jesse with my scent still on your body." The minute the words left his mouth, he knew his remark wasn't the smartest one he had ever made to a woman—particularly not this woman.

Her face paled, then the blood rushed back to color her skin a rosy coral. "You bastard! You bedded me for the same reason a dog wets down a fence post—to mark your territory!"

He dropped the pillow and quilt and seized her arms to drag her against his body. "I bedded you because I love you and because I wanted to leave you with a memory and to make one for myself."

He set her away from him and bent down to pick up the pillow and quilt. He straightened up and walked to the door before turning to face her again. "Take away the fact that men walk upright on two legs, there's not much difference between men and dogs. Yes, I did mark you, and be damned if I'll be sorry for it."

He had barely closed the door behind him when he heard glass crash against it and smelled the scent of rose water. He'd seen Mattie cry and he'd seen her hard as nails and he'd seen her white with rage, but he'd never seen her so mad as to throw things, particularly an expensive bottle of perfume.

He thought it might be a good sign.

Not until he heard her start to cry did he wish he had listened to Jesse McDade, who knew her better. He should have gently freed her to see Jesse and make her choice instead of acting like a jealous fool hellbent on forcing her to make up her mind.

He should have trusted her like he said he would.

He should have—but he didn't. And now—when it

was too late—when the last card was played, he
wanted to burst back in and comfort her. Instead, he
gripped the bannister until his knuckles turned
white. He never knew until then that he was such a
hard man.

Or such a cowardly one.

He leaned against the bannister and listened to
his dream made flesh tear herself apart with sobbing, and was too afraid to ask if she cried on his
account or Jesse's.

CHAPTER

31

Leon held his horse down to a slow walk, putting off as long as possible the chore of picking up the mail in Tascosa. He hated the town and didn't understand why his mother always shook her head in sorrow over its half-deserted condition. It wasn't like Tascosa had ever made Mattie Hunter welcome. So far as Leon knew, some of Mattie's most troublesome times had happened in Tascosa—times told in half-heard tales. Such as the day his mother told the Canadian River ranchers to their faces that she wouldn't build her share of the drift fence.

Leon frowned. But she had built the drift fence—or rather his father had, and Mattie had never ordered it torn down until after the Big Die Up. He wondered why she'd changed her mind. His mother wasn't known for being wishy-washy. When she set her mind on something, nobody wasted his time arguing with her—except maybe Tom.

Except lately.

Lately Tom had been sleeping in the bunkhouse and he and Mattie hadn't been arguing. Matter of fact, they hardly even talked anymore except to say "Pass the salt" at the dinner table, or when Mattie handed out orders about the ranch, and then Tom mostly listened.

Little Rachel was too young to know anything was different, but Leon noticed Joe was looking wan and pinched—like he hadn't been sleeping good, or maybe was crying at night when nobody could hear him. Leon remembered doing the same thing when he was younger and Grandpa Corley had brought him back to the Bar H after his pa was murdered.

Leon gripped the reins a little tighter as he felt his belly begin to cramp. Anytime he thought about his pa's murder, his belly started hurting. It hurt all the time lately—since Jesse McDade had come back from prison last week.

In fact, most of the troubles on the Bar H started with Jesse's arrival. Not the dusty pastures or poor calf crop—that was the drought and the grasshoppers—but Tom sleeping in the bunkhouse and Joe's peaked face and his ma's sick look—and his own bellyache.

He took to eating his meals in the bunkhouse with the few hands left who rode for the Bar H brand to avoid sitting at the same table with Jesse McDade. He would not break bread with his father's killer.

On the other hand, he couldn't reconcile his memories of the man he had loved as a child with the hard-faced stranger who never smiled and whose silver eyes sometimes looked so sad.

Nor could he reconcile his memories of the mother he had worshiped as a child with the hollow-eyed woman who seemed to be held together with basting stitches.

Sometimes Leon felt as though his life had been

cut asunder. There was his life as a child riding with the hands across a prosperous grassy kingdom; then there was his life after his return from his grandpa's home in Pueblo. Those he trusted as a child—Jesse, Mattie, Jubilee, Hank Wilson and Red—he could not trust as a young man.

Sometimes he sorted through his early memories—images blurred with the passage of child into manhood—and could not bring into focus a portrait of his father. He found that most frightening of all. It was as if he had never possessed a father, but rather had been begot by a phantom who took human form only for his conception, then vanished into indistinct memories.

No one would tell him anything of his father other than when he was born and what color hair and eyes he had and how he had died after beating Mattie. No one left that out, but no one—not even Jubilee or his grandpa—would tell him what kind of man his father was nor why he had beaten Mattie other than a disagreement over the land.

The land, thought Leon bitterly. That was another difference between his life as a child—the heir apparent of that Hunter woman—and his life now. Once he had loved the land, but now he saw it as a rival that stole away his mother's affections from his father.

He envied Robert his uncaring disregard for the past, or more properly, he envied Robert's youth at the time of their father's death. Robert could not remember a life without Tom; could not remember a life when his mother did not focus on the land; could not remember Jesse McDade.

Lost in his bitter thoughts, he did not realize he had reached Tascosa until his horse nearly walked over one of the "girls" who lived in its Hogtown section, a blonde whose bedraggled dress testified to a hard life in a dying town where coins were scarce.

Leon tipped his hat to the girl whose aging face spoke of too many men with too little love and too much hard lust. "My pardon, ma'am. I was thinking of something else and wasn't watching where my horse was going."

The girl—and Leon decided she was a girl not much older than he if somewhat more worn of face—smiled at him with carmine lips and put her hands on her hips in a pose he found more pathetic than provocative.

"If you really want to make amends, you might entertain me for an hour or so. We can borrow my friend's house. She lived far enough away from the river that her place didn't get washed away in the flood like mine. Lucky I wasn't there or I might be dead instead of standing here talking to you."

Her empty eyes said maybe she wasn't so lucky to have survived, and Leon felt pity mixed with lust—or what he thought might be lust since his britches suddenly seemed too small to hold his rapidly growing member. He'd never had a woman before, but he'd overheard enough from the cowboys to know what to do—or thought he did—and this girl looked to be too desperate to criticize his performance if somehow he didn't measure up to her more experienced customers. There was a first time for every man, and who better to teach him than a girl who, like him, was without a home.

He licked his lips and found his mouth dry. He tried to remember what the cowboys said the going rate was for hired women and couldn't. "I might be interested in sharing a little time with you. I'll pay, of course, so you won't be out any." Immediately he worried that he sounded too crass and tried to take away the sting of what amounted to buying human flesh for an hour. "It'll be a way for me to make up for my horse nearly running you down. Would a dollar be enough, do you suppose?"

He held his breath waiting for her reply, suddenly wanting to be with this girl more than he had ever wanted anything before. Standing there in her cheap red dress that showed too much of what looked to be a generous bosom, and a face that showed too little hope, she promised an hour's forgetfulness in a life that could use a little.

She nodded. "A dollar will be fine."

Leon swallowed and held out his hand. "Put your foot in the stirrup," he directed, moving his own out of the way. "And grab my hand and I'll pull you up. We can ride to your friend's house. With all this mud it'll be nicer for you than walking."

The girl backed away a step. "I can't ride astride like a man. I'd have to show my legs."

Leon was puzzled. If he had the way of things right between a man and a woman, she'd be showing more than just her legs as soon as they got to where they were going. He beckoned to her. "Come on. Nobody will care. Nobody will probably even see you."

She shook her head. "You would see. I may be" — she glanced away a moment as if she didn't want to look at him— "a working girl, but I have my pride. I do some things that folks don't think are proper, but I don't do others." She spread her hands with their nails bitten to the quick. "I can't explain it except to say that everybody ought to have the right to hold fast to one rule they don't break. Maybe it's nothing much to you, but not riding like a man and showing my legs is my rule."

"But my mother rides astride," said Leon without thinking.

The girl nodded. "But she's that Hunter woman. She does as she pleases and no one can run her out of the Panhandle. I hear even the law can't touch her."

Leon pulled his hand back. "You hear wrong. And don't be talking about my mother."

The girl's empty eyes filled with desperation and she reached out and touched his knee. "Please don't be mad. I'm just repeating what other folks are saying. I don't mean to be disrespectful."

Hesitantly she stroked up his thigh and Leon felt himself break into a sweat and his thoughts swirl away in a mist. "I'll walk with you since you're so modest," he heard himself saying in a thick voice he didn't recognize as he slid off his horse and boldly put his arm around the girl's waist. "My name's Leon Hunter, but I guess you already know that."

She nodded. "My name's Phoebe."

"Phoebe what?"

"Just Phoebe. A last name's not important without a family."

They walked toward a two room adobe shack just off Main Street. "You don't have any folks?"

She shrugged. "I had some when my life was different, but that was then. I don't live back then anymore. I live now—and now I don't have folks."

Leon understood. His life was divided into then and now, too, and at present, the now was of considerably more importance.

Later, stretched out on a rickety iron bed in the back room of the tiny adobe shack, feeling like he'd been turned inside out and hung up to dry, the then of his life came rushing back. He rose up on one elbow to lean over the girl who lay curled up next to him. "What did you mean about my mother?"

Phoebe opened her eyes. "The sweat ain't hardly dried on your chest and you're already worrying over what your mother's going to say?"

Swallowing painfully, Leon pushed back thoughts of what Mattie might think of his morning's adventure. "Decent women don't talk about things like we just done. Besides, that's not what I was asking you."

Phoebe sat up and pulled a ragged sheet over her breasts. Sweat had caked the heavy powder she wore and smeared her rouge, and Leon noticed for the first time how thin her face looked and how sharp her cheekbones were. She looked like Rachel's china doll with its painted face blurred, and he felt pity twist his heart again.

Phoebe tucked her hair behind her ears—baby-fine hair, Leon realized, soft as corn silk. "What were you asking, then?"

Leon sat up, too, making sure the sheet covered his male parts. "What did you mean when you said the law couldn't touch my mother?"

Phoebe looked down at her hands and quickly curled them into fists as if ashamed of their ragged, bitten nails. "I heard talk, is all. Folks are all the time talking about that Hunter woman."

"What folks?" demanded Leon. "Gamblers and whores and such trash?"

Phoebe seemed to shrink and her skin flushed crimson under the streaked powder. "I'm a whore," she whispered.

She was a whore. Leon knew that as well as he knew his own name, but he didn't want her saying it out loud. He kept remembering her refusal to ride astride and thought Phoebe had ways about her that were distinctly not whorish.

"Don't be calling yourself names," he finally said for want of anything better.

Startled, she looked at him, then ducked her head, but not before he saw fear in her eyes. "I'm sorry I ever talked about your ma. I ought to know better by now. I've been cuffed often enough for talking out of turn."

Leon pulled her into his arms and rested his chin on top of her head. Her hair felt good on his skin, and he wondered again how old she was. Older than time, he figured. Whoring wasn't the best way to stay young.

"I'm not going to hit you," he said. "I just have to know what folks are saying." He hesitated, then rushed on before he could change his mind. "Everybody at the ranch is closemouthed about my mother, and not real anxious to talk about my pa, either, but I got to know how it was with them. I got to know who to believe so I can have some peace. So tell me what you've heard."

Phoebe pulled away from him and tugged the sheet up under her chin. "Folks say she had something to do with your pa's murder."

"No! That's not true! My pa beat her," he said. "Nearly killed her is what she told me. Jesse McDade killed him so he wouldn't do it again. Ma didn't have anything to do with it."

She laid her hand on his shoulder. "I'm just telling you what I heard. That don't mean it's true."

Leon shrugged off her touch. "Go on. What else are folks saying?"

Phoebe fiddled with the sheet. "That she's Jesse McDade's whore and always has been. They're saying now that Jesse's out of prison, she's taken up with him again, and kicked Tom Miller out of her bed."

Leon heard again the taunts of his classmates when he was going to school in Tascosa. Whore and murderer were what his mother was called then, and seven years later nothing had changed. He covered his ears. "No," he whispered.

"Your pa beat her 'cause she was whoring with Jesse McDade."

"You quit saying that! She wasn't Jesse's whore!

Pa beat her because she wouldn't sign the papers to sell the Bar H."

Phoebe stared at him in disbelief. "Then why did Jesse McDade kill your pa? It weren't his ranch. It weren't any of his business."

Leon clenched his fists as her words rang in his ears, and all the years of doubts demanded to be answered. "Shut up, damn you!"

Phoebe cringed away from him, throwing up her hands to shield her face. "I'm sorry."

He felt guilty for scaring her and tried to pull her hands down. "I won't hit you. I promise. My ma would take a bullwhip to me if I did. She says a man who'd hit a woman is lower than dirt."

Phoebe let him lower her hands. "I'm sorry I called your ma a whore. I ain't a fit person to be judging her. There's times I've been hit that I wished a man dead, but I didn't have nobody to take up for me. Your ma's luckier than me. She had Jesse McDade."

Leon let go of her and climbed out of bed to dress. As he pulled on his britches he glanced back at Phoebe, still sitting in the middle of the bed staring at him with frightened eyes. She had forgotten to cover herself with the sheet, and Leon's gaze dropped to her bare breasts. Had his mother sat naked in front of Jesse McDade while he dressed to leave her? Had she spread open her legs for a man not her husband? Leon gagged at the thought of it.

"Leon, you don't have to go. Stay awhile longer. And—and you don't have to pay me nothing. I enjoy your company. You make me forget what I am."

He buttoned his shirt and picked up his hat. "I got to go. I got to ask my mother for the truth. She'll tell me. I don't remember her ever lying to me."

"Maybe you shouldn't ask. Things like that are private, and women don't always want to talk about them."

"Mattie Hunter is my mother!"

"But Leon, she's a woman, too."

He left without telling her that he could not abide thinking of Mattie Hunter as woman.

The shadows were reaching across the prairie toward the east when Leon rode up to the frame house that had never felt like home. His mother had sent him to Pueblo with Grandpa Corley before he'd had a chance to get used to the house, and when he came back to the Panhandle to live, Robert had already marked the three story headquarters as his own territory.

To Leon, the old plaza on the Canadian would always be home. It was there he was happiest. Riding across the dew-wet prairie perched on the saddle in front of his mother. Watching the branding and marveling that his mother turned pale at the smell of burned hair. Listening to his mother clap her hands and cry the first time he roped a calf. Smelling the scent of rose water when his mother tucked him in bed and listened to his prayers. Walking by her side while she picked wildflowers in the spring and talked to him of how beautiful the plains were to those who had eyes to see.

These were the times he remembered—and they had all happened at the plaza.

He walked through the front door. "Where's my mother?" he asked Jubilee.

The old man narrowed his eyes and pursed his lips. "Abouts time you were getting home. Near sundown and your mama worries about you young'uns being out after dark."

"I'm not a *young'un* anymore. I'm a man and I asked you a question."

Jubilee frowned at him. "Don't you be getting

snippy with me, Leon. And don't be acting too big for your britches neither."

Leon thought of the bulge that strained the buttons on his pants when Phoebe had rubbed his leg and burst out laughing. "I don't believe I have to act anymore, Jubilee. At times I am too big for my britches."

Jubilee's gaze sharpened and Leon felt himself turn red. "How come it took you near all day to ride into Tascosa and pick up the mail?"

Leon swallowed. He had been in such a hurry to get home that he'd forgotten the mail. Not that it mattered, he thought, straightening his shoulders. Nothing much mattered except talking to his mother.

"I need to talk to my mother, Jubilee. Where is she?"

"She be in her office, but she's busy."

Leon pushed by him and walked to his mother's office, opening the door without knocking. Mattie and Jesse stood facing each other in front of the desk. In the heartbeat of time before his presence registered, Leon saw the sad yearning on his mother's face as she looked up at Jesse. Her posture looked soft, as if she was about to flow into Jesse's arms.

Leon's heart starting pounding in his chest and he wanted to run back outside, jump on his horse, and ride for Tascosa and oblivion in Phoebe's arms.

Mattie turned, her face turning pale. "Where are your manners, Leon? You know you should knock before opening a door."

He forced the words out. "I want to talk to you—now!"

Mattie licked her lips and turned even paler as she studied his face. "Certainly. Come in."

Leon nodded his head toward Jesse. "Not with him. I want to talk outside. I don't like this house."

Jesse arched one eyebrow, and Leon thought he might scream out loud when he recognized the gesture as the same one Robert used.

"I'll speak to you after supper, Mattie. It seems young Leon has a burr under his saddle about something. I can wait," said Jesse, picking up his Stetson off Mattie's desk and walking toward the door. He stopped in front of Leon. "I loved you as a boy, Leon, and I'm sorry that what I did soured your affection for me. I feel the loss, but I understand why you might hate me. I wish things had been different but they weren't. I wish I could change the past in such a way that we could still be friends, but I can't. Hurting you is the only thing I regret."

Leon's throat hurt as he fought back both tears and accusations. The old love he felt for Jesse battled with his newfound hatred, and he thought he might tear himself in two. He heard the door close and let out a sob of relief.

He felt his mother touch his cheek and flinched away. "Outside. I'll talk to you outside," he whispered and turned to blunder through the doorway and run awkwardly across the living room and out of the house. Outside, he hesitated, then crossed the porch and walked toward the shadows cast by the huge cottonwood tree's naked limbs.

He turned and waited as Mattie hesitantly walked toward him. Her eyes glanced up at the tree, and he thought he saw her shudder. Her steps slowed and she paused outside the shadows. "What do you want, Leon?"

Leon felt his chin quiver and took a deep slow breath. "They're talking about you in Tascosa."

He saw her hands clench. "I should think the good folks of Tascosa had too much to worry about to be spending their time gossiping."

"How come they always gossip about you, Ma?

From the time I can remember, folks have talked about you."

Her face turned crimson and he saw the thin scar on her chin clear as day. Slowly she paled and it disappeared. "Folks like everyone to be the same and live by the same rules. It's comfortable that way. You never doubt what's right and never wonder whether you ought to act this way or that. When a person, a woman, chooses to live by her own rules and makes her own decisions according to what's best for her, it makes others uneasy. It makes them doubt themselves, so they find fault."

"Did you give them cause, Ma?"

Mattie looked past him at the tree. "I stood up for myself."

"Were you Jesse McDade's whore? Did you send him out to murder my father?"

Mattie swayed and Leon started to reach out to her, but she caught herself and stepped away. "I was never a whore, Leon, but yes, I did lie with Jesse. I earned the right to sin and I paid my reckoning for it. Jesse and I both did."

"And my father found out and beat you for it."

Mattie looked directly at him, her eyes as hard as always when she spoke of Samuel Hunter. "No, he didn't. He didn't raise a hand until Jesse quit as my ranch manager. Then he raped me again to prove he was stronger."

"Again?" echoed Leon, feeling as though the ground was shifting under his feet.

"Every time he lay with me was rape, Leon, but I didn't know the difference until Jesse taught me the way love should be between a man and a woman."

"But he was your husband."

"That didn't give him the right to abuse me, Leon. And it didn't give him the right to try to take away my land."

"Did you send Jesse out to murder him?" asked Leon again.

"No, I did not. I knew nothing about it for three days, but I kept Jesse's secret because he did it to save me."

"Because you were his whore!" cried Leon.

"No! Because Samuel Hunter was a bastard and a thief, and Jesse didn't intend to let him kill me and steal my land."

"It's always the land with you, isn't it? Did you ever think my father might have been kinder to you if you had just once put him ahead of the land?"

Mattie straightened her shoulders and to Leon's eyes seemed to grow taller. He saw her shadow lengthen until it nearly equaled that of the cotton-wood tree. "I tried to be the kind of wife that people expect a woman to be, but I might as well have tried to touch the moon. Samuel abused and despised me from the first day we married. He tried to make me feel ashamed of being a woman and I would not let him. He only wanted to sell the land because he knew it would hurt me."

"He was my father," said Leon.

"I know, but you are nothing like him. We cannot choose our parents, Leon. We take what we are given. I don't deny your right to honor Samuel as your father, but I do deny your right to force me to honor him."

"But I suppose you honor Jesse and give him what was my father's right!"

Mattie closed her eyes briefly, then opened them to reveal a grief so enormous that Leon nearly cried out in pity and confusion. "I honor Jesse and I gave him every part of me. I cannot explain what Jesse and I share because you wouldn't understand. You've never felt such a kinship yourself, and until you do, you will not believe it can exist. But it does,

Leon, and I pray you will find a woman who is the other part of yourself as Jesse is the other part of me."

Leon thought of Phoebe and blinked back tears as he looked at his mother. "Then it's true. You've taken up with Jesse again and turned Tom out of your bed."

A tear ran down Mattie's cheek. "No, that is not true. I honor Tom as my husband. It is Jesse that I have turned away."

"I don't think so, Ma. I think you'd see us all in hell before you'd cast out Jesse McDade."

He ran into the house and up the stairs while she called his name.

CHAPTER

32

"Leon's gone," announced Robert as he spooned sugar onto his oatmeal.

Mattie glanced at Tom. "Did you send him out with no breakfast?"

Tom laid down his fork, his eyes as calm and as hard as they had been all week, and Mattie felt the indecision that had plagued her since the moment he had walked out of their bedroom. "I didn't send Leon anywhere, Mattie. And I don't deny a boy his breakfast."

"I didn't mean to accuse you of being unkind, Tom," she began when Robert interrupted.

"I meant he's gone for good, Ma. His clothes are gone and so is his horse. I looked in the barn."

Mattie gripped the edge of the table in an effort to keep from fainting. "Dear God," she whispered.

Tom shoved back his chair. "I'll go look."

"I'll go with you," said Jesse.

"I can do without your help."

Mattie rose. "Stop it! Stop it, both of you. My son is gone. Can't you put away your jealousy long enough to look for him?"

The two men glanced at each other, and Tom finally nodded. "Don't worry, Mattie. We'll find the boy."

"I want Leon," said Joe and started to cry. Rachel, hearing her brother's sobs, began to wail in sympathy.

Robert put down his spoon and looked at Mattie. "I'll watch out for the little ones, Ma, if you want to ride with Tom and Jesse."

"No!" said Mattie, picking up Rachel. "I want all of you to stay with me. I don't want any of you to leave my sight."

"Don't worry, Ma. We're not going to run off. Joe and Rachel are too little, and I won't leave my land. Leon didn't feel the same about it as I do. That's why he could run off and I can't," said Robert.

Mattie stared at her second son, uneasy with his lack of grief. "Robert, Leon is your brother. Don't you feel worried at all about him."

Robert shrugged, the golden eyes so like her own expressing a wistfulness that seemed sadder than true sorrow would have been. "Sometimes I wanted to like him, Ma, but he always held something against me, and we ended up fighting. It might have been nice if we could have been real brothers."

"But you are real brothers," protested Mattie, panic making her voice strident. She could not deal with Robert's guessing the truth. Not now.

"I know that, Ma, but we didn't feel like brothers. We were too different and I couldn't stand his talk about Samuel Hunter. He used to go on and on about him. When I was little I used to get a bellyache every time Leon said his name so I'd start a fight to make him shut up and to make myself feel better. My belly didn't hurt when I was fighting. I used to get the worse end of the deal, but I never let that stop me."

"Robert! Why didn't you tell me?"

"You were sick from the beating, then you turned white as a sheet every time someone said something about him. I was scared of making you sick again."

"You remember that day Samuel beat me, don't you?" she asked, wondering how much harm her obsession with hating Samuel had caused her two sons.

Robert nodded, his face going tight. "I remember enough. I remember you shouting and your face all cut up and bleeding. And I remember riding to the Flying MJ and the look on Caroline McDade's face— like she hoped you'd die. I'll never forget that look, and I'll never forgive her either."

"Caroline had her reasons, I suppose," said Mattie, feeling again the horrible pain from the beating.

Robert cocked one eyebrow. "You ain't a real good liar, Ma. You ain't forgiven her either. And it doesn't matter what her reasons were. They weren't good enough."

"Maybe it's time to forgive and forget, Robert. Maybe if I had, Leon wouldn't have run off."

"Leon run off because he couldn't make up his mind who to believe—you or the gossips—and he finally couldn't stand his hurt any longer."

"What do you know about gossip, Robert?" Mattie asked, staring at this son who was old and wise and hurt beyond his age.

Robert gave her a level look. "I remember Jesse McDade coming in your bedroom that night. I never understood why he should look so sad, until I grew up. I reckoned some of gossip about you and Jesse

McDade must be true, but that didn't have nothing to do with why Samuel Hunter beat you, because you and Jesse must have parted company long before that."

"We had," whispered Mattie. "But how did you know?"

Robert sighed. "Why else would Jesse McDade look at you like you were a memory? Leon ought to have believed you, Ma. He ought to have known you'd sooner take a beating over the land than over a man. I would, too. Then I'd get up and kill the man who beat me."

Mattie leaned back in her chair, suddenly frightened for her son. Robert was too much like her, too absorbed by his love of the land. She wondered if he would ever love enough to give it up as she had been ready to do for Jesse.

As the day wore into night and she paced the floor waiting for the men to return, Mattie knew she had not yet paid her full reckoning for her weakness for a man not her husband. For all her talk of choosing her own way, Leon showed her that there was no escaping the cost of that choice.

When Tom walked in near dawn the next day, she knew by his expression that he had no good news. "We tracked him as far as Tascosa, Mattie, then we lost him. We think he might have taken a girl with him."

"A girl?" asked Mattie. "He doesn't know any girls in Tascosa."

Jubilee shuffled his feet, then burst out. "He took your sidesaddle, Miss Mattie."

"What kind of a girl would run off with a young boy?" she asked.

Tom sighed. "Mattie, he's seventeen. He's a man."

"What about the girl's family? Surely they'll help us search."

Jesse stepped up beside Tom. "She doesn't have a family, Mattie. She's a whore named Phoebe."

Mattie sank down on the sofa and began to laugh. "He ran away from me because he thought I was a whore, but I guess he likes whores better than he thought if he chose one to travel with."

Her laughter turned to sobs and she stretched out full length on the sofa and buried her face in her arms. She heard voices and the door slamming, then felt someone lift her up in his arms. She knew without opening her eyes that it was Jesse. If she were dead, she would still recognize his scent and the feel of his arms.

"I'll take her upstairs, Tom," she heard Jesse say.

She opened her eyes. "No. Outside, Jesse, under the cottonwood tree where it all began. It's fitting that it end there."

She met Jesse's silver eyes and saw the dawning knowledge. He nodded. "All right, Mattie."

She pushed against his shoulders. "I'll walk. I walked before."

He let her down and followed her outside. The bare branches of the tree glimmered in the waning moonlight and rattled in the faint breeze. Mattie leaned against its trunk and looked up at Jesse. "I gave you up once before to keep my son. It was years ago when you quit as my manager and collected your bonus from my father. I wanted a divorce, but my father told me that the court would probably take Leon away from me and give him to Samuel. I chose Leon over you, and now Leon chose a whore over me."

She glanced away, unable to meet his eyes. "He learned about us, Jesse. That's why he ran away. He couldn't face my adultery. And it was adultery. I've finally admitted that. I never did before. I argued myself into believing that what we did was right and that other folks were wrong to judge us. I never really repented of what we did. I never paid a reckoning."

She felt Jesse step closer and closed her eyes. Never again would she be alone with him. Never again would they be close enough to touch.

"Mattie, what do you call marrying Tom Miiler if not a reckoning?" he asked.

She opened her eyes to look at him again, seizing the time to memorize his face, this man who had known all the different Mattie's as she had grown from timid girl to strong woman, who had supported her until she could stand alone as the equal to any man, who had given up his freedom that she might be safe.

"I call Tom Miller a second chance, Jesse."

It was Jesse who looked away. "Does he hold your heart, Mattie?"

"He holds a part of it, Jesse, as you do. You would not believe me if I told you otherwise."

His eyes glittered as he turned his face toward her again, and for the first time in her life she feared Jesse McDade. "I could change your mind, couldn't I? I could force Tom Miller out of your heart."

"Yes," she whispered. "I won't deny it. But I'm asking you not to. I'm asking you to let me have my second chance. I'm asking you to leave as I should have done when you first rode up. I lost my son and wounded my husband because I did not. Giving you up is my repentance, Jesse." She closed her eyes. "I would die for you, but I cannot live for you."

When she opened her eyes again, he was gone.

Jesse rode into the Flying MJ just as the sun rose on the first day of his exile. His time with Mattie had always been measured in stolen minutes and hours, but there would be no more such stolen time. From this day forth, she would exist only in his memory as he would exist in hers. She was as the dead to him, as he was to her. She would live for Tom, and he would . . . live and find such small pleasures as he could. He still had the land—and he had a daughter he didn't know, and realized suddenly he had never known.

Dismounting, he tied his horse's reins to the hitching post, and stepped inside his house for the first time in seven years.

Caroline stood by the piano looking much the same—heart-shaped face, hazel eyes, glossy chestnut hair without the silver that lightened his own. She was not quite so slender as he remembered, and time had traced a few lines of discontent about her eyes and mouth. Still a handsome woman, he supposed—if a man didn't know her.

He glanced about the room. "Everything looks the same."

She heaved a sigh, and he remembered she always did that when she was displeased. He also remembered how much he had hated that trait in her. "The sofa is new, Jesse, and so are the mattresses and all the curtains. Those horrible grasshoppers got into the house and ate everything. I can't imagine why Tom Miller didn't do something."

"Tom Miller had other things on his mind besides keeping grasshoppers out of an empty house."

"I'll venture that *she* didn't lose her furnishing to those horrible insects."

Jesse took two quick steps and seized Caroline's arm. "I've come back, but I have a few rules by which we'll live, Caroline, or so help me God, I'll ride off and leave you to the mercy of this land. The first rule is that you will never mention Mattie again, and neither will I. The second is that you will not keep my daughter from me as you did before with your talk of her needing to sleep, or my being too dirty and crude to touch a tiny baby. I will be a father to her and to any other children we might have, and you will not stand in my way."

"Children?" she asked, flinching away from him.

He nodded. "We will share a bed and I will lie with you when the urge becomes greater than my distaste. We will make a life together somehow in spite of our feelings for each other."

"You wronged me!" she burst out.

"We wronged each other, Caroline. The ledger is closed on the past. The future is what we make of it, and perhaps in time we can learn to deal fairly with each other. I can't promise you more than that. If that is not enough, or if you can't abide me, then tell me now, and I'll let you go free to live wherever you wish."

"I won't leave you alone on this ranch."

She spat out the words like venom, and he knew that she had not changed at all and he had just begun his reckoning. Like Mattie, his repentance was in living.

"Where is my daughter, Caroline?"

"In the kitchen," she said, reluctantly stepping aside to let him pass.

Jesse walked into the kitchen and saw the stranger who was his daughter. Curls black as a crow's wing hung past her shoulders, and silver eyes like his own seemed too big for her thin face. Other than her pointed chin, she looked nothing like Caroline—certainly not in expression. Her eyes were wide and fearful and held no secret shadows.

She was a child without defenses—and Jesse feared for her.

"Louisa, I am your father and I've come home to protect you."

CHAPTER

November 1899

Tom thought the good Lord must have had Tascosa in mind when He warned against building your house upon the shifting sands that time and change might sweep away. To survive, a town needed folks and commerce and Tascosa had neither. Month by month since 1890 when the railroad bypassed it as a trading center, and the XIT had moved its headquarters, Tascosa's population had dwindled as one house after another, one store after another, was abandoned. The land around it was suitable only for grazing, not farming, and the big ranchers had long ago refused to trade in its stores. The bridge over the Canadian had never been repaired after the flood of 1893, and the river's altered course lapped too close to the heart of the town for anyone's comfort. Tascosa, once the county seat for ten counties, drowsed beside the Canadian in an ever-growing silence. Only the county officials, a few families stubbornly hanging on to nearly bankrupt businesses, and the Mexican families who first settled there remained. A few gamblers and a girl or two still hung on to fleece the cowboys and drifters who rode in on Saturday night to drink and play cards in the last remaining saloon.

Tom and Robert and Jubilee rode down the old Tascosa–Dodge City Trail from the north, angled across a vacant lot to Spring Street and down to Main. The old business district was busier than Tom had seen it in years. If a man peered down the street with half-closed eyes, he could pretend it was '86 or '87 again, and Tascosa was on the verge of a boom. Of course, only a half-blind fool would not have seen the handwriting on the wall in the form of the barbed wire surrounding Tascosa, but Tom remembered a number of such fools. The fact was Tascosa had hold of most folks' imagination, and nobody had wanted to admit the town was doomed, landlocked in the middle of the big, fenced ranches with no way in or out except across those selfsame ranches whose owners didn't give a tiddly damn whether Tascosa lived or died.

But Lord Almighty, it had been a lively place while it lasted. Even Mattie mourned the little cow town, which surprised Tom. He couldn't recall her spending a single happy occasion inside its boundaries, but he guessed she identified Tascosa with the days of open range. The town grew with open-range ranching and died with the coming of barbed wire even if not everybody admitted it was dead. Mattie still had a soft spot for the open range. He guessed all the old-timers did—judging from the number of horses and buckboards lined up along

Main Street—else this reunion hosted by the old Equity Bar for any man who rode the open range would be a bust.

He chuckled to himself. Mattie had been a mite miffed that only men were invited until he pointed out that ladies always put a damper on drinking and lying, and Tom suspected there would be a lot of both. Not everyone from the old days would come. Temple Houston had moved to Woodward, Oklahoma Territory, and Charlie Goodnight wasn't much for a party since he considered parties a poor excuse for stopping work. He didn't figure Abner Taylor from the XIT would come, but probably a few of the common hands would. Lee wouldn't be there, of course, since he sold the LS to Charlie Whitman in '93. Lee had been a cantankerous old bastard, but Tom missed him. If nothing else, Lee had kept things stirred up and prevented boredom. He figured Mattie wouldn't agree, given the number of times she and Lee had gone toe to toe over one thing or another. Or maybe she would. Mattie had a fondness for the old days.

Tom chuckled again. It was hard to think of himself and Mattie as being old-timers—particularly not Mattie. She was thirty-nine years old last January, heading toward forty, but she could still turn the heads of young men. She hardly looked older than when he'd first met her, and he had never grown tired of loving her even though age had slowed him down some. He was about as close to sixty as he was to fifty and a man's blood didn't heat up as fast. Maybe his age accounted for the fact that Mattie had not quickened with another baby after Rachel. Or maybe the Lord thought two children was all Tom Miller was due.

Plus Robert.

Tom was as fond of that boy as if he had fathered

him instead of Jesse. Maybe it was because he was Jesse's son that Tom loved him. Maybe it was guilt that he could watch Robert grow into manhood while Jesse would never know his eldest son. Or maybe it was because he could never admit his own affection for Jesse McDade. Another time, another place, they would have been friends, would have enjoyed visiting together. But not now and not here. Mattie would always stand between them.

"What you laughing about, Tom?" asked Jubilee. "Folks gonna think you getting addlepated, riding along laughing to yourself."

"I'm thinking about getting old, Jubilee." He didn't add his thoughts about Jesse. Those were private.

The man scowled. His hair was thin and completely white now, and his shoulders were rounded and his back bent. Tom wasn't certain how old Jubilee was, but he figured he must be just shy of eighty.

"There ain't no sense in thinking about getting old, Tom," said Jubilee. "You gets that way whether you thinks about it or not."

"You have a sour disposition tonight, Jubilee," said Tom. "Maybe I should have left you at home with Mattie and the young'uns."

Jubilee scowled again. "I ain't gonna be left behind. I is an old-timer just like you. Older, in fact. I been here since '77. I just got the miseries, is all. Anybody ought to have stayed to home, it's Robert. He's too young to remember how it was before barbed wire and railroads."

"I remember," said Robert in the deep drawl that never ceased to make Tom uneasy. Robert sounded too much like Jesse McDade. Looked too much like him, too. Way taller than six feet with broad shoulders and lean hips and that silent way of walking like Jesse's. If his hair was black instead of that gold-streaked brown, and his eyes silver instead of Mattie's yellow brown, and his mouth more thin lipped, Robert Hunter would have been branded as Jesse's wood colt. As it was, nobody had guessed but Tom and maybe Jubilee.

"You don't do no such thing," said Jubilee to Robert. "You was still too young to ride a horse by yourself when barbed wire started sprouting up like weeds."

Robert grinned in that lazy way of his. "I listened to the hands talking. Hearing stories and imagining is nearly as good as living it—but not quite. I wish I had known what it was like to ride over the prairie and not meet another white man for days. I wish I had been the oldest instead of Leon."

"Don't go talking like that in front of your mama, Robert," said Jubilee. "She still gets all upset sometimes when she thinks of Leon."

"If Leon was any kind of son, he'd have written Ma if he was still alive. He was a fool to throw away his family and his land over a father he made up out of whole cloth."

"Don't be judging a man till you walk a mile in his moccasins, Robert," remarked Tom.

"I'm not," said Robert. "I was in the same boat as Leon, but I was smart enough to pick the pa I wanted instead of whining after one so lowdown he'd beat a woman. You been a pretty good pa, Tom. Not much I'd change about you."

Tom felt tears wet his eyes and wiped them dry with his bandanna. He hadn't cried in a coon's age, but Robert's offhand remark touched him. He loved Mattie's sixteen-year-old son as much as he did Joe, but Robert wasn't one to accept affection easily.

He reached out and squeezed Robert's shoulder. "Guess there's not much I'd change about you either except maybe to hear you tell an old man a little more often that you approve of him."

Robert shrugged. "I'm not much on handing out compliments. Too much empty talk as it is, but I felt like I ought to tell you tonight." He shivered and Tom saw goose bumps rise up on his arms. "I don't know why I felt that way."

"Doesn't matter," said Tom, dismounting and tying his horse to the hitching rail. "I appreciate it all the same."

He pushed through the door into the Equity Bar. Its two large rooms were full of cowboys and ranchers, wagon bosses and wranglers, some barely old enough to shave and others aged by the Panhandle wind and dust and sun and snow. The slap of cards and rattle of dice echoed from the back room where the gambling tables drew a crowd. Men in boots and high-crowned hats lined the long mahogany bar in the front room. Tobacco smoke rose in lazy circles to form a gray cloud near the ceiling. Deep laughter, loud voices, the jingle of spurs, the clink of glasses greeted every man who walked in the Equity Bar with the promise that for this one night he was free to relive the time when every man chose his own fate and stood tall on the prairie and cast a long shadow—the time when a man held his land by his own efforts and not by the charity of the state of Texas—the time before bankers and syndicates, railroads and farmers, when men were fair because they chose to be and not because the law forced them to be.

The time when ranching was a calling and not a business.

"Look there, Tom," said Jubilee, gesturing toward a table in the corner of the main room. "It's Jesse and that Scotsman what has the place next to Miss Mattie's. I ain't seen Jesse in two, maybe three years—not since he put up that fence between our place and his. Lordy, Lordy, look at that gray in his hair."

And the hard lines on his face, Tom might have added but didn't. The fact was, they were all older, all harder, like sandstone changed into granite by the alchemy of time and the brutal demands of the land. A man changed, or a man quit. It was as simple as that.

Jesse looked up and nodded at Tom without any animosity that Tom could see. The bitterness still lurked in Jesse's eyes, but Tom figured it always would. Doing the right thing didn't necessarily leave a man feeling content.

Tom gave Robert some money. "Buy us all some beers, son."

Robert arched one eyebrow. "Me, too?"

Tom slapped the young man on the back. "I figure I ought to buy you your first drink, Robert."

Robert gave him a fixed stare. "Why tonight?"

Tom thought it an odd question to go along with Robert's odd stare, but he guessed the boy was just surprised. "A man never knows if an opportunity might come along again so he grabs it when he can." He squeezed Robert's shoulder. "Don't be making such heavy water out of being treated like a man instead of a young'un."

Robert shook his head like a man dazed by the hot sun and gave Tom an anxious look. "Thank you. Pa," he added—the first time he'd ever called Tom that.

Tom felt tears sting his eyes and grinned. "I reckon I like the sound of that. Son," he added deliberately. He cleared his throat. "Get along with you now and get that beer. Jubilee and me are gonna take the weight off our legs at Jesse McDade's table."

Robert hesitated, his eyes flickering toward the

table in the corner, then nodded, and walked to the bar, leaving Tom to puzzle over his odd behavior.

"That boy do come all over queer sometimes," said Jubilee. "Miss Mattie allus thought Leon was the one to be bruised easiest by living, but I thinks Robert is. That boy sees too much and feels too much some of the time."

Tom shook his head as he threaded his way through the crowd toward Jesse's table. "He's young, Jubilee, and the young don't have thick hides. Prick them and they easily bleed. He'll grow one with age—just like you and me have. There's a lot to be said for age. It calms a man so he can better weigh his life. And this night I find myself content."

Jesse looked up as Tom paused by the table. "I didn't expect to see you here, Tom. I don't remember you as being much for drinking and carousing."

Tom pulled out the chair and sat down. "A man oughtn't to miss a wake for a passing age, so Jubilee and I came."

"In other words, you came both to praise Caesar and bury him?" asked George Faulkner, extending his hand toward Tom.

Tom shook hands with the Scotsman. Faulkner had aged along with the rest of them, but it was less obvious. His gray-green eyes had a few more lines at the corners, and his hair boasted a few silver streaks, but his aristocratic features seemed no less youthful than they had always been. He and Mattie were a pair, Tom decided. Both holding age at bay.

"That's about the size of it, I guess," said Tom to Faulkner. "And Tascosa seems a fitting place to do it. I reckon it's passing into history right along with us."

"Jubilee," said Faulkner. "You have seen more of life than the rest of us. Have we—these ranchers and cowboys—made history, or has history made us?"

Jubilee took a long pull at the beer Robert gave him, swallowed, then cleared his throat. "Well, I tells you, Mr. Faulkner. I reckon we all just stumbled into history, but if we hadn't been strong, we wouldn't have lasted long enough to be sitting here talking about it."

"A profound observation, Jubilee," said Faulkner before turning to Robert. "Young man, as a representative of the future, what is your opinion? In the words of Mr. Rudolph's last editorial, will you cuss us when we are gone?"

Robert sat down, his eyes darting from one man to the next. "Some will, I reckon—those who can't measure up to what you did. But I don't feel that way. I wish I could have been one of you instead of being born too late."

Jesse swallowed his drink and slammed the empty glass on the table. "Don't live for what's already passed you by, Robert."

Robert gave Jesse a long look, and Tom admitted to himself that he owed McDade a greater debt than he supposed. All that the other man wanted, Tom Miller possessed: Mattie Hunter and Jesse's son.

"I don't live in the past," said Robert. "But I can't help noticing the tracks all of you left."

Faulkner shoved back his chair and climbed on the table, his head barely clearing the ceiling. First one man noticed him, then another until all in the crowded room fell silent to gawk at the Scotsman. The curious silence distracted the men in the gaming room, and they abandoned their gambling to fill the archway between the bar's two rooms.

Faulkner bowed to the crowd. "Gentlemen, this young man here" —he gestured at Robert— "this harbinger of the future among us relics of the past, has called us heroes, favored by the gods to bring civilization to this windswept land. Let us lift our glasses high and drink to ourselves, for there will not soon be a generation to equal ours."

He lifted his glass as cheers broke out and men with leathery faces and gnarled hands stood a little taller. "To the heroes among us!" he pronounced.

Tom had to admit that nobody could equal Faulkner for eloquence even if he did overdo it a mite given the present company, which included a goodly number of old hands who had been known to carry mavericking to the point of rustling. Whether they were heroes or not depended on which side of the barbed-wire fence a man stood.

A thin man whose sunken left cheek bore the scar of a bullet wound threw his glass at Faulkner. It missed the Scotsman and chattered against the wall behind him. "I'll be damned if I'll drink with a bunch of rich ranchers who hogged all the land and kept us nesters from making an honest living."

An old cowboy, his bent back and awkward walk testifying to painful joints from too many years riding half-broke horses and sleeping on the ground, laid a swollen hand on the speaker's shoulder. "Now, Blackie, I reckon you're exaggerating a mite. I don't recall the living you made being altogether honest. Seems to me your herd increased every time the LS herd decreased. Some folks might call that rustling."

Blackie shoved the old cowboy away. "Shut up, Ben Scroggins. You always sucked the LS hind tit. Wouldn't even back up the cowboy strike when we was trying to get what was due us."

Scroggins fell back against the bar, and Tom saw him grimace with pain. "I reckon it was my right to sign on or not sign on, Blackie. I didn't see no percentage in changing one boss for a set of bosses."

Tom stood up. He hadn't recognized Blackie at first since his hair had gone white and one side of his face puckered up from that scar, but he hadn't forgotten the man's sour disposition. Time hadn't sweetened it any. "Blackie, leave Ben alone. The cowboy strike has been over and done with for a long spell. No point in riding back over that ground. Let's all have another drink and enjoy being heroes for an evening."

"Heroes!" spat Blackie. "I see men poor 'cause they were held back by you ranchers. I see stove-up cowboys put out to pasture 'cause you fenced them out of work."

"Things change," said Tom. "We got farmers and towns now. Can't have cattle running loose over a man's crops, and it just don't take as many men to herd pastured cows."

Blackie pointed to his scar. "You see that? You ranchers done that to me. You outlawed my brand—called it a maverick brand—and sent the sheriff out to take my cattle. I didn't cotton to that and put up a fight. One of the posse shot me and left me to heal up."

There was enough truth in what Blackie said to make Tom uncomfortable. Some nesters had been run off their property for no better reason than they filed on a few sections that happened to be inside the boundaries claimed by the big brands, and there had been blood shed. But in a whole lot of cases, the nesters were stealing a start—rustling somebody else's cattle to start their own herds.

"There was good and bad on both sides, Blackie, but that's no reason to tar everybody with the same brush. I lost my place, too. Sold out after my spread was fenced in by the LX."

The crowd was sorting itself out, Tom noticed, with old nester ranchers and maverickers on one side, and big ranchers and cowboys who rode for the big brands on the other. He saw Hank Wilson and Danny Boone and a couple of Jesse's Flying MJ boys easing toward them with their hands resting on their guns. Tom frowned and shook his head at Hank. He could smell the anger in the air—like an old wound breaking open and leaking pus—and didn't want anybody aggravating the situation.

"You done all right for yourself though, didn't you, Tom Miller. Married up with that Hunter woman and rolling in clover."

Tom heard the scrap of boots against the wooden floor behind him and saw Jesse McDade step up beside him. "Blackie, you ought to mark your targets better," said Jesse. "Mattie Hunter supported the cowboy strike. She hired blacklisted cowboys and got thrown out of the Stock Association for her trouble the same as I did. And scars? Well, Mattie has a few of those, too, and one of them is from being shot by a trail boss when she barred him from trailing cattle with tick fever across her land."

Jesse stared at each man who crowded around Blackie in support. "Tom and Mattie worked hard for what they have, and they stayed on the land during the drought when a lot of settlers ran, but I guess it's like Robert said—some folks will cuss us because they can't measure up to what we did."

"You ain't any better than any man here, McDade," said Blackie. "And a damn sight worse than most. I don't know anybody else in this room who shot two men in cold blood 'cause he didn't like the way one of them treated his own wife."

There wasn't a sound to be heard in the Equity: no shuffling of feet, no jingle of spurs. Tom wasn't even certain anyone was breathing.

Jesse's eyes turned the dull gray of a knife blade. "Killing you isn't worth going to prison, Blackie, but if I were you, I wouldn't say anything else that might make me change my mind." He nudged Tom toward the door. "We all came here tonight to talk over old times, and we did what we came for. I'm just damn sorry the only old times some of us remember are the bitter ones."

Faulkner doffed his hat at the crowd. "A good night to you, gentlemen. Don't let our departure spoil your evening."

"And it's good riddance, too," said Blackie, his mouth twisting itself into a sneer. "We don't want to listen to the leavings of a foreign syndicate any more than we want to listen to our own homegrown bastards like McDade."

Jesse started toward Blackie, and Tom grabbed his arm. "Let it go, Jesse. He's trying to start a fight any way he can, and I'm not in the mood for it."

Jesse let himself be pulled out the door, and Tom let out a sigh once they were in the street. "Some folks got to blame everybody else for their troubles," said Tom. "And I recollect that Blackie was always good at that, and he ain't changed none."

"You should have shot him, Jesse," said Robert. "One of you should have, anyway. None of you used to put up with his kind of talk."

Tom sighed again. "That's the difference between being young and old, Robert. You learn not to let talk draw blood."

"All the same," began Robert when Jubilee interrupted him.

"You hush your mouth, Robert. You ain't never seen no gunfights and bullets opening up a man's carcass till you can see his innards. Until you does you ain't got no call to be telling us what we should have done."

Jesse's eyes and hair glittered in the moonlight and his breath left puffs of vapor in the chill air when he spoke. "We aren't heroes, Robert. We're just men who outlasted what the land and other men threw at us, and part of that outlasting was knowing when to walk away."

Hank Wilson, along with Danny Boone and Jesse's men, backed out of the Equity's door, their hands still resting on their guns. "We best ride if we're going to, Tom," said the grizzled foreman. "There's too much liquor fueling ugly talk in there for my peace of mind."

Tom stepped in front of Jesse and reached for his horse's reins when the Equity's door burst open and several men crowded out. "McDade!" yelled one of them.

With the light from the open door in his eyes, Tom couldn't be sure who yelled, but he thought he recognized Blackie's voice and sighed. Blackie just wasn't going to let his discontent lie.

"Blackie," Tom called out, then heard the roar of a .45 at the same time its bullet slammed into his chest. He clapped his hand over his wound and stumbled against his horse's neck. The animal neighed and danced sideways, and Tom guessed his horse didn't like the smell of fresh blood. Tom didn't much like it either—particularly since it was his own.

Tom saw Blackie jerk, then half fall, half stumble back into the Equity as the sound of a shot close to Tom's ear nearly deafened him. He tried to find some charity in his heart for the old mavericker, but all he felt was mad clear through. Be damned if he was ready to die, and be damned if he wanted to die because years ago Blackie had stolen some cows and got caught in the act. He grinned through his pain. A man just never outgrew his arrogance at thinking that he had a choice of when to die.

He felt his legs fold up under him and sank to the

ground. He heard cursing and more shots, then felt hands grab him under the arms and begin dragging him away.

"Hang on, Tom," said Jesse. "I'm going to haul you around the corner between the Equity and John King's old drugstore and leave Jubilee to guard you while the rest of us take care of any of Blackie's friends who still feel the need to fight."

Tom felt himself propped up against a woodpile and had just enough strength left to grab hold of Jesse's shirt. "You send Robert back here, too. I don't want that boy trying to kill anybody and maybe getting killed himself. He don't have the practice at killing the rest of us do, and I don't want him to learn." Tom coughed and tasted blood as it filled his mouth and rolled down his chin.

Jesse clasped Tom's shoulder. "I'll see to him. I owe you my life, Tom. If you hadn't answered Blackie so he thought it was me, you wouldn't be sitting here leaking blood."

Tom managed a weak laugh and had to spit out a mouthful of blood before he could answer. "I always did talk when I should have listened, Jesse, but don't you be feeling too guilty. Blackie might have hit me anyway. I recollect he always was a terrible shot."

CHAPTER

34

Jesse drew in a breath of death-tinged air. He glanced around the shabby room in the Exchange Hotel, now crowded with men whose hands were still stained with gunpowder. Gunpowder and blood—the smell of death. Hank Wilson had a bandanna wrapped around his arm where a bullet had creased it. Danny was a little worse off. A shot had caught him in the thigh and torn a hunk of flesh out. He'd bear the scar of this gunfight in the shape of a hollowed-out spot just above the knee on his left leg. Even Jubilee's face was bloody from being hit with splinters when one of Blackie's cohorts emptied both barrels of a shotgun into the woodpile.

Not everyone was lucky. One of his Flying MJ boys rested in another room with a sheet pulled over the ugly hole between his eyes. Blackie and his friends lacked even that. Their bodies still lay where they had fallen—in the street, inside the Equity, in the weed-choked lot behind the bar. Tomorrow the sheriff and whoever still lived in Tascosa could clean up the blood and bury the bodies. Jesse didn't care.

He heard a smothered sob and put his arm around Robert, who stood at the foot of the bed looking at Tom Miller. The Andersons, who ran the Exchange Hotel these days, had offered a room and a bed to the wounded man. Not that Jesse had cared about that either. If the Andersons hadn't offered, he would have simply taken over the hotel by gunpoint if that's what it took to keep Tom Miller from dying in an alley behind a woodpile.

And Tom Miller was dying. His skin was that telltale gray that foretold death, and blood kept bubbling out of the hole in his chest in spite of the bandage Mrs. Anderson had wrapped around him. A trickle of blood dribbled out of his mouth periodically, and Jubilee would wipe it away. Tom's eyes were closed and sunken under his thick, jutting brows.

Robert let a sob escape his tightly pressed lips, and Jesse stroked the boy's thick, gold-tinted hair. "Don't fight it, boy," said Jesse. "Let the tears out. Tom Miller is worth grieving for."

Startled, Robert turned his head toward Jesse. "I never thought you and he liked each other very much."

Jesse smoothed a lock of hair out of Robert's eyes. "We did and we didn't. Of all the men I've ever known, Tom Miller was the finest. If things had been different between us, I would have loved him like blood kin. Maybe I do anyway. I don't think I'd hurt this bad otherwise."

Robert drew a breath that rattled from suppressed tears. "Isn't there anything we can do? I could ride to Amarillo for a doctor."

Jesse clamped his hand on the young man's

shoulder. "You couldn't get there in time, and Tom's lung shot anyhow—close to the heart. His chest is filling up with blood. I never knew a man shot that bad to live. Besides, I want you here in case he comes to. I want him to die with somebody who loves him holding his hand. He does love you, Robert?"

The young man swallowed and nodded his head. "I never called him pa until tonight. I think I pleased him when I did. I hope so, anyhow. I just wished I'd called him pa sooner."

"Don't grieve about it, Robert. You picked the very best time to tell him. He'll be leaving us shortly, and he'll leave with your words ringing fresh in his ears instead of stale from being said too much without feeling."

Hank Wilson stirred from his seat by the narrow window. "You reckon if we try to sew up that hole it would help any, Jesse?"

Jesse shook his head. "I don't think so, Hank. We might make it worse. Without any way to leak out, I'm afraid the blood would just fill up his chest and choke him. I don't want to take that chance."

Robert grabbed his arm and jerked him around. Golden eyes pierced Jesse's own—eyes harder and older than only a few hours ago. "We can't just let him die without trying something, Jesse. Anything, goddamn it, anything."

More than Tom Miller would die this night, thought Jesse. The youthful innocence of Mattie's second son would die also, leaving a man's knowledge of his own vulnerability in its place.

"I'm sorry, Robert."

The young man froze—like a wolf sensing the hunter—than shuddered. "You mean that, don't you? You and my pa are bound together. You're gonna be less than you were when he dies."

Jesse felt a chill sweep up his spine at hearing the boy's words. Such perception was unnatural in one so young. "That's right, son. When Tom leaves, he'll take part of me with him—and part of your mother, too. It's always that way with good men."

Robert let go of Jesse and stepped away. "Then I think you best wake him if you can. I doubt Tom wants to sleep his way into the grave. It could be he wants to leave a little of himself behind for each of us."

Jubilee tenderly wiped Tom's mouth again, catching the thin trickle of blood with a clean rag torn from one of Mrs. Anderson's sheets. As each rag turned red and wet with blood, Jubilee dropped it into a washbasin sitting on the floor next to his feet and picked up a clean, dry one from a pile stacked on a table beside the bed.

The basin was filled with bloody rags.

Jubilee looked up at Robert. "We wake him up and he's gonna hurt something fierce."

Jesse studied the unconscious man, clenching his jaw against his own tears. He'd known Tom Miller as long as Mattie had—and maybe in a certain sense knew him better because they were both men and shared a man's way of thinking.

"Let's see if we can rouse him, Jubilee. He won't care about the hurt as much as he'll care about fighting off dying as long as he can."

"Lordy, Jesse, it's downright mean to let a man suffer when he can go easy."

Jesse leaned over the bed and laid his hand against Tom's brow. The skin was cold and slick with greasy sweat, and Jesse knew that Tom wouldn't live much longer if they didn't wake him up. "He'll want to see Mattie, Jubilee, and asleep, he's letting go of life. Awake, he'll fight a little longer—maybe even long enough for Faulkner to reach the Bar H and bring her back."

Jesse slid his hand between Tom's head and the pillow and lifted him up. "Jubilee, wipe his face with a wet rag. Hank, get me a glass of water with whiskey in it. Bleeding like he is, Tom's got to be thirsty. Robert, come over here and hold his hand and call to him. Besides Mattie, I'm gambling he'll come back for you before he would anybody else."

Jesse never knew later whether it was the whiskey or the cold, wet rag, or Robert's hoarse voice calling his name over and over again, but Tom's eyes finally opened as the hours crept toward that darkest part of night just before dawn when men most often died.

"Robert, are you all right? Did Jesse keep you safe like I asked him to?" Tom's voice was weak, and deeper than usual as if he were calling to them from some distant place.

"I didn't get shot, Tom."

Pain glazed Tom's eyes, but didn't reduce the alertness in their depths. "That's good, son. I worried about you. I didn't want us both residing on that bluff above the Canadian and leaving your ma to look after the place and the two little ones without any help."

"I'll watch over her, Pa."

Tom smiled, then coughed up blood that Jubilee wiped up. "You be careful at it, though. Your ma don't like men lording it over her." He stopped to draw a breath, and Jesse flinched at the bubbling sound he made. "And Robert, trust Jesse if you need a man's help."

"I can take care of myself and Ma, Tom. I don't need nobody's help."

Tom lifted his head, his hazel eyes suddenly bright. "Promise me you'll trust Jesse."

Robert looked confused, but nodded. "I promise, Tom."

The dying man let his head fall back against the pillow. "Thank you, son," he said, closing his eyes briefly.

Jubilee leaned over him anxiously. "Lordy, is he gone?"

Tom opened his eyes suddenly. "Not yet, Jubilee. I'll hold on awhile longer." He smiled. "We used to have some good talks around the kitchen table at night, didn't we?"

"Yes, sir," agreed Jubilee. "We had us some times."

"Did I ever tell you that you brewed up undoubtedly the best coffee in the Panhandle?"

Jubilee's chin quivered. "Don't believe you ever mentioned it, Tom."

"I can practically smell that coffee. I wish I had me a cup right now."

Jubilee got up. "I'll go see if Mrs. Anderson might borrow me her coffee pot."

Tom clasped Jubilee's hand. "You do that—old friend—and take Robert with you."

"No! I'm not leaving!" said Robert.

"I can't make you, son, and I won't ask anybody else to force you, either, but I'm asking you to mind me one last time. I want you to remember me with some life still in me, not as an old gray husk spraying blood and pissing all over himself as he dies."

Robert's mouth twisted, then he slowly leaned over the bed and pressed his lips against Tom's forehead. "Good-bye, Pa."

Tom didn't try to hold back the tears that rolled down his cheeks, or maybe he lacked the strength, Jesse didn't know which. "Good-bye, son. I liked being your pa for a little while."

He watched the aged negro man lead Robert out, then turned his head toward Hank and Danny.

"Hank, I can't think of a man I would rather have had on the place than you."

Hank cleared his throat and reached down to squeeze Tom's hand. "I'm gonna miss riding out with you, Tom."

Tom smiled. "I reckon I might miss it, too. Don't know if there are horses where I'm going."

"I don't know much about religion and such, but I can't imagine God would ask a cowboy to spend eternity without a horse."

"I suspect you're right, Hank," said Tom. He looked over the foreman's shoulder toward Danny. "I'm gonna miss you, too, boy, and I'd appreciate it if you'd make sure Robert don't climb on any half-broke horses. Sometimes he lacks judgment."

"I'll see to it, Tom," said Danny, limping over to squeeze Tom's hand.

Tom sighed. "Good-bye, then, boys. Jesse here will see me out."

"You best hang on, Tom," Danny said. "Miss Mattie's on her way. That Mr. Faulkner went to fetch her."

For the first time Jesse saw desolation in Tom's eyes. "I'll do my best," he said.

Jesse picked up a clean rag and wiped Tom's mouth again. "I figure Mattie will be here in another hour. Faulkner planned to run his horse to death getting to her if that's what it took, and I imagine Mattie will do the same."

"I reckon she will, Jesse. Mattie's always been a determined woman—but soft, too, when the time's right. I'd sure like to see her one more time."

"You hold on to that thought, Tom, and you'll last."

Tom looked up at him, his eyes as calm as always. "I don't think so, Jesse." He choked and coughed, spraying blood over himself and Jesse's shirt. He drew a shaky, bubbling breath. "I'm sorry as hell to be dying, McDade, but it's not how long a life is, it's how good it is that counts. My time with Mattie made life good, but I reckon I knew all along she never was really mine. But I was always hers, and she knows it, so I'm content."

Jesse felt tears of his own roll down his face. "Damn it all, Tom, she was yours. She sent me away."

"At best I borrowed her for a spell, but it's closer to the truth to say we shared her. She's a part of both of us."

"Tom, if I thought it would save your life, I'd curse Mattie Hunter to her face."

Tom studied his face. "I believe you mean that, Jesse."

"I do."

"That's a mighty generous offer and if I wasn't about to die I'd take you up on it." He smiled and lifted his hand to clasp Jesse's. "Next to Mattie, I'm gonna miss you the most, McDade."

Jesse's throat hurt from trying to avoid crying. "My God, Tom, I'll miss you, too."

Tom's eyes closed and the intervals between the bubbling breaths grew longer. Jesse held on to his hand so Tom would know he didn't die alone and waited for the end.

Just before dawn—when night was fading into day—Tom's eyes flickered open. "I'm sorry as hell about something else, McDade."

Jesse leaned over to catch the faint words. "What else, Tom, and I'll try to make it right."

Tom's skin was bleached of all color now until his face looked ghostly. "I'm sorry as hell I can't stick around to see how this all turns out."

"How what turns out?"

Tom's bloodless lips smiled one last time. "You and Mattie. I'm dead, but you two got living left to do. Knowing the both of you the way I do, I expect you will do as you please and the devil take the hindermost." He took one shallow breath and blood poured from his mouth.

"Damn it," said Jesse as he slipped an arm under Tom's shoulders and lifted him up so he wouldn't suffocate on his own blood. "Don't you die until Mattie gets here."

"I loved her," whispered Tom, each word accompanied by a gush of blood. He gripped Jesse's hand. "Tell her."

"I will, Tom. I promise."

"Thank you, Jesse, and good-bye."

Jesse held Tom until the light faded from his eyes, then lowered him to the bed, and kept him company while they both waited for Mattie.

CHAPTER

All the flowers were dead when Mattie buried Tom beside her daughter in the cemetery on the bluff, so she cut cedar branches to decorate his grave and promised him bouquets of roses come spring.

Dressed in black crepe and swathed in a heavy veil, Mattie clutched the hands of her two youngest children as she said a silent farewell to their father. The pungent scent of cedar swirled by her on the wind as she conjured up Tom's image.

"I'm sorry I was too late to say good-bye, Tom. I rode as fast as I could, but you were already gone when I arrived in Tascosa. Jesse said you died just as the sun was rising, so I'll always know you're close to me at dawn."

The mourners filled the small cemetery and stretched out across the prairie. Every cowboy who ever rode with Tom, every rancher who ever passed the time of day with him, every merchant who ever traded with him came to pay their respects. From every corner of the Panhandle the grizzled, leathery men who tamed a land—the pioneers who outlasted blizzards and prairie fires and drought and grasshoppers—came to honor one of their own who preceded them into history.

"I've heard so many overblown compliments about you, Tom, that I hardly recognize the man they're describing, but no one said the words that best fit you. No one said you were a patient man."

She could hear Tom's soft chuckle in the wind that whispered through the cedar branches on his grave. *"Folks don't like to speak ill of the dead, sweetheart. I guess they mistook patience for plodding, and there's not much exciting about a man who plods along one step at a step—except he generally always gets to where he's going in the end."*

"Mattie, my condolences on your loss."

Tom's voice faded out of Mattie's imagination as reality intruded and she felt Robert nudge her shoulder. Belatedly she extended her hand to the man who stood in front of her. "Thank you, Mr. Faulkner."

Faulkner pressed her hand between both of his. "I will miss him. Not only did I rely on his advice on ranching matters, but I enjoyed his conversation. He was a wise and tolerant man."

"Yes, he was. Very tolerant." Mattie's voice broke and she felt tears spurt from her eyes. She swallowed and tried to stem the tide. Her grief was too private to share with the other mourners.

She felt Faulkner trying to peer through her heavy veil. "He was also beloved, wasn't he?" the Scotsman asked.

Curiously, she didn't feel that Faulkner was prying. Perhaps because he had been at Tascosa with

Tom—had even killed one of the men involved in Tom's murder. She owed Faulkner just as she owed all the others who had fought Tom's killers. Finally she could forgive him for Samuel.

"He was very much loved," said Mattie.

"Then my regret for his death and your loss are redoubled. May you endure your mourning with patience."

"As Tom would do?" asked Mattie.

Faulkner's faint smile held both humor and grief. "He was a very patient man."

Mattie squeezed the Scotsman's hands. "Thank you, Mr. Faulkner."

He freed his hands, stepped back, and bowed with a languid grace before moving on.

She looked after him thoughtfully. George Faulkner had lived in the Panhandle fourteen years, but was still a stranger to most folks who distrusted his aristocratic and very reserved ways. Yet the Scotsman was the one person who rightly called Tom a patient man and appeared to understand all that virtue entailed. How ironic that the same man who so misjudged Samuel Hunter could so accurately judge Tom Miller.

Another mourner claimed her attention and she put away the puzzle of George Faulkner. He had defied her understanding for years at odd times when she would catch a glimpse of warm understanding and regret in those gray-green eyes followed immediately by his usual amused expression, and she supposed he would continue to do so. Figuring him out would be a welcome diversion when grief became too much for her mind to bear in the empty years to come.

She heard Tom's chuckle again in her mind. *"Mattie, you always look too deep in a man's heart when his secrets are hanging about his neck for all to see. Underneath his fancy foreign ways Faulkner is a very simple man much like me."*

Mattie shook her head in denial, and felt Robert pinch her arm. "Ma, you just shook your head no when Mrs. Anderson told you Tom was a good man. She gave you a real queer look."

"I didn't hear her. I was listening to someone else's voice."

Robert's eyes were filled with sorrow—and understanding. "I know, Ma. I feel Tom close to us, too, but folks will think you've lost your wits if you talk to him."

She swayed and clutched his arm. "How did you know?"

Robert glanced down at her. "I reckon Tom left a part of himself behind to comfort us as long as we need him. I talked to him myself last night while I was keeping watch over his body."

Mattie felt herself turn cold. "Dear God, you're mad and so am I."

Robert's eyes were steady and showed no dazed look of insanity. "He loved us too much to let us go so soon."

Mattie shook her head. "No, Robert, it's just my memory putting words together in my mind. Tom is gone, murdered by a bastard for no good reason, and he's buried at my feet." She tilted her head to look toward the sky. "Dear God, I'll miss him so."

Through her thick veil and blinding tears, she glimpsed a tall man standing at the head of Tom's grave jerk his head up to stare at her from tortured silver eyes. In the second before she fainted she thought she saw another man—a man with calm hazel eyes and a mouth that always smiled so easily—gently push Jesse toward her.

* * *

Jesse rode over on the third day after Tom's burial and waited under the cottonwood tree while Robert fetched Mattie.

He saw her step out of the house and caught his breath at the sight of her ravaged face. She was as bloodless as Tom before he died and her cheeks were hollowed out and blue smudges underneath her eyes made them look bruised. She looked frail and ill as she paused at the bottom of the porch steps before slowly walking toward him.

He caught her hands and felt how bony were her fingers. Her flesh was melting away like snow under a summer sun and he turned cold at the thought that she, too, would slip away from him. "Mattie," he whispered. "Mattie, I'm sorry."

She looked up at him, the golden eyes as beautiful as ever. "I've been expecting you, Jesse."

He rubbed her cold hands, feeling how loosely her wedding band turned on her finger. "How did you know I'd come?"

For the only time in his life Jesse could not decipher Mattie's faint smile. "I knew."

"I have a message for you from Tom."

She searched his face. "Of course, I should have thought of that. Duty drives you here. I don't think you would have come otherwise."

"Surely you didn't want me to come, or was he right? Do I still claim more of you than you offered him?" He squeezed her hands until she grimaced. "Tell me, Mattie. Is it grief stealing away your appetite and disturbing your rest, or is it guilt?"

"Was it grief or was it guilt that so tormented you at Tom's funeral, Jesse?"

Her voice was serene as she turned his question back on himself, and he was suddenly furious with her. "Damn it, I didn't know how much I'd miss him—how much I loved him—until I sat in that shabby room and watched him bleed his life away knowing that bullet was meant for me. Yes, I grieve. And yes, I feel guilty for taking any part of you away from him."

"What was his message to me, Jesse?"

"He said he loved you. I meant to tell you at his funeral, but you fainted before I could."

"It's just as well. Tom was wrong to think his funeral was the proper time to say out loud what I never said and should have while he was alive. And it is not grief that takes away my appetite and keeps me awake at night. It is the need to confess, but I could only confess to you."

He released her hands and turned away. "I don't want to hear your transgressions against him, Mattie. You'll have to rid your conscience of them some other way."

"You cannot refuse to hear me, Jesse, or Tom would have given his message to someone else. But he didn't. He gave it to you. You are my link to him. He will hear the words he needs from me only if I tell him through you."

He turned around and clasped her shoulders, feeling again how frail she was, how close she was becoming to a wraith, and felt his grief expand to encompass the wife Tom had left behind. She was suffering and he could not turn down her plea. For all his guilt he could not turn away Mattie Hunter.

And Tom had known it.

"Tell me, Mattie," he whispered.

She tilted her face up to his. "I loved him, Jesse, and I arrived too late to tell him. I loved him not with the passionate intensity with which I loved you, but with a deep, quiet strength that matched his. I will miss him more than he might ever have believed."

Jesse felt tears begin to flood his eyes. "I never knew you felt so deeply about him."

She caught a tear on her finger. "I believe he

wanted you to know, Jesse. He wanted to absolve you of your guilt. That part of me you hold was never his for the taking. Love freely given cannot be snatched back and passed along to the next convenient person. Love will die if treated so."

"Do you think Tom heard you, Mattie?"

She closed her eyes and cocked her head as if listening. "I believe so. I think I hear him calling, but so faintly." Her eyes snapped open, so filled with loss that Jesse wanted to cry out. "Somewhere in my soul a banked ember flickered out and a warmth left my life. He's truly gone now, and I'm once again alone."

Jesse looked at the bare branches above their heads. "Did our tree survive the drought and grasshoppers, Mattie?"

Her eyes were puzzled. "The uppermost branches died, but yes, it survived."

"And each spring it buds out again?"

"Yes, of course. That's what living trees do, Jesse."

He stroked his hands along the tops of her shoulders, down her arms, and clasped her hands again. "Before he died Tom said we still had living to do, Mattie. I believe him now. We're like the cottonwood tree. We'll survive our grief as it survived the drought."

She pulled away from him. "But not today, Jesse. Not today and not for all the tomorrows I can foresee."

Beyond his own grief, beyond his own loneliness, at the far edges of his soul Jesse knew the other reason Tom had sent him to Mattie. "You won't bury yourself. I'll not allow it."

She straightened her shoulders as she always did when challenged. "You have no say over my life, Jesse McDade."

"We are not done with each other, Mattie Jo Hunter. Tom knew it. I know it. One day you will know it, too."

D.R. Meredith's grandmother drove a covered wagon in the Oklahoma Land Rush of 1889. Her father passed along to her tales of Jesse James and the Younger brothers that he had heard as a youth in Missouri. Lawmen and outlaws, cowboys and Indians, homesteaders and gamblers were not mythical characters to her, but real people her family knew.

After graduating from the University of Oklahoma, Meredith followed her husband to Texas. Although a prize-winning author of eleven mystery novels, she took a holiday from crime writing to create a duo of historical sagas set in the Texas Panhandle. Drawing on her own family's oral traditions and on tales told to her by children of the early settlers, as well as years of research, Meredith has written stories rich in local history and stunning in their portrait of a woman fighting for her place in a man's world of nineteenth-century Texas.

Acclaimed by *Texas Almanac* as one of the state's ten best mystery writers, D.R. Meredith lives in Amarillo, Texas, with her husband and two teenage children. She edits a column on Western literature for *Roundup Quarterly*, a publication of Western Writers of America and Texas University Press.

▣ HarperPaperbacks *By Mail*

EXPLOSIVE THRILLERS FROM THREE BESTSELLING AUTHORS

CAMPBELL ARMSTRONG

Agents of Darkness
(0-06-109944-9) $5.99

Mazurka
(0-06-100010-8) $4.95

Mambo
(0-06-109902-3) $5.95

Brainfire
(0-06-100086-8) $4.95

Asterisk Destiny
(0-06-100160-0) $4.95

BERNARD CORNWELL

Crackdown
(0-06-109924-4) $5.95

Killer's Wake
(0-06-100046-9) $4.95

LEN DEIGHTON

Spy Sinker
(0-06-109928-7) $5.95

Spy Story
(0-06-100265-8) $4.99

Catch a Falling Spy
(0-06-100207-0) $4.95

For Fastest Service—
Visa & MasterCard
Holders Call

1-800-331-3761

MAIL TO: **Harper Collins Publishers**
P. O. Box 588 Dunmore, PA 18512-0588
OR CALL: **(800) 331-3761** (Visa/MasterCard)

Yes, please send me the books I have checked:
☐ AGENTS OF DARKNESS (0-06-109944-9) $5.99
☐ MAZURKA (0-06-100010-8) $4.95
☐ MAMBO (0-06-109902-3) $5.95
☐ BRAINFIRE (0-06-100086-8) $4.95
☐ ASTERISK DESTINY (0-06-100160-0) $4.95
☐ CRACKDOWN (0-06-109924-4) $5.95
☐ KILLER'S WAKE (0-06-100046-9) $4.95
☐ SPY SINKER (0-06-109928-7) $5.95
☐ SPY STORY (0-06-100265-8) $4.99
☐ CATCH A FALLING SPY (0-06-100207-0) $4.95

SUBTOTAL .... $_____
POSTAGE AND HANDLING .... $ 2.00*
SALES TAX (Add applicable sales tax) .... $_____
                    TOTAL: $_____
*ORDER 4 OR MORE TITLES AND POSTAGE & HANDLING IS FREE!
Orders of less than 4 books, please include $2.00 p/h. Remit in US funds, do not send cash.

Name _____

Address _____

City _____

State _____ Zip _____ Allow up to 6 weeks delivery.
                                 Prices subject to change.
(Valid only in US & Canada)

HO281